GODDESS
SAVE
THE KING

By

A.R. Fagundes

Goddess Save the King

Copyright © 2017 A.R. Fagundes

Copyediting by EbookEditingServices.com

Formatted by Ebooklaunch.com

ISBN: 0-692-80589-3
ISBN 13: 978-0-692-80589-3

This book is dedicated to my awesome parents.

"You (humans) shall evolve into divine beings to allow insight into your origins, so that you may finally see you all originate from the same place, the same love. Do not forsake your brothers and sisters in times of need, or suffering, for it is in those moments that your species will achieve greatness."

-Message of the first Prophet

"The paired diviners shall rise when the earth is at its worst to annihilate evil before its end. The planet will be returned to the divine in its purest state in which it was at its inception, so that life may begin again."

-Message of the second Prophet

"The destruction of the earth is finite. At 3000 CE the world ends, after the divine reap the holy and banish the lingering evil forever."

-Message of the third Prophet

PROLOGUE

Year: 1861 CE
Planet: Rioria of the Virgo Stellar Stream Galaxy
Land: Starlands
Kingdom: Theris, kingdom of the elves

In the king's suite in the palace of Ividia, tucked away in the center of Theris, darkness shrouded the room. Light tried to peek through where the curtains met but failed. The room was in disarray as if it had been ransacked. Vases that used to hold fresh flowers lay shattered on the floor. Tables were overturned. Pillows were torn in half. A settee that was once positioned at the end of the bed had been kicked against the wall; its broken pieces scattered on the floor.

In the darkness, the king sat on the floor with his back against the side of the bed, his head in his hands as he silently wept. The cry of a newborn echoed from down the hall. The king sobbed loudly in response to the sound: the sound of loneliness. There was a faint knock at the door. The king didn't move. The door slowly opened, and a single visitor entered.

"My Lord," the visitor attempted gently. "It's time. We need you to let us bury her."

The king had fought everyone in the palace to halt the burial process and managed to stall it for almost a week. He wasn't ready to let go of his queen. The king's head lifted from his hands. He stared at the ceiling, trying to get a grasp on his reality and succeeding only long enough to give the order for the burial before he retreated into a grieving oblivion.

He reached for the small glass sitting on the tray of untouched food that had been brought to him hours ago. His anger rose, triggering him to throw the glass against the wall, sending shattered pieces to all corners of the room. One small piece of glass ricocheted and struck his cheek. A small drop of blood pooled at the corner of the mark as he ripped the shard from his face. The wound healed within seconds. He stared at the shard in his hand and burst into tears again.

CHAPTER 1

Year: 2963 CE
Planet: Earth of the Milky Way Galaxy
City: Lost Angeles, formerly Los Angeles

Tessa Hill stood in a long line of customers waiting at the 3-Wear to pick up her latest order. The 3-Wear replaced many abandoned dry cleaner storefronts before the last war, and few remained. After the collapse of manufacturing, ready-made clothes became an item, on a long list of items, that grew in scarcity. The remaining human population rolled with the change, merging technology with pre-existing clothing to reuse the textiles. The process took minutes, but the demand was high, so customers must return the following day to pick up their orders.

When people brought their old clothes to the 3-Wear, they chose new styles in which their clothing would then be reduced, reused, or recycled into new designs. The technology broke down the existing garments to thread-level to re-color and re-build an old blazer into a new peacoat. Had this been an earlier time in human history, those who invented such technology would have bragged about how much their creation cut waste and made the earth a better place. However, the truth was that the technology was needed for survival now, and no one knew or cared about who invented it.

Survival was now humanity's primary concern.

Tessa finally made it to the front of the line and handed the cashier her ticket. It had a small claim number printed on one end of it. The cashier took the ticket and disappeared into the backroom to find her order. Tessa drummed her fingers on the countertop as her gaze wandered around the space. It wasn't much to look at, with only blank white walls and two chairs. The cashier returned with her order then requested payment. Tessa noticed a small card stapled to one of the hangers that held her new purple sweater. She tore it off and opened it. She stilled as she read it. Her attention lifted to the cashier, who only offered her an apologetic look. Tessa gathered her clothes and darted out of the 3-Wear. She threw herself into her car, shoving the new clothes into the passenger seat before scrambling for the card. She shook her head as tears fell. She'd been looking forward to this new sweater for months. It took that long to afford the process for one item. Now, she'd never look at that sweater with the same excitement again.

Tessa sighed, dried her tears, then drove to the address noted on the card, cautiously avoiding freeways as she ventured west. Due to many collapsed freeway ramps, it became a way for stragglers to trap and loot unsuspecting travelers. Twenty minutes later, Tessa pulled up to the intersection of Olympic Boulevard and Main Street in Santa Monica, California. She peered out the window to find what used to be the Santa Monica Police Department building. It used to be a small building, but when the world started to change for the worse, the building grew and now sprawled over two city blocks. Tessa trembled as she looked down at the card in her hand. Once she gathered herself, she slipped out of the car and made her way to the abandoned building's entrance.

After a few strained attempts, Tessa pushed open the front door that had been boarded shut after the last war. She moved through the dilapidated police station, noticing there were no working lights, but there were enough holes in the building to light her way. She unfolded the piece of stationery in her hand. It was designed with a modern, minimalist aesthetic in mind, with the letters QC in silver at the top of the card. She found herself rubbing it between her fingers from time to time during her search. Paper this fine wasn't available for public consumption anymore. Nothing so crisp, so moneyed, was easy to come by.

Unless it came from Quantum Corporation.

Quantum Corp. was one of the last remaining corporations in the world. Their almost solitary existence did not deceive the remaining few million humans on Earth. Whispers traveled with details of the entity's evil doings subsidized by the governments left in the world. Its agents were tasked with destroying anything the organization deemed a threat to it and controlling every human on the planet, particularly the more gifted ones.

Everyone knew the QC was why people went missing and were never seen alive again.

As it was, the earth was on its last lap. Thirty-seven years to go, then the planet would go up in smoke. Fire, actually, as promised by the last prophets who had come and gone with their riddle-like messages. Of their many decrees, only three messages were clear to the masses.

The first was that humans' biology would advance like their own over the coming centuries, allowing humans one final chance to redeem their species by motivating them to face the growing evil in their world and help those who couldn't help themselves, thereby securing their place in the afterlife.

The second message was a bit convoluted, and it had sparked the last war. The prophet spoke of the coming of the diviners, which no one understood. Did that mean more prophets would travel to Earth or was it more of a horsemen-of-the-apocalypse event? Many humans believed the diviners to be angels of death, sent to rid the world of evil one last time before its end.

The third message was that whether or not the humans chose to change for the better, a timer for the destruction of all life on Earth was set for 3000 CE. No extensions.

The arrival of the prophets tore at the fabric of reality, opening portals worldwide. The humans who couldn't handle the prophets' ultimatums escaped their fate through the portals. Some portals were gateways that led to beautiful new worlds, but many did not. The problem with portals was that not everyone could see them. The more evolved humans could see them in plain sight, commencing the QC's interest in locating advanced humans. It was the chance to acquire gifted agents and take over this world and others.

After the prophets visited, the population was not protected from the cataclysms that nature brought forth over the centuries that followed. As repeated disasters diminished the human population, technologically advanced infrastructure was an included casualty.

Tessa noticed that the once leading-edge technology used in the precinct had been ripped from the walls or destroyed. Looters, she knew. This type of technology could only be sold to the remaining rich, as electricity was no longer in abundant supply to utilize anyway.

Tessa reopened the folded piece of stationary. It had the police station's address, an office name, and a password written in neat script. Everyone knew that if you received a message from the QC, you didn't ignore it, and you didn't tell anyone you received one. If you did, two people disappeared, instead of one.

Tessa wandered past offices and finally found an interrogation room with the hallway window blacked-out. The placard on the door contained the name of the office she needed to find. It was the placard for the chief of police's office. Someone thought it was cute to move it from its originally designated door. A small screen was paired with the knob on the door. She turned the stationary's written surface toward the screen, and it scanned the card's information. The door unlocked, and she stepped inside. She jumped in surprise when the door slammed shut and locked behind her. All that was in the room was a two-way mirror on one wall, a monitor hanging from one corner of the ceiling, and a chair. The rest of the room showed signs of neglect.

"Miss Hill," a robotic voice vibrated from the monitor speakers, filling the room.

Tessa turned to the monitor, then at the two-way mirror. "Yes?"

"Have a seat," the voice instructed.

Tessa struggled to maintain a neutral expression as she seated herself. The thought of not leaving the room alive remained at the forefront of her mind. Still, she had enough confidence to ask, "Why am I here?"

A deafening pause. "Quantum Corp. requires your services."

My services? She was no one noteworthy. She was a hospital administrator at the only hospital left in Lost Angeles, with only a boyfriend to call family. She had nice friends, though. She tried to see them every week, as the lack of family remained a painful reminder of her solitary existence.

"We have assigned you to a reconnaissance mission."

Fear crept up her spine. "You want me to spy on someone?"

More silence. "Quantum Corp. has substantial enemies, Miss Hill. Two of which are included in your circle of friends."

No! Tessa dreaded as her hands fisted in her lap. "And you want me to do what?"

"Relax, Miss Hill," the voice said. "Once your job is completed, you will be set free."

"I'm supposed to believe that?"

The voice chuckled. "Your limited abilities aren't a threat to us, Miss Hill. We want big fish. Two, specifically." Tessa shook her head and looked away from the two-way mirror as she crossed her arms over her chest. "The Everly twins pose a great threat to our national security." The voice's tone was reasonable, adequately masking its deception.

They pose a great threat to your organization, Tessa thought. Tessa didn't know about the twin's extensive abilities, if any, but they were exceedingly wealthy. Even in such terrible times, money still had the power to keep information hidden and individuals protected.

Silence settled in the room.

The monitor turned on and showed footage of the twins, Adaline and Asher Everly, who couldn't have been much older than seventeen at the time. Adaline was being interrogated in a newer-looking room than the one Tessa was being held, only to have Asher tear through a wall to rescue her. Realization lit Adaline's face, then she reached one hand for the two-way mirror. Her telekinesis shattered the glass then choked the life out of the three men in suits who observed her from the other side. An electrical current radiated from Asher. He channeled it into the outlets and fried the building's circuits until the entire structure blacked-out.

"The Everlys are murderers, Miss Hill," the voice said as the monitor went black.

"It kinda looks like your fault," Tessa snapped back. She knew Addy and Asher to be very kind people. Addy had been her friend since they met in medical school.

"Regardless," the voice silenced her. "Humans with extensive abilities cannot be allowed to live among the general population."

Because they can rally against you, Tessa thought.

"Your job," the voice continued, "is to collect information on their daily whereabouts, activities, and most importantly, the use of their abilities and their strengths in those abilities."

To add to their arsenal of advanced humans, Tessa knew. She was glad the Everlys had never shown her the range of their abilities, just the ones that most humans had. After watching the video, Tessa entertained the possibility that her friends were more powerful than demonstrated. The Everlys were practiced, intelligent, and at the top of their class in medical school. Surely they would be just as honed in their gifts as they would be their surgical abilities. The twins were right in their decision to reveal nothing of themselves that may cause the QC to notice them. Yet, here was Tessa being pressured to turn against her friends.

Wait, the QC couldn't have known of Adaline's abilities upfront, or they would have simply tried to snatch her from the streets, Tessa thought. They must have called her in to turn on someone else... like they're doing to her. Adaline showed the strength to bulldoze the authority they used to implement fear to the masses when they thought she was a less evolved human.

"And if I say no?" Tessa inquired.

Silence.

"You won't leave this room alive," the voice finally responded.

Tessa exhaled hard. She didn't have any substantial abilities to save herself like Adaline and Asher did. Tessa only had the standard two abilities that most humans had: accelerated healing and supervision.

"What's expected of me?" she asked.

The voice explained that she would need to return to that same room each week, on the same day and time, to report back on her findings of the Everly twins, most importantly Adaline. After the voice shared the details, it paused before asking Tessa, "Are you with us, Miss Hill?"

Tessa's defeated gaze lifted from her lap into the two-way mirror. "I'm with you."

CHAPTER 2

D r. Adaline Everly appeared on the roof of the Griffith Observatory wearing her sweeper gear. The Observatory had been commandeered by the QC right after the end of the last war. Once the remaining world governments knew that the diviners lived in the United States, the rest of the world turned on the American government and waged war in an attempt to destroy the ones who were meant to return the planet to the divine. Although the United States emerged victoriously, all sides had committed irreparable damage to each other. The U.S. desisted its efforts in aiding other countries and instead channeled all its resources into repairing itself.

Once the war was over, and the U.S. had withdrawn from the global unity system, Quantum Corp. was born. The other countries used the QC to infiltrate the United States to find the diviners for the sole purpose of annihilating them. What remained of the CIA, FBI, and NSA curbed some of their advances, but once the QC started kidnapping advanced humans, the organization became a significant threat. The U.S.

agencies had difficulty keeping up until they began recruiting advanced humans of their own. Still, the QC proved to be competent at evading the U.S. agencies.

Adaline shifted her molecular structure as she walked through the Observatory walls, now the QC's West Coast headquarters. Not very conspicuous, Adaline thought, as she scanned the extensive technology the QC was using to track her and her brother. The QC knew where the Everlys lived and where they worked, but no matter what tactics they used against the twins, the QC always failed. The twins were unbeatable.

Agents charged at Adaline once they noticed her. She continued her mission, unfazed by their presence, freezing agents in their momentum as she searched for information. It wasn't information she needed, but it was information she promised to someone else. She came upon the main room, where the walls were covered in screens showing data, maps, and pictures. Many of which were of Adaline.

"That's a bad angle," she said aloud at one hardly flattering image.

She spun as she heard movement behind her and locked eyes with a large man in QC quasi-military gear. He delivered a kick to her face that should have thrown her to the floor. Adaline's head snapped back before she wiped the blood that ran from her nostril. Her nose realigned itself, and the injury healed in seconds.

Adaline chuckled as her eyes glowed white. "You call that a kick?"

The man's face paled as he witnessed the amount of energy radiating from her. She stepped forward and kicked her left leg out, her foot colliding squarely with his chest. The force sent him flying until he smashed into a wall and sank to the floor unconscious.

"That's a kick," she said with a smirk.

She searched the agents' souls suspended in the air, looking for the one who had the most information to turn over to the CIA. She stopped in front of a man in a gray suit who looked to be more of a pencil pusher than a field agent. She snatched him by his neck.

"You will do nicely," she said to him. As she touched him, he became unfrozen. The man's eyes widened in fear before he squirmed and begged for mercy. "The best joke I've ever heard is when evil begs for its life," she admitted. With a thought, she snapped the necks of all the agents who remained frozen and let their bodies fall to the floor. The horror on the man's face of whose neck she held was all the reward she needed. Her eyes ignited with white flames, causing the facility to catch fire as she teleported away with him in hand.

"You are the only lucky one today," Adaline told her detainee as she arrived at the exchange point a few miles away.

"It's about time," a familiar woman's crabby tone hit Adaline's ears before she turned to see the Director of the CIA, Carmen Fields, staring at her. Carmen was flanked by three black hover-Hummers, containing teams of agents. All the agents were pointing guns at Adaline.

Adaline chuckled. "Guns? Seriously?"

Carmen sighed. "You spooked them when you appeared out of thin air."

Adaline grinned. She enjoyed teleporting. It was the one ability that made her feel the freest. She could not be trapped by anyone or anything.

"At ease, gentlemen," Adaline said humorously, as she held up the QC agent and dangled him in front of them. "I come bearing gifts."

A loud explosion erupted behind Adaline, where the Observatory used to sit on the cliffside. The dome that once held an impressive telescope fell down the mountainside, detonating another explosion of its own upon impact.

Carmen rolled her eyes. "Was that really necessary?"

Adaline shrugged. "Obviously."

Adaline and Carmen's interactions were always derisive. Adaline knew she was one of the two most powerful beings on the planet and has had trouble with any human who thought they had authority over her.

It was the same dynamic from the first day they met. It had taken a lot of Carmen's time to track down Adaline and Asher Everly because their medical practice was the perfect cover. Finally, Carmen transferred to the CIA's West Coast office for a few weeks to arrange a surgical consult with Adaline. There were many hurdles that one had to go through to successfully obtain an appointment at Everly Surgical Institute. Finally, after much due diligence, Carmen found herself in their waiting room. A nurse greeted her and showed her to an examination room before taking her vitals. The nurse excused herself, and Carmen was left alone to snoop around the room before Adaline entered. A few minutes later, there was a knock at the door, causing Carmen to quietly scramble back to her seat on the examination table. The door opened and in walked Dr. Adaline Everly with a clipboard in one hand and a pen in the other.

"Ms. Carmen Fields," Adaline said, without looking up from the clipboard. "Ninety-seven years old, complaining of mechanical issues with hips and legs." Adaline finally faced Carmen, who sat quietly. Carmen was stunned at first upon seeing Adaline because the doctor's physical body emitted energy, unlike anything she'd ever seen. "How long has the problem been going on?"

Carmen cleared her throat. "On and off for about ten years."

Adaline pursed her lips to one side, then set down the clipboard and crowded Carmen's personal space. "Relax," Dr. Adaline said to Carmen as she waved a hand over Carmen's body like she was scanning for something. "So," Dr. Adaline said nonchalantly, "did you find anything good?"

"Beg pardon?" Carmen asked, confused.

"In my drawers and cabinets that you were searching before I entered," Adaline said. "Did you find anything?"

Busted, Carmen thought. "How did you know?"

"I always know," Adaline said simply, as her eyes met

Carmen's. "What are you doing here, Director Fields?"

"I thought you always know?" Carmen asked.

Adaline smirked. "I do. I also allow people the chance to tell me themselves."

"Why?"

"It's amusing to find out just how much people lie," Adaline said, smiling to herself. For some reason, that truth never got old because it varied from person to person and made the experience entertaining.

Carmen took a deep breath. "I've been searching for you and your brother for quite some time." Adaline nodded, knowing that was true, allowing Carmen to continue. "After the war, the two of you were never seen or heard from again." Also true. "What you both did for your country was truly remarkable."

Adaline rolled her eyes as she began to pace the examination room and listen to Carmen. Nothing the Everly twins did was for the sake of the country. There wasn't much of one left. The twins did what they did to protect lives, lives that wanted the diviners safe.

"What you did for Captain Monroe was nothing short of miraculous," Carmen gushed. "He was supposed to be lost due to his extensive injuries. Dead. Not only did he survive, but he also walked out of intensive care like he'd never even endured a paper cut in his long life."

Adaline smirked to herself as she thought of Jim, whom Carmen referred to as Captain James Monroe of the U.S. Marine Corps. Jim was her father's best friend. They had served side by side for decades until her parents died tragically in a car accident. Adaline and her brother always knew it was not an accident.

"We need you again," Carmen said.

"How annoyingly predictable."

"The QC is growing in number and in brutality."

Adaline's head snapped up with an amused expression. "For whom?"

Carmen sighed. "For anyone who is not an advanced human."

"What do you want me to do for you?" Adaline asked her, mildly entertained.

"I need to infiltrate the organization and bring it down from the inside," Carmen explained. "To do that, I need information."

"You need captures, not kills," Adaline concluded.

"Precisely."

Adaline eyed her. "Why do you want to save a world that's doomed in less than forty years?"

Carmen shrugged. "We don't know if that's true."

Adaline's eyebrows lifted. "You're joking? Three prophets tear through the fabric of our reality to tell us the world is done, give us a specific date, and you want to believe the date is arbitrary and their message subjective?" Carmen shifted on the examination table. "Understand this, Director, this world is done. I suggest you explore the portals you know of and find a new world where you can live out the rest of your life. Forget this one. Evil is embedded in most humans who walk this planet."

"I don't care if you say we are doomed," Carmen said. "We have to try to save it."

Adaline stared at the Director, then shrugged her shoulders before reaching a glowing hand into Carmen's abdomen. Carmen gasped at the move and froze.

"Well, if you are going to choose to be delusional," Adaline said, as she looked the Director in the eyes as her own glowed white, "then you should be in top physical health." Adaline yanked something from the Director's abdomen and hip joints, pulling free a black void then throwing it on the floor. It coiled like a large snake in the form of black mist. Carmen stared in horror as she scrambled back on the examination table.

"Relax," Adaline said, annoyed. "Just don't touch it." Adaline placed her palm over the Director's abdomen and filled her torso with white light. The Director felt a surge of energy, increased blood flow, and a change in her posture of how her legs carried her body.

"Stand up," Adaline instructed her.

Carmen slid off the examination table before putting her weight on her feet before letting go of the edge of the table. She bent her knees then straightened her legs, amazed by how her body felt.

"Director Fields," Adaline said to Carmen with arms folded, "our purpose is not to preserve evil in any form but to extinguish it from the earth."

"I understand," the Director said, as she straightened her clothes. "But you need to be open to the possibility that you are wrong."

Adaline burst into laughter, making the moment awkward for the Director.

"I have my orders, Dr. Everly," the Director tried to remain stern. "By order of the president, I am to find the two of you and enlist your aide in capturing QC agents to use their information to infiltrate their organization. Will you help your country?"

Adaline chuckled. "Unbelievable." She thought for a long moment. "I'll humor you. And when I do remember to leave one alive, I'll bring the agent to you. You are not to interfere in my and my brother's purpose. If you do and get caught in the crossfire, the damage is on you."

"Thank you," the Director said. "I'll be in touch." Carmen gathered her things before Adaline turned to leave the room.

"Oh, and Director," Adaline said over her shoulder, "the day you try to order me around is the day our agreement ends." The door to the examination room slammed shut behind her.

*****

At the drop-off point, Adaline handed over the QC agent.

"Here. A new toy."

Agents rushed to arrest the QC agent, who went with them willingly to get away from Adaline.

"Everly!" a familiar voice said.

Adaline turned to see CIA agent, Blake Harris, coming toward her. "Hey, Pyro!" Blake was one of the few CIA agents Adaline would interact with outside of Carmen. He was an advanced human, equipped with more than the standard two advanced traits all humans possessed.

Blake chuckled. "Any chance you can teach me a little more today?"

"Only if you pay attention this time."

"I didn't mean to make that ice cream truck explode," he said sheepishly.

Adaline gave him a sidelong glance then laughed. "Okay, fine. If you practice control in your spare time… preferably near a large body of water."

He smiled. "Done!"

"Okay, hold out your palm and make a small flame." He did as instructed, and a small flame burst forth. "Good," Adaline said. "Now make it hotter." The flame grew. "Not a bigger blaze — Keep it small and focus on increasing the temperature."

Sweat ran down Blake's face from the heat as he struggled until Adaline put her hand on his shoulder. "This is how it's supposed to feel." She guided her pyro ability to flow down his arm. A powerful white flame burst from his palm. "Do you feel that?" she asked, as she passed her free hand through the flame. "Notice the difference between the heat of the first flame and how this flame leaves your hand cool and burns clean."

Blake stared at his hand, dumbfounded by the power he wielded. "That's incredible."

Adaline smiled and took her hand away, extinguishing the white flame. Blake was still staring at his hand. "Keep practicing." Adaline turned back to Carmen. "Are we done?"

Carmen nodded. "We're done. I'll be in touch."

Adaline teleported to the front entrance of Everly Surgical Institute in Santa Monica. A piece of paper taped to the front door of her building caught her attention. She peeled it off to examine it, noting the above-par use of crayons that depicted her and her brother with wings. The drawing showed them saving people. Adaline loved new fan mail, especially when it came from a child.

"Diviners," echoed in a child's voice like a soft whisper in the street behind her. She glanced over her shoulder and noticed new graffiti on the side of the building across the street. It showed her and her brother defeating QC agents. The words "Save us!" were tucked in the corner of the impressive artwork.

"Sorry, guys," she muttered under her breath. "But there's not much left to save."

A noise behind her reset her focus. She smiled and turned to identify her opponent, but her face was met with another kick. Then a team of QC agents immediately attacked her.

"I'm gone for ten minutes," she growled, as she kicked one agent so hard he landed in the intersection. "And you fuckers have the nerve mess with me in front of my pretty building." She waved her hand and teleported them to the backside of the building, next to the dumpsters. Their faces were filled with horror as they tried to move but failed against her power. She opened the dumpsters with a thought before one agent piqued her curiosity. She let him speak.

"You are the devil!" the agent exclaimed. "You will die a horrible death soon, you witch!"

Witch? That's a new one, Adaline thought. Talk about a downgrade.

A dry smile on her face held while she scanned the agent's soul record. She perused his past, not from just this lifetime, but all the ones that came before it. She wasn't surprised to see that he had always been evil, all the way back to his time as a Nazi officer stationed at Auschwitz.

"So, let me get this straight," Adaline said, as the agent floated in the air in front of her, "in this lifetime alone, you have tortured and killed six people, all of whom were innocent, yet you did it for the thrill of it. You raped your daughter for three years since she was seven years old, beat your wife to a pulp on an almost daily basis, and made her an outcast to all of her friends and family, making her feel isolated and dependent on you, all the while making your co-workers think she deserved it because you put on a show to them that you are some stand-up guy... and you're calling me the devil?" Adaline's eyes blazed with white light.

The QC agent trembled as his thoughts raced. "What are you going to do? Torture me?"

"I'm not a torturer," Adaline admitted with a smile. "Well, that's not entirely true. But the one waiting for you on the other side is quite skilled in the craft. Allow me to arrange a meeting." Before his eyes could widen in horror, she snapped his neck along with those of the other agents. When she dropped their bodies in the dumpster, the lid slammed closed.

Today was trash day.

What a hate-mongering dick, she thought, as she recalled the agent's devil comment. She stilled as she felt eyes watching her, but she didn't search for them. She knew they were innocent eyes, eyes that belonged to a child, a child who continued to succeed in finding her.

"Diviner," whispered the innocent voice.

Adaline's head snapped in the direction of the child to find no one else around. Impressive, she thought, before her cell card buzzed. She pulled it out of her pocket to read the message.

"Shit," she said, as she read that Mr. Nelson was going into cardiac arrest. Adaline closed her eyes and thought of the locker room on her office floor. In seconds, she had arrived at her locker and scrubbed-in for surgery.

A young woman trailed Adaline as she bolted for the operating room. "Hello, Dr. Everly."

"Hello, Maddy," Adaline acknowledged her brother's physician's assistant.

"Dr. Everly sent me to fetch you."

"Asher needs to stop giving you admin tasks," Adaline muttered behind her surgical mask. Before Maddy held open the door to the operating room, Adaline said to her, "Change your rotation to my schedule. I will train you. I can't have a physician's assistant doing receptionist work."

"Yes, Dr. Everly," Maddy said as she continued to hold the door open. "Thank you."

"And tell Dr. Meza that I'll be ready to meet with her to review her psychological assessments after I'm done with this surgery. You will also be in that meeting."

"I'm on my way to her office."

"Perfect." The door to the operating room closed behind her as she saw Asher standing over Frank Nelson's open chest cavity.

"A little help!" Asher called to his twin.

"What did you do this time?"

Asher's eyes narrowed on her. "You know this is not my fault."

She knew, just like she knew Frank Nelson's health records upside down and backward. This surgery was mostly a result of the patient's own doing. The other half of the blame fell on the surgeon who opened him up the first time and implanted artificial valves he shouldn't have added. Mr. Nelson's fault stemmed from the prophecy's downside: warning humans that their biology would evolve to be like the prophets. As a result, illness and disease became far more literal, and it could manifest in the body very quickly.

Patient Frank Nelson was still mourning his son's loss, ten years after the child's passing. Something that he had done often with his son was play catch in their backyard. Because he continued to grieve as if it were the day the boy died, Frank Nelson manifested a heart condition and carpal tunnel syndrome in his throwing hand. When his health showed signs of failing, Frank Nelson came to Everly Surgical Institute to see the best surgeons in the world, to salvage his body and perhaps the rest of his life. After all, the guy had a wife and a daughter who still needed him. He came to see the Everlys just in time. His body was about to give up, and when it reached that point, death came quickly. However, with Frank Nelson going into cardiac arrest in the middle of surgery, it appeared death was trying to claim him sooner than the Everlys expected.

Adaline stood over Mr. Nelson's open chest cavity and held her hand over his seizing heart. Pure white light spilled from her palm into his body. The heart strained with difficulty, then accepted the light.

"Now give it a jolt," Adaline said to Asher.

He put his palm next to hers and released an electric current from his hand into Mr. Nelson's heart. The heart gave a labored beat, then another, and another, until it surged to life.

Asher let out a sigh behind his surgical mask. "That was close." Adaline nodded.

The twins stood over Mr. Nelson as Asher began to close the man's chest cavity. Mr. Nelson responded wonderfully to the anesthesia, and Asher was on his way to finishing the surgery in record time. Asher's hands worked so fast that his fingertips could not be detected, even with the evolution of human sight. Adaline stood by for her final role in the surgery.

"Time!" Asher said as he lifted his hands from the patient's chest, his work completed.

Adaline checked the time. "Twenty-two minutes and thirty-three seconds."

Asher smiled. "New record!"

The twins high-fived over Mr. Nelson.

"Your turn, Addy," Asher said as he pulled down his surgical mask before leaving the room.

Adaline smiled down at Mr. Nelson as she rested her hands

over his incisions while white light flowed from her hands, filling his chest. His tissues healed rapidly, with some of the staples pushing out of his skin. His new heart was briefly jostled by the contact with the light, again.

"No, no," she whispered aloud. "C'mon now."

The heart surged to life and continued with a strong, steady beat. Adaline removed her hand once he was fully healed, pulled her surgical mask down, and smiled at a job well done.

Back in the locker room, Adaline changed into her street clothes. Such a simple act like taking the time to change clothes reminded her that although she and Asher served a greater purpose in the face of the earth, they had to remember to take the time to act human. These moments granted them pockets of time to reflect on the day, but Adaline secretly dreamed of a day when she didn't have to "act human" anymore. However, she didn't dwell on the thought of freedom because the twins had yet to figure out a way to obtain it. As far as they knew, there was only one way: die with the world and be freed in the hereafter. It was a retirement they were guaranteed because of all the evil they have faced during their countless lifetimes, along with the evil the twins would face as they swept the earth clean of it.

Adaline shook the thought as she noticed she stashed her sweeper gear on one of the shelves in the locker before she had gone into surgery. She couldn't leave the clothes at work, so she added them to her bag that she set at her feet. When Adaline pulled her zip-front hoodie from its hanger, her bag tipped over. She heard a few items spill out of it as she shrugged on her last layer of clothing then scanned the floor.

Where did her lip balm go? Her gaze shot around until she spotted it halfway across the room. The coast was clear, so she reached her hand out toward the lip balm, and it rolled back to her before floating into her hand. She popped off the cap and liberally applied a layer to her lips before shoving it back into her bag and heading home.

Everly Surgical Institute was a state-of-the-art private medical facility that the twins opened once they had finished their surgical residencies. Celebrities, world athletes, and heads of state (of the states that were left) flew in to meet with them if they were to have surgery for any reason. After Adaline's first run-in with the QC and their parent's death, the twins packed up their lives and fled New York for Lost Angeles. They were brilliant students who had finished high school early and decided to go pre-med at one of the most exclusive universities in Southern California. They intended to leave the past as far east as they possibly could manage, without leaving the U.S. Neither of them detected any sign of the QC until they began practicing medicine on the West Coast. Since their parents left the twins a substantial inheritance and a few military connections, the twins decided to go into business for themselves. This served two purposes: they could practice medicine and utilize their powerful abilities to help others, and it would provide a front until it was time to fulfill their purpose.

The twins decided they would contribute to their failing world by considering the prophets' messages: to help others and expose the world's evil. They both knew that they couldn't do the latter without an escape plan and had been trying to devise one. All they were missing in their strategy was a refuge and perfect timing. They knew the QC had an extensive network, but the Everlys wanted to do everything possible to avoid being caught by surprise, so the timing was critical. In the meantime, they were diligent in covering their tracks in everything they did, from work to play.

A steep, cement staircase was stacked against the west side of their surgical building, leading down to a private parking lot. Asher stood at the top of it, waiting for his sister, so they could play their daily game. The twins had dealt with many hardships from a young age, so when the opportunity came to cater to their inner child, they took it.

Asher tightened the straps on his designer backpack that

held his favorite tech-toys. Adaline hurried over and pulled the straps on her bag tight, too. She needed perfect momentum because her brother moved as fast as his hands did during surgery. This was an ability she was still working on herself.

"Ready?" he asked.

"Go!" She took off before him.

"Hey!" he called after her. "Cheater!"

She laughed over her shoulder as she pounded down the stairs. Asher tried to zoom past her with his accelerated speed, but she grabbed at his backpack, causing him to stumble. She gained a few steps ahead of him, giggling the whole way. With five steps left to reach the bottom of the staircase, he regained traction and blazed right past her. His momentum generated a tailwind that caused her hair to fly over her face, distracting her from executing an abrupt stop, but the momentum threw her forward. Although prepared to stick her landing, her brother stepped in and caught her. He set her on her feet.

"I know you could have handled the landing, but I don't like to see you fall," he said.

She smiled up at him. "You're always saving me."

Asher's chest puffed with pride. He always felt like a hero in his sister's eyes. Adaline was the only woman in his life who built him up, and he would do anything for his twin. Other women just wanted to take from him, and his billions were at the top of their shopping list. Asher was very protective of his twin for more reasons than that, though. As many special abilities as they both had together; individually, Adaline was the one of them who had the most gifts, as well as the greatest strength in her gifts. Asher was the only one who knew about most of her gifts, and vice versa. They didn't talk about their abilities with anyone else, and when they did speak, they communicated telepathically. It was a perk of being a twin in their era. Since the human species had shown signs of evolution, most of the population had experienced advancements in life spans and shared a few of the same abilities. However, anyone who had more than the usual two abilities did not talk about it.

There were two apocalyptic events; the first kicked off in the year 2050 CE, and the second rippled throughout their world beginning in 2460 CE. As disaster continued to strike over the next few centuries, bringing the world population to the threshold of extinction, people finally started to accept their abilities. It was what linked them, versus focusing on some unimportant difference as a reason to hate each other. Even so, if a person had more than two abilities, they weren't discussed. It didn't matter how many governments were toppled and resurrected in the past nine hundred years; one truth remained: governments desired control over the best weapons. Advanced humans with multiple abilities equaled the new age of weapons.

The twins didn't risk speaking a single word about their abilities in front of anyone. They had experienced enough loss to understand it was best to not share, making each other their only support system. Their secrecy decision excluded their parents, who the QC killed once they got a front-row preview of Adaline and Asher's abilities.

Humans who lived in this post-apocalyptic world still wrestled with one unforgettable old habit. As much as they advanced, biologically or otherwise, they still had the insatiable hunger for more. Even with the collapsed manufacturing industry where items were hard to acquire didn't stifle the unquenchable greed that caused humans to consume. This selfishness was the center of why the world still hadn't reached peace.

Adaline pulled into the garage of her Malibu beach home, and Asher did the same at his house next door. Asher's house was a smart-home of a sleek, modern design, whereas Adaline's home was simple, highlighting her personal touch in her décor. It showcased the depth of her knowledge of other cultures that no longer existed and collections of fallen trades, like the film and music industries. She relied on a few of the luxuries of technology but didn't go as overboard as her brother, who was always hungry for new tech toys.

She turned off the engine of her car, and her mind searched her home for uninvited guests. She didn't have enough fingers to count the number of times QC agents were hiding in her home, waiting to take her down. That snowball's chance in hell ended with their dead bodies dumped into the ocean. It had been three months since the last home invasion, and the bodies still hadn't washed up onshore. She zeroed in on two men sitting on her balcony, carrying feelings of weariness and contentment. She smiled before exiting her car.

Adaline enjoyed taking her time to decompress from her surgery-loaded days by performing simple tasks that most people didn't do for themselves anymore. She liked to cook, bake, read, and putter around her house. Adaline opened the sliding glass door that led to her balcony, alerting the two salt-and-pepper-haired gentlemen lounging on her patio to her presence. "Good evening."

"Addy?" Both men acknowledged her and stood up.

"Hungry?" Adaline asked them.

"Yes, ma'am," one said.

"Asher isn't fixing anything good for dinner?" Adaline asked them.

"He never does," the other said.

Adaline chuckled as she recalled losing count years ago on the number of microwaves that had exploded under Asher's misuse. "Come on in."

"Thank you," they echoed and wandered into the house. Adaline started making dinner for everyone as the two men chose to sit on the bar stools at the end of the kitchen island. They were her father's oldest friends. The one wearing his favorite tattered baseball cap was Captain Anthony Harper of the U.S. Marine Corps, and next to him sat Captain James Monroe, also of the Corps. When the last war came to an end, her father, Colonel Michael Everly, rushed a critically injured Captain Monroe to his children in hopes they could save his best friend's life. The twins had just come from sharing the front line alongside the Marines, so they didn't hesitate to help Jim. At first, they lost him for a minute, but Adaline managed to revive him.

Captain Anthony Harper froze in shock when he witnessed what Adaline did to save Jim. At that moment, he understood why he fought in the war: to protect these kids. He and Jim dedicated their lives to it. They taught the twins to fight in hand-to-hand combat and coached them in training their instincts. When their parents were killed by the QC, Jim and Tony quickly took care of the burial arrangements, then moved to the West Coast to keep an eye on the twins while they finished medical school. As time passed and the veterans aged, now the twins kept an eye on them. Once the Everlys made a name for themselves as surgeons and opened their private practice, they bought the homes around their own, one for Jim and one for Tony. It turned out to be retirement at its finest.

"We brought groceries," Tony said, as he set a bag on the counter.

"That's very thoughtful of you," Adaline said, and she opened the bag to find fresh vegetables. "Are these from your patio garden?" Tony nodded with pride. "They look amazing," Adaline said before checking to see what meat she had in the refrigerator. "How about chicken and veggie stir-fry?"

"Mmm," Tony hummed with a smile.

"That sounds mighty fine," Jim said. His southern drawl was more pronounced when he was hungry.

Adaline set to work and quickly had full plates of chicken and veggies placed in front of everyone. She pulled up the barstool between Jim and Tony before digging into her meal. They ate in silence. The Marines weren't much for conversation when food was involved. At the end of the meal, the three of them caught up about their days, and Adaline shared her QC agent drop-off to the CIA.

Tony commended her with a nod. "Very good."

"I wish I was younger," Jim admitted. "I would love to fight those bastards with you." Jim is where Adaline and Asher got their potty mouths.

Adaline chuckled. "It would be an insult to your level of fighting ability."

Jim's chest lifted with pride, and he nodded before taking the last bite of his dinner. The men cleaned up after themselves and said good night to Adaline. They left to check on Asher and ask him about his day, too.

Once Adaline determined that her tasks were completed for the day, she followed her routine of meditating on her patio until well past sunset. Meditation was an otherworldly experience for her. Sometimes, in Om-drunk hysteria, she could open her eyes during the meditation and see small globes of white light dancing around her. If one approached her, she could inhale it and let it circulate through her body. She knew many secrets as to how the universe provided for the people who lived in it. The problem was that humans chose man-made avenues for their brains to concentrate on, so they could "check out" from their demanding lives for a time. She struggled to teach this to Asher. He was gradually catching on because he still liked to check out from his stressful days in destructive ways. Adaline knew peace was always a deep breath away and that everything she truly needed to care for herself existed within her. Aside from tamping down the QC when they came sniffing around, which kept her in constant sur- vival mode, she was content with most of her life. All she was missing was great love.

She loved Asher, Tony, and Jim, along with a few close friends. But to have the lifetime love of a man, and to return it? No dice. It didn't help that her lovers kept dying due to the QC's relentless recruiting attempts.

Adaline took a seat on her patio and closed her eyes. Imme- diately, her brow furrowed as she detected another presence. Not a person. Not an animal. Not technology. Energy. She opened her eyes and looked around, then headed down the stairs to the beach. Wandering to the backside of the staircase, Adaline found a small, purple portal opening hovering a few inches from the ground.

That's new. She walked up to the side of the portal, her bare feet sinking into the cool sand. The portal was shaped like an oval and stretched to about five feet tall. She touched it with the tip of her finger, which went straight through to the other side. She pulled her finger back for a moment then slipped her entire hand through. She felt the cool temperature of impending dusk, just like in her world.

She shrugged. Only one way to find out for sure, she thought before she slowly stuck her head through the portal. On the other side, a vibrant, burgeoning world awaited her. She'd never seen so much green! She gasped and ducked back out of the portal, reeling at what she saw.

That can't be right. Most portals led to hell-planes, and humans who tried to escape this world were devoured by monsters or unbearable terrains and weather conditions. She decided to explore it and retrieved her shoes from the patio. A moment later, she shrugged on a jacket and stepped through the portal. She examined her surroundings of this new world.

Hmm, the ledge of a riverbank, she noted the portal's location from the other side. Not ideal. She kept her balance effortlessly, stepped further away from the riverbank, and hurried up the bordering trail. She tensed when she felt eyes on her.

On a small hilltop across the river, Prince Theodon's pointed ear twitched as it picked up on the royal guards ordering someone to stand still across the river. He turned to see a female raise her empty hands in the air, then held still for whatever instructions followed that she clearly didn't understand. The guards rambled off several questions to her, none of which she answered. He focused on her.

A human female! A tall, pretty one.

An outsider.

Theodon froze in realization as a moment from his past rushed to the forefront of his thoughts. He stumbled upon the eternity ponds by accident as a youngling. He had been out hunting on his own when he fell through the roof of an undiscovered cave that was only known to be a hill. Young Theodon didn't know of the cave's entrance, let alone its existence, which was odd given that very little is ever abandoned in Theris. What's broken or shut down is generally repurposed into something else. Elves were very efficient when it came to optimizing the function of all structures in their communities. Their long lifespans resulted in their having to endure each other for millennia without unlimited space.

Young Theodon hopped to his feet, pointing his loaded bow in all directions in the darkness around him. The only light came from above, from where he had fallen, and from a staircase across the room. As Theodon scanned the room for potential threats, he saw many books, candles, and tightly-rolled scrolls stored on shelves. The symbols he saw carved into the candles made him back away from them immediately, and he moved toward the staircase.

There was a time when evil lived there; he knew it just by the feel of the place, yet he still descended the staircase. The never-ending curiosity that came with youth pushed him to find the origin of the glow. Three glowing ponds awaited him in the underground cavern. The water glowed blue, and each pond seemed bottomless.

What is down there? Young Theodon stepped to the edge of the middle pond and searched its depths with his superior sight. During his exploration of the pond, he stumbled and fell into the water. Although he knew how to swim better than any youngling his age, his father made sure of it, but what happened to Theodon while submerged paused his fight or flight response. The water swirled around him, showing him scenes from his life. He saw images of his father scolding him, of his grandfather loving him, and of his father's instructions as he taught young Theodon how to handle a sword. The water picked up speed and fast-forwarded to the not-so-distant future. Young Theodon saw himself at a thousand years old. He was still having adventures, always exploring, but he evolved into a solid warrior. He was smarter, faster, and braver than he was at that moment. He was going to be everything young Theodon yearned to become. Then the water revealed a new scene; two she-elves, both very beautiful, and both from noble families. One was trying to catch Theodon's eye while the other simply wanted to be his friend. Both would succeed. And of the two, one would betray him. Young Theodon couldn't see their faces because they were both turned away from his view. But both females had the same light-colored hair.

The next scene showed him to be a little older than in the previous scene. He was captured, and he was being tortured by an entity he could not see beyond the darkness that surrounded his older self. Young Theodon cried out at the scene and tried to reach for his older self, but it changed quickly to something new.

The third scene shown to him was of his father interacting with a female who looked different from the elves. His father's happiness was evident when he kissed the female and embraced her, with an older Theodon standing nearby. The young Theodon was amazed at the open expression of his father's love. She was the key, the key to his father's happiness and perhaps his own.

Could it be real one day? Could his father find happiness again?

Before young Theodon could revel in the potential future happiness he would get to experience, an arm shot down through the surface of the pond and grabbed him by the collar of his shirt. Just as quickly, young Theodon was pulled from the water and laid out on the ground as he coughed up water.

Now, over one thousand years later, Theodon stared at the

human whose wrists were being bound by the royal guards and recalled that humans hadn't visited Theris for nearly a millennium. Theodon hurried from his hilltop and crossed the Pilia River to get back to the palace, where he knew the guards would bring her. As he hustled, he heard the guards order her to walk between them as they escorted her to the palace where she would be brought before their king.

CHAPTER 3

A daline remained silent in this new world, mostly because she didn't speak the language. Although, she was excellent at evading questioning with humans of any language. After all, there were only six languages left in her world, and she was fluent in them all. None sounded like what these soldiers yammered at her. As they escorted her along a path, she assumed they would bring her to some authority figure, given the insignia on their uniforms that screamed archaic aristocracy. During the walk, she took the time to take in as many details around her as possible. All the guards were male and had long hair that reached past their shoulders. The colors of their hair were all lighter variations in tone. No black hair. No dark brown. One guard walked in front of her, one behind her, and one on either side of her. Focusing on the guard in front of her, she accessed his soul record. Adaline had become exceptionally skilled in this ability, quickly scanning records to find specific information. She discovered that the guard in front of her was extremely loyal to his king.

A king? Adaline thought, unable to resist rolling her eyes. *Just what I need, some guy who has been conditioned to order people around.* Adaline was an unapologetically stubborn person. No one could tell her what to do, mainly because she was more powerful than anyone. Adaline could respect the guard's sense of loyalty because it was rare in her world. She observed that the guard was generally a good soul and tended to reincarnate into positions that landed him in the service of others who became great leaders.

Hmm, he might want to think about breaking that karmic circle. But people's individual soul journeys were not her business unless they were evil. She just wanted to know if she was working with good people or not. That knowledge made a huge difference in how she chose to conduct herself. If he were evil, she would have to always be on guard. She decided to allow the guards to be suspicious, for now, then she would convince them she was just a tourist.

They ventured down a long entryway that led to a palace. It reminded her of some of the most remarkable buildings her species had ever constructed, which no longer stood. The palace was the perfect marriage of royal grandeur and art nouveau, and it blended seamlessly with the thick forest that surrounded it. She remained distracted by the architecture as the guards dragged her up the front steps of the palace. They ended up in a beautifully decorated large room with a massive throne positioned on the far end of it. The guards halted close to the throne and ordered her not to move. She figured their firm pointing at the ground in front of her meant "stay."

When did I become a golden retriever? Adaline thought before chuckling to herself. *Alert the medical board!*

One guard left the room. Adaline guessed he was fetching someone.

Ha! She swallowed a chuckle at the follow-up dog joke.

From a separate entrance, someone hurried into the room with a curious expression. Adaline focused on his features. He was as tall like her, and he had long, black hair that he wore in a half-braid that hung down his back. She admitted that he was handsome as he analyzed her. He made a tentative approach and dismissed the guards from her sides. She could tell by the guard's actions that they acknowledged someone of higher rank before backing away from her. He stepped closer.

He must be a royal, she thought, after noticing the embellishments on his attire. He looked young, but not too young to be a king if she remembered her human history correctly. He appeared to be in his early thirties in the way of the Old Age. The Old Age was when humans aged faster, which lasted until 2050 CE when the prophets visited the earth. Their arrival accelerated human's biological evolution into higher beings. As a result, their lifespans lengthened as the speed of their aging slowed to a crawl. In the Old Age, Adaline appeared to be in her late twenties, when she was eighty-five. She snapped back from her thoughts when she noticed the royal's pointed ears.

Her eyes widened in surprise. *An elf!* Her excitement must have shown on her face because he smiled.

"Hello," he said to her. His pronunciation was shaky because he hadn't used English in a long time.

"Hello," she echoed, as her dark eyes searched for hints to his character. She read his soul record, and she smiled at what she saw: A loving son, a good soul, a gifted warrior, and lots of neglect in his early years of this incarnation. Her heart hurt when she read the latter. She wouldn't delve into those details now because she was merely content knowing she was speaking to a good person.

"What is your name?" he asked her. His bold gaze brightened with contentment at the sight of her as if he knew something she did not.

"You first," she replied while eyeing him suspiciously, even though she was relieved he knew English. Her eyes widened as she felt a surge of energy coming toward her. "What is that?" His head tilted.

Her eyes shot around the room in alarm, struggling to process the surge of incoming power. The elf tensed when he noticed the change in her. Adaline swayed on her feet and stumbled. The elf stepped with her; his hands held her elbows to help her remain upright. Considering what he knew about her, he wouldn't let her out of his sight, but his concern was growing. Once she was steady, the double doors across the room burst open, and in walked a stunning sight. A taller elf garbed in luxurious robes strode confidently into the throne room while calling out in an accent she couldn't define. "Theodon!"

"Yes, Father," the elf in front of her responded in English, without taking his eyes off an unstable Adaline.

Adaline's eyes widened. *That is his father?* She hadn't even begun processing his physical appearance yet, as she was still stuck on an important detail: the king was a source of pure power, of natural magic. Adaline found that most people didn't understand the terms were one and the same. Adaline had never seen a natural source before in her life, except when she astral projected to other planes of existence. However, she never witnessed it in her waking state — and it was rarely in the form of a person. Pure magic existed only in conditions of nature on other planes beyond the earth. The king had it rippling off him without pause, and she noticed vibrant colors in each ripple. As he moved closer, his aura merged with hers. The sensation triggered alarm as the overlap sizzled with untapped sensuality.

Whoa, easy Killer, she thought, as she stepped back in hopes to better process her visceral reaction to his presence. His energy crowded the space and saturated her own, activating her adventurous and playful nature. It felt old, transcendent, and regenerative. She sighed hard when she felt the endless years of his life. He was ancient, at least a few millennia or so. She could feel his stare penetrate her without meeting his gaze as she continued to explore his energy. He was curious about her, yet he had limited patience, although unlimited time. His equally cold demeanor didn't help, but his energy drew her to him, even though she wouldn't dare move closer.

Cluster-fuck of a lifetime, she thought, as the warmth of his aura sent goosebumps down her body to the tips of her toes. Her gaze lifted to his face, and she was stunned again. Since he appeared to be in his late thirties in the Old Age, the king was a walking contradiction. His long mane was the color of the midnight hour's glossy void, and it was manageably tucked behind pointed ears. His immense, wide-set gaze mirrored the lush foliage of the kingdom. Mesmerized, Adaline finally noticed a slim fitting crown molded across his forehead that dipped into a point between his eyebrows. She'd never known a male to first appear vicious before it registered that he was also beautiful.

Yes, beautiful.

His sharp cheekbones and aristocratic nose added to his regal appearance. Although refined in mannerisms, the word diva popped into her mind to describe him. She almost smiled at that. She read his soul record and found that underneath the refinement was a burial of harsh experiences and pain.

Loss. Profound, dark, intense loss. Unmanaged pain. And it wasn't recent, but he still carried it with him every day with the detached, cold, façade he had put in place to avoid feeling it. She was confused at the contradiction of his positive energic field versus his soul record.

Why? she thought before she continued to read. She read of the loss of his queen during the birth of his son. Her face fell when she came across the details. As he struggled to process the loss, there were brief, precious moments between him with his son. Adaline tried to reach far back in his record to see what kind of male he was before the loss and finally succeeded. Pure joy flooded her heart as she felt his as she saw that he was the happiest elf in the realm. All conditions of wild and plant life were connected to his mood. When he was pleased, flowers bloomed, and trees produced fruit in abundance. The sun shined without a cloud in the sky. She could even hear the echo of his laugh as she continued to read.

That is the most beautiful sound, she thought, as her gaze remained distant.

She stopped reading and glanced over her shoulder out a window that overlooked the kingdom. It was dreary outside. No direct sun was in sight. The plants and trees appeared thick and were still green, but no flowers were in bloom. It looked like the kingdom merely existed instead of thrived.

She reassessed his energy, scanning forward in his record to the present. She read he had a cold demeanor (which was staring at her at that moment), a silver tongue, and he preferred isolation. This was easy enough to rationalize, but there was also a caged ferocity, an animal wildness brewing beneath the surface of his angelic features. His unusually sharp canines added to the physical evidence that he carried a hidden, barbaric nature.

He was dangerous.

Adaline wondered if facets of his personality were hidden because of his rank or if it was due to social cues. Regardless, this walking contradiction put Adaline on high alert to maintain her guard. She also found herself trying to understand why she thought his pointed ears were attractive.

The king froze at his son's use of English, and his focus narrowed on the visitor his son was holding up by her elbows. Not a pointed ear in sight.

A *human.*

The king focused on her as his stride slowed. He moved with predatory grace as if he hadn't yet decided if he were going to stalk or attack this particular prey. He noticed she was tall for a female human and quite beautiful, in absurd looking clothes. She was the epitome of calm until his ear twitched as he discovered her racing heartbeat. She wielded a significant amount of power that billowed off her alluring form. Possessing power was something he never knew humans accomplished since they had always seemed a less evolved species. Her dark, doe-eyed gaze stayed on him as he neared. It didn't escape his attention that she wanted to move away from him. A moment earlier, he noticed her captivated expression on him, as if she was reading the most exciting page from the book that contained his long life. Then she saddened at whatever she discovered. His icy stare caught her attention again after she seemed to be finished.

Adaline could tell the king was extremely aware of her, but she noticed more as she scanned him.

Symptoms.

Not one had ever gotten past her. Her brow furrowed with concern as she noted the cloudy coloring in the whites of the king's eyes when he glanced to one side. She moved closer to take a look, disregarding that she was in the early stages of incarceration.

Uh oh, she thought.

He immediately leaned away from her, shocked that she would step into his space. No one would dare to come closer than a few yards from him, outside of his son. And aside from their staff, females were not allowed in the palace.

"Who are you?" the king pinned her with a glare.

"I'm a human who needs a vacation," she said, as she continued to examine his face.

He moved away from her, his hands tucked behind him as he walked a circle around her. His blatant appraising of her went unopposed by her as she noticed his energy became easier to endure the longer she interacted with it. She wanted to purr at the feeling of being enveloped in its warmth as she rocked back and forth on her feet. She pretended to whistle before the sound of a child crying caught her attention. She froze.

"Where's that coming from?" she asked Theodon.

Theodon smirked at her, delaying an answer to her question. "What is your name?"

"Dr. Adaline Everly," she blurted out and stuck out her

bound wrists, extending one palm a little further. The prince eyed her hand before he understood she offered him a greeting. He put his hand in hers before she slowly shook it. The tension between them calmed, and they both smiled. The child wailed again.

"I'm Prince Theodon Iolas Sleone of Theris," he returned.

"A prince." She nodded in approval. "Sounds like a decent gig."

Theodon chuckled.

"Doctor, you said?" the prince inquired. She nodded. "Meaning?"

Oh right, she thought, searching for an elf-equivalent word for doctor. "Physician?" He squinted one eye and tilted his head like the word didn't quite register. "Medical professional?" He shook his head. "How about healer?"

He nodded. "That one we know."

"Good," she said with a wide smile. "What's wrong with the child?" The child's pain reflected in Adaline's body. She had to bend over, put her hands on her knees, and take a deep breath before standing again. The blending the child's ailments and the king's energy was a heady combination, especially now that he was standing closer to her, his gaze on her unshakable.

"What are you doing in my kingdom?" the king interrupted.

Her attention lifted. "I found a portal at my home. I decided to explore it and ended up here." Her breathing was returning to normal, but she could still sense the child's pain. "Bring her to me."

The royals did a double-take.

"You are not one to issue orders, Human. You are moments away from landing yourself in my dungeon," the king said coldly.

This elf didn't understand who he was threatening, she realized. Adaline chuckled, which made him angry. "Threatening me won't be the smartest decision you've made today." Theodon's eyes widened at Adaline's tenacity.

The king tried to crowd her. "What do you want with the

child?"

"What is your name anyway?" she asked with borderline indifference, purposely to further irritate him.

The king's nostrils flared as his voice boomed, "I am King Aureon Oenuil Sleone of Theris, Lord of the Starlands. You will answer my question, Human or your freedom is mine."

Theodon's eyes shifted from his father back to Adaline.

"My freedom cannot be taken. And you should consider negotiating instead of threatening me. It might work out better for you." Adaline's conviction was sobering to the elves. "You're fortunate. I normally don't give warnings." She dared to wink and smile at the king.

Aghast at her behavior, the king was speechless as Theodon stood wide-eyed in silence. The guards moved in, ready for the order to seize her. Adaline's face was on Theodon, but her eyes lifted to meet the king's as they began to glow white. "I wouldn't do that if I were you." The king held her glowing gaze before he finally waved the guards away. He didn't waiver from where he stood, nor did his stare fall from her. The human was proving more interesting as time passed.

Adaline let the light fade from her gaze. "Bring her to me."

"For what purpose, Human?" the king sneered.

"I'm a world-class... healer... on my planet," she hesitated to change out the world surgeon, a word she earned at a young age and many times over. She stumbled on her feet and gritted her teeth. Theodon rushed in to help her stand again, but she waved him off. "She's in a lot of pain." It was awful to feel the pain of small children because they couldn't communicate what was wrong, so the feelings she detected were magnified. The poor things could only cry. She'd done an impressive amount of pediatric surgery in the past, but she knew the child wouldn't need any of that. However, she was uneasy that she would be forced to reveal one of her abilities to these elves. "If she continues to go untreated, she'll live maybe another one or two miserable years."

Theodon signaled to the guard to retrieve the child. No elf present would admit the child had been back and forth to the palace many times to use the king's personal healers with no lasting results. A moment later, the guard brought in the fussy youngling. Adaline didn't want to reveal more than one ability, so she extended her wrists toward Theodon for him to free her.

"Will you try to run?" Theodon asked.

"I never *try* anything." She paused. "I promise to heal her and give her back to you once I'm done." She lifted her bound hands and extended her pinky finger. "Pinky promise."

Theodon glanced at her finger. "This is binding in your world?"

"Oh yeah," she said convincingly. "Nations sign peace treaties with it."

The prince's eyes narrowed on her before he shrugged, then reached for her with his pinky finger. Adaline interlocked them together. "Promise."

"All right." Theodon paused to deliberate before cutting her wrists free. Adaline stroked her wrists and noticed a few scratches. No matter, she thought. They had already healed as the prince handed her the child. The baby continued to wail through the exchange. The sound echoed down the palace halls. All the elves present gritted their teeth at the sound due to their own highly-sensitive hearing.

"What's her name?" Adaline asked Theodon. The little one looked to be not yet two years old.

"Farryn," Theodon replied.

"It's okay, little Farryn," Adaline cooed at the little she-elf as she snaked her arm around the child, securing her to her chest. "I've got you." Adaline's hands were already glowing with white light, just as her eyes had earlier.

"Da," Farryn baby-talked as she pointed one little finger at Adaline's glowing hand.

One guard said something in urgency to alert the prince, then pointed to Adaline's hands while staring in shock.

Adaline smiled at the guard. "Afraid of a little light, huh?" Theodon was about to move in defense of the child. Adaline held up one glowing hand. "Not a good idea." His eyes locked with hers. "You will cause harm to her if you interrupt the process. Just trust me." He sighed hard but remained focused, ready to pounce at any moment if needed. Adaline admired him. He was prepared to defend a child that could not protect itself. She looked forward to being great friends with Theodon. She glanced at King Aureon out of the corner of her eye. He was perched over her shoulder, eerily still with his attention on her hands. It was like being watched by a predator that waited for her to make a wrong move, so he could justify ripping her to shreds.

Okay, no pressure. Adaline's hands worked on Farryn as she continued to talk and coo at the child. Farryn's crying faded as her glowing hands covered the child's tiny body. Adaline found where the illness was rooted before sinking her hand into Farryn's small intestine. A moment passed before Adaline pulled the disease from Farryn. The child squirmed as the prince and the king watched, enamored by Adaline, as she uprooted a black mist from the child and cast it aside. It floated to the ground then slowly dissolved. Farryn regained color in her cheeks.

"Look at those rosy cheeks," Adaline cooed at the baby, who started to laugh and reach for Adaline's face, understanding who was making her feel better. Adaline noticed Theodon approach the mist that was dissolving. "Don't touch it."

"Why not?" he asked.

"Do you want to get sick?"

Theodons shrugged. "I'm immortal."

"That means nothing in this case," Adaline replied honestly. Theodon backed away from the mist. "Good decision," Adaline commended. "As heroic as I'm feeling today, I don't have the luxury of time and energy to save a child *and* a prince in one day." She winked at Theodon. The corner of his mouth lifted.

Adaline rested her hand on Farryn's belly, and she flooded

the child's digestive system with light. The child glowed for a moment, giggled, and tried to kick her chubby legs. Adaline scanned her body one more time before deciding that her job was done. The glow in her hands faded. Farryn cried out a laugh and reached out with grabby hands. Adaline chuckled and bounced the little one in her arms before looking at Theodon.

Theodon remained frozen in shock. All he managed to do was stare at the child, back at Adaline, then back at the child. He'd never seen anything like it from his father's healers, and they were the best in the world. *Where did that light come from?*

Adaline glanced over her shoulder to find that the king had moved closer. Very close. A few inches away from her shoulder was much too close. *His presence is really affecting me,* she thought, as she felt a tightening in her chest, but she shook it off and handed Farryn to Theodon. "I kept my pinky promise." Theodon remained fixated on the baby in his arms. "She'll be okay."

"How do you know?" the king prodded.

Their eyes met as he rounded to stand in front of her. "Because it is divine healing." He lifted his brow at her, unconvinced. She smiled.

"What is the purpose of your visit to my kingdom?" his tone was warmer than earlier.

She thought about it for a moment. "Well, now that I'm here, I wouldn't mind a social outing of some kind." She felt like she was on vacation because no one knew her here, let alone any inclinations about the extent of her abilities or life purpose.

She was free.

King Aureon's gaze ran up and down her person as he tried to determine how much trouble she was going to cause him before dictating, "You will be escorted everywhere you go in my kingdom while you are here."

"I'll look after her," Theodon offered.

Adaline grew excited at the idea.

The king was uneasy about his son going off with this...

questionable human. He allowed it because expressing emotion wasn't a strength he wielded. It hadn't been for over a millennium, so there was no sense in starting now. The king gave them his back and strode from the room while calling over his shoulder to Theodon, "Do not let the little human out of your sight."

After the king left the room, Adaline shot Theodon a look and pointed after the king. "Who the heck is he calling little?"

Theodon grinned as he offered his elbow to her. "Come. I know just where to take you."

CHAPTER 4

King Aureon stood with his feet planted wide on the balcony that extended from his private suite. Standing still like a warrior in effigy with his hands tucked behind him, he let his mind connect with his kingdom. His eyes closed as the breeze swept his dark hair over one shoulder and rustled the hem of his robes. He let out a long exhale as he connected. Within seconds, he heard the leaves falling from trees, birds feeding their young, spiders diligently weaving their webs, birds taking to the sky, and rivers running over rapids.

He heard everything — Including the heartbeat of the new human refugee that had raced once she laid eyes on him. He thought he would have the upper hand over her based on her attraction to him, but he was wrong.

Dead wrong.

Dr. Adaline didn't do as expected of her species, nor of her gender. She demonstrated to be firmly planted in her intelligence, cleverness, and power versus her heart's emotions.

She was... surprising.

Aureon quickly left his son and the human behind in the throne room as soon as he could get away without suspicion. No one would have been the wiser of the reason behind his hastiness because of his neutral countenance. Although he knew he must hide his reaction to her, the weather didn't hide it at all. Sunshine peeked through the overcast day, and the wind pummeled the trees. Elves moved indoors due to the wind's strength due to the turmoil in the king's heart he couldn't yet navigate.

He closed the door behind him when he first returned to his suite and stood with his back to the door. His chest heaved as his anger boiled. Because emotions had once taken everything from him, he now allowed himself to express only two. The first to surface was anger, which quickly tripped into rage. Those were his safe places because they were clear and defined.

Awareness was only good for detecting enemies.

Attraction was only good for casual encounters, in which he didn't partake.

And love. Love wasn't safe.

Love died.

His rage boiled over as he grabbed the console table next to him, lifted it over his head, and threw it at the adjacent wall. The sound of the impact eased his temper. Acting out had been soothing since Theodon's birth.

The shift he experienced when positive emotions struggled to surface was jarring when he discovered the attraction he felt for the human. His thoughts centered on Adaline and how her dark doe-eyed gaze penetrated through all the barriers he had erected in his mind to protect himself. She observed him intentionally like she already knew all his secrets. Yet, as she peered into his psyche, she withheld any judgment against him. Her knowing look made him feel vulnerable, and that would not do.

He noticed that her feminine characteristics were a contradiction to the energy he detected as he approached her. She wielded significant power, and once her eyes started to glow, he knew not to push her further or else endure her wrath. The fact that a female could possess greater power than his own was tantalizing and bothered him also.

As he listened to his kingdom's sounds while trying his best to reset his mind, he decided he would watch over Farryn and note any progressions or deterioration. He would not focus on the shine of Adaline's long, dark brown hair, her porcelain skin, her cleverness, her unmistakable hourglass shape, or wonder how soft she must be to the touch.

I will not go there, he thought, as his brow furrowed before trying to shake the image.

He would also forget how aware he became of her before laying eyes on her and how she seemed to be of him. He would find a fault in her armor, exploit her talents, and he would have her banished from his kingdom as soon as he had evidence of wrongdoing because if he didn't have it, his son would fight his decision.

But before he could kick her out, he had questions about her healing ability.

Lots of questions.

Questions that might take time for him to ask.

Then he would make her leave.

Forever.

Yes, that is it, he thought, before his focus drifted back to the harsh winds. He inhaled and exhaled, prompting the winds to ebb.

Regardless of how he felt, there was one order of business to handle. His mind reached into the minds of his subjects. His telepathy's strength was how announcements were made to the kingdom, and this was a message he must disclose.

"Humans have returned to Theris," the king said to his subjects in his native tongue. Before he could receive any responses, he let the connection fade. Elves were talented at picking up languages, and when the last humans visited Theris was no exception.

He released a defeated sigh, acknowledging his instincts warning him that he would have no control over Dr. Adaline but not yet accepting it. He returned to focusing on his kingdom's sounds as he searched for an external source to be his inner peace.

CHAPTER 5

"So, I have questions," Adaline admitted to Theodon as he escorted her.

"That does not surprise me," Theodon chuckled.

"It doesn't?"

"I would be disappointed if you didn't," he remarked. "You seem to be a curious person."

Adaline squeezed his elbow. "You got me."

"Go on," the prince directed.

"So… your father," Adaline began, "I noticed he emits a substantial amount of energy. All other elves around him do not. Is that a king thing, or is that a him thing?"

Theodon smiled. "It's both. Aside from the strength elves gain with age, new kings inherit their predecessors' intelligence and strength. However, my father has done significant work on himself over the past millennium to evolve. As a result, he's achieved a level of…"

"Godhood," Adaline finished.

"Yes."

"Do his subjects worship him as such?"

"Most do, yes."

"Wow."

"Your intrigue is amusing."

"Why?"

"You exhibit great power as well, yet you are amazed to notice the same in another," the prince pointed out.

"That's a fair observation," she said to him. "But consider that I've never met elves before today, let alone didn't know they would be so evolved."

The prince's forehead crinkled. "Are not the humans of your world like you?"

Adaline chuckled. "Not even close. My brother is the only one on my planet who is like me."

"Then you know exactly what it feels like," the prince pieced together, "to have many who love you, worship you, and fear you all at the same time."

Adaline thought for a moment. "You're right. Well played, Theodon."

Theodon nodded with a victorious smile. "Next question, Dr. Adaline."

"Are there different types of elves?" she asked.

"Yes," he said before explaining. "There are four types of elves: Tearuine, Drearian, Ileotil, and Brao."

"Which are you?"

"I'm Tearuine," he said. "The royal bloodline is always Tear and speaks Tear, among the other languages."

"Is there prejudice against elves from different groups mating?" she asked.

His eyes narrowed. "That doesn't matter."

"But you said the royal bloodline is always Tear," Adaline threw back.

"Because Tear genetics are dominant," he stated. "My mother was Brao with fair hair and eyes, but if one elf in a union is Tear, the children born from that union look Tear."

"No exceptions," Adaline stated as she perused his features, noting all that matched his father's. The only minor differences were that Theodon's eyes were slightly closer together, and his jaw was a little wider.

"None," he confirmed.

That's interesting, she thought.

"Next question."

"Are there only elves on this planet?"

Theodon sighed. "Unfortunately, no. There are only elves in Theris."

"Theris?"

"The name of my father's kingdom." She nodded and waited. "Beyond our borders are… very dangerous beings."

"Okay. Stay in Theris at all times — got it."

Theodon chuckled. "Yes, please do." There was a pause in their conversation. "Next question."

"How old are you?" she inquired.

"I am 1,102 years old. Next question."

Whoa, Adaline thought as she stopped in her tracks. If Theodon was a little over a millennium in age, how old was his father?

"And your father?" she asked.

"You should ask him," Theodon encouraged.

Her eyes narrowed on him. She couldn't be cross with him because he was so kind. Instead, she skipped the argument.

"Do elves have timeshares?" Adaline asked, half-joking. His head tilted. "It's a vacation home where a person can split ownership with a few others to cut costs, but they still get to go somewhere nice two weeks every year."

Theodon smiled. "You only want to visit Theris two weeks a year? That's a shame."

Adaline's heart softened. "I don't think your father would be happy to see me wandering around Theris more often than that."

Theodon pursed his lips and shrugged. "He might surprise you."

Adaline peered over at Theodon for a moment, not fully understanding what he meant by that comment.

They turned down a pathway with a thick canopy of trees overhead that made it impossible for moonlight to penetrate, but there were shrubs at knee-level that glowed, illuminating their path. The entire natural world of Theris emitted pure magic, the same that rippled off the king. Magic could be found in its raw state like it was in the kingdom, but once it was practiced and mastered, it became power or ability. Adaline knew all humans carried it within them, like her and Asher, but they never practiced it to find their souls' true depth.

"That's incredible," Adaline whispered while staring in admiration at the glowing foliage.

Theodon smiled. "You should see the ones in Drearia. Every plant glows at night and in different colors." Adaline's eyes widened in surprise at the idea of illuminated shrubbery as far as the eye could see. "Even the insects glow," Theodon added.

"That's terrifying," Adaline admitted.

Theodon laughed before he led her down a quiet path where the trunks of trees were narrow, and the surrounding wildlife grew quieter. They arrived at two trees that crossed halfway up their trunks, forming a natural archway. The forest was thick around them, so much so that Adaline didn't notice the crossed trees were a door until Theodon gestured for her to enter. Adaline surveyed the entrance, apprehensive about going in first. She couldn't see a few inches past the trees, and she couldn't hear a sound of what was inside. She eyed Theodon with suspicion.

The prince smiled. "You said you wanted a social outing, Dr. Adaline Everly." He exaggerated his gesture for her to enter again. "I have delivered."

Adaline squared her shoulders to the entrance and focused on her abilities if she might need one or two on the other side.

Her focus shifted to Theodon as the corner of her mouth lifted. "Call me Adaline."

Adaline stepped into the unknown and landed in a venue packed with the glowing plants that Theodon had described. There was no use for lighting because the glowing foliage lined the space, traveled up the walls, and hung down from the ceiling. Booths and tables were carved out of the space, with some tucked away in a rare dark corner. A few tables had more privacy afforded to them by draping vines that acted as curtains to keep out prying eyes. A glowing stream flowed through the venue. Adaline noticed a few elves sitting on the bank of the stream with their feet hanging over the side, kicking around the water as they laughed and socialized. Adaline was frozen in awe of her surroundings and hadn't noticed that Theodon was quietly waiting beside her.

"Are we in Drearia?" Adaline asked him.

The prince chuckled. "No. The owner is Drearian and transplanted all of the plants you see to create this place."

"It's beautiful," Adaline commented, as she realized that the longer she remained in Theris, the more magical it seemed. Everyone around her was of an advanced species, making her feel less isolated than she was in her homeworld. Maybe this world is the final step in our plan after we finish serving our purpose on Earth.

"I'm glad you think so," a female's voice came from behind her.

Adaline spun to see a beautiful she-elf smiling back at her. She was tall with olive skin and covered in dark tattoos of vines wrapped around her body and framed her face. As much as her silver hair color should have aged her appearance, the she-elf looked to be about Adaline's age.

The female formally acknowledged Theodon. "My Lord." Theodon returned with a nod.

"I am Eleona," the she-elf said to Adaline.

"I'm Adaline," Adaline replied, entranced by the she-elf's large, dark blue eyes.

"It is nice to meet you, Adaline," Eleona said to her. "I haven't had the pleasure of interacting with a human in quite some time." The she-elf was surprised to hear English in her club and quickly followed it to find the speaker. She adored the last humans that visited Theris because they were her best customers.

"How long ago was that?" Adaline asked.

Eleona mulled over her memories. "Just over a thousand years." Theodon nodded in agreement.

"A lot has happened to us in that amount of time," Adaline admitted. "Hopefully, the ones who last visited weren't too much trouble."

Eleona cast Theodon a knowing look before both elves chuckled. "It was nice meeting you, Adaline. Should you need anything, just speak it." She vanished as quickly and quietly as she arrived.

Adaline faced Theodon. "Tell me the truth. The last humans that visited Theris were basic, weren't they?"

Theodon was amused by her question. "Come. My table is this way."

Adaline latched onto his elbow, and they moved through the venue that was flooded with music. Male elves' gaze stuck to Adaline as she gripped the prince's arm. She noticed their eyes reflected, like a cat.

"If you see the reflection, it means they want you to see them," Theodon whispered to her.

"The elf method of getting hit on. Nice." The prince laughed. "Isn't that a bold move for them to make if I am walking with you?"

"It means the female must be so beautiful that the curious male doesn't mind courting death for the chance to be near her," Theodon replied with a playful nudge.

Adaline smiled to herself as she blushed before she squeezed his elbow. "Smooth talker." The prince laughed. Heads turned to the prince as if they were shocked to hear him laugh. Then all eyes moved to Adaline, the source of his laughter.

"Right this way." Theodon gestured for Adaline to enter another dark passageway. She stepped through without hesitating and noticed that she'd entered a private bar. Of course, it was packed with the same kind of plant life that filled the main room. The group of elves sitting at the bar turned around when they entered. They studied Adaline for a moment but stopped when Theodon entered. They cheered.

"There he is!" they shouted in Tear as they all raised their glasses.

Theodon was, once again, at Adaline's side. "Good evening, everyone," he said to them in English to signal a language change.

Adaline leaned over and whispered, "Your "own table" is a private bar?" Theodon nodded and winked. Adaline shook her head. "It's tough being the prince."

"Theodon," a male elf said in a thick Brao accent as he approached.

"Uncle," Theodon acknowledged in English. Landon gauged Adaline, understanding his nephew's use of English once he recognized her species.

"She's stunning," Landon said to Theodon in English.

"She's standing right here," Adaline said, annoyed.

Theodon chuckled. "Dr. Adaline, this is Landon Elacan, my uncle."

Landon gave her a clipped bow as he took pleasure in checking her out. He was handsome with his honey-blonde hair that was intricately braided to keep loose strands off his chiseled face. Almond-shaped hazel eyes, dimples, and a dazzling smile hinted to Adaline that he must be quite a hit with the females. Must be Theo's mother's brother, Adaline reasoned, after recalling the dominance of Tear genes. There was no way Landon was directly related to the king.

"Hello," she said to Landon.

"Dr. Adaline," Landon slithered closer.

Adaline put her hand on his chest to halt his advancement. "Right there is fine."

Landon smiled. Females never curbed his advances. They were always happy to see him. Little did he know that Adaline was reading his soul record, and she wasn't surprised to find that Landon was all about his womanizing ways. He became that way after his sister died. She had been the only female figure in his life for some time, so he sought comfort in the arms of different females every night.

People latch onto the most predictable coping mechanisms, Adaline thought.

"It was nice meeting you," she said to Landon with a genuine smile, then she told Theodon, "I'm going to get a drink." She left them for the bar. Landon's lust-filled gaze raked over her stunning figure as she walked away.

"Uncle," Theodon said knowingly in Tear.

"She's…" Landon returned in his nephew's native tongue.

"Yes, she is," Theodon said. "More importantly, she is off-limits."

Landon's ogling eyes snapped to his nephew. "You're joking."

"You know I am not good at telling jokes," Theodon said firmly. "Dr. Adaline is a friend of the crown and will not tolerate your behavior."

"*She* won't tolerate it?" Landon sputtered.

"Dr. Adaline?" Theodon raised his voice, and Adaline turned away from the bar, "Would you be so kind as to show my uncle evidence that you will not tolerate his cavalier behavior?" Adaline's eyes glowed white, along with her fingertips. She smiled at them mischievously.

Landon's eyes widened in shock. "Fine."

Adaline let her light fade as she returned her attention to the bar and picked a seat between one male elf and one female.

"A human!" the female said excitedly.

"An elf who speaks English!" Adaline mimicked her excitement.

They both burst with laughter and introduced themselves. Theodon smirked at their playfulness before taking his usual seat at the far end of the bar on the other side of Forb and Bole. Landon sat on the far side of the prince. Forb slapped the prince on his shoulders.

"We leave you alone for a few days, and you return with a stray human," Forb joked.

Bole peered over at Adaline. "Is she house-trained, Theodon?"

Adaline leaned back in her chair as she caught wind of Bole's joke. "Outside of the occasional accident on the throne room rug, I'm still working on it."

The males laughed.

Forb signaled to the barkeep about Adaline. "Whatever she wants to drink, I will gladly pay for it." Forb caught Adaline's eye. She smiled. He raised his glass to her, and she nodded in return. Then she continued her conversation with Talia and Roserie as if it had never been interrupted.

"I like her," Forb admitted to Bole and Theodon.

"You like all females," Bole joked.

Theodon's almost spat out his drink. Forb slapped him on the back again until Theodon returned to laughing.

Roserie observed Theodon closely. "He laughs easy today."

Adaline sipped her drink before glancing at it, then Theodon, who was laughing at something Bole said. Bole raised his glass in Adaline's direction. She nodded before reading his soul record. She was sad to find memories of the loss of his little brother at a young age, neglect from his father in following years, and… jealousy of Theodon. Adaline wasn't entirely surprised by the latter, but it was rooted in treachery.

"Laughter is a good thing," Adaline admitted to the females.

"You misunderstand," Roserie explained, "he seldom laughs. Yet, here he is, laughing since the moment he entered the bar with you."

Adaline didn't miss Roserie's jealous undertone. Did she have a crush on Theodon? Adaline thought the possibility odd since the she-elf chose to sit on the opposite side of the bar from the prince to make puppy eyes at him while he sat next to his uncle. She started reading Roserie's soul record, but her focus was cut short by Talia.

Talia nudged Adaline. "You've changed things, human." The she-elf winked at her.

Adaline sensed their desire to probe, to extract as much information from her as possible. Once Adaline discovered that Talia and Roserie came from noble families, Adaline understood that the one thing that didn't change from one species to the next was when things grew dull, gossip and drama passed the time. Any information members of the royal houses gathered could be used against each other, allowing the holder of said information to elevate their rank or simply in the royal family's eyes. This stream of thought inspired Adaline's curiosity about everyone present. So as the night continued, she juggled light-hearted conversation as she read everyone's soul records in detail.

Adaline smiled at Talia. "If I can manage to get his father to laugh like that, I expect to be made a living saint!" Both females erupted with laughter. "Do we have a bet?" Adaline challenged slyly.

Talia and Roserie glanced at each other and smiled. "We'll take that bet."

"Sainthood, here I come!" Adaline hollered before setting her empty glass down and hailed the bartender. When Adaline on the bartender as Talia and Roserie continued to talk, Adaline froze for a moment in awe of the she-elf's features. She wasn't Drearian or Tear, that Adaline knew right away, which sparked further curiosity about who she was and what she was doing slinging drinks in a place like this, even if it was a classy place. She looked like she should be perched on the wealthy patron side of the bar.

"What would you like to drink?" the she-elf asked Adaline.

Adaline abandoned her thoughts. "The same thing would be great. I don't know what it's called."

The pretty bartender glanced at the glass. "It looks like a Savory Sunset."

Adaline thought for a moment to compare the name of the beverage to the image the name suggested. *Accurate,* she thought. "Did you create this beverage?"

"Yes."

"I'll have another Savory Sunset, please," Adaline said, then paused before adding, "and your name."

The she-elf didn't hesitate. "Coming right up!" She moved to the other end of the bar to mix the drink before calling over her shoulder, "And my name is Sacha."

Adaline grinned as she thought, *No, its not.*

A few hours passed as the laughter and drinking continued.

"So," Adaline said to Forb, "how far can you hear?"

"It depends," Forb admitted. "The older the elf, the further the distance he can hear, and the more he can hear within that space."

"Feel free to humor me with details," Adaline said, waving him on as she sipped the drink that rested in her free hand. She was enjoying learning about the abilities of elves. Tonight, she found out that families could telepathically communicate with each other. Elves that are far older and more practiced, generally at least 5,000 years in age, can develop the ability to communicate with elves outside of their lineage. It was rare, but it could be done. Their five senses were substantially more advanced, which captivated her curiosity. She would ask detailed questions to Theodon later, but she continued to ask general questions to the prince's friends.

"A young elf of about one hundred years old can hear up to

a mile away," Forb explained. "But in that mile, he can only hear obvious sounds like rivers, winds, and large animals, versus a thousand-year-old elf that can also hear all of the wildlife in between."

"Including insects?" Adaline asked. Forb nodded. "That's impressive," Adaline admitted before sipping her drink.

"How about you, Adaline?" Forb asked. "How far have humans come since they've last visited us?"

Adaline smiled before admitting, "We've been through a lot since then. Our biology has evolved for the better, and our life spans are much longer." Forb nodded. "We need less outside of ourselves to survive, but old habits die hard."

"What do you mean?" Talia asked her.

Adaline sighed. "We still haven't let go of wanting more, of needing new, now and always. This greedy mindset has led to our downfall." A downfall that was approaching sooner than most humans who were left wanted to admit. Her serious admission brought the conversation to silence.

"Well, that was a buzz kill," Bole commented, which caused everyone to laugh and return to lighter conversation. The males' conversation graduated from intelligent interactions to brute strength challenges as the drinks continued to flow. Landon and Bole faced each other to honor an arm-wrestling challenge. Their strength caused the wooden bar underneath them to crack, so they moved to a stone table. Money was laid on the table before their hands locked together again.

"Ready?" Forb said. "Go!"

Adaline watched their roughhousing, appearing as if she was tuned out to everything going on around her. That was far from the truth. She felt Roserie's scheming intentions as the she-elf flirted with Theodon from across the bar with her beckoning gaze and sensuous smile.

Talia whispered to Roserie, "Why did he even bring the human with him?" Roserie glanced at Adaline and giggled.

Adaline read Forb's soul record and found he was from a newer noble house, and his father was an elder that served the king. Forb enjoyed his friendship with Theodon and was a good-natured elf.

Good, Adaline thought. *Hopefully, his motives will never change.*

It was the other patrons calling Theodon friend who bothered her. Adaline read about Talia's scheme for the crown once before and failed and how Roserie was attempting the same through Theodon. That didn't sit well with Adaline as she noticed the males were trying to get Theodon to participate in their shenanigans. Bole beat Landon, which didn't make sense to Adaline because Landon was clearly older and stronger. Roserie had disappeared from the bar, and a minute later, so did Landon. Adaline was determined to investigate their exit as Theodon took his uncle's seat across from Bole. The pile of money on the table grew. She approached Theodon and Bole before their round started and said, "I play winner." She searched for the bartender. "After I find the lady's room."

Theodon lifted his chin to the far hall. "Down the hallway. It's the last door on the left."

"Great, thank you." Adaline turned on her heel and headed for the restroom. She slowly walked the long hallway toward the last door on the left, but she stopped when she heard two voices grunting and moaning their way to ecstasy behind the only door on the right. She hurried past the door, put her back to the wall, and cloaked herself in her force field. A minute passed before the voices settled and the door opened. Out walked Landon tying the lace-up fly of his pants as he headed back to the bar.

Wait for it, Adaline thought. Another minute passed before another emerged, and Adaline's heart sank when she saw Roserie. The she-elf finished fixing her skirts then walked toward Adaline to enter the restroom. After the door closed behind her, Adaline dropped the camouflage as she combined what she witnessed with what she read earlier. She knew Roserie was crown-hungry, and she also knew that Theodon had feelings for Roserie. Now she's overheard Landon pleasuring Roserie. Adaline shook off the shock and nonchalantly walked into the restroom. She sidled up to the sink and began washing her hands next to Roserie. They exchanged minor chit-chat until Adaline dried her hands.

"Do you like Theris so far?" Roserie asked her.

"You know, I do," Adaline said. "It's meeting intriguing people, like you, that's convinced me to continue to visit in the future."

Roserie assessed Adaline's expression for a moment before giving a practiced smile. "You're so sweet. Thank you!"

Adaline held open the door to the restroom with her foot. "You're welcome. Shall we?"

Roserie exited the restroom in front of Adaline, who seethed with anger for a moment before she heard, "Adaline! You're up!" She saw Theodon stepping away from the table after Bole's challenge to the prince. She didn't believe for a minute that Bole won on his own accord and chalked it up to Theodon's humility. Adaline's eyebrows lifted at the pile of money on the table as she slid into the seat across from Bole.

"Double or nothing," she said to Bole as Forb stood over them. Their eyebrows lifted in surprise at such a bet. *I'm going to play this weak human card until the wheels fall off,* she thought, as she smirked and set her elbow on the table. "What?" Adaline said to Bole, who was still shocked by the bet. "It should be easy money, right?"

"Where will you get that kind of money?" Forb asked.

Adaline tilted her head toward Theodon. "This guy is going to loan it to me."

Forb and Bole laughed but stopped when Theodon nodded, accepting the commitment. Bole finally took Adaline seriously.

"All right," Bole said with a shrug.

Adaline smiled as they locked hands, and Forb rested his

over both of theirs.

"Ready? Go!" Forb said before lifting his hand.

The smug grin on Adaline's face didn't falter as Bole pushed against her unmoving arm. His muscles starting to ripple as he pushed harder, and his teeth gritted through his struggle. Adaline checked her manicure on her unoccupied hand. Her strength stunned Forb, and Adaline smiled and winked at him. She glanced at Theodon, who wore a contented smile on his face.

Her eyes narrowed on him. "You didn't really lose to him, did you?" Bole continued to struggle against her strength. Theodon looked at her meaningfully. "I knew it," she said before she slammed Bole's hand against the stone table. The momentum threw the elf out of his chair and cracked the table in half. "You're a nice guy, Theodon." She got up from the table and grabbed the stack of cash, then pretended to count it. "Do you want your money back?"

"No, you won that fairly," Theodon confirmed.

Forb, Bole, and everyone else in the bar gaped at Adaline.

"Well, fair is debatable," Adaline jested before she fanned the bills in her hands. "How much is this, anyway?"

"It's enough to keep you sitting pretty for quite a while," Theodon wisecracked.

"Was that?" Adaline leaned toward Theodon. "Was that a joke?" Adaline couldn't stifle a laugh as she pushed his shoulder.

Theodon snickered. "Are you ready to leave, Dr. Adaline?"

"I am," she said. "I have a feeling the end of that last drink is going to hit me soon, and I should probably be lying down when it does."

Theodon offered her his elbow. "Then let's be off."

By the time Theodon had escorted Adaline back to the palace, midnight had come and gone. Theodon didn't think about the possibility of a human reacting differently to elfin alcohol, since it's been so long since he'd seen a drunk human. Adaline and his friends seemed to have a good time together, so they continued drinking until Adaline's arm-wrestling win. Theodon noticed Adaline wobble when she first tried to stand after her victory, and he remained mindful of her intoxicated state during their return to the palace. Now, he had a drunken human doctor's arm wrapped over his shoulders to help her remain upright as they walked through the palace. She was a little giggly and even burst into laughter a couple of times, but other than that, she was far more entertaining than anyone he'd ever shared drinks with.

"Theodon," Adaline said in as serious a tone she could muster. She had an important confession to make, and she couldn't let any more time pass without sharing it.

"Adaline," Theodon replied.

She chuckled before getting sidetracked. "Is it okay to call you Theo in front of others?"

"Can I call you Ada?" Theodon shot back.

Adaline giggled. "No! That's silly…"

Theodon smiled before saying truthfully, "I'm afraid you cannot call me Theo in front of others." Unfortunately, etiquette for addressing royals withstood all bonds of friendship.

"Darn, I like that name."

"So do I."

Walking through the palace halls triggered Theodon's recent memory of his father's first meeting with Adaline earlier that evening. Watching the two of them being drawn to each other gave him hope. Hope for his father and hope that what the eternity ponds shared with him as a youngling was true: that the key to his father's happiness would lie within a beautiful outsider who knew what to do with his pain. That tiny sliver of hope gave him the motivation to happily show Adaline around Theris and to watch over her.

Adaline was able to keep up with Theodon and his friends' antics once the drinks started pouring. She could take a joke and throw one right back. Adaline had intelligent questions about elves and their history. She took the time to evaluate the information they shared before responding and listened to learn, not to reply. Theodon figured she had honed that habit due to being a "doctor," as she called it. He escorted her down a long hallway that was lined with doors to bedroom suites. Theodon's suite was near the end, as was the king's suite which rested behind large double doors. He was about to stop at the door to a room on the right side when she lost her footing. He snatched her by the waist and held her in place.

"Whoops," she said.

"I've got you," he said, taking all her weight, which was slight for his elfin strength.

"I have something to tell you," she said to him as she rebalanced. How could she possibly say it without it sounding ominous?

"Does it have anything to do with the questionable looks you threw my way before you beat Bole?" Theodon asked her.

"Yes," she confirmed. Theodon nodded. "It may upset you," she said truthfully as her brow furrowed. Theodon stopped walking and awaited her big reveal. "I'm a little drunk, so…" she sidestepped, "I think I should just show you." She reached for his face and settled her palm against his temple.

Theodon gasped at the charge of power as his eyes snapped shut before information flashed through his mind: the sensations, feelings, and images Adaline picked up when she passed the meeting room where his father met with the elders as they left the palace, the details of the soul records of his friends, and bits of Adaline's conversation with Talia and Roserie. Adaline removed her hand, and Theodon's eyes flashed open.

"What did you do?" he asked her.

"I showed you," she said. "There is deception in your house. It's deeply rooted and disguised as friends and counsel."

"Theodon," a voice came from behind them.

Theodon glanced over his shoulder to see his father standing in his sleep robes. He wore no crown, and his loose hair was tucked behind his pointed ears.

"Father," Theodon acknowledged.

"Getting dizzy," Adaline said in a soft voice as her knees gave way.

Theodon turned to catch her, but the king had already accelerated down the hallway so fast that his form blurred, and he swiftly scooped Adaline into his arms. Theodon stepped back and swallowed a smile as he noticed his father's concerned expression while examining the human in his arms who was on the verge of passing out.

The king's head tilted. "Door."

Theodon opened the nearest bedroom door, and the king entered while cradling the inebriated human against his chest. She was still lovely in her state of dizziness. The king closed the door behind him with his foot. Outside in the hallway, Theodon smiled openly, turned on his heel, and headed to his room. That small sliver of hope he carried for his father grew that night. He wouldn't allow what Adaline showed him to tarnish this moment of contentment yet. He'd consider the rest tomorrow.

Back inside the guest suite, the king was still gazing down at Adaline. She'd begun to doze in his arms, periodically murmuring a few words as she rested her cheek against his chest. *This will not do,* Aureon thought, but he couldn't reason setting her on the bed just yet. Finally, he pulled back the covers and gently set her down before slipping off her shoes and tucking her legs under the covers. He studied her zip-front hoodie and wondered if that should come off too, but he concluded he may be crossing a line by removing it. Then he struggled to convince himself that a line hadn't already been crossed.

He recalled what she had shared with Theodon about deception in his house. As he brought the covers up to her shoulders, he wondered how she could possibly know about it. For centuries he'd been building a case against the elder who was at the root of it all. He always came up short in his findings, for this elder was far older than Aureon, making it tricky to keep up but not impossible. Was Adaline somehow the elder's pawn? The idea was sobering to Aureon. Could all of what had happened before rise against him so many years later?

The blankets' coziness caused Adaline to stretch like a cat before she curled on her side facing Aureon. He couldn't remember the last time he'd done anything as domestic as tucking someone into bed. *Such a foreign feeling.* He stood over her, brows still drawn, as his hand hovered over her hip. The hunger for her curves was undeniable as she continued to occupy his thoughts, which hadn't ceased since they met. It wasn't merely desire, but a carnal need to be physically close to her, to want to do things with her. Things that elfin males were not supposed to think of doing with their females. Where has this lust-filled fascination come from? He'd gone more than a millennium without feeling an ounce of desire. Still, within the moment of laying eyes on her, he experienced an overwhelming need that he had never come close to feeling, even in his younger years.

"Mmm," she purred through her sleepiness at the feeling of his energy before she muttered, "Sexy ears."

His eyes widened in surprise at her admission before locking onto her full pout. He sank to his knees, still hovering over her as she fell asleep. She looked sweet when she slept. She was far from being the brilliant doctor who wouldn't put up with anyone trying to control her and would talk back to anyone, regardless of their rank. Her cleverness amused him. He leaned in and placed a soft kiss on her cheekbone. The sensation caused her to shrug back her shoulder, exposing her neck to him. His eyes narrowed on her skin and ate up every detail of her softness. She relaxed and nuzzled the pillow with her cheek, found a comfortable position, and settled.

"Dr. Adaline?" he asked softly.

"Hmm?" she answered, her guard down due to her intoxicated state.

"Why have you come to Theris?"

She yawned. "To get away."

"From?"

"Bad humans," she whispered.

Aureon thought her answer ominous and attempted to obtain more specific information with this investigative opportunity. "Is there a male who watches over you?"

"Uh-huh."

The king fisted his hands at his sides. Here he was tripping over himself for this... this... this human when she had no reason to stay in his world. She wasn't like the last humans who searched for refuge in Theris. She was merely a visitor and nothing more. He released his anger then decided on one more question.

"Do you wish to return to Theris?"

"Um-hmm," she answered before falling into a deep sleep.

He wouldn't interrogate her further. He knew his tactics weren't exactly admirable. One didn't have to live as long as him to understand that. But the opportunity to learn without causing damage, or an admission of feelings without her remembering, was enticing. He heard her heartbeat normalize, and her breathing deepened. Then an energetic field of white light covered her like a cocoon. Curious, the king touched it with the tip of his finger, only to receive a burning jolt in return. He yanked his hand back.

A force field?

The only reason she would need such protection would be if she were of great importance or in constant danger, he reasoned. *Perhaps both?* Regardless, it was a survival tactic and the fact she needed one was alarming. He struggled to dismiss the fact that the physical boundary made him want her more than before, as he was not accustomed to restrictions.

After a moment, he decided he would continue to play the long game with her, as it was his strength, for he had nothing but time. He would continue to treat Dr. Adaline with suspicion until he could prove, without a doubt, that she was not the pawn of the elder he'd been tracking. His attraction to her could be orchestrated, he reasoned. But how could someone get it so right?

He quietly closed the door to her room and assigned a guard to stand watch before heading to his suite to turn in for the night.

CHAPTER 6

The next morning, the king and the prince sat at their breakfast table, waiting for Adaline to join them. Meanwhile, they discussed the differences in humans between Adaline and the ones they met almost a millennium ago.

"They were not advanced like her," Theodon mentioned to his father. The king silently agreed as breakfast was placed in front of them. "She's intelligent," Theodon stated. The king nodded. "Clever." Another nod from the king. "And-"

"Too smart for you," Adaline cut in from the entrance to the dining room.

The elves' gaze lifted from their plates.

Adaline's stern countenance and penetrating remained on the king as she approached the table and seated herself across from him.

"Good morning," Theodon greeted her.

She allowed her serious expression to break for a moment. "Good morning. Thank you for showing me around last night. I really enjoyed spending time with you."

The prince nodded. "The pleasure was mine."

Then Adaline turned back to the king, and her features went cold, surpassing the impact of the king's usual cold stare. Aureon had the need to shift in his seat.

"What's wrong?" she asked him. "Afraid you're in the hot seat?"

Theodon's focus remained on Adaline as he chewed his breakfast, curious as to why she was upset.

"Theodon," she said while staring at the king, "tell me what happened after we returned to the palace last night."

Not yet understanding her asking's purpose, he assumed she was too intoxicated to recall, so he obliged her. "I escorted you back. You were a little unstable to walk on your own. So, I took you to one of the guest suites." Adaline's eyes blazed with fury at the king. Theodon's eyes shifted from Adaline to his father before continuing, "Father appeared and caught you when you became dizzy. He took you into the suite."

"Thank you, Theodon," she said and then directed her next question at the king, "Then what happened?"

Silence.

"Nothing?" she said to him. "Just keeping more secrets to stack on top of the ones you already have?"

"Is there something you wish to accuse me of, little human?" he asked in a low, eerie tone.

"Accusation implies room for innocence," she challenged. "Something you are not."

The energy rolling off him was defensive and angry.

"What are you talking about?" Theodon asked.

"Your father decided to interrogate me while I was drunk," she said to Theodon, her fiery eyes never leaving the king.

"You are one to talk," he sneered at her.

"Excuse me?" she said, baffled.

"You are here for adventure, and you leave behind a male at home who is meant to protect you," he said to her, rising to his feet with his hands on the table, ready for the verbal confrontation to escalate to wherever he deemed necessary.

Adaline didn't allow him to use his height as an obstacle. She stepped onto the seat of her chair so she could look straight down at him while she reprimanded him. Theodon's eyes widened in shock as the situation escalated. He put his flatware down and readied himself for… well, he didn't know what, yet. He figured he would have to jump in between them to save her because she was a human, but he'd witnessed her power. Instead, he waited to act.

"That male is my twin, you ass!" she yelled at him with her hands on her hips. "My brother! You're damn right – He's the one male protecting me, just like family should because the rest of you are takers, like the information you siphoned from me last night that isn't yours! It was none of your damn business, and you have no right to it. I don't care what your rank is in this world. All royals in my world are dead, and that's exactly what your title is to me. Nothing. Zero." Her eyes and fingertips glowed as she waved her hand at him, making him stumble back down to sitting in his seat and locking him into place. She stepped down from the chair, placed both hands on the table as she leaned forward. Her voice turned vicious as he struggled against her power. "And it's not me that needs protection." Theodon quietly rose from his chair. "If this were my world, I would have ended you. The only reason I haven't is because of him." Adaline pointed a glowing finger at Theodon.

After the bullshit he pulled last night, I can't fathom how Theo turned out so good if Aureon was all he's had, she thought.

The king ceased struggling against her power once he felt the foundation of the palace shake. Her power was far greater than he expected. Still, her words hit him with a more significant impact about how important it was to her for information about her to be unknown. It meant that the force field she slept under was to protect her because she was important, he realized. He wondered about all she was for her to be diligent in keeping personal details about herself concealed. Was her twin like her? What had happened in her world that made her so secretive?

What he did was wrong, Aureon knew that, but kings don't apologize. Instead, he tried to stick with his original plan: suspicious until proven innocent.

"Who are you to speak to me this way? Do you know who you are accusing?" he snarled.

She leaned close to his face while her voice quieted to a serious tone. "Oh, but I do… and very well." Her eyes flickered with light. She stared into his eyes as the epiphany hit him while tears pooled in her own: she did know him. That's why she looked at him intentionally when they first met. She could see him, all of him, and even after learning so much about him, she still stayed for a night.

"You're fortunate. No one has ever lived to have the chance to disrespect me twice," her voice cracked before her head tilted. "Do we understand each other, now?" She didn't wait for his response because she felt winded, punched in the gut with the reality of Theris when the dream was what she wanted. *This isn't home.* She wouldn't be free here like she'd hoped. She sighed and stepped away from the table, dropping her telekinetic hold on Aureon before addressing Theodon.

"Theo," she said with a small smile and tears in her eyes, "it was very nice meeting you. I wish you the best." She headed toward the palace entrance she was dragged through by guards the day before.

"Will you return?" Theodon asked as he stepped away from the table. Adaline glanced over her shoulder, shook her head, and headed for the portal.

No! the king thought, but he did not outwardly react. His soul attempted to use his emotions to shake his consciousness's depth free after being dormant for so long. He had a millennium to practice tamping his feelings down to barely a whisper, and the honed lack of reaction was emotionally crippling him.

Theodon rushed after her. "Please don't make this decision now," he pleaded with her as he followed her out of the palace. It was new for him to beg due to his title.

"It's already made," she said with conviction.

Theodon hurried to keep pace with her as she backtracked to the portal. "Wait. Had he not interrogated you, when were you planning to visit?"

She thought about it before returning to her hastened pace. "In five days."

Theodon clapped his hands victoriously before he stopped her. "That's perfect." She looked at him like he was crazy if he thought she was setting foot in elf-land ever again. "Please listen. What my father did was not right. I can tell you that had it been my grandfather interrogating you, he would not be sorry in the least."

"Your father isn't sorry for what he did," Adaline said. "He's sorry he got caught. He assumed no one would hold him accountable because a king doesn't abide by boundaries." Just like when humans had royals.

"That's fair," Theodon said. "The difference is my grandfather would have thrown you in the dungeon for yelling at him because he believed he had every right to whatever he wanted at any given time."

She crossed her arms over her chest and raised an eyebrow at him as she recalled Aureon's first threat to throw her in the dungeon. "Apple doesn't seem to fall far from the tree, Theo."

He tilted his head at her with a conscience-stricken expression before saying, "This is the point I mean to share with you: when you got upset with him and, as you said, held him accountable... and not to mention, threatened him, he cared."

"I know he did," she said. She didn't miss the look of realization on the king's face or his feelings that came with it.

Theodon's brow furrowed. "Then why are you leaving?"

"Because he betrayed the trust he hadn't earned, yet," she

stated. "I'm not going to repeat extending to him the opportunity to gain my trust, then become hysterical when he disappoints me as if I can claim I never saw it coming. That's insane! You are expecting me to trust someone who has always been the way he is and therefore will never change when it's my safety at stake."

Theodon's brow furrowed. "How do you know he will do it again?"

"Because it happens every time, Theo," she said. "Men in my world are supposed to protect me; however, there are only three men who deliver. The others want information about me to gain the upper hand, trap me, exploit me for personal gain, or kill me. So, tell me, Theo, why should I trust your father, who is obviously in it for his own personal gain?"

Her truth hit Theodon hard, causing him to sigh as his hands rested on his hips and his eyes fell to his feet. He searched for something that would make her reconsider. He knew that if she could get past this and give his father a chance to make up for his wrongdoing, he would surprise her. However, she'd have to allow him the space to do that.

Theodon took her hands in his to draw her attention. "I understand the fear behind the possibility of past pain recurring in one's life, but I've known him much longer than you. You must know that he never wants females around for any reason. However, you slept down the hall from him last night after he tucked you into bed. There was a time when the most beautiful subjects flooded the throne room to crack his façade, and he crushed their hopes every time." His grip on her hands tightened while his attention dropped to them. He finally met her gaze again. "For once, I see hope for him. It's in the curious way he looks at you and how he responds to you. If there's a chance, any chance, that you can digest his mistake, the coldest elf in the kingdom might find happiness with the cleverest human I've ever met."

Well, damn, Adaline thought to herself with a sigh.

A beat passed.

"Why do you want me to be with your father?" she asked

Theodon.

"Because I see something there, Addy," Theodon answered.

Adaline smiled softly at his use of a nickname for her. "I can't promise you anything," she informed him. "If I do decide to come back, it will be in five days." Theodon let out a sigh of relief. "Theo," she held his attention. "If I come back. Understand?"

He nodded before gesturing down the road. "Your consideration is all I can ask for, Dr. Adaline. May I escort you the rest of the way?"

"Yes."

"Also," Theodon added, "I should remind you that you still have a bet to win."

"That's a low blow, Theo," Adaline muttered before she kicked a small rock out of her path.

Back at the palace, the king slumped back against his throne. *You idiot,* he thought as he rubbed his temples with one hand. *She fled, and you did not even move.* What kind of male had he become? Moments later, his son stood before him, clearly upset.

"You have five days," his son informed him.

The king remained silent while watching his son. They stared at each other, knowing that this one human has changed everything.

Theodon switched to telepathy. "Leave it to you to upset the one female you had allowed in our home in a millennium by being something she's experienced many times before — a male who was supposed to protect her but didn't. Excellent job at betraying her trust, Father." He crossed his arms over his chest.

Aureon didn't snap at his son, nor did he need to be further chastised. He narrowed his eyes on the prince, prompting Theodon to conclude his rant versus continuing it.

"You might have a chance to right this wrong in five days," Theodon said in his father's mind before storming from the throne room. "I suggest you begin thinking about your apology."

CHAPTER 7

"**A**sher is wondering what's wrong with me," Adaline admitted to her friend, Tessa, who was sitting across from her. She glanced at the cards in her hand. They sat at a table in the common area of the Hall of Lost Arts. After the world caved in on itself, humans had a hard time resurrecting the arts and extracurricular activities tied to mass manufacturing. It was rare to have a Hall of Lost Arts in one's area, and it usually took over a ransacked library. At a Hall of Lost Arts, people could check out books, music, board games, movies, or decks of playing cards. The hall even offered classes on dancing, painting, drawing, and the like. Since supplies for these hobbies were scarce, the items could never be removed from the facility; hence the common area provided to use them.

"I'm trying to figure out what's wrong with you," Tessa admitted as she sorted her cards according to suit. "You meet this guy, he screws up big, and you are still mulling over it. I don't get it. You've usually drop-kicked all memory of them off your beach house balcony by now."

A couple of days had passed since Adaline's fallout with the king, and she was surprised it still bothered her. She felt attached to the situation because of Theodon's confession before she left. It was as if she had to return, and the one thing she hated most was being told what to do. However, she couldn't dismiss an intuitive nudge pushing her toward the king because he was someone significant to her. She just didn't know what yet. What she did know, however, was to withhold two details from Tessa: that the "people" they were talking about were elves and royal elves that lived on a distant planet. Also, Adaline sensed a shift in her friendship with Tessa over the past week. She hadn't taken the time to investigate it, so specific details went missing from their girl talk until she did. Both women kept flipping their cards until a pair of aces came up.

Tessa's hand covered them first, and she grinned at her victory. She took the pile and added the cards to her hand, rearranging them as she integrated her winnings. Adaline's eyes narrowed in playful suspicion. Their game continued, along with their conversation.

"If you think this guy is worth the hassle," Tessa said while scanning her cards, "then, by all means, go for it. You really don't take the time to invest in men outside of Asher because of how much they've hurt you. I know this because I was on the sidelines watching each one go up in flames... literally, in one case."

Adaline glanced at Tessa and sighed before staring at her cards, vacillating between which to play while considering her friend's rationale. Tessa's comment about Adaline investing only in Asher hung in Adaline's mind, which wasn't true, but that was due to Tessa not knowing about Jim and Tony —

and that would not change.

A smile grew on Tessa's face as she witnessed her friend gain a realization. "I think there's something you may be overlooking in this situation." Adaline played her next card. Tessa played hers before saying, "I think you may have more power in this situation than you realize."

"You have my attention," Adaline replied while focusing on the cards in her hand.

"Remember when I was dating Nick, and I vented about how we were far into a relationship, but I still hadn't met any of his friends or family?" Tessa asked her.

Adaline nodded. "And I told you that all you needed to do was to cut to the chase and make your needs known. Tell him what you need, so he could consider how important it was for you. And that if he really cared about you, he would provide you with what you need."

"Yes!" Tessa chirped.

"What's your point, friend?" Adaline said as she played her next card.

"You have his son rooting for you. You successfully treated the little girl they brought to you. His son enjoyed taking you out to meet his friends. His friends liked you," Tessa listed.

Eh, that's only horn-dog Uncle Landon... and maybe Forb, Adaline thought.

"All you are doing is making his son look like the better option," Adaline admitted.

Tessa shrugged. "Then maybe you should consider dropping one for the other. No judgment there." Adaline laughed. "You are acquiring allies," Tessa said as she played her next card, not paying close attention to the game. "Good ones."

The conversation paused as they played another round. The pile of cards between them was building up to a game-changing stack.

"What I'm saying is-" Tessa tried to reiterate.

Adaline's hand slipped in to cover the two kings that sat face up on the table. She smiled wide. "You're saying I have all the cards.

CHAPTER 8

At House Miathan, a shouting distance from the palace, Talia wandered through her family's sprawling estate. She crossed a small bridge over a spring that ran through the property, and she continued through an oasis in search of her father. On the far end of the oasis was an intricately built canopy that protected Graydon Miathan's desk from the elements. He was sifting through papers spread in front of him.

"Father," Talia acknowledged.

"Yes, my dear?" Graydon asked as he continued to search for a lost document. His eyes narrowed on the papers in front of him, highlighting his crow's feet. This subtle sign of aging proved one thing: Graydon Miathan was ancient. Talia waited to speak again until prompted by her father.

"I am looking for a letter that holds an update regarding an important pending project," her father admitted. After he decided to pause his search, he asked her, "What brings you all the way out here today?"

"I thought you should know that Theodon brought a human to Eleona's a few nights ago," Talia informed him.

Her father caught a stray strand of his long blonde hair and re-tucked it behind his ear as he considered her statement. "What of it?"

"She's-"

Graydon's eyebrows lifted. "It's a female?"

"Yes, Father," Talia confirmed. "She's different from the ones who came before her."

"Pssh," Graydon huffed. "That species is not far from being a single-celled organism."

"This one is different, Father," Talia warned.

"How so, my dear?"

"She beat Bole at arm wrestling," Talia revealed. "And she looked at us as if she could see through us. I think... I think there is more to her, Father."

The elder pursed his lips and nodded. "One human cannot derail our plans, my dear, no matter her strength. Their species is obsolete, and she will only get herself killed if she gets in our way. Another casualty, nothing more."

Talia preened with pride at her father's confident words. She's hung on each one since she was a child, and he came home with the news that she would one day marry Prince Aureon and be the next queen of Theris. However, that dream came crashing down when King Cerus allowed his son to choose his bride so Aureon could marry... her. Talia's thoughts of Queen Aravae were never polite, even before she married Aureon. Aravae was from a new noble house, whereas House Miathan was an ancient dynasty.

Graydon and King Cerus had a falling out when the king sent for the elder to speak privately about the change in plans for their children.

"How could you do this, Cerus?" Graydon argued. "This arrangement has been planned since their infancy! What am I supposed to tell my daughter? She has been looking forward to this union since she was a youngling!"

Cerus shook his head in defeat. "I understand your situation, old friend, but I cannot allow my son to repeat my tragic history or that of the kings before me. The only way the crown is bearable to serve is with a king's true mate at his side. My son has found his mate. If he doesn't have that bond, he has nothing, as my life has proven. I will not allow an unfulfilling existence to be repeated in the life of my son. A king should have the same opportunities for love and family as any other elf. Your daughter should be allowed the same freedom." Cerus originally planned, to no one's knowledge, to move forward with the arranged marriage, had his son not found his mate by a certain age. To Cerus' relief, Aureon met Aravae in record time, and he's never seen his son happier.

"We are not any other elves!" Graydon shouted before he lunged at Cerus and snatched the equally ancient king by his collar. "My daughter is supposed to be queen! Your son will pay for this!"

Cerus' shoulders grew defensive as his gaze turned predatory on his longtime friend. "Be careful of your words, Graydon," Cerus warned in an eerie tone. "My son is already more powerful than me. Should you cross him, I have no doubt he will not hesitate to bring his wrath down upon you and your house. He will make sure there isn't a single Miathan left to walk the Starlands."

"So, you plan to allow your son to marry this... this... female from a farce of a noble house?" Graydon spat out.

"House Elacan is a new noble house," Cerus defended, "and rightfully so. Cristatus deservedly earned the honor for his family as he fought by my side when I was up to my ears in Crae! The question you still haven't answered to this day is: where were you?"

Deafening silence hung between them.

"You never told me what was so important that you'd abandon your duty to your king, to fight alongside me," Cerus admitted, glassy-eyed. His heart was breaking because there was a time with Graydon was his closest friend. They grew up together and fought side by side over millennia, but greed had rooted its way in Graydon's heart, and it was tearing Cerus' in two.

"I miss one battle that you ended up winning. What of it?" Graydon sneered.

"Not one battle," Cerus' voice became a whisper. "One war."

"My house has been loyal to the royal family since ancient times!" Graydon exploded. "We are supposed to be rewarded for standing by the Sleones for so long!"

Cerus cast Graydon a worried look. "Are you saying your loyalty comes at a price? Your friendship, too? Is what I should have known this whole time? That you expected a payout for your allegiance paints you in a different light in my eyes, and it saddens me." Cerus' head hung as he paced.

Graydon fumed. He didn't care about Cerus' sadness. Graydon only wanted to finally reap the benefits of being close to the Sleone family, so he tried to merge with it through his daughter's marriage to Aureon. Now, he wouldn't collect the reward for all his planning.

"You are mincing words," Graydon accused. "You know I deserve this!"

...*to rule,* Cerus detected in the subtext of Graydon's exclamation.

Cerus approached his friend and rested his hand on his shoulder in an attempt to de-escalate the situation. "That's why we are blessed with love and offspring, so we all may feel like kings in the eyes of our families."

"To hell with your sentiment!" Graydon threw Cerus' hand off his shoulder and stormed from the room.

"I warn you of your gluttonous heart, old friend," Cerus' words cut through the air, stopping Graydon in his tracks. "If it controls you, now, and you choose to seek retribution against something as beautiful as two elves in love, know that I will not hesitate to act against you."

Graydon hesitated to glance over his shoulder at Cerus.

"And I will not restrict my son from doing the same," Cerus ended.

Graydon rushed from the palace and, from that day forward, hatched his scheme against the Sleones. The first phase had worked: the poisoning of the queen. It wounded the new King Aureon significantly. Even better, there was no evidence to charge anyone with the murder, so the royals announced that she passed due to complications during childbirth. The second phase of the plan was gaining momentum, and should the prince not marry who Graydon deemed best for his own interests, the enemies of Theris would pillage the elf kingdom to ruin. And the third phase, well, the third phase, Aureon could not fathom the horror Graydon ensured would destroy House Sleone forever.

So, for Graydon to hear that Prince Theodon was consorting with a human female was continuing to fall in line with the elder's plan, and he had no problem getting rid of her, too, if she became a nuisance.

"Don't worry, my dear," Graydon said to his daughter. "This will all be over soon, and the Sleone's will rule Theris no more."

CHAPTER 9

A daline reflected on her conversation with Tessa as she walked to her car in the Hall of Lost Arts' parking lot. Most vehicles drove themselves, but Adaline didn't want technology dominating her life. Most people handed their lives over to machines without thinking twice, and Adaline shuddered at the thought of giving up autonomy.

That's what got us in trouble in the first place, she thought, as she drove away.

On the ride home, she considered what happened during her brief time in Theris: the food, the drinks, the elves.

The king.

She remembered when she and Theodon returned to the palace from Eleona's. Aureon stood further down the hall before dizziness overtook her. Theodon kept her hoisted on her feet, and in the next second, Aureon scooped her up in his arms. She felt his concern, curiosity, and captivation, which ignited her fury when she woke the following day and realized his deception.

Socializing with Theodon's friends revealed that elves were far more advanced than humans could ever hope to become. It would take thousands of years for her species to have a chance of catching up, but humans had less than thirty-seven years left. Her eyes watered as she pulled into her garage as a realization hit: the elves are what humans could have been if humans could have just eliminated their greed. Yet even in their final years, humans continued to enslave themselves with things they didn't need, thinking more stuff would solve their problems when the answer was less. The answer was within, she knew, and it was clear that the elves knew that, too.

Theodon and his friends answered numerous questions she had about their species. The elves didn't need technology to connect; they were already connected to the planet, its creatures, and families had telepathic abilities among themselves. Some elves were able to develop the ability to communicate beyond the family bloodline, and Theodon revealed to her that the king could connect with all minds in the kingdom. It was how royal decrees, invitations, and announcements were made to ensure everyone received the correct information.

By nature, elves were fast, stealth, and were built like Adaline remembered dancers to look like in her world: ethereal in appearance, strong in body, and graceful in their movements. It was clear to Adaline that the males hid a facet of themselves, burying their wild nature, only to channel it on the battlefield. However, the prince contradicted this discovery, as he seemed to possess the capacity to be open and vulnerable. Collectively, the majority of males shelved that characteristic, replacing it with refined mannerisms. Examples of the king's behavior filled her mind.

Repression kills, Adaline thought.

She considered when the king tucked her into bed, then kissed her on the cheek. The sweet memory was ruined by his interrogation of her. Aside from his trickery, she thought his brief show of affection was a bold move, given how cold he was to her during their first interaction.

Unless the affection was part of his scheme too, she thought as her face fell. "Just a pawn in another man's game," she whispered. Trusting him was no longer an option, so she strategized a plan for if she returned to Theris. Then she wondered about the extent of the king's abilities versus those of his subjects. The rank of king implied that Aureon was superior in some form. Perhaps she should explore that if she returned.

The thought was sobering: returning to Theris. At that moment, she accepted that she would. She would have smiled at the idea, but she remembered using her abilities to reprimand Aureon before leaving. He may want nothing more to do with her. As she exited her car and wandered to Asher's house, Adaline reasoned that Aureon wouldn't have made it this far in his life if he couldn't handle being reprimanded.

She headed down to the basement of Asher's home, overhearing her brother sparring with Jim. Tony critiqued Asher's form while Adaline pulled her gloves out of her bag and slid them on before entering the room. Asher had started an hour before her because her time with Tessa ran late.

"Look who's finally here," Tony jested when he saw Adaline. Tony always wore a big smile.

Adaline smiled as she walked up to him and planted a kiss on his cheek. "Hey, boss."

"See?" Tony said to Asher, "Your sister shows me she respects my authority. Why can't you do the same?"

Asher paused between swings to say, "If you actually believe she respects your authority, then she really has you fooled, old man."

Tony laughed as Jim took another swing at Asher, who blocked and retaliated.

"All right," Adaline said, as she shifted her weight from one foot then the other before she let her bag slide off her shoulder. "Stop picking on Jim."

"Would you rather I pick on you?" Asher pushed.

"Is that?" Adaline leaned forward, then glanced at Tony, "Is that a challenge?" She pretended to dance around the space like a professional boxer trying to stay light on her feet.

Tony grinned. "I think it was."

"I'm stepping out of this line of fire," Jim conceded with his hands raised before backing away from Asher.

Adaline took her place across from her twin, shifted her stance as her eyes started to glow. "Ready?"

Asher smiled as a white electric current rippled over his own. "Ready."

The twins collided with a sonic boom, shaking the house and breaking the windows as their sparring session continued for the next hour. They always fought as close to full strength as possible to become better fighters, and Asher's basement was the perfect cover. When they were finished, Adaline shifted the house's molecular structure back into place as if the trauma to the foundation never happened, and everyone headed upstairs to the kitchen as the shards of glass reformed the windows.

"So, something interesting happened this weekend," Adaline shared.

"Oh?" Jim said, intrigued. "Let's hear it."

"I explored a portal," Adaline admitted.

"Addy, that's dangerous," Tony warned.

"What's going to happen, Tony? I'll die?" Adaline asked. They all knew that was practically impossible. Tony sighed and held up his hands in defeat. She turned to Asher. "It led to a kingdom of elves that are biologically advanced, like us."

"So, you're thinking?" Asher tried to see where she was going with this.

"I think I should continue to learn more about this place," she said, "to see if we have a final step to our plan."

Asher froze once he realized what she was implying. "It might be a home for us?"

Adaline smiled. "Maybe."

The use of the word "home" affected Asher deeply. It had been many years since the twins had one. Home implied safety and love. Now, they just lived in houses. Asher's eyes pooled with tears until he chuckled. He reached his hand across the countertop and covered his sister's. "We can have a home? I never thought that would happen again."

Adaline squeezed her twin's hand. "Give me some time to explore. I kinda hit a snag with a few elves that live there."

"What do you mean?" Jim inquired.

"The royal family is technically a good family," Adaline said. "But others are plotting against them, and I have a feeling it's going to get... messy soon."

"What are these royals like?" Tony asked.

Tall, gorgeous, with extensive trust issues, she wanted to blurt out as an image of the king surfaced in her mind.

"The prince is very nice," Adaline admitted. "He reminds me a lot of you, Asher, minus the techaholic tendencies."

"Hey!" Asher exclaimed.

Tony chuckled. "It's true. I don't know anyone who needs a robotic unicycle."

Asher crossed his arms over his chest. "It's instrumental to my lifestyle." Adaline laughed when she saw Jim roll his eyes. "So, you were saying the prince is a noble, heroic god of a man, just like me."

"Actually, it's the king who is kind of a god..." Adaline trailed off.

All three men's eyebrows lifted.

"So, yeah," Adaline muttered as she rubbed the back of her neck. "About him..."

CHAPTER 10

C ommander Hunter Nash punched the wall in the observation room that peered into the interrogation room containing a terrified Tessa Hill. She was instructed to return to the abandoned precinct with information about the Everlys. Only, she didn't have the information they needed.

"Goddammit," he seethed.

"Miss Hill," the commander said into the microphone that masked his voice. "You were told to retrieve personal information about the Everlys, information that would help us, and we would let you go. You have failed."

Tessa shook in her seat as tears spilled down her cheeks, sure they would kill her now.

"They don't reveal anything," Tessa stressed. "They speak generally about their lives, and they conduct themselves normally. If I probe, they'll know something's off." *Please don't kill me,* her mind cried as her face contorted in a harsh sob.

"Let's give her one more shot," Agent Jackson Bale suggested to Commander Nash.

"Are you insane?" Nash asked. "She'll run straight to the Everlys and tell them everything!"

"She's too terrified of what we will do to her if she fails, again," Bale argued. "Plus, she's just one woman."

"One woman the Everlys will crucify us for if she ends up dead and they find out about it," Nash reminded him.

"They won't find her," Bale assured.

"What are you insinuating?" the commander inquired.

"I'm saying that maybe it's time we accelerated the Max-Program," the officer stated. If Miss Hill failed, again, she could be their next subject for their top-secret program.

The commander pursed his lips, his interest piqued. "That's not a bad idea."

"Hmm." Bale smiled as both men stared out of the two-way mirror at Tessa. "Don't worry, she'll come back with information next time."

"Well then," the commander said, "give her new instructions and let her go."

Minutes later, Tessa hurried out of the police station. Once she ran to her car and locked herself inside, her façade broke, and she sobbed uncontrollably with her forehead pressed against the steering wheel. Her life was on the line, and it was effortless for the QC to erase her from the world.

She had to do something. She had to act.

What am I going to do? She thought before an idea emerged, and her tears stopped. She scrambled to fasten her seatbelt, started her car, and floored the accelerator into traffic.

Meanwhile, King Aureon reached into the minds of the Alloralla family.

"I would like to see Farryn today," he spoke into their minds in Tear.

"Yes, Your Majesty," the mother and father immediately replied.

Within the hour, little Farryn was carried into the throne

room by her mother, who appeared to be uncomfortably pregnant. Her discomfort set off an alarm in Aureon's mind. He listened to the baby she carried. His eyes widened for a moment upon discovering she was carrying twins, and one baby's heartbeat was faint. Farryn's father accompanied them. The parents caught sight of the king and rushed to bow before standing to meet any further requests.

Aureon rose from his throne, and his eyes never left Farryn. She appeared to be as happy as ever. He tucked his hands behind his back and descended the stairs that elevated his throne to observe her closely. His green gaze reached beyond the surface of Farryn's biology into her digestive system, her immune system, her cardiovascular system until he had searched her entire little body. A few minutes passed before he finished. Astonished that he saw no trace of the disease, he opened his arms to hold the child. The mother didn't hesitate to hand Farryn to him. Even so, Aureon noticed the mother's anxiety about handing over her child to a powerful person with a known temper, and he was compelled to relax her suspicions. Little Farryn reached for the king and cried out with a happy laugh. Aureon smiled to himself as he lifted her and settled her against his chest. He kept searching her biology as he spoke to her parents for any clue he might have missed.

"I have not held a child in a long time," he admitted in subtle admiration. The parents smiled and relaxed. "Not since my own son was little."

Little Farryn tried to join the adult conversation with a few mumbled words in Tear as she patted the king on the shoulder and let out a squeal. She thought the king's big green eyes were pretty toys; therefore, they must be touched. She reached for his face, earning a shocked gasp from her parents as her little hands landed on the king's cheekbones. A corner of his mouth lifted before he took the opportunity to search her brain again. He found nothing wrong – no trace of the illness. In fact, the child's energy levels were optimal, far from where they were first brought to the palace. Remarkable, the king thought before handing her back to her mother.

"Thank you, Your Majesty," the mother said as she took Farryn. The king gave a clipped nod.

"It's a miracle, My Lord," the father said, pulling his wife against his side.

The king didn't comment at first. He noticed how happy the family was now that their daughter was healed and had the chance to grow up. "It is quite a phenomenon," the king replied. "Thank you for bringing her to me." Both parents bowed to the king before leaving.

Aureon refrained from instructing them to make him aware of any changes in the child. It seemed they needed a victory to revel in, and he would let them have it because he knew firsthand what it was like to hope for a child to live through a deadly illness. As he reflected on when he almost lost Theodon when he was little, Aureon's shoulders slumped. He re-buried the memory and returned his attention to Farryn's healing and the light that had passed from Dr. Adaline to the child.

What was that light, and where did it come from? He thought of her response of it being "divine" and wasn't satisfied with that. His mind raced to develop hypotheses for reasons a human could possess such significant power. He fell short.

Farryn's dramatic recovery didn't sway his thoughts from the possibility of Adaline being a pawn to distract him. In his mind, his attraction to her had such a carnal impact on him that it could not possibly be real; therefore, it must be fabricated. The king sighed, weary of his years of being on guard against enemies in his own kingdom that he could not fully identify, aside from one. He had to keep up appearances as he continued to search for evidence that would finally allow him to punish the guilty parties that Adaline tried to warn Theodon about the night they returned from Eleona's.

His thoughts strayed to that night when he carried Adaline to bed. How was a being that powerful so soft to the touch? She was trusting and vulnerable in her tired and intoxicated state... and he took advantage of her. *Not my finest moment,* he thought, as he began brainstorming an appropriate apology.

CHAPTER 11

A daline sifted through a chest she kept in her closet that contained journals, maps, photographs, and other trinkets her ancestors collected over the centuries. It was a collection initially started by their ancestor, Jocelyn. She was a loyal follower of the prophet who announced the coming of the diviners. The prophet honored Jocelyn's loyalty by informing her the diviners would be born into her family in the form of twins. The prophet continued giving Jocelyn information about the diviners and their purpose, so Jocelyn began recording it in a journal, hoping the information would reach the end of her lineage - the twins.

Thankfully, it did, as her family was secretive about their knowledge that the diviners would be their descendants. Each generation was conscious about collecting information they deemed would help the twins better understand their purpose and gifts. There were also news clippings and boxes of military medals and certificates. The twins were the first to stray from their military-lineage to become doctors. However, that was not the information Adaline was searching for at the moment. She was lost in thought while thumbing through photographs, smiling to herself at the ones of her and Asher when they were little. Her heart clenched at the photos of the two of them with their parents. After allowing herself a moment to yearn for happier times when they were all together, she set the photos aside and picked up Jocelyn's second journal in the series. The twins read all the content contained in the chest when they were younger. But now, it felt like it was time to review it all, considering the pending end of life on Earth.

Adaline flipped through, recalling a section Jocelyn had written about the growth of their abilities. Adaline knew how to exercise her current ones and awaken dormant ones, which took a lot of time and energy. Now, she desired to expedite the process. Finally, she reached a passage that mentioned, "Abilities can be received through a direct connection with the divine."

Hmm, Adaline thought. *Direct connection. I thought we were already directly connected?* Adaline closed the journal and arranged the journals in their proper order before closing the chest and stowing it away. She considered the idea until she found herself on her large patio that overlooked the Pacific Ocean. She sat on her meditation pillow, folded her legs, rested the backs of her hands on her legs, closed her eyes, and focused.

Direct connection with the divine, she kept whispering in her mind. At first, the images she saw while meditating defaulted to what she came to know as a peaceful place for her, then the images changed. Everything turned white, and she couldn't decipher walls from ceilings in the endless space.

"Hello," someone said behind her. Adaline spun to see a translucent being of white light. His blurred features begged her to take precautions.

"Hello," she replied as she tried to analyze him. When that didn't work, she read his soul record. "Ah!" she hollered, and her eyes snapped shut. Searching his soul record was like opening the door to the surface of the sun, searing her retinas.

"Careful," the being said as he waited for her eyes to regenerate. "Don't let your curiosity get you hurt."

"Could have used that warning earlier," Adaline shot back, blinking her eyes as the tissues regenerate.

"All better?" the being asked.

"Yes," Adaline confirmed. "Who are you?"

The being gave a small smile amused that Adaline was such a forthright human, leaving no room for unanswered questions.

"I am what you are searching for," the being stated.

"A direct connection to the divine," Adaline repeated. Her tone revealed she wasn't convinced yet. She'd projected to many planes of existence and had met dozens of beings who falsely claimed their rank and knowledge.

The being nodded.

"Do you have a name?" she inquired.

"Not one that can be pronounced with a human tongue," the being admitted.

Adaline pursed her lips. "You must be ancient then."

"Quite the contrary, diviner," the being stated. "I am infinite. Eternal. Old and new, and ever-changing."

Adaline drew a parallel that this being, and the prophets that returned to Earth, spoke similarly to how they revealed information. Therefore, this being maybe legitimate in his claims.

"All right, I'll bite," Adaline said. "What do my brother and I need to do to awaken dormant abilities at a faster rate?" She knew that the number of abilities they wielded, and the strength in those abilities, might be the key to their surviving the end of the world. The twins had to prepare if it might be true.

The being nodded at Adaline's question. "Return here, and I will give you the key to awakening more abilities, but only a few at a time."

Adaline's brow furrowed. "Why only a few?"

"To give you all at once would cause a similar harm as when you tried to read my soul," the being confirmed, as he let his words hang in the air for a moment, "But far worse. You can only awaken more than that when you are in your true form, and you bond with your twin to fulfill your purpose." Adaline remained rooted in her thoughts. "Because you are still of a human biology, you must give yourself time to acclimate before returning for more."

"What happens when we awaken all abilities?" she asked.

"You will be fully divine on Earth," the being said. "Fortunately, you may not need all abilities to fulfill your purpose on your planet, but you will have them nonetheless."

That's good to know, she thought.

"Your brother still has many obstacles in comparison to you," the being said.

"How so?"

"His attachment to earthly possessions inhibits him from arriving at this plane on his own. Therefore, he will be behind in his abilities versus yours," the being revealed.

"He already is," Adaline stated. "Would you be open to an incentive program?" The being's head tilted. Adaline was about to use a word that didn't come naturally to her. "May I please give him his first awakening to encourage him to evolve his own soul?"

"You dare to ask me to trust that you would take your abilities and your brothers, trusting you to correctly distribute them?" the being challenged.

Adaline paused. "Yes."

"Why?"

"Because my soul record substantiates my credibility," Adaline stated matter-of-factly.

The being smiled as the human proved herself far from being a pushover. "Hold out both hands."

Adaline didn't hesitate to do as instructed. The being formed two balls of light, one in each hand. The small globes burned with a golden light until they burned bright white.

"Yours is the one in your right hand," the being indicated.

"And your brother's is the one in your left."

"Is it a simple insert to the heart?" Adaline asked. The being nodded. "Okay," Adaline said to the being before she said a phrase that was slowly becoming less foreign to her, "Thank you."

The being smirked. "You are welcome."

The scene faded, leaving Adaline sitting on her patio alone, once again. She peered at the light balls that rested safely in each palm. She studied the one meant for her.

"Moment of truth," she whispered before pushing the ball into her heart until it sank into her chest. Her heart rate accelerated, as did her breathing while the new abilities unlocked and melded to her soul. Her breathing normalized as every cell of her being felt the surge in power. Her eyes shone brighter.

"Ash," Adaline spoke into her twin's mind, "Get over here. You've gotta try this."

CHAPTER 12

There was one day left to reveal if the human doctor would return to Theris. Theodon lifted the strap of his full quiver over his head to secure it across his back as he exited the palace. He tested his bowstring while walking down the front steps, then heard a child fuss. His attention lifted to see a long line of elves, both adults and children, filling the walkway to the palace.

Theodon addressed one of them in Tear, "Why is everyone in line?"

The elf bowed before addressing the prince. "We heard of the healing of the Alloralla's baby girl, Farryn. Is it true, Your Grace? Is there a female who can heal us?" The elf's hopeful eyes searched Theodon's neutral expression.

Theodon exhaled slowly, understanding the ramifications of publicizing Adaline's healing abilities. He nodded to himself before informing the elf, "I will return with an answer."

The elf was delighted to get a helpful response from a member of the royal family.

Theodon hustled back into the palace and found his father in his library, standing over a large manuscript. The king's finger shot across the page in a blur, keeping up with his speedy reading.

"Father," Theodon addressed the king.

"Son," the king said without looking up.

"We have a problem," the prince admitted. The king glanced up from the page. Theodon walked over to the balcony attached to the library and gestured to the long line building down the palace's front. The king strode over to his son's side, his hands clasped behind his back, and peered over the edge.

"The human doctor has generated an audience," the king said.

Theodon watched more elves flock toward the palace to get in line. "They won't be dispersing anytime soon."

A moment of silence passed as they continued observing the growing line of subjects.

"Tell them they can return tomorrow," the king said.

Theodon's head shot up to look at his father, shocked that he would welcome so many into the palace. He must have a motive, Theodon thought. "For what purpose?"

The king smirked as he made a leisurely return to the text he was reading. His mind developed an ideal scenario. "She will choose what she wants to do about the line when she arrives."

"If she arrives," Theodon interjected.

The king shrugged, dismissing the comment. "We have witnessed how she reacts when her choice is taken." The king flipped to the next page in the large manuscript. "She wants a choice? She will have it."

Theodon tried to determine his father's motive and concluded faster than he expected. If the king allowed her to choose, then he would get a preview into the extent of her abilities. The opportunity for her to reveal more about her power piqued the king's curiosity.

Theodon shook his head. "You never learn, do you?" He turned on his heel, storming from the library as he muttered under his breath, "You are going to apologize for meddling only to betray her again." Theodon hoped, but differently than before that the human doctor possessed wrath. One that she would rain down on his father if he chose to go through with his plan.

CHAPTER 13

"**I**t feels like I'm stuck in a euphoric state for a few days," Asher said about his awakening process from his perch on the roof of a high-rise building in Century City. Asher was thrilled when his twin brought him his first light-ball-upgrade. He was a fan of trading-up whenever possible, and it didn't bother him that it came from a being Adaline couldn't identify.

"Then it subsides after the third day," Adaline finished. She playfully kicked her feet back and forth as they dangled off the side of the building. Asher nodded as they watched the streets below, waiting for QC agents to reveal another covert office location at any moment.

"So, we automate this," Asher proposed. "We absorb it and feel light-headed for a few days, absorb it for another two, exercise the new abilities for another two, and repeat the process each week until we know everything,"

"Just like finals week in college," Adaline joked.

"We ended up acing those too."

"Well, we were the youngest kids on campus. What else were we going to do?"

Asher's chest rose with confidence. "Oh, I kept myself plenty occupied."

"If by occupied, you are referring to sorority row, then yes, you were quite the busy medical student."

Asher grinned. "I was thorough in all of my examinations."

Adaline playfully nudged her twin. Asher chuckled before noticing a woman running for her life on the street below, with three QC agents closing in on her.

"Look, Sis. Minions!"

"How great would it be to have minions?"

"The best," Asher whispered enviously.

"The only thing the QC has that we don't," Adaline stated as agents spotted them and started scaling the building. Asher nodded to his twin, who stood and pushed off the roof, floating a few inches above it. Asher latched on to the metalwork on the building's façade, allowing white electricity to shoot from his hands and down the structure. The agents were electrocuted, their bodies twitching and convulsing before their grip unlatched from the building, sending them falling to their deaths.

"Shall we show them what they're missing out on?" Asher asked.

Adaline smiled. "We shall." She plummeted feet first while Asher gained traction against the building as he ran down the side of it. He zoomed past his sister as the terrain under his feet changed from building to the pavement. His acceleration gave him ample time to scout their surroundings as Adaline's fall slowed to a float before her feet planted softly on the ground.

A blur flew past Adaline as she heard "Diviners" echo off the buildings surrounding them. She looked around for the origin of the voice but found no one.

"I think we have a little speedster following us," Adaline said into Asher's mind.

"Cool," Asher replied. "We'll catch him later." Asher was thrilled at the possibility of finding another speedster like himself.

The three QC agents chasing the woman stopped and redirected their efforts once they spotted the twins.

"Incoming," Adaline said to Asher. Asher took his place at his sister's back, smiling as more agents funneled in their direction.

"Well, at least we can't say today was boring," Asher admitted. Dozens of agents ran at him as his eyes rippled with a white electric current.

Adaline chuckled as her eyes glowed. "Always the optimist."

The twins let the first wave of agents in to fight them in hand-to-hand combat. They needed the excitement. Then the second wave came and fell, and the twins integrated their new abilities into their fighting style. Asher pivoted to punch another agent square in his jaw, asserting his might. The impact sent the QC agent flying until he slammed into the next building.

"Whoops!" Asher said before he looked at his fist in surprise.

"An upgrade?" Adaline asked.

"I guess so," Asher said as he continued to examine his fist.

Adaline laughed before she kicked an agent square in the chest. "I think we should wrap this up."

"Good idea."

"I have an upgrade, too," Adaline said cleverly. She turned to Asher and put her hands on his shoulders before instructing him, "Palms straight out, and let the current fly."

Asher unleashed the electricity from his hands and held them out as instructed. His sister channeled her fiery white light through him and out his hands, turning his white electric current into a searing death ray.

"Now spin," she said to her brother. She stepped in time with him as he spun, slicing all standing agents in half. The cut was so hot that it cauterized the bodies.

"No blood, no foul," Adaline said, patting her brother on

the shoulder.

"Impressive," Asher said as they surveyed the damage.

Adaline nodded in agreement as she took in the body count around them. "Good times."

"Ready to go home?"

Something massive landed in front of them. It touched down with an impact that cracked the pavement under its feet. Towering seven and a half feet tall, it peered straight down at the twins, whose eyebrows lifted in surprise.

"Um, not yet," Adaline said, staring up at the creature. "It seems we've earned a bonus round."

The inbound's massive chest heaved as it stared at them. Adaline skimmed through its soul record.

"It's a partial artificial," Adaline informed her twin. Adaline concluded that the QC successfully resurrected the long-dormant Max-Program, where they pieced together advanced beings and then modified them into monstrous killing machines.

"Which part?" Asher asked, perplexed while surveying the behemoth.

The massive creature charged them, plowing into Asher. The monster smashed him through wall after wall of the building behind them. Once the beast hit a steel beam, slowing his lethal momentum, he took a blade that was latched onto his wrist and brought it down on Asher, but it disintegrated in his hand. The creature became enraged then followed it to see where it was going. Adaline drew the molecular structure of the blade into her hand, allowing it to reassemble. She touched it, and it shocked her.

"A blade with an electric pulse," she called to Asher, whose body was imprinted into the steel beam that held up the building.

"Well that's not nice," Asher said while finally peeling himself free. His broken clavicle snapped back into place, and the bone knitted itself together immediately. His right shoulder realigned and sank back into its socket with a snap.

Adaline shifted the structure of the metal in her hand to form a new blade. She asked the creature, "Are you being controlled, or do you choose to harm us of your own free will?"

The being was caught by surprise, as he was briefly mesmerized by Adaline's molecular manipulation. He growled, "No one can control me!"

"That's what you think," Asher said before he electrocuted the creature from behind.

The creature's body seized then Asher stepped aside as the beast's knees gave way, smashing into the ground. Adaline took the new blade and slammed it through the creature's skull. A moment later, it toppled over to one side, dead.

The twins looked at each other and shrugged before Asher said, "Okay, now let's go home."

CHAPTER 14

The following day marked the fifth day, the day Adaline would return to Theris. She stood over her expertly made bed, scanning the options she laid on the comforter to take with her.

Asher perched on the corner of the bed. "So, have you been practicing?"

"What are you talking about?" Adaline said as she fidgeted with a few items before packing them in her small bag.

"Remember what we discussed?"

"Ash, we've covered a lot in the past few days."

"That's true," he agreed. "I'm referring to the conversation we had when you mentioned that you threatened the king of a land we might want to move to once our world ends."

"Ah, that one," Adaline said before quieting.

"So… have you been practicing?"

Adaline was silent for a long moment as she organized the items in her bag. "No."

Asher chuckled. "You were able to say it to me… once."

"We were five."

"I know," Asher said, "I remember it clearly. You stumbled and collided with me. When you saw you knocked me over, you said...."

"I'm s-s," Adaline struggled.

"Come on, Addy!"

"S-sorry!"

"Yes!" Asher clapped his hands, entertained by her uneasiness.

"Ugh..."

"I know those are hard words for you," Asher said. "But they may prove effective if you believe Theris would be a good home for us."

Adaline sighed. "I know."

"You'll do fine," Asher encouraged.

"Yes, she will," a voice said from behind them.

Jim was standing in the doorway with Tony. Both men were adjusting holsters wrapped around their shoulders before putting on their jackets.

"What do you two think you're doing?" Adaline asked.

"We are going with you," Tony informed her.

Adaline's eyes narrowed. "Why?"

"We didn't like how this king upset you," Tony admitted. "So, we'd like to escort you back and check out the situation to make sure you are in a safe place."

"That's really not necessary," Adaline stated.

"Oh, I like this idea," Asher said, amused.

Adaline eyed Asher while wondering if he was crazy. She knew the answer.

"We are not negotiating on this, Addy," Jim told her. "If this is a place you think we can call home, then he needs to understand that it's not just you that won't put up with his lousy behavior."

Adaline's eyebrows lifted. "And you are going to tell him that?"

"In so many words, yes," Jim confirmed.

"This I gotta see," Adaline said. She decided she was satisfied with what she'd chosen and finished packing her bag. "Let's go." She flung the bag over her shoulder and headed for the portal.

Sunrise was breaking over the horizon, and most of Lost Angeles was still asleep. No one would see them leave. Adaline stepped through the portal and up onto the riverbank in Theris. A moment later, Jim and Tony were at her side. She heard a throat clear before she noticed a royal guard standing alone. He appraised her, then Jim and Tony.

"Dr. Adaline?" he asked her in a heavy accent. He was still getting used to using English after not using it for centuries.

She stood tall. "Yes."

He nodded in greeting. "I have been instructed to escort you to the palace."

Let the games begin, she thought, before telling the guard, "Thank you." She followed him with Jim and Tony trailing her. It was easier to take in the sights this time around.

Theris was thick with foliage and tall trees. Everywhere she looked was covered in green. Still, no flowers bloomed, but the sun shined freely. As the guard led them through the front entrance of the palace, Adaline noticed a long line of elves standing on the side of the path. Adults and children were lined up as if they were patiently waiting for something.

Or someone.

Adaline leaned toward the guard. "Is it a holiday or something?"

"Pardon?" the guard replied.

"Why is everyone lined up?"

The guard smiled. "They are here to see you."

Huh? she thought. "I don't understand."

"Word traveled of how you helped the Alloralla's daughter,"

he told her.

Ah, so that's the game, she thought; to get her to show her gift in a public forum. She could fix that, as she had no problem revealing the extent of the power of a single ability, for she had many.

Many of the elves in line nodded in her direction; some even smiled at her. Children waved. She waved back and smiled.

"If I'm going to do this, I will need some assistance," Adaline told the guard.

"That can be arranged," the guard replied.

They were in the throne room by the end of their conversation, and Adaline was happy to see Theodon waiting for her with a big smile on his face. She greeted him with a hug. He planted a quick kiss on her cheek before he embraced her.

"You brought friends," Theodon stated after he let her go.

"Ah, yes," Adaline said before making introductions. "Theo, this is Jim Monroe and Tony Harper. Gentlemen, this is Prince Theodon."

Theodon stepped forward to greet the Marines, extending his hand for them to shake, properly executing the custom he learned from Adaline. Jim grasped the prince's hand before shaking it firmly. Then gave him a clipped nod and a, "Hello." Tony did the same.

"It's nice to meet you both," Theodon said to them. "Will you be staying with us as well?"

Tony shot Jim a look before Jim said, "We don't plan to, no. Thank you for your hospitality."

"Of course," Theodon said with a smile before addressing Adaline again. "I'm glad you're here," he said as he gestured toward the palace entrance. "You have generated quite a crowd."

"I saw that," she said.

"What would you like to do about it?" he asked her.

She looked at him for a moment. "You ask me as if you think I have a choice."

There was that word again: choice, Theodon noticed.

112

Having her own was important to her. "Of course you do."

She shook her head. "No, friend. I don't." He looked at her questioningly for a moment. "In my world, doctors make a vow to treat people who are ill," she explained. "There's no choice involved, only action," she stated. Theodon nodded in understanding. "And there are a few things I'll need to make this work."

"Name them."

Within minutes, Adaline had her own office set up in an enclosed room in the palace to avoid prying eyes. She set her bag down and pulled out a small surgical kit. Theodon explored the room and noticed her organizing her tools. When his attention fell on the tools, his eyes widened with alarm because they looked like small torture devices.

She faced him. "I need you to be really honest with me about some information I need before I begin regarding elfin biology."

Theodon smiled. "Of course, ask!"

Afterward, the guard from earlier knocked on the door and formerly addressed Theodon before speaking to her. "Dr. Adaline, everyone is becoming restless."

Adaline had an idea then pointed to the guard. "Theo, can he assist me today? I need someone to vet patients."

Theodon turned to the guard. "Darius, you will be assisting Dr. Adaline for the rest of the day."

"Yes, My Lord," the guard said with a salute to the prince.

Theodon asked Adaline, "Is there anything else you need?"

Adaline sighed at the reality of how her gift worked. "Fresh food. A large plate of it. A pitcher of water and a glass."

Theodon eyed her curiously, smirked then nodded. "Done. Anything else?"

"Can I use the throne room for about ten minutes?"

"Yes."

Adaline instructed Darius, "I need you to corral all elves with common sicknesses from the line and send them to the throne room immediately. After that, I'm going to deal with the most serious cases for the rest of the day." Darius nodded. "Can you gather them quickly?"

"Yes, Dr. Adaline," the guard confirmed, turned on his heel, and used his elfin speed to process everyone in the line outside the palace. Within minutes, the guard wrangled sixty elves into the throne room.

Impressive, Adaline thought as she walked in and scanned the room. The elves had formed a circle.

"Addy," Tony said, as he stepped up to her side, "are you sure you want to conduct such a large demonstration?"

Adaline put her hand on his shoulder and tilted her head toward the crowd of people. "I'm killing two birds with one stone, Tony. I'm treating sick people, which I'm very good at, and I'm playing what the king thinks is his game when it's actually mine."

"How do you figure?" Tony asked.

"Because I will win in numbers," Adaline smiled. "Therefore, I win the game, which requires me to reveal only one ability in the process while I keep the rest private."

"Fair enough." Tony nodded before he informed her, "Jim and I are going to take a look around."

"Don't get into any trouble," Adaline warned as she eyed them suspiciously. She knew what kind of damage the two of them could cause if they wanted.

"And deprive us of fun? You ask too much of us," Tony jested before he winked at her.

Adaline chuckled as the two men disappeared down the long hallway. Darius kept pace alongside Adaline to the center of the throne room, and she asked him to translate for her.

"Everyone, I need you to join hands," Adaline stated.

The elves looked at her and then at Darius, who echoed the request in Tear. The elves held hands with those immediately next to them. Adaline scanned the room to make sure everyone made a closed circle of joined hands. She searched to find which two in the circle appeared to be the weakest links and found them to be two little girls who looked like they had the worst case of the flu anyone could ever tolerate. Adaline approached them.

"Hold my hands," she reached out to the two children. They glanced at each other in confusion. Darius repeated the command, and the two little ones unclasped their hands and reached for Adaline's.

"Everyone inhale deeply and exhale fully," she said. The guard repeated the instructions. Adaline felt the room relax. "This will take about twenty seconds and is not painful," she said. The guard repeated the message. "Continue to relax," she said before she began to draw on her white light. Her torso glowed before radiating the light to her extremities. The elves gasped. "Relax," she warned. The guard repeated her warning. The room settled.

The light in her chest divided and funneled down her arms before light shot from her hands, sending the light through each elf in a domino effect. Everyone in the room tensed for a moment at the sight of the light coming toward them, then relaxed after it passed through them. Adaline released the children's hands.

"Check to see how you feel," Adaline instructed the room. Darius translated her statement.

Everyone monitored their breathing, as well as their senses and their movement. Looks of surprise were exchanged before their eyes found Adaline. Those who didn't speak English nodded in her direction with smiles, and she heard a few "thank yous" from the few who did.

"You're welcome," she said before addressing Darius.

"That was amazing!" he exclaimed.

Tip of the iceberg, she thought to herself.

"Thanks," she said to him.

"What is next?"

"I need you to make a separate line of those who are

terminally ill or disabled, and I will start with them."

"Terminally ill, Dr. Adaline?"

"Dying," she stated plainly.

"Yes, Dr. Adaline," he turned on his foot and went to work.

The food and drink she'd requested were delivered to her office. She thanked the servant for providing it as she swept her long hair into a smooth ponytail. She stared at the food, knowing she was going to burn through all of it within the hour. Sustenance aided her ability, but she usually didn't need it when treating humans. She assumed her body would burn through the food faster when healing beings with longer life spans, so she figured it was best to prepare. If she were weak, she could not help anyone. The situation reminded Adaline of her emergency room rotation in medical school.

"How the mighty have fallen." She chuckled at the thought in comparison to her world-renowned surgical practice.

There was a knock at the open door, and she turned to find a mother holding a small boy. The mother's concerned expression moved from Adaline to her boy and then back to Adaline.

"Hello," Adaline said in greeting. "Which of you needs help today?" Adaline eyed them.

"My son," the mother said with a thick accent. "He has always had trouble moving."

Adaline waved her in and asked her to set the boy on the table. The poor little guy had trouble sitting upright on his own. Adaline pushed pillows around him to prop him up.

"What's your name?" Adaline asked the boy.

"His name is Net," the mother spoke for the boy who was too little to know English.

"Net," Adaline echoed and smiled.

The little boy smiled in return. Adaline asked the mother questions about Net's condition. She had to use her stethoscope and reflex hammer, the latter being a tool she hadn't touched in decades. After examining the boy, she narrowed his illness to cerebral palsy. His advanced biology was trying to heal it and was semi-successful, but the disease seemed to be putting up a fight.

Adaline pulled up her stool to sit in front of the boy and held out her hands. "Net, let me see your hands." The mother translated for her son, and the little boy hesitated. At his mother's urging, he finally set his little palms in Adaline's. She smiled at him, easing his tension.

"Now hold on, okay?" she said and heard the mother translate. The little boy nodded without a word, and then Adaline's hands started to glow. The mother gasped. "It's okay. This won't hurt him." Adaline turned back to Net to see his eyes widen in shock at her glowing hands.

Adaline laughed. "It doesn't hurt, right?" The mother asked her son if he was in pain. Net shook his head and giggled. Adaline's smile was short-lived when she noticed the black mist circling in his head. "Close your eyes," she told Net. The mother quickly translated the instructions. The boy complied before Adaline sank her hand into his brain. She grabbed the mist and yanked it out of his body. He jolted forward at the release as Adaline flung the mist to the ground. Upon contact with the floor, the mist began to disintegrate. She laid her glowing palm against his forehead, filling him with as much healing light as his body would accept. The light traveled from his brain, into his arteries and veins, before spreading throughout his body. When finished, Adaline looked him over to note any changes. His muscle mass had already improved.

"Okay, now let's see how we did," Adaline said as she lifted him off the table by his underarms and set his feet on the floor. "Take the time to steady yourself before you take off." Adaline knew Net couldn't understand her, but he got the gist of it when he had the strength to use her long legs to lean against as he obtained balance. A moment passed before he stood, and he smiled up at his mother. His mother had tears in her eyes upon seeing her boy stand on his own for the first time. Net lifted one foot, then the other, testing his range before he took off running out the door. Theodon was passing by in the hallway and caught Net with one arm. The boy giggled. The mother sobbed in relief after witnessing what she thought was a miracle.

"There are two more things, Mom," she addressed Net's mother as she moved closer to her. The mother nodded as she tried to wipe her tears away, but new ones continued to take their place. Adaline smiled in understanding. "First, he needs to do a lot of physical activity to rebuild his muscles. So whatever children do to play that involves a lot of movement, that's what you need to have him do to give him the chance to catch up to other boys his age."

"Of course," The mother sniffed and nodded quickly.

"And the second thing," Adaline moved into the mom's personal space, "is you."

"Me?" the mother asked, confused.

"Parents go through so much emotional turmoil when disease touches their children," Adaline explained. "It anchors stress in the body, which usually manifests into its own illness in the future." The mom nodded in understanding, and the tension she carried that was tied to her confusion eased. "Is it okay to touch you?" Adaline asked as she closed the rest of the distance between them.

"Yes," the mother nodded. She was ready for release. That's when Adaline's part in a patient's healing was easy to facilitate.

"Relax," Adaline instructed as her left hand started to glow. "And close your eyes."

As soon as the mother's eyes closed, Adaline's glowing hand penetrated into the mom's body with ease. She reached into her chest, touching her heart, her lungs, and her stomach, then she saw the mist. The mother carried it in her neck, shoulders, and chest.

Common places to carry stress, Adaline thought. She spread her fingers within the mother, swirling them around to gather the mist before she curled her fingers around it and pulled it free from her system. The mother coughed hard, and Adaline slid her other arm behind her back to steady her. "Easy," Adaline said to her. "Breath as deep and even as you can." The mother regained her breath and stood with strength and balance.

Her expression filled with awe. "It's gone."

Adaline smiled at her. Doctor-patient relations were clinically detached for Adaline, but this mother wouldn't have it. She flung her arms around Adaline and cried her thanks.

Adaline patted her arm. "You're very welcome."

When the mother finally let go, Adaline said, "It looks like you will be plenty busy now, trying to keep up with your boy."

Theodon joined them to hand Net back to his mother. The mother hugged her boy close and turned back to Adaline. "I would have it no other way." Then the mother left with her son, who was giggling as she tickled him in her arms.

Theodon moved further into the room. "That was incredible."

"Thank you," Adaline said as she shuffled over to the table and poured herself a tall glass of water. She chugged half of it before facing the prince, deciding that she wouldn't eat in front of him. As much as Adaline liked Theodon, she couldn't trust revealing any information about herself that he could potentially share with his father, even after all she knew about him. She understood that family came first, which included the sharing of information.

Meanwhile, Jim and Tony finished wandering the palace and returned to the throne room. It was completely empty of the large gathering of elves that packed the space earlier. They took their time learning the room until Tony wandered close to the throne. He noticed there was no gold and no jewels embedded in the woodwork. The throne was embellished only by the artist who carved the design from wood and nothing more. Whoever carved it was genuinely gifted, Tony concluded, as he got lost in the scenic display that covered the left wall that flowed around the throne and continued on the right wall.

"It is the story of the creation of the world," a voice filled the space behind Tony.

Tony turned to see a tall, statuesque elf standing behind him. He wore richly colored robes and a crown. The resemblance between him and Theodon was almost uncanny.

"You must be the king," Tony said evenly. The king gave him a clipped nod. "I'm Tony."

"And I'm Jim," Jim said from behind the king before he walked around to stand next to Tony.

"It's a nice place you have here," Tony commented.

"You flatter me," the king remarked. "You must be here with Dr. Adaline, I presume?"

"We are," Jim confirmed. "We came to check on Addy and make sure she arrived okay."

"And to make sure nothing was going on that would upset her again," Tony added.

The king tilted his head at the two Marines.

"See, King," Jim said, not caring of the formalities in addressing Aureon. "Addy came home upset after her first visit to your kingdom. When we found out why we thought it best to take the time to introduce ourselves."

The king's eyebrows lifted in amusement. However, he couldn't mistake the jealousy he felt when he heard Jim call her Addy. A nickname implied a close bond, which was something Aureon didn't have with her.

"Are you here to threaten me?" the king inquired.

"No," Jim said. "Although our skill sets remain sharp."

"Very sharp," Tony echoed and nodded.

"And it is that skill set that brought me, Tony here, and Addy's father together, in long-lasting friendship until the day he died," Jim explained. "Tony and I made a promise to him that we'd watch over Addy and her brother; to keep them safe. And as you have probably figured out, Addy doesn't need to be watched over every minute of the day." The king's eyes stayed locked on Jim. "That doesn't mean a person can't hurt her feelings or her heart," Jim stated. "It's almost impossible to do either, yet you've succeeded."

A pregnant pause filled the space between them.

"The point is," Tony took his turn, "Addy is like a daughter to us both, like family. And we protect our family. I'm sure you would do no less for your son, who seems like a nice enough young man."

The king's gaze swept from Tony back to Jim, knowing the older man wasn't finished.

"We want what's best for Addy," Jim said. "And if she likes to visit here, then that's fine with us. I also understand that when she first came here, she was a stranger who was probably watched closely for security reasons. From this point forward, no more of that will be happening."

"Or else?" the king asked.

"No or else," Tony said. "It's simply in your best interest to treat Addy with respect." Tony knew that if anything terrible happened to Adaline while she was in Theris, she would be the first to avenge herself, and Asher would arrive in tow. At that point, the king would wish to deal with Tony and Jim over the twins.

The tension radiated between the three males for a long moment. None of them conceded.

"Father?" Theodon entered the throne room, then stopped in his tracks when he sensed the tension.

Tony was the only one to acknowledge Theodon. "Hello, Theodon."

The prince smiled and resumed his approach. "Hello."

"Father," Theodon said to Aureon, "Dr. Adaline just cured a little boy's legs! He can walk now. It was incredible!" The Marines looked at the king with smug, knowing, close-lipped smiles plastered on their faces. The king suppressed the urge to roll his eyes. "Come," Theodon said to his father, "you should see all she is doing." He turned to Tony. "I'm sure you are well aware of her talents."

"We are," Tony admitted with a smile.

"Addy is capable of miraculous things," Jim added as Tony nodded.

The prince led them from the throne room and down the hall, just as another shocked elf exited Dr. Adaline's pseudo-office. He looked at his hands, flipped them over, then looked some more.

"I can see!" he shouted in Tear, before turning to see the king and the prince standing in the hallway. The elf's attention froze on Aureon in his opulent robes, recognizing his king's divine energy anywhere. And, now, for the first time, he could see the ruler he'd felt for centuries. Then the elf noticed Theodon – and uncanny resemblance to his father. "Your Majesties," the elf gave a rushed bow. "My apologies." He quickly backed away from the royals.

A moment later, Adaline exited her office and was looking after the elf that had just left. The king watched as Tony and Jim immediately walked over to her, and her instant reaction was to smile upon seeing them. Jim squeezed her in a hug as he told her what a great job she was doing.

"Thanks," she said as she blushed barely enough for anyone to notice.

"Do you feel safe here now?" Tony asked her. She nodded without a doubt.

"Do you need us to stay?" Jim asked her.

"No, I'll be fine," she assured him.

"All right," Jim said. "Then we'll be on our way."

"I'll walk you back," she began to say before Jim and Tony wouldn't have any of it. They wanted her to stay and continue helping people like they knew she loved to do.

"All right," she finally said. "I'll see you in a couple of days."

"Bye, Addy," Tony said as they made their way back through the throne room and out the front entrance of the palace.

"Bye!" she called after them. The king watched her look after them. Her expression turned from joyous to concerned. Considering their age, she probably watched over them more than they watched over her at this point in her life. She turned to walk back into her office and stopped when she saw the king. She held his gaze for a moment before she re-entered her office in silence.

A moment later, Darius poked his head into Adaline's office. She signaled to him to bring in the next patient. Hours went by, as did plates of food and pitchers of water. Adaline saw dozens of patients while the king and the prince periodically passed by her office door. A young male left her office with a big smile on his face, happy to be able to breathe evenly. Darius poked his head into her office again.

She nodded before saying, "The next patient will be the last of the day." She yawned quietly and stretched her arms overhead.

The king posted nearby once he heard the hint of fatigue in her voice. Theodon tensed when he heard it, too. Both elves took stations on each side of her office door but far enough away to not crowd her space. Darius escorted an old elf to her office and opened the door for him. The old elf addressed both royals formally before stepping over the threshold and closing the door behind him. The royals glanced at each other.

"She's doing too much," Theodon communicated telepathically with his father.

"It's her choice," the king replied.

Theodon's eyes narrowed at his father's use of that word, then they both listened in to Adaline's final consultation of the day. The old elf greeted her, then took a seat on the examination table.

"Hello, Dr. Adaline," the elf said to her. "You are causing quite a stir out there."

"Am I?" She smiled at him.

He nodded slowly, and a smile spread across his face before admitting, "It's a wonderful thing to see."

"What are you here for today?" She canted her head to fish for his name.

"Alvis."

"Alvis," she echoed.

"I'm afraid it's my heart."

Adaline reached for her stethoscope, but she didn't rise from her chair. "What symptoms have you been experiencing?"

Alvis exhaled evenly with his hands on his knees as he leaned forward while naming off his symptoms. Once finished, he struggled to regain his breath, proving true one of the symptoms he shared with her. Adaline didn't have to touch him to know he was experiencing heart failure. Without a word, she approached him and scanned her hand over his heart. Through gritted teeth, she yanked it back then peered at Alvis as her eyes watered.

"There's more to this that you haven't told me," she said to him. "Care to share?"

Alvis finally nodded.

Adaline slid her stool in front of Alvis and retook her seat as he explained the greatest mistake of his life: how he treated his mate poorly to the point where she'd finally left him. He never emotionally recovered. The two royals standing outside the office shot each other a look as Alvis' story struck a chord for them both.

"I've been a mess ever since she left," he admitted. "The symptoms didn't show up until I was around 6,000 or so years. They've been getting worse ever since."

Adaline's arms crossed over her chest as she concluded something that sounded like a fairytale but was quite real, "As a result, you are dying of a broken heart." Pause. "How old are you now?"

"7,452 as of two weeks ago," Alvis admitted.

"Happy birthday."

His shoulders fell. "It wasn't."

"I'm sorry."

"So am I."

Silence floated between them. Alvis sniffed and nodded before saying, "I should have been better to her. I should have given her everything she needed from me, but I didn't. And it's too late."

Theodon couldn't bear to listen anymore, so he turned his back to his father and left the palace. The king stayed to listen to her speak, hanging on to every word. He found himself forsaking his original intent to expose her abilities, surprised that his ulterior motives concerning her effortlessly fell away and were replaced with regret and admiration.

"How do you figure that it's too late?" Adaline said although she could tell he was deteriorating rapidly.

"Because the pain is rooted deep," Alvis said to her. "I feel it in my soul. I came to you today to ask you to help with the pain because I am certain I will pass on soon. Just get rid of the pain. Can you do that?"

Adaline caught herself in an emotional pickle. "Yes, I can do that." She knew he wouldn't last long enough for the pain to return.

Alvis left her office feeling relieved of discomfort, and Adaline closed the door behind him. She shuffled over to her table, where food and water awaited her. She plopped into the chair and muttered, "A hell of a first day." She snacked on the food.

After she finished, she shuffled over to the examination table to lie down to give the food time to be absorbed into her system. The door to her office creaked open. Adaline thought it was Darius checking on her, but it wasn't.

She heard firm, quiet, measured steps and then saw the color of his robes. She didn't lift her gaze because her eyes were still hurting. And if she never saw him, she'd know it was the king from the extent of the emotions that rushed over her that didn't belong to her. She didn't say a word while she watched the king take her chair and move it to sit in her field of view before he pulled the train of his robes to the side and sat down. Even when he took a seat in a simple chair, the action was executed with precision and grace.

She wanted to vomit.

His eyes scanned her with his glacial stare, unreadable to anyone else but her. She could feel his concern for her well-being which softened her attitude toward him.

Remember, she reminded herself of her conversation with Tessa, *you are holding all the cards.*

She tucked her arms under her head for support, ready for whatever he had to say. He didn't like that her heartbeat was strained or how low her energy level had plummeted. The only thing he decided was reasonable was the fact she chose to lay down.

"Are you well?" he asked in a low whisper.

"I've been worse," she admitted.

He didn't like that answer, especially the truth that emanated from it. Adaline barely noticed the muscle that ticked under his left eye.

This will not do, he thought. "What do you need to regenerate?"

She smirked. "You can understand why I have no intention of sharing that information with you."

Silence.

His frustration boiled under the surface of his face as his hands fisted on the arms of the chair. He wanted to help, but he didn't have Adaline's trust, so she would limit what he could do for her. He deserved that, he knew, but he didn't do well with restriction. The only variable that kept him from erupting was that she was within his reach. She slowly pushed herself up to a seated position. He automatically stood with her as she rose, alarmed by his reaction to her movement. She finger-combed her hair back into place and fixed her shirt before she slowly lowered her feet to the ground. He stepped closer to her as she found her footing and stood to her full height. As fast as her body seemed to be regenerating, he saw the weariness in her eyes.

"What do you need?" he asked her again. He'd give her anything so she would no longer feel the way she did.

Adaline allowed her gaze to penetrate his icy stare as she thought about what she needed most, and she didn't feel the least bit sorry about it. She never did. "Dinner in my room. A hot bath in a tub that will fit me. Oil for said bath that will make my skin feel soft and smell pretty. And a foot massage."

He thought about her requests then nodded. "Done." She gave the biggest smiled she could, given her energy level. "I'm going to escort you to your room," he told her, then turned to offer her his arm.

"I can make it on my own."

"You can," he said, "but you do not have to."

She thought about his words for so long that it made him burst into action. He leaned down, shrugged his arm under her bottom, and lifted her off the ground. He pulled her against his body as he searched her face. "I prefer you not to walk at all."

The shock by his direct move had her clutching his shoulders to maintain balance. It didn't matter where she grabbed him to steady herself; he would never let her fall. They arrived at the door of her suite. He gauged her reaction as he slowly set her feet on the ground, leaving one hand to hover over her back until he was certain she could maintain balance. He opened the door to her suite and gestured for her to enter.

"Is there anything else you need?" he asked her.

She thought for a moment before saying, "My bag from my office."

"Dinner, oil, and the bag will be delivered shortly. Ena will be along to show you how the bath works. The foot massage will be delivered after you have bathed and settled," he stated matter-of-factly.

She nodded sheepishly. "Thank you."

He tucked his chin to her, indicating the smallest of bows, then left her to her bath. She entered the bathroom and noticed a massive tub that could fit at least three people in it.

How did she miss that during her last visit? No matter, she was prepared to make up for it right now. After playing with the two levers on one wall, she jumped back when a flood of water shot through a large opening in the wall, filling the bathtub in a cyclone pattern. There was a knock at the door.

"Come in!" she called from the bathroom while she stared at the tub in awe.

"Ena, Dr. Adaline," the servant called.

"Hi, Ena!" Adaline called back to the she-elf entering her room.

"I'm setting up dinner in your room," she called. "Is everything all right?"

Adaline kept staring in amazement at the massive cyclone tub. "I'm so awesome right now, Ena."

"It sounds like you have figured out how to use the tub," Ena stated. "Be sure to leave the levers on during the duration of your bath."

"Thank you, Ena," Adaline said, still staring at the tub.

Once Ena left, Adaline snapped back to reality and turned off the tub, remembering food was waiting for her in the other room. She gobbled it down, relieved at the tingling sensation her body gave off as it regenerated. After eyeing the tiny side plate of desserts that had been included on the tray, she was tempted to skip dinner and go straight to dessert. However, she knew she had to treat eating as refueling after the long day of healing immortals. Then she'd savor each sweet morsel. She lounged for a few minutes with her hands folded on her stomach. A satisfied smile crossed her face. She grabbed the bottle of oil Ena had left on the table, popped the lid, and took a whiff. *Divine!* she thought. *It's tub time!*

CHAPTER 15

K ing Aureon stood under a canopy of trees, surrounded by the elders of each of the noble houses in Theris. All of the elfin males present were 7,000 years at the youngest, himself not included, and most of them came from ancient noble houses, except two. The newest members were Ensatus Aetrune and Flavial Usleon. They were awarded nobility due to their acts of heroism in the war against the Hexaborgs over 1,100 years ago. Graydon Miathan opposed their promotions at no surprise to Aureon. However, Cerus stood by his son's decision, who was newly crowned king before the war. Aureon liked the newest members of the elders' circle because their perspectives were refreshing and unbiased. They also were not yet jaded by the long years of their lives, unlike the others. And Flavial was the closest person Aureon would ever consider calling a friend.

"I think it's fantastic that the human has been able to heal our sick," Flavial chimed. "She has revealed to us ways disease can still end us. We can have the healers fully research her findings. It's a blessing she chooses to visit Theris."

Indeed, Aureon thought.

"I agree," confirmed Ensatus. "Perhaps she can train our healers?" He turned to address Aureon directly. "Is her healing ability superficial or organic in nature, My Lord?"

"From what I have witnessed, it is an organic anomaly," the king offered. He decided he would share little about her as he reflected on how drastically his agenda had changed regarding Adaline. It switched from desiring to take advantage of her power to protect her from harm.

"That's unfortunate," Ensatus commented. His fingers steepled in front of him as he paced away from the king. His thoughts circulated in his mind searching to find another way for the new human to further aid the elves.

"What do we care about one mortal?" Mouriel Olostuil asked. "Her life will be over in a moment, giving us false hope that all can be healed forever."

A few elders nodded in agreement. The elder preferred not caring about anyone else's business unless it directly affected him or his family—otherwise, good riddance.

"Even if she can provide us with insight as to why we can still sicken, no matter how evolved we become?" Flavial posed the question to the group. "Our lives end through ascension or death, and death usually results from battle and should *only* result from battle. So we should be at a point in our evolution where we understand the reasons why we can still sicken, even if it's a rarity. We owe it to ourselves and our children."

Aureon's focused on Flavial's logic, which was sound.

"You hold this human in too high regard, Flavial," Graydon argued with a dismissive wave. "She's just a human. She will have no lasting impact on our people. She will visit. She will help. She will leave. One day, her short life will be over, and we will all still be here living our long existences just as before."

Aureon heard one of the elders sigh at Graydon's last statement. The years had taken their toll on the mind and body. Not the centuries, for they passed quickly. Aureon discovered from personal experience the millenniums jaded them, which was too early for the lesson to surface in an elf's life.

"Then we are all agreed," Flavial stated. "Whether she's helping or harmless, it is fine that she visits."

"Yes," they all echoed. A few nodded.

Most of the elders exited the canopy under the moonlight to adjourn to their homes. However, Aureon felt Flavial's presence remain.

"My Lord," the elder addressed him. Aureon pivoted to meet Flavial's gaze. "If she's truly doing good, then she should stay," Flavial said reasonably, "However, I fear that because she is of a delicate species, she could be in danger if left to wander alone."

"What do you suggest?" Aureon asked, knowing well that Adaline didn't need supervision, but he played along with the elder's ignorance of her power.

"That she remains under the care of the crown, My Lord," Flavial recommended. "If anyone is equipped to keep her safe, it's you and Theodon." Flavial secretly hoped that the human healer could help the king, as Flavial remembered the king's rage and pain that came when his queen died. Aureon nodded. Flavial shrugged. "Maybe there is an exchange that would interest her." Aureon continued to listen.

"If she needs to get away from her world, as you stated, to take a vacation," Flavial pointed out, "Perhaps a trade of a place to live for her healing gift?" Aureon nodded at the idea, although he concluded it unnecessary as he would provide whatever she needed when she visited. "Those are the extent of my thoughts on the matter," Flavial admitted. "I hope I have the honor of meeting her soon." Flavial felt his words were well received, and he gave a shallow bow before bidding the king good night and leaving the canopy.

Everyone either wants her to stay or does not care if she does, the king thought with relief. It was an ideal situation. Then, triggered by the king's worry, a blossom opened in the tree overhead and fell from the canopy. Aureon reached out his palm, and the flower landed in his hand. Upon examining it, he was amazed to find the blossom from the tree, which was usually bright pink, was now a deep purple.

Change, he realized. He felt a shift in the kingdom the day she arrived, just as he did when she left and then returned to his world, again. *Now the environment is responding to her because I do,* he thought. But, unfortunately, the elders, except for Flavial and Ensatus, did not respond well to change.

Aureon allowed the blossom to fall to the ground and departed the canopy for the palace. He had an apology to deliver before the little human went to sleep, and he couldn't manage to shake Mouriel's words regarding Adaline's mortality. "Her life will be over in the blink of an eye, therefore giving us false hope that all can be healed forever."

CHAPTER 16

A daline was relaxed and moisturized from head to toe as she searched the dresser drawers in her room for sleepwear. Choosing a dark pink tunic and long pant set with a robe in the same color, she layered herself in the soft fabrics and tightly tied the robe's belt. As she turned down her bed for the night, she heard a knock at the door.

"Come in!" she called as she removed the decorative pillows from the bed and set them aside. Someone clearing their throat behind her, who clearly wasn't Ena, caused her to spin. The king stood in forest green sleep robes with his jet hair half-braided down his back, pausing before crossing the threshold between the suit foyer and her bedroom. He carried towels in one hand and a small vial of oil in the other.

Oh, no, she thought. *No, no, no, no, no, he is not touching me*. It was fear of what she would do because of how his touch might feel. She already knew how good his energy felt just by being in the same room. His touch? A terrifying thought.

He detected her increased heart rate as he watched her shift on her feet before sitting the towels and vial on a side table. He moved furniture around at the foot of the bed in silence. After a minute, two chairs faced each other with a small footstool between them. Finally, he gestured for her to take a seat.

No, she thought hard.

He noticed her apprehension. "Please."

"Why?"

He exhaled as he attempted this new avenue. "It is my apology." Suspicion filled her gaze. He gestured, again, for her to sit. A moment passed as she read him because she didn't trust that he had no other agenda. And she wasn't surprised that she was right. Although he took the time to learn how to give an impeccable foot massage, his intention toward her was far more primal; he wanted to touch her. He knew he damaged things between them and wanted to rectify the situation with an act of catering to her needs. However, he wanted his hands on her just as badly. She stifled a shiver as she continued to read him. She saw that he was well-practiced in concealing his emotions, but doing so proved challenging for him as he was overrun with feelings. He desired her body writhing beneath his as she succumbed to pleasure. But as much as he wanted her, he had the patience to wait for her to be willing, for he had endless amounts of time.

He's playing the long game, she thought. *Smart elf.*

All she had to do was decide if she wanted something to happen between them, and she didn't have to decide now. While she took measured steps to the furthest chair, her watchful gaze never left Aureon. He sat in the chair across from hers, covered the footstool with a towel, and shrugged off his outer robe. Adaline noticed the king's sleepwear was intricately stitched around the neck and cuffs, molding perfectly to his muscular chest and shoulders.

Wow, she thought before averting her gaze to her seat. Her own robe would stay on, she decided, as she slid into her chair. Her layers of clothing began to feel like protection against him, no matter how flimsy her reasoning or how much her body was starting to respond to him.

"How was your dinner, Dr. Adaline?" he asked, trying to tear through the palpable awkwardness with casual conversation. Using formalities almost helped.

"It looked amazing, Your Majesty," she admitted. "I even had the opportunity to savor some of it."

He eyed her curiously before he patted the footstool, prompting her to rest her feet. The skirt of her robe fell away, leaving her soft pajama bottoms in full view.

"I do not understand," he said as he curled the other side of her robe's skirt under itself to tuck it away.

She conceded that if he was going to take the time to cater to her, she would have to share with him. "After the day that I had of healing beings that are older than I will ever be, food is only viewed as fuel, not something to be enjoyed."

He nodded in understanding as he cuffed the pant legs of her pajamas. He was careful not to touch her skin until it was time to begin. "Do you need the same replenishment when you treat humans?"

"No," she admitted. "My normal eating and sleeping schedule serves me fine."

He felt like a bigger jerk than before when he recalled telling Theodon that Adaline could decide what to do with the endless line of elves that camped in front of the palace when she returned. Had he known that it would drain her, he would have had everyone return to their homes and let Adaline pace herself with treating his subjects a few at a time throughout her visits to Theris.

But his ulterior motives got in the way…

He released an exhale through his nose that caused his shoulders to stoop as the realization proved abrasive. *No matter*, he told himself. *I am here to make amends.*

"Is something wrong?" she asked, knowing he was fretting to himself.

"Yes."

Silence.

"Do you want to talk about it?"

"No."

He noticed the scars on her feet and fumed at the idea of someone harming her. She sat up in her chair, feeling his building rage.

"Who did this?" he said, pointing at the lines on her feet. She had one on top of each foot as well as on the sides.

"Oh, that's nothing," she said. "I had to have a corrective surgery to balance my feet." His expression was unconvinced. "In my younger years, I had a growth spurt that happened quickly. As I tried to find my new posture for," she gestured at her curves, "everything that was growing, my feet grew a little funny. It hurt to wear most shoes, so I had surgery to correct my feet. Then I learned how to properly stand to support my new body."

"How fast did you grow?"

"Six inches in height over fifteen months," she admitted. "All other areas followed suit."

She caught him staring at her boobs for a moment and smirked. Males were the same no matter the world or universe. His focus reverted to her feet, where he leaned closer and lightly touched the hairline scar on the top of her foot. She swallowed a gasp and wanted to pull away, but not because his touch was unwanted.

"The scars are still sensitive," she hissed as she backed her toes from the edge of the footstool, but he wrapped his hand around her ankle. Their eyes locked as he set her foot back into place.

"I will not do that again," he promised. He didn't want anything to ruin this moment, and Adaline didn't know how she would get through the rest of this evening with him massaging her feet if the smallest of his touches caused a visceral reaction.

"Relax," Aureon whispered, still holding her ankle. He waited for her breathing to normalize before he let go of her to pick up the damp, hot towel he had between his feet. He unfolded it carefully and put a small corner of it against her feet.

"Too hot?" he asked.

"No."

He proceeded to wipe her feet with the hot towel while being mindful of each of her toes. She watched him quietly as he was clearly focused on every action he took. Finally, he swiped the towel over the inside arch of her foot. She squealed and yanked her foot out of his hand. His eyes shot to her face as she blushed.

"I'm ticklish there," she confessed as she slowly returned her foot.

The powerful human is ticklish, he mused. What other surprises will he find out about her? He surveyed her expression as he put the towel to her inside arch again and applied pressure when wiping her skin. She hissed through her teeth at the sensation as she gripped the armrests of the chair. However, it wasn't bad enough to tear her foot from his grasp again.

"Better?" he asked, clearly entertained.

She nodded before she finally relaxed in her chair as she watched him, searching her thoughts for conversation to lighten the mood.

"Does my being ticklish amuse you, Your Majesty?" she asked.

"It amuses me greatly, Dr. Adaline."

"Why?" she asked. "And it's Adaline."

He locked eyes with her for a moment as her name rumbled in his chest. Goosebumps scattered over her legs, capturing his notice. He wanted to drop the towel and pounce on her, to muss up her perfectly brushed hair and to kiss her lips until they were swollen, but he held his position.

A beat passed.

"Because it's a vulnerability I did not expect," he said.

"What did you expect?"

He thought for a moment. "Less than the same as the humans who visited Theris long before you."

That is a fair assumption, she thought. "So... short life span, slow healing, poor sight," she listed.

"Unable to hold their drink," he chimed in.

Her eyes widened, and she giggled. "How do you know that?"

He smirked as his eyes stayed glued to the task at hand before telling the story. "The last time humans visited, Theodon was still a youngling. That is when an elf is under a century old." She nodded as she continued to listen. "The humans were under the impression that their world was coming to an end," the king explained. "And once they found Theris, their attitude revolved around constant partying because they felt they successfully escaped the end of their world."

Adaline chuckled at the result of Y2K in human history.

"And because Theodon was still a youngling, which is when we tend to be quite reckless and restless," the king said, "he would carry on with the humans who were out celebrating every night."

Adaline watched him with a small smile on her face, noticing his features lightened when he talked about his son.

"Theodon would be so happy to go out and join them, and he would forget how each night of partying with them ended," the king recalled with a chuckle.

What a beautiful sound.

"Because our alcohol is so strong, and the humans couldn't hold their drink, one would always end up vomiting on Theodon." The king started to laugh. "And he would come home furious, with the front of his tunic covered in it every night."

"Yet he still went out with them the next night?" Adaline chimed in.

"Yes!"

They both burst with laugher.

"Poor Theo," Adaline said.

The king's laugh dwindled.

"Maybe I should apologize to him on behalf of my species," Adaline joked.

The laughter subsided, and the king let the hot towel drop to the floor. He picked up the vial of oil. Anticipation ate at them both about their first oily contact. He clasped his hands together to warm the oil then picked up her foot. He stacked another pillow underneath her calf to allow her foot to hang off the end. He rubbed the oil from the tips of her toes and up her ankle. Then he kneaded his thumbs into the pads of her feet.

"Oh!" she gasped, alarmed by how good his hands felt. "You're going to get oil on the pill-," she tried to get out, as she heard him inhale deep and exhale hard.

"I do not care," rumbled from his chest as he caught her gaze. She seemed easily spooked as she attempted to look away, but he ensnared her with his emerald stare, hoping she wouldn't pull away from the moment. But, instead, her dark gaze connected with his, and he saw fear rooted there.

"What are you afraid of?" he whispered as his eyes searched hers.

"Nothing," she blurted.

He clutched her calf so she couldn't pull away. "I know. You are powerful. What is spooking you?"

She settled back into the chair before she finally admitted, "Emotions."

If you only knew, little human, he thought as he sighed, which she seemed to mimic. He noticed it calmed her more, although he could tell some anxiety lingered. *I need her willing*, he thought. *Need to win her*. He also needed to make an effort to learn her and acknowledged the opportunity in front of him.

"It is all right for me to continue?" he asked her.

"Yes," she said after a pause.

She reclined in the chair before clasping her hands on her stomach and closing her eyes. Her body turned into the consistency of a puddle as Aureon diligently worked on her limbs.

"You do not strike me as the type to be scared of anything," he said after a long silence.

"There's nothing to be scared of anymore," she said ominously.

He noticed her voice wavered. "Was there at one time?"

"Why are you so curious?"

"There must be a reason why you sleep with a protective barrier at night."

She lifted one eyelid to peer at him. "You've watched me sleep?"

He stilled as they locked eyes.

After another bout of silence enveloped them for some time, she focused on what he was doing. "Why did you learn this?"

He thought about earlier in the week when he had experienced his first foot massage. He rarely indulged in such self-care. He viewed it as a luxury until he experienced it for himself. What helped was his impressive ability to watch something done one time, it didn't matter what it was, and he would be able to mimic it to perfection from that point forward. It didn't matter the length of the task or the level of detail. If he focused on it the entire time, he could replicate it without error, and it was committed to memory forever. So, he didn't learn it because this was a luxury in which he would partake regularly — He learned it for her. And the fact she requested a foot massage after a tiring day added to his determination to make the process as enjoyable as possible.

"To show appreciation to a good doctor," he said, silently hoping this wouldn't be the only foot massage he would give her. A beat of silence passed before he added, "And to apologize for my behavior during her first visit."

"I thought kings don't apologize," she murmured. His eyes

widened in surprise as he never voiced that thought. "Relax, I'm not a mind reader," she confessed. "Yet." A smile spread across her face. "It wasn't hard to guess."

"Am I so predictable?" he inquired. Age did that to elves, after all.

"Well, the last thing I would have ever predicted would be getting a foot massage from a king who threatened to throw me in his dungeon the first day I met him."

"I had never met a confident, mouthy being who had such a problem with authority in my long life," he muttered.

"Neither had I," she whispered.

They both chuckled. They were similar in power in that they were both the most advanced of their species. So naturally, they would both have a problem with authority, restriction, and rules they hadn't made themselves. Aureon's hands ran up the sides of her calf muscles, to her knee, then massaged her muscles on his way back down to her ankle.

"Mmm," she purred as she shifted in her seat and her eyes slid closed. "That's nice."

Quite nice, he thought, as his gaze ate up the length of her strong, shapely legs before he was distracted by the sight of her pant cuffs sliding up to her thighs. Aureon struggled to tamp his emotions down as the image of stripping her naked, tossing her onto the bed, and taking her until she moaned his name flooded his mind. He shook the thought, alarmed. *That's not what elves do.* Females expected gentleness from their males in all things.

So why the raw hunger for the human?

Adaline drifted off to sleep in the chair while still reclined before the king finished her foot massage. He wiped the excess oil off her limbs, and his hands then uncuffed her pants before he approached the chair in which she dozed. His eyes locked on her legs again. Grabbing the skirt of her robe, he covered her legs before lifting her from the chair. She started to stir, and knowing he'd get resistance from her if she came out of it entirely, he quickly instructed her, "Arms around my neck."

She complied without hesitation, and he carried her while she remained silent. He could still hear her slightly elevated heartbeat, and he clutched her closer to his body as he gently delivered her to bed. When he slipped her legs under the crisp sheets and pulled the edges of the blankets up to her shoulders, she shimmied onto her side until she was comfortable. His brow knitted with concern as he wrestled with not wanting to leave her alone and wondering when he should ask her about the details of her healing gift.

"Hmm?" she moaned, sensing his feelings.

"Still awake?" he asked while lowering himself to meet her gaze.

Her eyes opened, and she took stock of his feelings. "You have questions for me." He nodded. "Can we discuss them in the morning?"

"No patients tomorrow?"

"No," she said. "Tomorrow is all about me." She stretched like a cat as a smile spread across her face. Then, she returned to lying on her side. "Can we speak before I venture out?"

She thought to leave him? He didn't like that idea, but he wouldn't dare restrict her. It was something he reviled and wouldn't wish on another being of comparable power. But, on the other hand, it did matter to him that she remained nearby to be under his protection. He would speak to her about it in the morning. He nodded as he rose to his feet before exiting her suite.

As the door to her suite clicked into place behind him, he heard her whisper gratefully, "Thank you."

CHAPTER 17

The following morning, Ena was in Adaline's room resetting the furniture from the previous night. Adaline requested breakfast in her room, and Ena obliged by bringing it to her. Adaline nibbled on her breakfast while scheming, smiling to herself as she pulled out the bikini she needed for her adventure that day. *I wonder if his emotions will noticeably change when he sees me in this.* He was clever at hiding sudden changes in his mood until she witnessed it happening in their private interaction last night.

Must be related to his rank, she thought. He probably used neutralizing his expression as a negotiation tactic, so he wouldn't give away his desires in a situation until he knew what everyone else involved wanted.

Clever elf, she thought, as she changed into her swimsuit. She smiled when she recalled the foot massage he had given her the night before. The focused intent on his face while executing the task perfectly was a moment that resonated with her. Although he knew how to give a good foot a massage, he really wanted to do an excellent job for her.

And he did.

She had woken up feeling heavenly this morning after spending the night rubbing her calves together because of their softness.

"Thank you for your help, Ena," she said to the servant, who worked quickly around her, as Adaline checked her hair in the mirror.

"Not a problem, Dr. Adaline," Ena said while smiling.

Adaline considered getting everyone to drop the doctor in her name, but that wasn't important right now. She stood back from the vanity mirror to appraise her bikini with the matching cover-up... that really didn't cover much. She slipped on her flip-flops and exited her suite. A few guards posted along the hallway gawked at her until she asked one, "Where is the king?"

The guard cleared his throat before he pointed down the hall. "In his study, Dr. Adaline. The seventh door on the left."

She proceeded down the neverending hallway until she found the seventh door on the left. She knocked and heard an emotionally detached, "Enter." Twisting the knob, she pushed the door into the room.

Adaline entered a quiet, intricately decorated space. She scanned the art on the walls, the books on the shelves, the furniture, and the architecture. So many nuances in the room reminded her that she was in another world. Her world didn't have books widely available anymore. They were scarcer than playing cards and board games.

Someone cleared his throat, and she pivoted to see the king blatantly staring at her from his desk. His pupils devoured his irises as he looked her over. His emotions channeled down his arms into his hands, one fisted while the other snapped the pen he was using in half.

Her clothes, if that's what they were, were so tiny and... accessible. Aureon's mind delved into the touches he could give her and the soft moans she would return if he snatched her up

144

and sat her on his desk right now. He salivated as he imagined brushing his lips against her neck. He shook off the indecent thoughts immediately. *What is happening to me?*

Aureon wondered if she understood the effect she had on males. His smooth stride to meet her didn't expose his concentration on how he conducted himself around her. But he did remain on one side of the oversized chaise in the center of the room, allowing it to separate them.

"Is something wrong?" she feigned innocence before nonchalantly stepping toward him.

Ah, she knows, he thought.

Between his tall frame and the height of the crown he wore today, he towered over her. His hands clasped behind him as his gaze bore through her.

She stopped in front of him. "You wanted to speak with me?"

"Where are your clothes?" he asked in a low growl while his hands fisted behind his back.

"Oh," she said, "I'm going swimming today, so I'm wearing my swimming suit." There was no point in trying to explain the term bikini. Instead, the king explained to her that elves didn't swim for the sake of leisure but for survival. "I don't know if you've noticed, but I'm not an elf," she said with a big grin.

"Where do you plan to swim, Dr. Adaline?" he asked, knowing there were no rivers nearby that were less than dangerous, except one that was too far away to access on human feet.

"A little bird told me that there are beautiful pools of water all throughout your private garden, and there is a huge one surrounded by a half-circle of trees that the sun peeks through to warm the water," she divulged. "That is where I will be spending my morning."

"Those pools are purely decorative."

"Not today," she replied, still grinning from ear to ear. "You have questions for me if I remember correctly."

Aureon was thrown by her cheerful attitude. He offered her his hand and escorted her to take a seat on the chaise while he continued to stand, pacing around her in large circles.

"Your healing gift," he started. Adaline nodded when he glanced over his shoulder to make sure they were on the same page. "It doesn't work on just physical injuries," he stated before pausing to look at her again.

"No."

"Can it work on old emotional injuries?"

"Yes," she admitted. "The older, the better."

"Why?"

"Because old pain is usually the easiest to let go of for the person carrying it," she explained. "By the time someone comes to me with an old emotional issue, it's like they are asking for permission to finally let it go."

There was a beat of silence.

"Usually, that's the case," she amended as she shifted in her seat.

"And if not?" he asked her. He came to a stop and crossed his arms over his chest. His attention drifted to her curves that wiggled when she moved without the support of real clothing.

She shook her head. "It can go a couple of different ways depending on the steps taken."

"Go on," he urged her as his focus on the matter returned.

"If a patient starts a healing session with me but stops the process before the session is finished," she said, "they will have to deal with a substantial amount of emotional fallout to release the remaining pain on their own, or come back and finish the process with me. Which is less painful and a faster process."

"And the other option?"

"They die from it."

"How is it possible to die from emotional pain?"

"It's easy," she said. "People tend to carry what is no longer theirs to bear for decades, giving the pain enough time in the

146

body that it manifests into physical illness. Essentially, we curse ourselves. The illness won't leave until the patient decides to unburden themselves."

"So, one can heal themselves."

"Yes," she said. "That's something I stress to my patients to learn in my practice at home."

"Do they?" he asked, truly curious about her life in her world.

Her face fell. "Few do."

It was clear that fact bothered her, and it was evident to him that she tried her best to motivate those who came to her for help. He resumed his pacing as he processed the information she'd shared, as well as maintain the physical distance between them.

"Why did you choose to share this with me?" he finally asked her.

Without skipping a beat, she said, "Because what you are carrying in your chest will kill you. Your symptoms are beginning to show." Pause. "You are running out of time." Adaline figured it out after she handed Farryn back to Theodon once the child was healed. The tightness in her chest she felt wasn't from Farryn nor Theodon but from Aureon, who had moved closer to her.

Another pause.

"And you have a good son who deserves to have his father around for as long as possible," she whispered.

"How do you know where it is?" he asked defensively, dismissing the comment referring to Theodon.

"Aside from your behavioral cues," she said, as she thought of the first day she met him and began reading his soul record, "that is an ability I will not reveal yet."

"And you would help me for Theodon?"

She appraised him. "Ask me the real question." Aureon stopped pacing before his attention lifted to her. Her head tilted. "Go on." His intense gaze bore through her without revealing a word. "Am I attracted to Theodon?" Adaline took a moment to give the king an elevator stare, and a smirk crossed her mouth halfway through her perusal. "I am not."

Adaline rose from the chaise and her gaze changed from appraising to honest. "If you consider choosing to heal, I will tell you that there is a question I ask all of my patients with emotionally based illnesses before moving forward with treatment." He remained silent. "Is this something you *want* to get rid of?" she explored his eyes for the truth. "Really assess that question because there are a lot of people who want to hold onto their suffering. If that's the case, I can't help you." She let a moment pass to let him think about her words. "Is that all you need from me right now?"

That was a loaded question for him. The only response he could muster was a stiff nod as he stepped out of her line of sight to the door.

"Pool time," she said with a smile before she headed out. He was at a loss for words at the sight of her backside, perfectly shaped and barely covered, walking away from him. He fisted his hands at his sides, denying reaching for her. "Oh!" she stopped and spun around. "How do I get an invitation for someone outside of the palace to join me at the pool?"

His eyebrow crooked as he considered if he wanted anyone else seeing her in a scantily clad state. "Who?"

"A female named Sacha," Adaline shared. "She's a bartender at Eleona's."

"I will send her the message."

Adaline nodded before adding, "Please specify in the message to let her know to bring clothes she can swim in recreationally."

He was amused at the idea because telling such a thing to an elf was ridiculous. "I will disclose the details."

"Thank you," she said with a bright smile before leaving the room.

He sank back onto the chaise she had just vacated and rested his head in his hands. *She will be the death of me*, he thought. A moment of silence passed, and he realized that his pending doom was of his own doing. He didn't have any symptoms that he could identify yet. What could she see? And how much time did he have?

CHAPTER 18

A daline conceded to her inner child upon entering the king's garden by running down the path that led to the pools. Laughing the whole way, the heads of curious elves who tended the garden popped up from behind bushes and shrubs to locate the origin of happiness. A few of them eyed each other, giggled, then returned to work. Adaline's jog slowed as she approached the pool Ena had mentioned to her earlier that morning. The trees were tall and thin, and their many branches grew in artistic patterns that reached for the trunks alongside them, creating a natural boundary around the pool.

Once Adaline moved a lounge chair next to the pool, another servant rushed out to her when he saw her handling the oversized chair by herself.

"Dr. Adaline!" the words rushed out frantically. "I can do that for you!"

"It's okay, I've got it," she said as she nudged the foot of the chair the way she wanted it. "But I could use one more chair. I have company joining me." The servant nodded and fetched another chair. "Thank you."

"You are welcome," he said. "If you need anything else, just speak it, and it will be brought to you."

"That sounds amazing, thank you," she said. "What's your name?"

"Gesso," he gave a slight bow.

Adaline smiled. "It's nice to meet you."

"And you," he said before he was gone as quickly as he arrived.

She shed her cover-up and slid her sunglasses up the bridge of her nose before she stretched out on the lounge chair. She lazed in the morning sun, choosing to refrain from getting into the pool until her guest arrived.

"Adaline?" a female voice asked from behind Adaline's chair.

Adaline sat up and looked behind her to see Sacha standing alone with a tote over her shoulder.

"Good morning," Adaline said while standing to greet Sacha.

"I received a message from the king," Sacha sounded confused, "…to join you for a swim?"

"Or to lounge," Adaline clarified. "Whichever you prefer. Come! Sit." She patted the armrest on the chair next to her. Sacha casually took her seat and set her tote down. "Are you hungry?"

"Thirsty," Sacha said as Gesso approached a moment later. Sacha spoke to him in the same elfin language she heard the guards use when they escorted her to the palace on her first day in Theris. Then, Sacha turned back to Adaline and smiled. "So, what's the story?"

"The story?" Adaline asked.

"Why am I here beside a pool that's not meant for swimming when you were carrying on with the prince and his friends who seem like they would be open to this sort of thing?"

Adaline smiled. She already liked Sacha.

"First off, just because they were his friends doesn't mean

they are also mine," Adaline clarified. "Because of that, I found there to only be three honest souls in that entire bar, and you were one of them." Sacha smiled. "Now, let's be honest souls and admit our real names," Adaline said while eyeing Sacha purposely.

Sacha nodded at Adaline's words as she found them fair. "My name is Sorsacha Olostuil."

"Ah," Adaline said. "And that doesn't sound like an ordinary name."

"My family's house is an ancient noble bloodline," Sacha confessed.

"And their beautiful descendant is slinging drinks in a bar for other nobles because?" Sacha smiled to herself at Adaline's compliment.

"Because I made a mistake," Sacha admitted.

Adaline's brow knitted. "Did you?"

Sacha's nose crinkled. "No."

"But it's a mistake in the eyes of your family." Sacha nodded. "So, you did what you thought was right, and you were punished for it, anyway," Adaline said, recalling the details of Sacha's soul record from the night they met at Eleona's. She grabbed her beverage and offered it as she smiled. "I think we should drink to that."

Sacha smiled wide and clinked her glass with Adaline's in celebration. *This human is far more interesting than the last ones who visited Theris.*

Over the next few hours, the females laughed, joked, swam, and splashed each other. The time seemed to fly by as the fun was neverending. Asking Sacha to join her was the perfect icebreaker for Adaline to learn more about the female elves of the kingdom and elfin history. Especially recent history, considering all that had happened to the Sleones since Theodon was born.

Theodon checked on Adaline and noticed Sacha as he walked up to the side of the pool. He found both females to be waist-deep in the water. One was talking while the other was laughing.

When Sacha saw Theodon, she executed a formal bow while in the pool. "My Lord."

"Sorsacha." Theodon nodded to her before turning to Adaline. He couldn't stifle his natural inclination to smile upon seeing her, regardless of knowing she was at the center of their reckless behavior.

"Are you here to join the fun, Theo?" Adaline asked, shafting royal etiquette by using her nickname for him.

He raised an eyebrow at her in an attempt to get her to bend, but he couldn't. He was a kind person, and he often laughed when Adaline was around. Adaline arched her eyebrow back at him. He swallowed a smile.

"Is that a yes?" Adaline asked.

"No," he said, with his eyes smiling. "I'm simply checking on you."

Adaline exaggerated whispering to Sacha, "He's still learning to trust me." Adaline winked at Theodon.

"Well, if you were swimming in my pool and weren't supposed to, I'd still be working on trusting you too!" Sacha shot back. Adaline's mouth dropped open, and soon as Sacha laughed. Adaline splashed her. Sacha gasped. "You will regret that, human!"

"Bring it, elf!"

The water war ensued as the two females splashed each other while facing away from each other to avoid getting hit in the face.

Theodon chuckled. "I see everything is in… order. I will check on you again later." The females didn't cease-fire to say goodbye to him.

After taking a break from swimming, the females lounged and chatted about everything Theris-related. They revisited the subject of Theodon, and both wondered if he felt left out of the fun they were having. However, he probably didn't think it was appropriate for the prince of the kingdom to strip down half-naked and jump into his father's pool that wasn't used for swimming. Such recklessness was only tolerated from younglings.

These royals should let loose occasionally, Adaline thought.

The king heard their fun and laughter from the balcony above them as he read in his library. When Adaline was alone, he would peer over the side, curious about what she might be doing. She started by lounging in the sun in her bikini. He still couldn't fathom clothing so small. He stared at it, transfixed by the tiny bright pink triangles that covered her curves. He stifled a groan when she rolled over onto her stomach and untied the back of her top as she lay in the sun. His eyes could pick up on the fullness of her breasts when she leaned up when Gesso approached her, asking her if she wanted something to eat.

As Sorsacha joined her, which he thought was an intriguing choice for a pool guest, he found himself rushing back to check on her whenever he heard a female holler, "Cannonball!" followed by a giant splash.

She is going to hurt herself, was the thought running through his mind.

Girl talk flowed between the females, and elfin males were not exempt as subject matter.

"So," Sacha nudged Adaline, "what are some differences you have noticed between elfin males and human ones?"

"Excellent question," Adaline said, as the king's pointed ears twitched as he listened for her response. "Well," Adaline began, "elfin males are generally in better physical shape." Sacha raised her glass to clink with Adaline's as an amen to that. Sacha sipped her beverage while Adaline continued. "Human males are generally less friendly," she admitted, "but I think that has something to do with all the tragedy my world has been through. It has left everyone in survival mode." Adaline was not exempt from that. She was reminded of it almost every night if she woke up in the middle of the night, only to see everything in her field of vision beat red in sync with her heart, indicating that she carried too much stress. Sacha nodded in Adaline's direction while listening. "Elfin males are generally helpful and highly intelligent," Adaline admitted. "Although, there are some accomplished males where I'm from." Her brother, for one. "However," Adaline said while holding up her drink, "human males are more open about the nature of their sexuality than elfin males."

Sacha spat out her drink. "How do you know?"

The king's knuckles turned white as he gripped the banister hard as Adaline's words hit his ears. He was prepared to slaughter whatever male dared to touch her while she had been in his kingdom.

"Okay, I haven't been intimate with an elf," she said, "but I've noticed an obvious contrast: males on both Earth and in Theris protect the females around them. Females are rare and appreciated in my world, but males do not suppress their sexual need for females. Whereas elfin males hesitate and measure every single response when they are interacting with a female. I assume they act similarly in bed."

Sacha nodded. "There's a reason for that."

"I'm listening."

"You may have noticed that Theodon is not that way," Sacha stated.

Adaline thought for a moment. "That's correct; he is not. He's kind and open, no matter what."

"That's because this behavior was affixed to a particular generation before he was born," Sacha admitted. Adaline nodded. "Close to 1,114 years ago," Sacha began, "the king's soldiers were at war on the northern border. It was a hellish one and seemed neverending. At the time, Theris allied with the Allo, who are a bloodthirsty species of monster warriors. They fought alongside each other for years, and the Allo's violent nature impacted the king's soldiers. Bringing them back into normal society was tricky, and Cerus had to find a way to rein them in."

"Cerus?"

"King Aureon's father," Sacha clarified.

"He doesn't have a title?"

"He passed his title to his son before the beginning of that war. It's not usually done, but he chose to step down and crown his son king."

"Why?"

Sorsacha shrugged. "Some say Cerus knew the war was going to be a long one, and he was weary of fighting. Perhaps he thought it best for the army to follow his younger, more resilient son into battle. So Cerus stayed behind to help the new queen while she was pregnant with Theodon. It seemed to work out for the best."

There was more to this story, Adaline knew. "What else happened?"

"Well, Cerus had to do a lot of damage control toward the end and continued it long after the war," Sacha admitted. "Soldiers were too violent to operate around civilians due to fighting alongside the Allo. But it turned out to be the easier of his tasks to handle. It was reining in the king that was the most heartbreaking." Adaline tilted her head in curiosity. "See," Sacha said, "Cerus had to curb the ferocity that was embedded in his son, so the king could go back to ruling the kingdom as if the worst never happened. Plus, Cerus had to help his son get through the grieving process of losing his queen soon after she gave birth to Theodon."

The information broadsided Adaline's stream of consciousness, and her eyes blinked wide in surprise. "So, Cerus had to raise a newborn, his grandson, until his own son came home from war to find out that he was finally a father. And a single parent."

Sacha nodded. "King Aureon came home to meet his new son, not yet knowing his queen had died, and he had to return to the front line in less than two weeks."

"Wow." Adaline exhaled as her heart sank in her chest. A moment passed before her heart surged with its normal strength, filled with empathy for Aureon.

The king had stopped reading to hear Sacha's retelling of the story, which was widely known in Theris. The details she shared were correct, except that there was so much more to share. It was his father's actions that prompted him to accelerate his soul work for the past thousand years, far beyond what he was already doing in his daily practice. *Perhaps I will have the opportunity to clarify someday*, he thought. The idea was enough to convince him to leave their pool time uninterrupted.

"Back to the reason for the story," Adaline said, steering their conversation.

"The answer is mostly yes; elfin males sidestep when interacting with females because they make sure to be gentle with them in all things. Most of the males around today are of the generation that fought with the Allo," Sacha confirmed.

Adaline nodded. "Does anyone know what Cerus did to rehabilitate them?"

Sacha finished sipping her drink. "None of them will say." Adaline's eyebrows lifted in surprise.

"Okay, aside from the general heartbreak that resulted from listening to that story, I still gotta say, getting what you need while being intimate with your partner is key," Adaline admitted. "And not at the cost of his authentic nature."

"What are you saying?" Sacha asked Adaline.

Adaline smirked, took a long sip of her drink, and pushed her sunglasses back up on her nose. "I'm saying that it's okay to let your male get a little rough in bed sometimes. It doesn't have to always be so sweet and gentle. Otherwise, intimacy gets repetitive and boring, which can be tragic for beings with such long life spans." She winked at Sacha.

"I completely agree," Sacha said to Adaline's amazement. "I've found variety helps."

"It seems that in the reining in of the soldiers," Adaline said, "their female counterparts have to reintroduce to them that it's okay to push the boundaries, and exactly how far."

"Otherwise, they won't go near it at all."

And if they won't go near it, the exchange remains the same, Adaline thought. Her mind wandered about what Cerus could have possibly done to instill such fear in his soldiers that none dared to utter a word about it long after his death.

Gesso interrupted the king's listening to the female's conversation. "My Lord?" he asked. The king gave Gesso his attention without speaking. "I have your afternoon meal for you, Your Majesty. Would you like for me to arrange it in here?" The king nodded, then gestured where he wanted his meal to be set up. "Also, My Lord," Gesso said, when he was done organizing the king's food, "the doctor is asking for more snacks for her and her companion by the pool."

The king drank from his glass before peering over the balcony to the beautiful human throwing herself back into the pool. She came up from an underwater handstand and shook out her hair before bursting with laughter. She was truly radiant and playful. She knew how to enjoy herself and managed to do so with a stranger. He wondered if her mood had anything to do with their private exchange last night. If so, that meant he found an avenue in which he could provide for her. He watched her intently as the realization brought him… contentment? Adaline's happiness made her appear far away, like he was peeking into a life that depicted something he could never possess, and his hands fisted at his sides. Her reality seemed out of his reach, regardless of if he yearned for the chance to experience it with her. Without looking away from her, he instructed Gesso, "Give her whatever she wants."

CHAPTER 19

The late afternoon sun and the endless swimming made Adaline yearn for a nap on her lounge chair, which she did after Sorsacha left. The king watched over her as she slept, making sure no one would disturb her. When Adaline awakened, she slipped back into the pool for one last dip. After a few handstands and flips in the water, she pushed up through the surface and stilled as the awareness of being watched crept up her spine.

Behind her, she heard the sniffing of something large. Slowly turning, she was amazed and terrified to find a large animal looking at her from the edge of the pool. A giant black panther with golden eyes stared back at her, unflinching. The king watched the two closely while he shed his outer robe and unsheathed his dagger in silence. He perched himself with one foot on the ledge of the balcony, ready to jump and fend off Cailu, the giant jungle cat that was curious about Adaline. Since Adaline's abilities were a guarded mystery, the king waited for a cue from her before he leaped into action.

"Easy, big guy," Adaline said to Cailu. The king saw her bring her palm to her lips, and she blew a glowing ball of white light in her hand. "I have a peace offering. If you accept it, that means I'm no longer a dinner option. Deal?"

She was a certifiable dork talking to a wild animal, a true predator, who was substantially bigger than the ones that used to be in her world. She brought the ball of light back to her lips and blew it like a kiss. It floated to Cailu, who sniffed the air as it approached. The ball touched his nose and burst, leaving the remnants of its healing properties on his snout. He inhaled deeply, then sneezed.

"Bless you," Adaline said.

Cailu shook his nose before inhaling the rest of the light. He stared at Adaline as the light ran through his body, healing his aches and pains. He appeared to have decided something regarding Adaline before he turned to trot back into the jungle.

"Okay," Adaline said, confused yet relieved. "That could've gone worse."

The king watched Cailu depart from the pool, leaving Adaline safe and alone. The big cat's reaction to her was intriguing to Aureon since Cailu viewed all living things as his prey. It took the king going up against the creature to "educate" Cailu that the elves belonged to Aureon and were therefore off-limits when it came to meal choices. And due to Aureon being thorough in his lesson, that education never needed to be repeated.

Cailu was the king of the jungle in Theris, which began less than a few miles northeast of the palace. The jungle marked the border into Drearia, where all plants and bugs glowed at night. In the darkest parts of the jungle, plants and insects also glowed during the day. No elf had ever returned from those parts, except for Aureon. He was so powerful and biologically advanced that he was connected to all living things in his kingdom. He could speak into the minds of his subjects or any animal, which was why the king was intrigued with Cailu's behavior toward Adaline.

The cat intended to see Adaline again.

The king lowered his foot from the balcony and sheathed his blade. He shook his head in amazement. The human was getting more interesting with each passing hour.

CHAPTER 20

A daline's focus was lost in the intricately carved ceiling of her bedroom suite as she listened to the silvery om vibration of the two moons that hung in Theris' night sky. She tucked in early for the night, but instead of falling asleep, she found her mind racing through the events of the day. Eventually, her thoughts settled on little Farryn. She stretched her arms over her head before preparing to project into Farryn's dreams. Adaline preferred this method to check on her patients after surgery. As a result, no patient ever needed to return for a follow-up.

Adaline exhaled and closed her eyes. A moment later, her spirit lifted then separated her from her sleeping body. Then, with a clear picture of Farryn in her mind, she stepped into the child's dream.

What Adaline saw filled her with amazement — a bright forest with animated flowers that sang songs and woodland creatures that played with little Farryn. It was a fairytale dream come true! Farryn laughed and squealed at a bunny that was sniffing her hand before she noticed Adaline.

"Da!" Farryn said happily with her little finger pointed at Adaline.

Adaline smiled. "Hello, Farryn."

Farryn waved and cried out a few excited words in Tear to Adaline. The little elf seemed happy to see her doctor. That's a surprise, Adaline thought. In her experience, kids didn't usually like doctor visits. Little Farryn reached her tiny hands out for Adaline, and Adaline didn't hesitate to pick her up.

"This is quite a dream you've got here," Adaline said. Farryn giggled. "I'm here to check on you," Adaline said as she tapped her finger on Farryn's tummy. Farryn responded by lifting the hem of her ruffled shirt to show Adaline her belly. Adaline chuckled. "That helps a lot, thank you." Adaline used her free hand to scan Farryn for any lingering problems and found none. She dropped her hand. "How do you feel?" She lightly tickled the little elf, who burst with giggles. "Good." Adaline smiled before setting Farryn back in the middle of bunnies and ducklings pining for her attention. "I'll leave you to your bunny fun." But the child reached up for her. Adaline leaned down. "What?" Farryn grabbed Adaline's face in her chubby little hands and kissed her on the chin. "Aw, thank you." Farryn giggled and refocused on her dream. "Be good," Adaline said as she exited the dream.

Where to next? Adaline thought. Her mind listed ideas as she loitered in the space between dreams and reality.

Adaline was curious about King Aureon long before listening to Sorsacha's history lesson by the pool earlier that day. Now, it made sense to Adaline why Aureon seemed dangerous when she first saw him. It wasn't just because he was the most powerful of his species or his age, bringing him abilities and wisdom. It was because of what state he returned home from war and the tragedy that awaited him. Adaline saddened. So much loss at once, she thought while shaking her head. Then she focused on Aureon and stepped into his dream.

Aureon's back faced her as he stood with his arms crossed over his chest. He stared at a giant vortex of water that connected to a river. The riverbanks were carpeted with flowers in bloom, and Adaline could smell their captivating fragrances from a distance. The vortex was taller than the king, connecting to the river like an on-ramp to a freeway. His feelings of contentment and wonder passed through her.

So why was he just standing there?

"This is the quietest you have ever been in my presence, Dr. Adaline," Aureon said.

Adaline smirked. "I didn't think it fair to spoil your dream just yet." She noticed he wore a lighter version of royal attire. His head held no crown, his shoulders no opulent robes. Instead, he was dressed in a short, sleeveless tunic that molded his muscular form, with long pants tucked into slim boots. His long hair hung loose and appeared soft to the touch like it had been brushed before going to bed. She stood next to him while her attention remained on the natural phenomenon. The river was an incredible force of nature, reminding her that she was a long way from her planet that had succumbed to ruin. "Please tell me this place exists in the kingdom."

The king smiled to himself. "It does."

"What is it called?"

"This is the Fotis River," he shared. "It is difficult to get to due to the terrain." A beat passed. "Yet, it is worth the struggle." She nodded.

Aureon moved closer to the vortex that swirled multiple hues of blue. The colors blended and separated at random.

Adaline noticed his long hair covered most of his back. She felt a nudge like she was missing something, so she pushed at the scenery in his dream, causing a breeze that briefly brushed his mane to one side. The bare skin on the back of his neck revealed the top of a scar. It looked like it could be a claw mark, but Adaline had never known an animal to have claws that large. Her eyes widened to see that the scar ran deep, and it wasn't one claw mark but three. She neutralized her expression.

"Why are you here?" she asked him.

"I thought about this place after your swimming escapade in my pool today."

Her shameless grin said much. "It was fun."

"It sounded… fun."

"You were listening?"

A moment passed. "Yes." He shifted his weight. "I used to come here in my younger years with friends."

Adaline smiled to herself as she pictured the king as a prince. She imagined him being young, reckless, and joking with his friends. But the mood quickly changed as she felt his sadness creep into her heart. She realized he was nostalgic about a fun time that was long gone, and much has changed since then.

Did the king relinquish his capacity to experience joy? *Excellent question,* Adaline thought and did her best to mask her feelings. However, because she knew he could read her heartbeat if her mood changed, she acted fast. She stepped behind him and sang his name.

Aureon turned to notice the mischievous grin on her face before she pushed him. The vortex sucked him up and carried him downriver. Adaline got a running start and jumped in after him. The water pulled her down the river like a slide. She discovered she could talk underwater as fish swam around her in schools. Larger ones stopped to be petted, and she was awe by the magic of it all. When she resurfaced, she couldn't stifle her laugher as she flowed downstream.

"Woo! Yeah!" Adaline hollered. Then she stilled when she heard a male laugh. Her eyes widened. Aureon. He was laughing.

Sainthood, here I come! she joked to herself before something grabbed her ankle and yank her under the water. Then, when her vision cleared, she saw Aureon pull her against him.

"The fun part is coming up," he said in her ear.

How is this not the fun part? Adaline thought.

A moment later, Aureon grabbed the back of Adaline's knees to tuck them to her chest before they both shot off the edge of the river. It ended in a waterfall with a steep drop into a dark pool. He launched her higher into the air before they plummeted into the water below. He straightened his form to hit the water feet first. Seconds later, Adaline cannonballed through the surface. When she finished rotating in the water and sprawled on her back, she idled to gaze at the light shining through the surface of the water. Filled with joy and wonder, she'd never felt so free to be out of control.

Aureon crowded her vision when he followed her to find what was keeping her from surfacing. His dark hair floated around his face, framing his handsome features. He looped an arm around her to pull her closer and explored her eyes. She couldn't hide her contentment from him, and she touched his cheek before a loud vibration rattled them both. They exchanged confused expressions before the sound repeated. Adaline felt the tug of her spirit back to her body because it was rustled to its waking state. A moment later, her spirit was yanked from Aureon's dream, and his hand passed through her when he tried to grab her.

Adaline's body absorbed her spirit, and her eyes flashed open at the sound of a loud roar coming from the garden. Her attention flew to her balcony as another roar echoed through the king's gardens. She slid out of bed, ran to the balcony, and peered over the side to find the large panther she had met at the pool.

Cailu quieted when he saw her. He turned his body around, pointing in the direction of the jungle as his eyes never left her.

Adaline knew what that meant - *C'mon!*

Was she really going to leave the palace in the middle of the night because a massive, wild animal wanted her to?

Yes. Yes, she would, she decided.

She hurried to change her clothes, grabbed her bag, and dashed to the gardens to meet Cailu. Her pace slowed as her eyes landed on the large cat, making sure she hadn't misread any signs, and he had lured his dinner down from the palace instead. What she missed for a moment was the large shadow behind him.

Realization struck as Aureon stood behind Caliu in black sleep robes. The breeze combed through his jet-black mane that reflected blue in the moonlight. *How pretty,* she thought, entranced yet jealous at his apparent lack of bedhead.

"Dr. Adaline," the king greeted her with slight irritation.

Adaline was shocked to see Cailu walk over to the king and butt his forehead to the king's hand until Aureon petted him in return.

In a throaty half-asleep voice, she asked, "How did you manage to get him to do that?"

The king smirked at Cailu. "We have an understanding."

Adaline had no doubt in that statement, as both creatures appeared equally powerful and wild. She felt an intuitive nudge, knowing she was missing something in plain sight, so she read through Aureon's soul record that included interactions with Cailu. She wasn't surprised to find the king battling the large cat, but what shocked her was when Cailu pulled a fast one and sank his claws into Aureon's back. The king yelled in pain before he hit his knees. Cailu moved to pounce on Aureon, but the king rolled out of the way. Aureon brought his blade up against the cat's throat and communicated with the giant beast in a menacing whisper. He spoke in a language Adaline didn't understand while his sword dug into Cailu's neck. Finally, the cat ceased resisting, and Aureon dropped his blade from the feline's throat. Cailu glanced at Aureon over his shoulder. Aureon tucked his chin to the cat. Cailu bowed his head in similar acknowledgment before returning to the jungle. Aureon tried to stand, but he wavered as the blood loss from the wound on his back made him dizzy. Familiar hands scooped up the young king before he could fall. Concern hung on Cerus' features as he appraised his son, who was losing consciousness. The old elf wiped a strand of hair away from Aureon's face before rushing inside the palace.

It was such a deep wound that Aureon's immortality couldn't fully heal it, Adaline realized as she recalled catching a glimpse of the scar earlier on the bank of the Fotis River.

"It seems Cailu is not here for me," the king said with a soundless yawn while stroking Cailu's thick fur. "He knows not to wake me in the middle of the night." Adaline noticed the king's annunciation highlighted his annoyance before his eyes lifted. His irises reflected light back to her. She couldn't curb the shiver that ran down her spine as she remembered Theodon's words about male elves' reflecting gazes at Eleona's. The king's eyes narrowed on her, noticing the change in her heartbeat and his nostrils flared. Finally, he stopped petting Cailu and clasped his hands behind his back while considering all possibilities before he spoke. "He is here for you."

"Why?"

Cailu turned his back, lowered his body to the ground, and waited.

"He wants you to get on," the king said.

Adaline's eyes widened in surprise. "That's hard to believe. He wouldn't come near me before."

"He is the king of the jungle, Dr. Adaline," Aureon informed her as he moved closer to them. "A king has the luxury of changing his mind at any time."

That's a loaded statement, Adaline thought to herself. "So, I'm supposed to climb on his back and trust that he won't devour me the moment I'm too far away for anyone to hear me scream?" Feigning weakness was a way to help her dodge the truth about her abilities. Especially when she was still determining how safe it was to be herself in Theris.

Her use of the word devour resonated with him, and his pupils dilated, forming a wild look in his eyes. He noticed Cailu was getting anxious; therefore, time was short. "Cailu will protect you because he needs you," the king said to her. "Regardless, I will make certain." The cat returned the king's attention. "Wait here," Aureon said to Cailu before telling Adaline, "I will return shortly." Aureon leaped onto the balcony off the king's suite, only to land without a sound.

"That was impressive," Adaline muttered before she caught Cailu looking at her. "What? Can you do that?"

A minute later, Aureon landed softly next to them dressed in dark clothes, with blades strapped to every limb. His wardrobe choice reminded her of her sweeper gear. Adaline was impressed with his daggers and managed to catch herself before she started drooling. "Nice hardware."

The king nodded in return as he mounted Cailu and held out his hand for Adaline to sit in front of him. She tightened her bag across her body and slid her hand into his. His touch was warm at such a chilly hour. She responded to his decisive actions because she shared the characteristic. He didn't hesitate to scoot her back against his chest.

"He travels very fast," the king shared. "Closeness is critical to making the journey comfortable." He indicated to lean forward and showed her what fur was best to grab onto. Then, he leaned over her, securing her body to Cailu's before he reached for handfuls of fur.

"Is this really necessary?" Adaline asked.

"It would be foolish to underestimate him," the king said, his mouth at her ear. Their proximity affected them. Aside from their overlapping auras that sizzled, they both experienced the same heated sensation upon contact when his chest touched her back. Even though he heard her heartbeat accelerate, he rejected the urge to wrap his arm around her. Instead, they settled into place, leaving them sandwiched to a large wild animal for the foreseeable future.

"Sounds like a voice of experience," Adaline shot back as she turned her head to catch his reaction. Her dark bedroom eyes caught him off guard, stealing his concentration from his reply.

The king held her gaze and repeated, "We have an understanding."

She quirked a brow at him. "You said that already."

They were silent as they regarded each other for a moment as their bodies hummed in anticipation. Finally, Aureon dismissed it, focusing on the task at hand, and spoke in Tear to Cailu without breaking his focus on Adaline. "Go."

Cailu's body lifted off the ground and took off into the night. Adaline's grip on Cailu's fur tightened as he picked up speed. The scenery changed from thick forest to dense, glowing jungle in a matter of minutes. Adaline was captivated by the lights, distracting her focus from her grip on Cailu's fur. She slipped, and Aureon's arm slid around her waist, pulling her against his body, allowing her to readjust her grip on Cailu. Surprised by the gesture, it took her a moment to thank him. He nodded as he effortlessly molded himself to Cailu, keeping his hand on the side of her waist for a while to make sure she wouldn't be thrown off.

At least, that's what she told herself.

Adaline heard something swinging through the trees above them. The jungle was so dense with fog that she couldn't see far in front of Cailu's nose, yet the cat galloped through the glowing jungle fearlessly, as if he'd taken this route a thousand times. Adaline covered the king's hand on her waist and squeezed until he did the same. They locked eyes after his grip tightened before she could see what was flying above them.

Elves. Drearians. Dozens of them flew through the trees, swinging on vines overhead. Adaline couldn't decipher any other features because they were covered in the same vine tattoos Eleona had, blending them seamlessly into their environment.

"Why are they following us?" Adaline asked Aureon.

"Something's wrong," the king said. Cailu's sense of urgency and the elves flying overhead at this late hour led Aureon to a decision. "If anything goes awry when we get to our destination, stand behind me."

She gauged the seriousness behind his statement then nodded. After all, this was his kingdom, and he would know how to resolve problems with his subjects best. Of course, Adaline had no desire to cause conflict, given how much she was starting to like Theris, but that may not be up to her.

Cailu slowed to a jog before stopping. Aureon dismounted the large cat and helped Adaline slide off. She shook out her cramping hands from gripping Cailu's fur for so long, then adjusted her bag. The large cat bit down on the hem of her shirt and pulled.

"Oh!" Adaline said. "Okay, I'm following you."

Cailu led the way to a small cave that was partially made of stone. The other part was a large tree. A few plants grew inside, and a soft glow lit the way to the back of the cave. Aureon followed closely behind Adaline, with his hands hovering over the grips of his blades strapped to his hips. They stopped in their tracks when they heard a guttural groan of struggle. They looked at each other for a moment. Aureon sniffed the air.

"It's his mate," he concluded.

Adaline's hand covered her abdomen as she leaned forward. "She's pregnant."

The king nodded then gestured for her to continue along the lit path behind Cailu. They came to the end of the cave and saw Cailu's mate lying on her side. She lay completely still and had a large, swollen belly. Adaline surveyed the pregnant cat. Cailu came up behind her and pushed his forehead against her back, nudging her closer to the problem.

"Message received," Adaline said to Cailu.

Aureon stood back with his arms crossed over his chest while Adaline analyzed the animal.

"Does she have a name?" Adaline asked without turning around.

"Nÿla."

Beautiful, she thought while kneeling in front of Nÿla's face to get acquainted with the feline. *Every patient deserves a consult.* The pain in Nÿla eyes was evident, and Adaline lifted her closest paw. The enormity of it swallowed Adaline's hands, yet Adaline sandwiched it between her hands the best she could before allowing her power to flow into Nÿla. Her glowing light traveled up the cat's arm and through the rest of her body. Nÿla's struggle to breathe ebbed.

"That's a little better," Adaline commented. She patted Nÿla's paw and gently set it down. Then, Adaline stood, always keeping one hand in contact with Nÿla, while moving down her large body. She heard Nÿla give a wincing exhale as Adaline touched her swollen abdomen.

"I know, it hurts," Adaline tried to calm the mom-to-be. Her hand skimmed over the side of Nÿla's belly as she opened her bag and pulled out her stethoscope with her free hand. She rested it against the pregnant feline and searched for heartbeats.

"One," she counted.

"Two."

"Three."

"Four."

Adaline hovered her stethoscope further down. "Five." She surveyed the ground before appraising Aureon, who remained silent. "Does the cold affect you?"

"No," he said.

"Would you mind donating your tunic?"

He gauged her for a moment, then unlaced the front of his black tunic that was layered over his long-sleeved shirt of the same color. He shrugged out of it and handed it to her.

"It's going to get dirty," she warned. Aureon shrugged his indifference.

Adaline took it from him with her eyes still on his, waiting for him to retract his help, but he didn't. She laid the tunic on the ground in front of Nÿla's belly, opened her bag, and took out what looked like a large notecard. Adaline flicked it, and it illuminated. Resting her hand over the glowing screen, and the card wrapped her hand in latex. She flipped her hand over for the process to be repeated. She covered her other hand in the same fashion then arranged her surgical kit on the tunic. Aureon's interest was piqued, indicated by his nonchalant wandering to

Adaline's side. After Adaline finished organizing, she glanced at him. She handed him the glowing card. "You don't think you get to just stand there and watch, do you?"

The king took the card and narrowed his gaze at Cailu. *The things I do for you,* he thought before he coated his hands the same way he saw Adaline do it. He quietly waited for further instructions because, knowing this little human, there would be more.

Adaline took a razor out of her bag and shaved the belly area where a C-section would happen if needed. Then, she stood over Nÿla's hindquarters and felt where the closest cub was to the birth canal. *Hmm,* Adaline thought, the cub hasn't turned. She petted Nÿla with her free hand.

"This is going to be unpleasant," Adaline said as a warning to Aureon. She focused on the cub under her hand and telekinetically turned the cub in the womb. Nÿla groaned in discomfort. Adaline's right hand illuminated, flooding healing light into Nÿla's womb. "I know. This isn't fun." Nÿla's reaction subsided as her discomfort ceased after Adaline finished turning the cub. "Okay," Adaline said to Nÿla as she tapped her belly. "Time to push."

Nÿla adjusted on her side before leaning on her upper half and pushed. Two minutes of pushing passed until the first cub's head was visible.

Adaline petted Nÿla's. "Good job." Adaline signaled to Aureon behind her to grab the scissors out of her hand and stand at Nÿla's rear end. "Get ready to catch."

Aureon crouched down, ready to hold Nÿla's first cub.

"When he's almost halfway out," Adaline instructed and demonstrated with her hands, "clasp him like this… gently but firmly, and ease him out the rest of the way when you feel her push. Give a little slack to the cord before cutting it."

The king reached forward, doing as instructed. And once the king had the cub cradled in his arms, he asked, "What next?"

"Lay him on the tunic," she said as she moved her surgical

tools to the edge of the tunic to make space for the cubs. "Then repeat the process until they are all out."

Adaline continued monitoring the other cubs in the womb to make sure everyone was in perfect sync. Cailu moved closer to Nÿla then licked her face. Adaline sent some healing light into her belly to help her cope.

"Okay," Adaline said to her as she patted Nÿla's fur again. "Now for the next one."

The process went on for an hour. Four of five cubs were lined up on the king's tunic that was spread on the ground. Adaline put on her stethoscope to listen for the fifth cub's heartbeat. It was faint. She felt the cub struggle under her hand. Nÿla's pain returned with a vengeance. Cailu jumped to his feet, fur standing in alarm.

"Something's wrong," Aureon stated.

"Shit," Adaline muttered as she reached for her scalpel. "I'm sorry," Adaline said to Nÿla as she held up her hands to freeze-hold Nÿla's feet away from her and to hold her head down so she wouldn't see what Adaline had to do next or harmfully react. Adaline coughed as she activated an ability she hadn't used in decades. Divine truth rang from her throat as she spoke, "Nÿla, sleep." Nÿla immediately fell into a deep slumber.

Aureon's eyes widened. "What are you doing?" Was that another power of hers?

"Saving them both," Adaline said as she made an incision in Nÿla's belly. Cailu snarled and poised himself to pounce on Adaline, but Aureon stepped in between them. The kings faced off, matching size for size, snarl for snarl. Cailu shifted his weight to pounce on Aureon, but the large cat froze midair. Aureon analyzed Cailu for a moment to make sure he couldn't move before returning to help Adaline. He marveled to himself at how even-keeled she was in the midst of chaos. After Adaline opened Nÿla's belly, she found the cub.

"Come here and hold him," she called over her shoulder.

The king was on his knees at her side with his hands out in front of him. A moment later, Adaline was handing him the fifth cub. The cub had the umbilical cord wrapped around his neck and was turning blue.

"Scissors?" she asked.

He leaned his hip toward her. "Side pocket."

Adaline grabbed the shiny handles cut the cord before untangling it from the newborn's neck. A moment passed before the cub breathed normally.

"Put him with the others and slide the tunic over in front of her face so she can do her part while I do mine," Adaline said while using her sleeve to wipe the sweat from her forehead.

Adaline carefully realigned the walls of the Nÿla's uterus and drew her finger over the incision. White light blazed from her finger, sealing the tissue as if it had never been cut. She did the same for the abdominal incision. Once finished, Adaline stood and put both hands over Nÿla's belly. "Now to expedite the recovery process." She saturated Nÿla's belly with white light that burned away all pain and swelling. Once the healing finished, Adaline released her hold on Nÿla after Aureon placed her cubs in front of her.

Adaline coughed as before. "Nÿla, wake up."

Nÿla shot awake, experiencing brief dizziness as she returned to consciousness. The new mom saw her cubs lined up in front of her and licked them clean. Adaline smiled and waved her hand, unfreezing Cailu. The large cat landed on the ground and glanced around in confusion before seeing his mate cleaning their cubs.

Aureon gaped at Adaline from behind her. He'd never seen anyone go to such an extent to save a life before. But, of course, Adaline would rather reveal her abilities to save Nÿla than for anything terrible to happen to the creature.

Adaline wandered over to the cubs. They started making whimpering and fussy sounds. "Uh oh, it sounds like someone is hungry."

Aureon took that as his queue, and he slid the cubs in front of their mom's belly to nurse. Four of them latched onto their mother quickly, but that fifth one kept seeking. Finally, Aureon lifted the fifth cub high enough to latch on to his mother. He retook his place next to Adaline, crossing his arms over his chest again.

"It looks like you won't be getting that tunic back," Adaline said.

Aureon admired the new family. "There are worse things."

Adaline smiled to herself as she peeled the latex off her hands and let the gloves float to the floor. As the latex came into contact with itself, it dissolved before reaching the ground. She assessed Nÿla, who was partially sitting up with her tail twitching to and fro. The large cat swiped at Adaline to bring her closer. Nÿla rubbed her face against Adaline's body.

Thank-you.

Adaline petted her. "You're welcome."

Adaline felt Cailu rub his forehead against her back, and she giggled. A cat-sub? A panth-wich! After letting her go, she packed her surgical tools in her bag, and her eyes met Aureon's.

"Ready?" she said before letting out a deep yawn. She covered her mouth with her hand. "Excuse me."

The corners of his mouth twitched as he was amused by her mortality. "Did you get enough sleep, Dr. Adaline?"

Her eyes glittered knowingly. "How could I sleep after being thrown from a waterfall?" His eyes widened as he realized she was present in his dream, not an imaginative part of his subconscious adventure. "I could really use a nap, but if I close my eyes now, I'm afraid they won't reopen for a long time." The humidity of the jungle did her no favors either, dotting her skin like morning dew. She used her sleeve to blot the excess water from her face.

He gestured for her to lead the way out of the cave. Adaline shuffled along the path, with Aureon and Cailu trailing behind her. They reached the cave's mouth and were greeted by a crowd of Drearian elves whose attention landed on the king, first, then they bowed. He nodded at them in return. They rose to stand, and all eyes fell on Adaline before erupting in cheerful victory in celebration of the birth of the cubs. A few elves rushed toward Adaline. The king said something quickly in a language she did not understand, as his arm shot out to shield her. The elves stopped in front of her. Aureon said something else to them. They all smiled and nodded their thanks to her. Aureon knew how handsy Drearians could be in their interactions, especially when they expressed thankfulness. He thought it best that Adaline learns about it through forewarning versus direct experience.

A platter of fruit was brought to Adaline. She gently cradled the intricately carved platter then searched Aureon's expression for direction.

"Those are yours to eat," he said.

"Now?"

"Yes."

"Thank goodness," she said before picking up a piece of fruit and tossing it in her mouth. She closed her eyes to savor it and chewed slowly. It was the most succulent and flavorful produce she'd ever tasted. "Mmm," she purred before opening her eyes to choose another one.

The elves rejoiced and celebrated around the two of them as Adaline ate fruit and Aureon stole a few pieces from her plate. Aureon issued a command to the elves, and a few rushed forward with chairs for them. He gestured for Adaline to take one, which she obliged. He didn't need to sit and rest, but he knew she did. He reached for a piece of fruit, and she playfully slapped his hand.

"No," she said firmly. Aureon's wild eyes narrowed on her for making such a bold move against a royal. "That one is my favorite." He understood her playfulness and chose another fruit. He was enamored by her, curious even. She was quite an anomaly.

"Are females in your world like you, Dr. Adaline?" he asked her. Then, he finally understood why Jim and Tony were protective of her after witnessing her abilities and how she used them to help others. If he factored in all he noticed about her, he reasoned that she must be considered valuable in her world.

"In terms of?" she asked.

He thought for a moment. "In terms of strength, abilities, sense of self, beauty."

Did he just call her beautiful?

"Women are hard to come by in my world," she admitted. "So, we are all a bit of a rarity."

"That is not what I mean," he said as his eyes pinned her attention. She noticed his eyes appeared brighter when surrounded by the dense jungle of the same color. She watched him tuck a strand of dark hair behind his pointed ear.

She smiled softly, understanding his question. "There isn't another woman like me."

He nodded, confirming his original thought: she was an anomaly.

Special.

She popped another piece of fruit in her mouth. "This," she pointed at the platter, "this is the best decision we have made today."

Aureon smirked at her goofiness. "The best decision was not getting on the back of a large panther that could kill you in one bite, Dr. Adaline?"

"Was that?" Adaline asked while leaning toward him. "Was that a joke?" She laughed. "You should try that more often." Her laughter got away from her for a moment.

He liked the sound of it and searched his mind to keep it going. "Or choosing to swim in a pool that was not meant for swimming?"

"Excuse me, Your Majesty," she exaggerated his title, "that wasn't our decision. That was purely my decision."

"It was not."

She cocked her head at him questioningly.

"You had to convince me to decide that swimming in my pool was a good idea."

She smiled. "And how did I manage that?"

"By wearing, what did you call it?" He thought for a moment. "Your swimming suit during our negotiations."

Adaline smiled wide and playfully pushed his shoulder. "You're on a roll right now." He nodded confidently, aware of what he was insinuating. "It's called a bikini," she said to him. He looked at her curiously as he chewed the next piece of fruit. "A bikini is a two-piece swimming suit."

He nodded as he brought the seeds from the fruit he ate to his lips and tossed them aside. "Those were hardly pieces." Adaline's eyes widened, and her jaw dropped. His lips stretched into a victorious smile like he won a point in a game they were playing.

"Is that a complaint, Your Majesty?"

He chuckled. "About that, I would never, Dr. Adaline."

His playfulness prompted her to eye him in fascination. "When's the last time you flirted like that?"

Although her view of him was genuine, it came off as a sultry expression to him. He surmised that she didn't know her subtle actions had passionate energy behind them. He thought about her question while he chewed, unable to pinpoint the exact number of years.

"It has been a long time," he admitted.

"How does it feel?"

His gaze smoldered. "Good."

She suppressed another shiver and changed the subject. "Have you thought about what we talked about this morning?" He nodded. "And?"

"I am still forming a decision."

"Fair enough," she replied. She surveyed the last fruit on the platter. It had a thick skin that was bright yellow with little purple knobs all over it. She wasn't sure how to proceed with it, so she eyed Aureon.

Aureon smirked and held out his hand, and she handed it over. He pulled out the blade on his hip. Then, with a demonstration of his superior dexterity, Aureon carved the fruit with remarkable speed and precision. She watched in silence.

"This is the best one," he confessed.

Adaline's excitement grew at the thought as she watched him finish. When he opened it up, she saw the layers of bright colors inside that led down to orange seeds in the center of it. It was so beautiful that she didn't want to eat it. He finally stabbed a slice with his blade and held it out to her. She quickly snatched it up and examined the colors. She still wasn't sure how to eat it.

He took a slice of the fruit in his hand and held it up. "Grown elves eat the whole thing, but younglings prefer eating only the inside fruit until the last band of purple before the rind."

She watched as he put the whole slice in his mouth before chewing. His eyes stayed on her, curious to see what she would choose. She nibbled on the inside of the fruit slice, and the sweet flavor exploded on her taste buds. A faint moan left the back of her throat as she closed her eyes. *Damn, that's delicious,* she thought before opening them again, only to see the king smirking at her. She ate the rest of the slice, rind included, with a big smile on her face before she exaggerated grabby hands. "Gimme another!"

He didn't hesitate to hand her another slice, but he kept the rest, so she would have to continue to ask him for more. Their lighthearted banter continued until the fruit was gone. Then she telekinetically snatched his blade from his hand before it floated to hers. He narrowed his eyes on her, but he failed to maintain a reprimanding stare because he was enjoying her company. She analyzed the weapon, impressed by the original design and curvature of the blade, then she spun it in her hand. Aureon's brows lifted, impressed by her handling. She finally handed it back to him.

"Very nice," was all she said.

He sheathed the blade as he saw Cailu walking over to where they were seated. Aureon rose to his feet to pet Cailu, and the large feline welcomed the touch. Adaline watched their interaction: Two kings in their own right. Both stood with the same unwavering confidence, strength, and power. Aureon offered his hand to help her stand. "Are you ready to return?"

She nodded while looking at Cailu. "Is there any chance he can go a little slower on the way back? I'm so tired that I'm afraid I may not be able to keep a grip on him."

He thought about what she said. "I will handle it… even if you did push me into a river."

Adaline feigned innocence. "What? That doesn't sound like me!"

Aureon's eyes narrowed on her, then her lips flat-lined to swallow a smile.

They mounted on Cailu's back the same as the night before.

Dawn broke during their journey back to the palace, and Cailu kept his pace to a steady jog. The king secured his arm around Adaline, holding her against him the whole trip. He felt her energy level drop as she grew sleepy and reacted by clutching her tighter.

Once they arrived back in the palace gardens, they said their goodbyes to Cailu, who trotted back to the jungle. He had a new family that needed his protection.

Aureon walked alongside Adaline into the palace as the sun rose on the horizon while he monitored her energy level. Then they ran into Theodon, who was wide awake and ready for the day.

Theodon surveyed his father, then Adaline. "Long night?"

She smiled at him. "I was quite an adventure, thank you."

Theodon grinned. He knew his father and Adaline had left with Cailu in the night. There had to be a good story behind it because Cailu rarely ventured close to the palace.

Adaline's thoughts were solely focused on the soft bed that was in her suite. Yes, her suite. She has officially claimed it, especially the massive bathtub.

"Would you both like to join me for breakfast?" Theodon asked.

"Breakfast before a long sleep is a good idea," Aureon said, mainly for Adaline. He didn't need much sleep initially, but he figured she would sleep for a while, and he didn't think waking up starving to be ideal.

Adaline agreed to have breakfast and shuffled into the dining room with the royals. She heard the king mutter something to the servants. She suspected that it was something along the lines of delivering the food faster because the servants picked up the pace shortly after. Then the three of them settled into their meals.

Finally, Aureon broke the silence. "Dr. Adaline, did you enjoy your afternoon of recklessness in my pool?"

Theodon shot Adaline a look from across the table while sipping his beverage.

Adaline met Aureon's gaze with an unashamed grin on her face. "Indeed, Your Majesty, it was so enjoyable that I will endeavor to do it, again, during my next visit... weather permitting."

Theodon choked on his drink. The king lifted an eyebrow at her. She smiled sweetly in return before popping a piece of bread into her mouth. She chewed without breaking eye contact. The tiniest of smirks caught the corner of his mouth, and she smiled brighter.

"You should try it yourself sometime," she said to Aureon before taking a dramatic turn. "Oh wait, you have!"

"You admit it," Aureon spat. "You were there."

"I admit nothing," she said, unable to look him in the eye before consuming the next tasty morsel on her plate.

Theodon, having no idea what they were talking about, shifted in his seat before changing the subject. "Have you recovered from your patient visits, Dr. Adaline?"

She gave his question some thought while she cut into her food. "I did before I over-exerted myself for the sake of adventure." She chuckled. "Soon, I will be at full power, again."

"Enough to examine me?" Aureon asked.

Adaline and Theodon fell silent.

"Are you requesting an examination?" Adaline asked.

A moment went by as Aureon chewed his food. Another moment passed after he swallowed. "I should know if anything is wrong."

"You already know the answer to that," Adaline said gently.

"I meant how much time-" Aureon began to say.

"-What is she talking about?" Theodon blurted.

"Nothing," Aureon tried to say.

"It's not nothing," Adaline said, not giving Aureon an inch to retreat.

The king sighed hard before his eyes shifted to Adaline. She lifted her chin in Theodon's direction, urging him to be honest with his son. Aureon turned in his chair. When attention met between father and son, Theodon's eyes watered.

"Dr. Adaline has made me aware of some symptoms," Aureon revealed.

Adaline noticed Theodon's grip tightened on his flatware. As she continued to watch him, she witnessed how deeply elves felt their emotions. She felt Theodon's anger, fear, frustration, need to cry, and his helplessness at the possibility of something happening to his father.

"Theo," Adaline whispered. The prince's focus shifted to Adaline. "Breathe."

The prince did as requested. His grip eased. "How bad is it?"

Silence.

"It's substantial," Adaline admitted. Her statement shook Aureon, even though no one present could tell by his countenance.

More silence.

"And he's going to be fine," she said to Theodon.

"How do you know?" Theodon asked. The shakiness in his voice revealed that he wasn't as practiced in hiding his emotions as his father.

"Because it's been discovered in time."

After Theodon regained his composure, he set down his flatware and extended his hand to her. "Pinky swear?"

Adaline felt like a jerk when she saw the flash of hope in his eyes as he made the gesture. She shouldn't have introduced something trivial to him as something important. She shook it away as she decided it would be meaningful from going forward. Adaline reached across the table and linked her pinky finger with Theodon's, and locked eyes with him. "I pinky swear."

The prince exhaled and nodded to her, trusting her word. Then, his attention fell to his plate.

"I will have answers tonight," Aureon finally said after a long silence. Adaline met his gaze and nodded.

Breakfast returned to be a silent endeavor. Theodon navigated his shock, unable to find anything else to say. And one hard-headed king continued overthinking the healing process he may soon choose to pursue.

CHAPTER 21

T essa rushed through her tiny apartment, tossing belongings into a duffle bag. Terrified that the QC would find out she was fleeing, her scrambling left her apartment disheveled, as if it had already been raided. Having no idea if she'd ever see her place, again, she varied what she packed between necessities and memories.

Tessa pounded down the stairs to the garage, hustling to a car that was covered. No one in the building knew who the vehicle belonged to except the building manager. She yanked off the cover and slid into the driver's seat. It took a moment to start the car. It had been her great-grandfather's car, a classic and one of the last made to run on gasoline. Once humans rode the electric car trend, hydrogen was next and quickly nudged electric cars out as competition. Then, when access to electricity became as scarce as the drinkable water supply, gasoline engines made a comeback. Her great-grandfather had loved the car so much that he passed it down through the family until it might be helpful again. Tessa's saving grace was always keeping the gas tank filled, so it would be ready at a moment's notice.

What a moment, she thought, as she shifted the car into reverse. She sped down Wilshire Boulevard a moment later until she met the coastline. After a few turns, she was on Pacific Coast Highway headed to Malibu. Praying that Adaline would be home, Tessa hoped her friend wouldn't be upset with everything Tessa intended to confess.

Tessa parked in Adaline's beach house driveway and hurried for the front door. She pounded on it frantically but was met with silence.

Where is she? Tessa thought as she tried to peer through a window. Tessa knew Adaline kept to herself and didn't venture out of her house much, except to go to work or to Asher's house.

Asher!

Tessa ran from Adaline's driveway to Asher's house next door. She knocked on his door and waited.

Silence.

Tessa trembled with fear as she wondered what she should do next since her plan A and plan B weren't home. She scanned her surroundings to identify anyone watching her but saw no one. She rushed back to her car and locked herself inside. A moment later, there was a knock on her passenger window that made her scream. She finally opened her eyes to see an older man covering his ears and gritting his teeth. Once she stopped screaming, he removed his hands and took a moment to look her over.

"Are you all right?" he asked, loud enough for her to hear through the window. Her heart was racing, and she shook her head. She was about to burst into tears for the third time that morning. The man's lips flattened, and he nodded. "You're here for Addy?" Tessa calmed at the familiarity she detected when she heard him say her friend's nickname. Her tears spilled over the corners of her eyes as she nodded. "I'm Tony."

She finally rolled down the passenger window and sniffed

back the next wave of tears. "I'm Tessa."

Tony nodded, knowing who she was because Addy talked about her on multiple occasions. The girls spent their social time together. But Tessa looked too upset for him to consider leaving her alone.

"Are you hungry?" he asked her. "I'm not much of a cook, but when it comes to pancakes, I am quite the professional chef. Would you like some?" Tony's warm smile stretched across his face.

"Where do you live?" she asked while trying to peer over his shoulder.

"I'm Addy's next-door neighbor." He pointed at the smaller beach house behind him. "Maybe she will be back after breakfast, and you two can talk."

Tessa tensed at the idea of going into a stranger's home, but if he was Addy's neighbor, then it had to be better than returning to her apartment and getting caught by the QC.

"Pancakes sound great," she said, trying her best to smile.

"Great!" Tony cheered. "I'm glad to have the company."

*****

Meanwhile, Asher had entered Theris, curious to see it for himself. Especially after Tony and Jim came home from their visit yesterday. Tony marveled about the energy ripples of color the king gave off and how the plants had a similar quality. At first, Asher could have cared less about the state of the elf world, but when the Marines shared their interaction with the king, and the magical nature of the plants, Asher thought it the perfect opportunity to multitask. First, he'd check to see what kind of land Addy had wandered into, make sure she was okay, then he'd explore the plant life for anything he could analyze in his basement lab.

He smirked as he remembered getting turned down by a woman he had almost successfully seduced. Once she found out he had a basement lab, she concluded he had to be a serial killer and couldn't leave his house fast enough. The laughter that miscommunication brought him was worth the minor case of blue balls. Before leaving the portal behind, he checked his surroundings, remembering Tony saying the palace was on the left.

So, what's to the right?

He wandered into an oasis of large green shrubs with tiny flowers. He took his time inspecting the plants, succumbing to his curiosity to the point he didn't hear someone approaching.

"Good morning," the voice broke through Asher's evil-plant-scientist-haze, and his head snapped around to see an elf standing behind him. Asher rose to stand and noticed the elf was almost the same height as him. His dark hair, porcelain skin, and green eyes made it difficult to look away, as he appeared doll-like. Asher noticed the elf was appraising him, too, and seemed to make his own conclusions.

"What is your name?" the elf asked.

"You first," Asher offered.

The elf smirked. "You must be Dr. Adaline's brother."

"I am," Asher admitted. "You figured that out quickly."

"You have similar coloring and features," the elf admitted and chuckled, "and you both deflect when it comes to giving information."

Hmm, Asher thought. "You must be Theodon."

The prince stepped forward and offered his hand to shake. "Prince Theodon Iolas Sleone."

Asher peered at Theodon's hand, then shook it. Both males eventually cracked a smile regarding their awkward exchange.

"Dr. Asher Everly," Asher said.

"You are both doctors?" Theodon asked. "Can you heal like your sister?"

Asher chuckled. "No one can heal like my sister." A moment passed. "The way I heal people is a little different." Theodon nodded. "Was my exploration causing trouble?"

Something Asher was accustomed to achieving.

"Not at all," Theodon said. "Just curious as to what you are looking for."

Asher thought it best to give Theodon the whole picture. "I have a lab outside of our medical practice at home. I'm always searching for plant life that can be compounded to cure diseases."

"In place of your sister exhausting herself by using her healing gift all day?" Theodon chimed in.

Asher lifted one eyebrow at the prince. "Something like that."

Theodon smiled. "Carry on, I will bother you no longer."

"Thanks, Theodon," Asher said, impressed by how cool he was being.

Theodon waved it off. "Not a problem. I think she should have a break, too."

"Did she drain herself?"

"She did, then she recovered, but she decided to go on a midnight adventure that seemed to drain her again," Theodon rambled.

Asher's eyes shot wide. "Where is she?"

"Oh!" Theodon realized he was too candid. "She's unharmed. She returned to the palace, ate two breakfast plates of food, and went straight to sleep. No one is allowed to disturb her."

Asher's protective nature toward his twin lessened once he heard she was resting. He knew after food and sleep she would be back to her otherwise resilient self.

"So, did she and the king kiss-and-make-up?"

Theodon pondered the question for a moment. "It demoted from open war to a stalemate."

Both males laughed.

"I expected worse," Asher joked.

Theodon noticed how the twin's personalities were similar.

They joked and laughed easily. *How nice it must have been to have each other while growing up.*

"Yes, and my father would have deserved it," Theodon admitted.

A pause passed between them as Asher wondered how honest the prince would be about his father, but he decided to ask the question was worth a shot. "Is he a good guy, Theodon?"

"He is," Theodon answered quickly. "But he did not handle the situation with Dr. Adaline correctly when she first arrived in the kingdom."

"Fair enough." Asher knew he didn't have to step in on his sister's business when it came to her choices in men, or males rather. She knew how to handle herself and wouldn't put up with being treated as less than she knew she deserved. She never came crying to Asher about being poorly treated in the eighty-five years they had spent looking out for each other in this lifetime.

"You don't seem worried," Theodon said to him.

"Neither do you," Asher shot back. The prince pursed his lips before shrugging his shoulders. "So Theodon," Asher said, desiring to make the most of their exchange. "I assume your time is in high demand, but I was wondering if you could give me a general idea about the plant life that grows here."

Theodon smiled. "I'd be delighted."

Hours later, Asher returned to Earth. Excited to test the plant samples he brought back from Theris, he didn't leave a single footprint in the sand as he sped back to his beach house. A loud explosion behind him made him spin to see a helicopter targeting Tony's house and QC agents propelling down from the airship. Fury rose within Asher, emphasized by the lightning tearing through the sky. He dropped the bag that held the samples and let the white electric current flow over his person. He quickly gathered enough energy to launch him into flight. As he descended on the helicopter, Asher reached for the sky, and a lightning bolt met his touch. He pointed his free hand at the machine, channeling the energy into it. The engine fried, and the airship plummeted, crashing on the beach in an explosive blaze.

Asher hovered over the gun-riddled hole in the roof of Tony's house. He saw a few QC agents down and an armed Jim standing guard over unconscious and bloodied Tony.

"I've got the rest," Asher said to him as he landed, and his electric current found every QC agent left on the property and electrocuted them to death.

Jim sighed. "I'm glad you're here."

Asher and Jim dropped to Tony's side to check his wounds. Asher touched one gunshot wound, and Tony hissed through his teeth.

"He's awake," Asher said, relieved.

"Those bastards are getting ballsy," Jim said as he surveyed the damage Tony incurred.

"It's a good thing they are terrible shots," Asher concluded, as he found wounds only in Tony's extremities. "I can fix this."

"Where's Addy?" Tony asked. He meant to ask where Tessa was. The girl was terrified the moment the first round came through the ceiling, and she ran.

"She's recovering from a long day," Asher shared. "But we can patch you up until she gets back to accelerate the rest of your recovery." Tony tried to sit up and winced. "I will move you," Asher said before he raised Tony up off the floor with his telekinesis. "You're both staying at my house from now on." Jim kept up with Asher's lengthy stride back to his home while still carrying his firearms, periodically checking behind them for the QC as lightning continued to flash overhead.

CHAPTER 22

A daline roused from sleep after dinnertime. Later that night, she walked beside the king, who led her to his study in silence. Adaline noticed his pace was that of a "dead-man-walking," yet instead of breaking the silence, she grasped his arm to help him tether his thoughts as his uneasiness washed over her.

"Don't be nervous," she whispered to him in the vast hallway. He wouldn't die today. She would make sure of it.

Aureon's gaze was thoughtful as he opened the door to his study and motioned for her to enter. She quietly made her way toward the oversized chaise that was the perfect size for him, noticing his hands remained tucked behind his back. His furrowed brow highlighted the worry he would never voice. As much as her heart ached for him, she knew her feelings wouldn't help him right now, so she switched to her clinically detached demeanor.

"It would be best if you set aside your crown, your rings, and your outer robe," she said.

In approaching his desk, he lifted the crown from his head and set it down. Then he shrugged off his outer robe and draped it over the back of his chair. He pulled his rings off one by one with a faraway stare out the window. Finally facing Adaline, he noticed her small smile. She gestured for him to take a seat on the chaise. He laid back and shifted while his nerves began to get the best of him.

Her voice was soothing. "Relax."

He took a deep breath and exhaled slowly. Adaline still felt his anxiety as she blew a ball of light into her hand. She held it close to his nose. "Inhale."

Captivated by the ball, a moment passed before he leaned into it and inhaled until the ball was gone. His eyes widened as he felt the light circulate through his system as a tingling, almost burning sensation. His body went lax.

"Better?" she inquired.

"Yes."

"Good." She sat on the edge of the chaise. "I'm going to have to touch you." His bold gaze locked with hers before he gave a firm nod. "It's important that you don't interrupt the process until I'm done."

Adaline's glowing left hand reflected in his large eyes. Her palm hovered over his face, neck, shoulders, and chest. She hissed and snapped her hand back, closing her fingers over her palm tightly. Upon examing her hand, he noticed her eyes were already watering.

"Are you all right?" he asked. The raw pain in her expression was something he'd never forget. Was that what he looked like to everyone else? *Maybe we should stop.*

"I'm going to work on your eyes," she said. "Is it all right to continue?" She knew it would be a painful process when what she felt in his chest was colder than dry ice and burned worse to the touch. His concern for what would happen to her if they moved forward washed over her.

"Will it hurt you?" he asked her.

"It will be taxing."

He didn't like that answer.

"The end result is always worth it," she stated.

"Has it hurt you in the past?"

She nodded. "It would often hurt a long time ago." She found herself recalling memories from her childhood. "Now, it's rare for it to hurt at all."

"What happened?"

She thought to herself before sharing, wondering if it was a good idea to share this particular story. Deciding honesty was best, she began, "When I was younger, a long-fought war finally came to an end on Earth. Those who fought returned home with physical and emotional wounds, unlike anything that I'd ever seen walk into my medical office."

"You healed them," he knew.

She nodded. "My father was a high-ranking officer in the Marines. It's a specific branch of the military in our country. At the end of this war, his best friend, Jim, who you met, returned home with many injuries... it was remarkable that he survived the journey." Adaline cast Aureon a knowing look before continuing, "My father asked Asher and me if we would heal his friend. So, of course, we said yes. He snuck us into the veteran's hospital where Jim was recovering. His body had endured so much damage that healing him affected me for three days."

The king's eyes widened. "We are not doing this."

"Yes, we are," she said. Aureon's head canted, wondering if she were mad. "I was eight years old when that happened."

His brow knitted. "So young." He pictured little Adaline being happy and so full of life then subjected to the horrors of her world. He disliked that image, that fact.

She shrugged. "What would you do to help those who risked their lives to keep you safe?"

He understood her actions, but he believed she should not

have made that choice at such a young age. *So why didn't her father protect her better?*

"Don't judge my father," she said to him. Aureon's gaze narrowed on her.

"I can tell by your feelings," she said. "My father originally planned to retire from the military, but then our mother got pregnant with Asher and me. He knew that we would be important for the world, so he changed course and fast-tracked his military career. He figured that if the time ever came, he would have developed the contacts to protect us. He was right, for a time."

"And what are you, Dr. Adaline?" he asked as his gaze danced over her. The little human never ceased to amaze him.

Adaline's gaze locked onto Aureon's as she sat silently for a moment. "I am a diviner," Adaline said before switching subjects. "Also, there was a silver lining to saving my father's best friend." Aureon sat quietly. "When Jim found out what Asher and I were, he promised my father that he would teach us both to fight so we could defend ourselves." Adaline smiled to herself. "He and Tony started training the both of us as soon as I recovered."

Aureon's eyebrows lifted. "You were excited to learn to fight?"

She nodded and smiled. "It was a defining time. It marked the beginning of learning to defend myself, my brother, and the practice of my abilities to strengthen them and learn new ones."

"How would you classify your fighting skills?"

Hmm, she thought for a moment. "I think the phrase "deadly thorough" pretty much encompasses it." She winked at him and smiled.

Aureon's regard for her lingered because he knew that if he took his eyes off her, he would miss something important, something revealing. He wanted to ask more about being a diviner, but he tucked the idea away for later.

Adaline sighed before she shook out her hands before her left hand brightened once more. "My point is that I am much stronger now," she said to him. Then, although his thoughts were still unsettled in his mind, she pressed on. "Are you ready?"

"Are you sure you want to do this?"

She nodded. "Absolutely. Are *you* sure?" He locked eyes with her for a moment before nodding. "I'll work on your eyes, first," she said before instructing him to close them.

The moment his lids sealed, her glowing hand reached into his skull, snatching up the mist that settled in the back of his eyes. Giving it a steady pull, she threw the mist onto the floor. Placing her hand over his eyes, she flooded his sight with white light before withdrawing.

"Slowly open your eyes," she instructed.

Aureon remained still, reveling in the difference of how he felt compared to a moment ago. Then, unhurried, he opened his eyes. After blinking a few times, his eyes widened in awe at the level of sharpness in his vision. Yet, it was the realization of his previous limits that shook him. Then his eyes landed on her.

Adaline smiled back at him. "I didn't think that green could get any brighter," she commented on the bold emerald hue of his irises that now possessed a slight iridescence. "Are you ready for the hard part?"

"Yes," he said assuredly, excited for what else could come from the process.

Her hands hovered over his chest, taking form like one would grasp a hammer and chisel. She glanced at him before she raised the hand that was the hammer and let it fall hard on the chisel that was her fist over his heart.

Crack!

Aureon's chest bowed, and his head flew back against the chaise as he gasped for air.

"Breathe," she said, "Focus on it. Count a five-second inhale, and a five-second exhale if you need to." Another crack happened as she chiseled the icy energy away.

Aureon's breathing normalized; however, his struggle did not, but that wasn't her most significant concern. Instead, it was getting past the ice to the mist, whirling like a cyclone in his chest.

It was dense, making it easy to latch onto but fast-moving.

"Almost there," she told him, before another swing of the hammer, then another. More of the ice began to fall away until she could see inside. Her hands glowed brighter as she reached inside his ribcage and nabbed the mist. Her chin lifted. "Hold onto the furniture." Aureon complied before she pulled the black mist free. His teeth gritted as she tugged, feeling the mist that was stubbornly embedded within him. Adaline managed to back away from the chaise and pull the mist to wrap around one shoulder, like a cowboy retracting a lasso. She braced one foot against the edge of the chaise; its resistance was enough to keep her from falling backward as she continued to pull and wrap. After a couple of minutes, she flung what she collected behind her. It uncoiled across the floor. As alarming as it was to notice the mist was so dense that it wasn't dissolving, she focused on what was left to remove.

Aureon noticed her eyes were bloodshot and her breathing shallow, but her determination was unwavering. Fear flooded him when he saw blood trickle from her nostril.

"Stop!" he choked out. Adaline's gaze shot to his as she attempted to remove the rest of the mist. She shook her head. It took all the strength he had to reach his hand around her wrist, his grip tightening. "S-stop."

Her eyes pooled with tears, knowing what was in store for him. "Stopping will cost you. For how long, I cannot say."

He tore her hand away with a painful roar, which sent her flying backward until she hit the floor with a loud thud. She looked up at the chaise, but he was gone. The door to the study slammed, sending the loud sound echoing down the long hallway of the palace.

Adaline rested her head against the floor, hoping help was nearby. She struggled to speak as loudly as she could. "Theo." Her eyes fluttered closed as her vision blurred. Before they shut, she saw a fuzzy outline of the prince standing over her. He was speaking to her, but his voice was a muffled sound in her ears.

All she could do was reach for him.

Theodon gently picked up Adaline and laid her down on the chaise. A few minutes passed as he watched over her, monitoring signs of her recovery. Finally, she let out a loud exhale before sitting upright. "Easy," he said. Her blinking slowed once her vision cleared. "Are you all right?" She rested her head against the back of the furniture and slowly nodded. He lifted his chin at the mist still resting on the floor. "Isn't it supposed to be gone by now?"

"When it's old pain, it takes more time to dissolve," she explained.

Theodon's brow knitted. "That's a lot of pain."

"And that wasn't all of it."

Theodon's concerned expression deepened. "What happened to the rest of it?"

Adaline and Theodon's attention shot in the direction of Aureon's painful cry at the far end of the palace. He fled to his suite while the icy damn of all the black mist that had gathered in his chest broke free. His body flooded with all the raw emotions that were harbored within him for so long.

A tear slid down Adaine's cheek. "He's still carrying it."

Theodon took a seat next to Adaline. "What will happen to him?"

She sighed. "He will have to deal with the fallout himself unless he lets me help him with the rest. But I don't think he will."

"Why not?"

"Because he stopped the process to protect me," she said as she wiped the blood from her nose. A moment passed before she admitted, "Which is actually a good sign." Theodon's focus shifted to the blood on her sleeve. "It may indicate he's finally ready to move on." Adaline noticed Theodon's brow furrowed with concern, the same expression his father wore before entering the study earlier that night. She shrugged. "Or he's just protective of females." Theodon knew her latter statement was-n't true.

Adaline covered Theodn's clasped hands with hers to get his attention. When his gaze lifted, she said, "If anyone can get through this, it's your father." Based on the extensive evolution of Aureon's soul, Adaline knew that the king could navigate the process and finish it sooner than a less evolved elf.

"How long?"

"That depends on him," she confessed. "I've seen people process it in a few days. Some take a week, while others need longer." Theodon nodded in understanding. She joked to Theodon that Aureon's mood swings might cause him to burn down the palace, but she knew Theodon could handle the damage control.

Theodon's eyes widened. "Are you serious?"

Adaline chuckled. "It's possible. Whatever emotions and actions he had when the grief first began will be amplified until he releases it all."

"Grief?" he asked and pondered the emotion for a moment. "Do you mean that he still carries grief for my mother?"

Adaline nodded slowly. "He's carried every ounce of it until tonight."

Theodon reflected on earlier memories. "I've never known my father to be any different than his present behavior. He's always been cold, calculating, intelligent, and isolated. And he always put being a good king first." The subtext, "instead of me," rang in Adaline's mind as she saw Theodon's eyes carry the emotion regarding what he was about to say. She grasped his hands again and waited.

"I always understood that my father was in pain. My grandfather was around when I was a youngling and kept watch over me. Time would pass, and I would always ask him if my father was still in pain. The answer was always yes. I always thought the day would come where he would no longer be in pain, and then he would come to play with me… but he never did."

Adaline attempted to steer the conversation to a happier notion. "Did you get to spend a lot of time with your grandfather?" Theodon nodded. Adaline squeezed his hands under hers. "I'm so glad that you had him for your earlier years. And I think it's wonderful he got to see you grow into an adult."

A tear fell from the corner of Theodon's eye as he gave a slight nod. "I miss him."

"I know," Adaline said as she felt his emotions. "You have a chance here with your father like you've never had before, Theo. He needs to get through this, and when he does, you will have the opportunity to learn the person he will choose to become. That can open avenues for healing the connection between you. As short as my life span is in comparison to yours, there's one something that I've seen repeat so many times that I now consider it a fact. It's that love can return to where it's been before. Your father has always carried an unconditional love for you, even if it's been buried, or you can't see it. A lot of grief came out of him today, so he will have the opportunity to reset to the point where I assume he will have trouble finding his new comfort zones for a while."

Theodon's head tilted. "How do you mean?"

"Well," Adaline said, "if he's used to being cold and isolated but no longer has reason to be, then what will he choose to be?" Theodon understood her point. "Because he will surely stumble throughout this process," she explained, "he will need you now more than ever. You will have to be the support system for him as he finds his way."

"And you will be a part of this support system, too."

"I will, Theo," Adaline whispered.

Theodon and Adaline heard the glass crashing and throwing objects against walls echoing from down the long hallway.

"You might want to check on him," Adaline advised. Theodon nodded and stood. "Theo, try not to interfere with his actions unless, of course, he could potentially hurt someone or himself. He needs to process the grief like he did before, and it seems like he was literal in his process."

Theodon nodded. "So, whatever he breaks, I shouldn't have it replaced until he's done?"

Adaline gave a small smile. "That's probably a good idea."

"What do you need in the meantime?"

She exhaled wearily. "Food, water, and sleep. I'll stay here to rest for a bit longer."

He nodded before carefully stepping over the mist. He hastened out the study door then broke into a run, heading in his father's direction. Adaline sank back into the chaise and closed her eyes until the food arrived.

CHAPTER 23

C ommander Nash tore his office apart in a rage when he saw the video footage of Asher Everly bringing down one of his stealth helicopters and laying waste to his agents. Agent Bale rushed into Commander Nash's office full of excuses and half-assed apologies. Commander Nash shot Bale in the head then call on another agent to dispose of the body.

"And after you are done with that, return for further orders, the commander instructed.

"Yes, Commander." The agent rushed his words to avoid any potential conflict with his superior officer. The agent hooked Bale's lifeless body under the shoulders and dragged it from the room. A moment later, a large screen appeared on the far end of Commander Nash's office with a young woman in a lab coat.

"Commander Nash, Dr. Clay would like to speak with you about the Max-Project progress immediately," she stated.

"Inform Dr. Clay I am heading to his lab now."

"Yes, sir," she said, and then the screen disappeared.

Livid that the first Max-Project monster of his rebooted program was so easily defeated by the Everlys, Nash's rage at the failure prompted him to give the order to attack a loved one of the Everlys, Captain Anthony Harper. To add insult to injury, Commander Nash discovered that Tessa Hill had fled her apartment to live with Captain Harper for protection, and the woman could not be found. After wondering why Miss Hill would escape to Captain Harper's residence versus the Everlys, Nash found that the Everlys, specifically Adaline, had gone missing recently.

They are preparing for something, Nash thought as he headed to Dr. Clay's laboratory. *We must be ready for all they will unleash.*

*****

Meanwhile, Theodon found himself wandering the streets of Theris that night after convincing his father to stay in his suite. Containing the king was like wrestling a wild animal, but then the king had a moment of lucidity and agreed to stay inside for the night. Subsequently, Theodon found himself needing someone to vent to, to seek comfort, but Dr. Adaline was sleeping for her own recovery. He enjoyed speaking with her but had no romantic feelings for her, and he needed the one person who knew how to draw his focus.

Roserie.

Little time passed before he found himself standing on the doorstep of her family's home. Instead of knocking, Theodon extended his awareness through the house until he found her consciousness and bid her come to the door. A moment later, Roserie's pixie features poked out beyond the gap in the front door. Theodon smiled in relief at the sight of her face.

"My Prince," she whispered as she bowed. "What brings you by so late?"

"I am sorry to disturb you at this hour, Roserie, but it's been a long day."

Roserie opened the door wider and stepped out, pasting on her best concerned countenance. "What happened?"

Theodon opened his arms and motioned for her to step within, having no desire to speak about the details of the day, nor would he, even if he could. Instead, she stepped into his embrace that enveloped her tightly as he tucked his nose next to her ear. He inhaled her scent. Immediately, Theodon's blood froze as the scent of another male hit his nostrils. It wasn't a scent from a hug or a kiss on the cheek. It was a scent that was intimate in nature and unmistakable.

"What's wrong?" she asked, noticing him recoil.

A sound of glass shattering hit Theodon's ears. One of his ears twitched, and he turned toward the palace.

Father, Theodon thought before facing Roserie. "I must go," he said to her before he broke into a sprint, causing the outline of his form a blur into the night.

CHAPTER 24

A daline awakened in bed in the middle of the night and peered over the side of the bed. There, her shoes were neatly arranged on the floor. *Theodon.* As her mind settled, knowing he'd watched over her, she relaxed against the pillows. She stared at the ceiling as the events of the day ran through her mind. It started well, even adventurous, yet it ended in tragedy.

Adaline cleared her throat and stretched before throwing her legs over the side of the bed. As she pushed herself up to sit, her shoulders remained stooped as she replayed Aureon's healing session in her mind.

Rubbing her eyes, she shuffled into the bathroom to stare at her tired reflection in the mirror as she brushed her hair back into a ponytail.

Adaline stilled as something amiss caught her eye. She leaned closer to her reflection and tilted her head back to see the dried blood left on her nostril. Sighing while reading for a towel to wipe it away, she shook her head. "Well, now you know what happens when you try to heal deep-rooted grief in a being that's far older than you will ever be," she said to her reflection. The life span of humans in her world averaged two hundred and thirty years, and Adaline knew the king was at least a few thousand years old.

What was she thinking trying to help someone so much older than herself?

Adaline released her self-berating thoughts. *Even if I knew the consequences for myself, I would have helped him anyway.* Now that she knew the ramifications of removing old pain from an ancient being, she'd have to find a way to build up her ability or find a way to treat them in stages. Maybe she could ask for an expansion of her healing ability during her next upgrade meditation?

Adaline nodded to herself as she finished cleaning her nose. The injury to her nose had regenerated immediately, but the reminder of what happened proved bothersome. Adaline shuffled back to bed, forgoing stripping off her clothes before slipping under the covers. Resuming her ceiling stare, she got lost in the details of how to best help older elves in the future. Finally, she closed her eyes and focused on the king. Her force field activated, covering her body as she sensed Aureon's all-encompassing energy nearby. But she failed to project into his dreams to check on his progress.

He must be awake. Why could Adaline feel his energy as if he were in the room?

Shocked, her eyes flew open to see Aureon standing over her with a feral gaze. He radiated rage, destruction, and madness.

Shit, Adaline thought before noticing someone else in the room.

Theodon was soundlessly perched in the doorway of her bedroom, his predatory focus narrowed on his father, ready to take him down if the king tried to move on Adaline.

The king chuckled, his madness swirling in his eyes. "Scared of me, little human?" Adaline and Theodon remained silent. "What?" The king gestured. "You do not like the results of your work?"

This wasn't her work – this was the extreme of all he carried that was being purged from his body, and it was terrifying.

As Aureon's fingers curled like claws, readying to strike, Theodon's feet left the ground. The prince's dive connected with the king's back, throwing them both into the wall next to the bed. Adaline jumped up from bed and scrambled out of the way.

Theodon gritted his teeth as he tried to restrain his father. "Get out of here! Now!"

"I can help," she said.

"Now!"

All right, she thought, as she bolted from the room.

"No!" the king bellowed and threw Theodon off him. "She's *mine!*"

Well, it's good to know his strength has returned, Adaline thought sarcastically as she darted for the palace entrance.

The king stormed after Adaline, who got halfway down the hallway before he was upon her. He reached for her shoulder the exact moment Adaline decided she would use her abilities to wrangle and rehabilitate him. For him, she would do this. The king's momentum froze in the air. Adaline faced him. She felt his shock as he remained fixed by her telekinesis.

"I was hoping I wouldn't have to use my abilities against you, again, Your Majesty," she said to him. "But you made me choose."

Theodon dashed out of Adaline's room and peered down the hallway. His eyebrows lifted at the sight of Adaline holding his father in suspension.

She peeked around the king to Theodon. "Are you all right?" He nodded as he jogged over to her side to examine his father, whose expression was livid for being restricted.

"Effective. Well done," Theodon said to her.

"Thanks," she said as her countenance remained neutral. "Is there anything that can contain him, long-term?"

Theodon thought for a moment before nodding. "There is… but you won't like it." He shot Adaline a knowing look.

Adaline sighed. "We need to do what's best for him."

"Can you move him, too?"

"Easily."

"Then follow me," he said before leading them out of the palace to one of the darkest places in the kingdom.

Adaline's sustained use of her ability to move the king took no concentration from her because telekinesis was a born gift for her. Born gifts never required practice to build the ability, as they already functioned at full power since birth. She followed Theodon closely as their surroundings grew more alarming as they trekked through the dark, narrow hallways of the dungeon. The guards were alarmed to see the prince, followed by a human female, with their immobilized king in tow. Theodon addressed a much older elf who wore a plain uniform adorned with medals different than others. Adaline guessed him to be the warden.

Theodon explained in Tear to the warden that he would need the proper facility to contain the king until his rage subsided. The warden fought with the urge to question the prince, thinking he may be attempting to overthrow the king. Adaline reviewed the warden's feelings and told Theodon, "He thinks you are plotting against your father." The warden stared at her in horror as his truth was revealed. His cheeks highlighted his shame as he faced the prince, awaiting punishment.

"The king went through a healing process to help get rid of old grief," Theodon explained to the warden. "He interrupted the process, which is causing negative side effects of madness that will last for a few days. He needs to be contained where he won't hurt anyone." The warden peered over Adaline's shoulder to see the king suspended in the air, the rage in his eyes unyielding. When no one burst into action, Theodon gave an annoyed sigh. "I can set him loose, and you can see for yourself when he tears all of you apart." The warden was shocked into further silence, so Theodon concluded it was time to pull rank. A snarl grew in his chest before he let it rip from his lips. "I am your prince! And I am ordering you to open the root box, now!"

Adaline's eyes shot wide at Theodon's demand.

The warden scrambled for his keys and hurried down a dark hallway. "R-right this way, Your Grace."

Theodon gestured to Adaline to go first, so he could bring up the rear. They descended further into the dungeon where the air deadened, the temperature rose, and sound was barely detectable. Adaline glanced over her shoulder to see the king still behind her with Theodon trailing them. They finally reached a room that had been expertly dugout for the containment system built into the space. It was a twenty-foot cube with thick metal slats built into the wall. Roots grew around each one. Adaline didn't think much of it until she set the king inside, and the warden locked the door.

"Don't let go of him yet," Theodon warned Adaline.

After the door was locked, a blue current rippled over the metal slats coming from the vines, adding further security to the cell. Adaline's eyes fell at the thought of the extra security needed to contain Aureon.

"Release him," Theodon said to her. Adaline sighed before setting the king on his feet and letting go of her hold on him.

Overtaken by rage, Aureon tried to inflict damage on his surroundings but gained no headway. He stopped for a moment, his chest heaving, glancing over his shoulder at his captors, who stared at him wide-eyed in surprise. A sinister laugh left the back of his throat. "Is this not what you wanted?"

The question was directed at Adaline.

The king stalked toward her, but she didn't retreat. It hurt to see him like this, but he made the decision to protect her. Now, he had to deal with the consequences unless he asked her to help him with the rest, which she knew he wouldn't do. Aureon grabbed the metal bars and howled at the electric shock. He jumped back, examined his healing hands, grinned, and charged the bars again. The shock rippled over his body, but this time he reveled in it, laughing the entire time before his gaze leveled on Adaline.

"Look at me now, little human," he snarled at her. "Your work at its finest!" Aureon tried to reach through the gap between the bars, but the current in those open spaces was more potent than the rest. He snapped his hand back with a howl again. His countenance furious, he approached the bars once more but with measured steps. The menace in his stare caused Theodon to sidestep, but Adaline remained planted as Aureon peered at her.

Adaline blew a small ball of light into the palm of her hand. Aureon, although mad, was mesmerized by the light, and she took advantage of the distraction. She whispered his name into the ball before blowing on it like a kiss. Floating gently through the bars, the ball collided with his face.

"Ahhh!" he shouted while trying to wipe away the light that sank into his eyes and inhaled through his nose, just as it happened to Cailu.

Theodon approached the bars. Adaline's arm shot out in front of him. A beat passed.

Aureon shook his head as his gaze cleared. The madness faded, and he rushed to the bars. "What is happening?" Adaline and Theodon both wanted to reach for him but held themselves back.

"What do you remember?" Adaline asked.

Aureon's gaze shot around until his thoughts focused. "We were in my study." Adaline nodded. "You healed my eyes then..." his voice trailed off as realization surfaced.

"It's okay," she said to him gently. "Because you stopped the process, you are going to feel like you are losing your mind for a little while."

"Why am I here?" Aureon asked.

"You started tearing the palace apart," Theodon confirmed before glancing at Adaline. "And you almost hurt people."

Aureon's eyes shot to Adaline. His alert stare turned glassy, and Adaline mirrored him as she felt how sorry he was. "I know," she whispered. "It's okay."

"What happens now?" Aureon asked Adaline.

"You can either have me help you with the rest, which I recommend," she said, "or you have to process these feelings and let them consume you until your body releases them. Feel every single one until you achieve equilibrium."

"Let her help you," Theodon urged.

The king's expression sobered as he recalled the blood that trickling from Adaline's nose. He shook his head. "I will do this alone." Adaline sighed. Theodon's shoulders slumped. The warden was still frozen in shock at everything he was witnessing. The king addressed the warden, "You will not release me from this cell until my son has deemed it time to do so."

The warden nodded quickly. "Yes, My Lord."

The king let out a long sigh before turning back to Theodon and Adaline. "Go."

They could see the madness returning, swirling over the color of his eyes. Adaline could feel Theodon's sadness and rejection, but she redirected his focus. "C'mon. You can check on him tomorrow." Theodon nodded and turned to lead the way out of the dungeon. Before Adaline followed him, she looked at the king as the pools of tears in her eyes spilled down her cheeks. "I'm going to stay and watch over you and Theo."

The king shook his head in protest. "No. You need to go where it's safe."

"Trying to tell me what to do has yet to work for anyone, Your Majesty," she said as she stepped closer to the bars.

"Get away from me," he said, his voice beginning to crack.

"I'm going to make sure Theo is all right while I help you recover," she told him. "To do that effectively, I need to share something of yours with him." A beat passed. "Do I have your permission to do that?" She activated her force field to cover from her fingertips to her elbow. He stared at her palm, then at her before he nodded. "Thank you," she said before she reached her hand through the slats. Placing her palm on his temple, his eyes snapped shut, and she quickly sorted through his memories of Theodon as a youngling. After a minute, she removed her hand and jerked away from the bars once she noticed the madness took over.

"Get out," Aureon hissed at her. Thunder rolled outside, bringing to Theris one of the most violent storms since the death of his queen.

Tears continued to fall as Adaline hurried to catch up with Theodon. Once she did, rain poured as Theodon's emotions burst from his chest. Yelling and arguing in the darkness with no one in particular as tears ran down his face. He tried wiping them away as quickly as they formed. Adaline's tears continued their free-fall as she listened to him while their clothes soaked through. As his anger grew, Theodon's intention to say horrible things about his father was stopped by Adaline shushing him.

"Listen to me," she said as she firmly held his hands. "You cannot hold this against him." Theodon's astonishment signaled to her that she must be joking. "He chose to heal," she said. "He gets credit for that. You need to understand everything you see him experiencing is an amplified version of the grief that struck him when your mother died."

Theodon froze at her words. *When your mother died.*

"He's carried it this whole time, Theo," she said with a sob as the rain washed her tears away. "He loved her so passionately that he carried the loss with him every day of his life since she died. To add to the emotional injury, one hundred years after the fact, which I understand isn't long for elves, he lost his own father who helped raise you while he was still trying to get his life together."

Aureon rooted himself into a new, cold way of being to cope with the loss. So, she understood how Theodon concluded his father never participated in his life, even though Aureon was more involved than the prince realized. Theodon's whole body shook as he wept. Adaline wrapped her arms around him as he sobbed.

"Shh," she attempted to console him. "He's going to be fine."

Anger burst from him. "How do *you* know? And why are you so forgiving of him?"

"Because he was there, Theo," Adaline said. "I promise you he was there."

"How could you possibly know that?"

Adaline stilled. "I can show you." Theodon's chest heaved for breath. "I can show you everything." She reached for Theodon's face and rested her palms over his temples.

Theodon's eyes snapped shut, and his father's memories flooded his mind. He saw himself as a youngling through his father's eyes. Theodon witnessed the times his father checked on Theodon after the prince had fallen asleep. His father always swiped whatever strand of hair was in Theodon's face and whispered, "I love you." The words struck Theodon deeply, as he could feel his father's love for him. Theodon saw his father showing his younger self how to use his bow and sword at a very young age because Aureon knew he could not be present for most of his son's training. He wanted Theodon to have proper form, even though the king knew he must delegate Theodon's training to his officers, who consulted with the king on the prince's training at every stage.

Theodon saw his father curl his body around his sleeping son at a time when Theodon was too little to be so sick. Aureon hadn't slept in weeks while doing everything possible to help Theodon, all the while hoping his son wouldn't die. Theodon felt his father's fear when he was in the middle of an elder's meeting and knew something was wrong with young Theodon. Moments later, Aureon crashed through the roof that sheltered the eternity ponds. The horror Aureon experienced filled Theodon's heart as he saw his younger self drowning in a cyclone of water. Aureon didn't hesitate to reach in and pull his son to safety. Theodon saw his father in a heated argument with his grandfather, who had taken his eyes off his grandson for just a moment, which allowed little Theodon enough time to scurry away to the eternity ponds in the first place. Cerus took the verbal beating, under-standing his son's fear due to his error, and did his best to apologize.

Theodon's resolve cracked in Adaline's arms as the scenes he watched overwhelmed him. Once she felt he couldn't take it anymore, she removed her hands and held Theodon. Crying hard as his knees gave way, she followed him to the ground, still hold-ing him. He threw his arms around her, clutching her tight as he buried his face against her shoulder and sobbed. She silently wept as she felt Theodon's surge of emotions as his body purged old pain, holding him until he finished. A long time passed before his sobs turned into labored breaths, his chest heaving until he breathed normally. Finally, his grip on Adaline loosened.

Adaline cupped his face and held his gaze as the storm rained down on them. "Now you see, Theo." Theodon nodded without a word. "Do you understand all you need to be for him, now?"

Theodon sniffed. "Yes."

"Remember, when you two get through his recovery, there is a chance for you both, unlike before. It's the chance for un-derstanding and repair," she said to him. "Not all fathers and sons that have that chance take it." He nodded, and her heart sank as she noticed he looked like a vulnerable little boy for a moment.

"How am I going to do this?" Theodon asked. "How do I enter into a rivalry that is older than I am and expect to win?"

Adaline clasped his shoulder. "Remember Jim?" Theodon sniffed, straightened, then nodded. "When Asher and I had sim-ilar obstacles, and the world was trying to come down on us, as this old rivalry is on you, Jim took us aside and told us, 'When you take claim over your life, people will fight you for it every day. If you build the habit to fight for it and keep it, you will become the person you need to be to handle the next stage of your life because it requires a stronger you.'" Theodon let out a loud sigh, accepting his new truth. Strength would be necessary to move forward. "*Fight*, my friend," Adaline encouraged him as she squeezed his shoulder. "Fight those evil bastards for trying to take what belongs to your family." He gave a firm nod before they finally walked back to the palace. They proceeded in silence for a while before Adaline reassured him. "I will not allow harm to come to either of you. So, if you need anything, call on me."

The corner of Theodon's mouth threatened to lift. "I will."

Adaline made a commitment to the Sleone's that she wouldn't leave Theris until both father and son got through the king's recovery. A weary sigh escaped her as she accepted that she would be an anchor for them both. After she returned to her suite, she took the rest of her waking moments to mentally prepare herself for what lay ahead for all of them.

CHAPTER 25

T he following day, Adaline stepped through the portal to Earth for supplies. She rushed through her house, grabbed her sweeper gear, and opened a second bag to pack a few things to hold her over while she helped the Sleones.

"Asher," she spoke into her twin's mind.

"Yeah, sis?" Asher responded immediately.

"Shit has hit the fan in Theris," she told him. "I'm returning immediately. Would you please tell my assistant to push all of my appointments to next week?"

"I'm listening."

There was a pause before her reply. "I found out what happens when I remove one thousand plus years of old grief from a far older elf king."

Asher thought to himself for a moment before finding the words his twin needed. "Was he terminal?"

"Yes."

"How much time did he have left?"

"Calculating for an elf's lifespan, I'd say about a decade," Adaline answered honestly.

"Given his grief was that old, and you say he is much older, ten years isn't much time."

Adaline sighed, but Asher only heard a pause on his end.

"Do you need me to go back with you?" Asher asked.

Adaline stopped from packing her sweeper gear into a duffle bag to consider his offer.

"No," she said. "I'm just feeling a little guilty."

The thought was absurd to Asher. "Why?"

"I meet this family for two seconds, and I find terminal health problems, as well as obvious indications of deception that's been pitted against them, so I've turned their lives upside down-" Adaline said before she was cut off.

"–Do you have enough evidence regarding the deception?" Asher asked.

"Not yet," she said. "I have significant pieces, but I need more information. It runs deep, Ash."

"How do you know?"

"It feels... ancient."

"Ah," Asher replied. The reading of soul records was not a gift he shared with his twin but sensing other people's feelings was one they shared. He was a little envious of the former ability. "Don't feel guilty, Addy," Asher said. "It sounds like your purpose with them is to clear away more than their inner chaos. Clear it all away and give them a full chance at happy lives."

"Okay," Adaline said after a moment of silence.

"When should I check in with you to make sure you haven't burned down the kingdom?"

Adaline chuckled. "Check on me around day four if you don't hear from me."

Asher nodded to himself. "If you need me sooner, say the word."

"You know I will," Adaline replied. "How's everything

here?"

"Did a sweep last night," Asher reported. "The QC keeps trying to beef up their weaponry, but it doesn't make a dent. They also sent a helicopter this time."

Adaline's eyebrows lifted. "What was the damage?"

"Tony got clipped in the shoulder." Asher sighed at that fact. "Jim provided cover fire until I got there. Now the QC is less a helicopter and a dozen or so agents."

"Wow," Adaline said at those sobering facts. "Do you need me to stay here for a day?"

"No, but if you could send a light ball to Tony before you go back, that would be great. He's just about healed up, but it would help. I'm keeping him at my place for a few days," he said to her.

"Light ball on its way," she said as she blew a ball of light into her palm. She whispered Tony's name in it and threw it in the direction of Asher's house. "We have less than thirty-seven years on this train wreck planet to go."

"Then what?"

She stopped packing. "Before we switch worlds?"

Asher had been giving her idea some thought since she first revealed the possibility. "Theris sounds like the one place we can truly be free…"

"To be ourselves," Adaline finished.

"I can't fathom what it would be like to wake up to that every day," Asher admitted reverently.

Neither could Adaline. To be free for the rest of her life? To not be limited to using the extent of her abilities to trigger the end of the world? To not go up in smoke with said world?

A dream!

A new endgame, if we live through carrying out our purpose, she thought.

"I'll check in with you in four days, big brother," she said to Asher as she threw the strap of her duffle bag over her shoulder and headed back to the portal. "Whether in this world or the next."

"Love you," Asher said.

"Love you, too," Adaline echoed.

The talk about switching worlds filled Asher with excitement and anxiety. He hurried to his garage and walked past his impressive car collection to access his storage vault on the other side. He unlocked the doors and pushed them open, finally ready to do something he told his sister he'd already done: pack for the end of the world. Adaline already had her "exit bags" packed, as the twins called them. Asher always figured he'd have enough time to handle this task, but now he pulled out four large duffle bags. He determined his packing ratio: two bags for medical/lab stuff, one for memories, and one for whatever he needed for his physical person. He figured that only extreme weather clothes should be packed in the latter bag, with a few other changes, and that's all since he would be making a lifestyle change upon leaving Earth behind.

Leaving Earth behind. That thought stilled his over-active mind.

Will we survive the apocalypse? He wondered. After a moment, Asher shook away the thought and elected for optimism before beginning to pack.

CHAPTER 26

T he next day, Asher headed into Everly Surgical Institute without his twin in tow. After dropping off his bag at his locker, he rounded the hallway to the small office next to his sister's. It was always an odd feeling when Adaline wasn't around. They made a solid team in everything they did together, making her absence palpable.

"Good morning, Nat," Asher addressed Adaline's assistant.

"Good morning, Dr. Everly," the petite blonde replied.

"You have damage control today."

"Oh?"

"Adaline will be out of the office all week," Asher explained. "Move her consults and surgeries to next week."

"What would you like me to do for those who traveled far to see her?"

"Give them the option of seeing me instead or allow them to stay in the recovery suites until their new appointment, so they don't have to leave and come back," Asher said.

"Okay. I'll start on it, now."

"And put Maddy back on my schedule for this week while Adaline is out. She needs to train up fast."

"I'll call her and ask her to hustle in early."

"Thank you, Nat," he said before rushing down the hall to scrub in for his first of twenty surgeries scheduled for the day.

"Dr. Everly?" his receptionist caught his attention as he was headed into surgery.

"Yes, Matt?" Asher said through his surgical mask, his hands in the air and his elbows tucked against his sides. The receptionist hesitated, looked back toward the waiting room, then back at Asher. "Out with it," Asher pushed.

"There's a Tessa here for your sister," Matt said. "She said it's urgent."

Asher rolled his eyes. *With Tessa, it's always urgent.* "Is she dying?"

Matt's eyes went wide. "No, Dr. Everly, but she does seem shaken."

That statement stopped Asher from further belittling as his brow furrowed. "Have her wait in my office until I finish with this surgery."

"Yes, Dr. Everly," Matt said, then returned to his desk in the waiting room.

Half an hour later, Asher pulled off his surgical mask and tossed his gloves as he headed to the locker room. He couldn't entirely change clothes because he had another surgery that began in twenty minutes. A moment later, he pushed open the door to his office to find Tessa sitting on his couch, sniffing back tears, as she blotted the corners of her reddened eyes with a tissue.

Not this shit again, Asher sighed at the thought. The only time he'd seen Tessa crying in the past was because some douchebag broke her heart after he had given her clear red flags from day one. Asher had no tolerance for stupidity. This was clearly a job for Adaline's capacity for compassion.

"What's going on, Tessa?" he asked as gently as he could

manage before he took a seat on the opposite end of the couch.

"You both are going to hate me," she started off, "but I had no other choice left." She wiped a tear from the corner of her eye with a tissue as she sniffed.

"Unlikely," Asher said. "But go on."

She sniffed again before handing him the piece of stationery she received from the QC at the police station. "I was given this." Asher took it, and his gaze froze on the silver letters at the top of the stationary. "They showed me footage of you breaking Adaline out of a similar situation they lured me into and said you must be captured. And if I didn't help them, they'd kill me!" Tessa burst into tears.

Asher looked over the note, front and back. "What did you tell them, Tessa?"

"I had nothing to tell them," Tessa said. "You guys only do normal things in front of me. I didn't know you could do more until they showed me the footage. They wanted me to report back to them every week, but I don't have any information to give them, so they are threatening to kill me if I don't bring them something."

Asher's anger stirred as he looked over the note. *Oh, I'll bring them something.*

"You never saw anyone's face when you would go?" he asked.

She shook her head. "No."

"And how many times have you gone to report?" he asked.

"I went the first time when I received the note, and one more time a week later," she said. "And then I planned to run from them when I came to see Adaline at her house, but neither of you was home. Your neighbor, Tony, startled me and invited me in for pancakes. I think they found me because the roof of his house was blasted through, and there were people dressed in black everywhere, so I ran."

Asher stilled to realize that she was at Tony's house when

he took down the QC helicopter. At first, it didn't make sense why the QC would target a retired Marine, but now that he knew Tessa was there...

"Thank you for telling me this, Tessa," Asher said. He began building a strategy on what to do next. "You can't leave this building. If you do, they will see you."

"What do I do?"

"You will move into my house, and Adaline and I will split watch over you," Asher said. "You cannot return home or to your job, or they will kill you." Tessa sniffed again as Asher's words sank in. "Do you understand?" Asher asked. She nodded. "Down the hall is Nat, Adaline's assistant," he told her. "If you need food or anything, just ask her, and she will make arrangements to get you what you need." New tears ran down Tessa's face. "Why are you still crying?"

"I'm thankful, Asher," Tessa said. Her eyes dropped to her lap as more tears fell. "Just thankful."

CHAPTER 27

A daline unpacked her duffle bag in her suite while Theodon slept through the morning. *Long night*, she thought. It was easy to convince herself to take a bath as she wandered into the large bathroom. Lost in her thoughts, while she turned on the levers to the tub and peeled her clothes off, Adaline noticed she was nowhere near the state of wonder she experienced the first time she saw the cyclone tub. As she sank into the water and leaned her head back on the edge, she focused on her breathing as her hands pushed the water around.

Defaulting to her clinical logic, she brainstormed a remedy to help Theodon. She settled on what she had done for Tony before leaving Earth. Once she had formed another light ball in her hand, she stared at it. The tiny flecks of light that swirled around in the ball distracted her from her stress. Each fleck was a symbol of profound healing in the palm of her hand, reassuring her that something so small could set right a wrong. She brought it to her lips and spoke the prince's name. Then, in the direction of Theodon's room, she tossed the ball of light. It disappeared through the wall and found its intended recipient.

That'll take the edge off, she thought while sinking into the water. Her eyes closed as her face floated above water.

Adaline was a strategist. She considered everything she did before she did it to ensure the best course of action to produce the best results. Asher was the same way. They would go over the patient's files the day before surgery. They would review tactics before going out on a sweep, no matter how many times they patrolled. And now reviewed the possible dangers for Aureon and Theodon over the next few days because they were both vulnerable. Theodon had never led a kingdom, and Aureon was unfit to rule. For how long was yet to be determined until she gauged his progress upon examining him later that morning. Those who plotted against the crown could get wind that the king is away because he rarely left Ividia, except to go to war. Adaline decided she would watch over Theodon, guard him against being preyed upon, and help facilitate Aureon's recovery.

Maybe I should have asked Asher to come to Theris, she thought. He could have kept an eye on Theodon as she focused on the king. She dismissed the thought and decided that she would retrieve her twin if she couldn't help them both through one day.

Perfect, she thought, before she dunked her head in the water. She wouldn't get to be wild and free in Theris like she hoped. She'd have to make a sacrifice and be a doctor taking care of patients and a diviner sweeping the streets of evil... again.

Ugh.

CHAPTER 28

T he storm lasted through the following evening to no surprise to Theodon. He knew his father's emotional turmoil ran deep, yet that's only part of what astonished Theodon once assuming the king's role. The duties overwhelmed him, as he had no idea how much his father did daily until now. The king always appeared composed, like he had complete control over every detail.

How did he do it? To suffer in silence for over a millennium and shoulder the demands of the crown? Unthinkable! Theodon wondered.

His father may have always been cold and calculating, but the king never let on at how much responsibility his rank required of him, let alone the stress that came with it. Theodon canceled all meetings his father had scheduled with any nobility, elders, or military officers and pushed them to the following week.

He will recover by then. The prince remained optimistic. Theodon couldn't afford to entertain a negative mindset, or he would give in to the stress of the endless responsibilities that lay before him. *How am I going to manage this for the foreseeable future?* He thought as he hurried to the throne room. The prince's shoulders lifted as he recalled all he learned about his father from Adaline last night. Knowing the truth fueled his motivation to take on the king's responsibilities until he recovered. With Adaline remaining in Theris for the next few days, Theodon was confident for the best results but wasn't so naïve to assume they would come easily. He noticed subjects were beginning to line up outside of the palace for Adaline, again.

Darius caught sight of the prince and hastened to keep up with him. "My Lord, Theodon!" he called after Theodon, who immediately faced Darius upon hearing his name. "My Lord," the guard addressed him again, less winded than before. "New patients are lining up outside for Dr. Adaline. When will she return?"

Coming back? Theodon's eyebrow lifted. "She is still here, Darius."

Darius's eyes widened. "Oh! Does she intend to see new patients today?"

"Not for the next few days. Dr. Adaline should return to the palace for lunch. You can ask her the details of her schedule then."

"Yes, My Lord." Darius turned on his heel, leaving Theodon to continue in the direction of the throne room.

In the dungeon, Adaline descended the carved dirt stairs to the isolated cell that contained the king. Theodon told her that he had delivered fresh clothes and all other necessities for the king to clean up for the day during his earlier visit. Adaline knew the king probably used what was brought to him as ammunition to throw against the walls in a rage, so she decided to take another set of clothes and toiletries.

Considering she arrived at his cell to see exactly what she predicted, she anticipated an interesting exchange. The king stood with his back to the far corner of the cell facing the rest of the space. His eyes were on her the second she rounded the corner from the stairs. He snarled at her and charged at her before colliding with the roots that wrapped the slats of his cell, shocking him before he jumped back.

Well, at least he's happy to see me, she thought. "Good morning."

"Get out!" he snarled at her.

Sweet talker, she thought. "No," she said before inspecting his cell. "Did you bathe and change clothes earlier?"

Adaline noticed a basin flung against one wall, drained, and turned on its side. Aureon was in the same clothes as the previous night, with dirty feet. *That's a no,* she thought. She addressed the warden, who had trailed her to the cell. "I need time alone with him." The warden was stunned, wondering why a human could possibly want to be alone with the king while he was in such a vicious state. "I am completely safe, and you cannot be privy to his treatment. It's confidential."

The warden shifted on his feet before he shrugged and turned to leave.

After he left, she faced Aureon. A smile tugged at the corner of her lips. "You are going to hate me after I'm done with you today."

"You have no control over me," he sneered.

"Oh, but I do," she confirmed. "I promise that I will only use my abilities to help you through your recovery and defend myself, if necessary." After that, they'd renegotiate. Maybe.

Aureon reached for her and was stunned that his momentum was halted, which only made him angrier. She continued to watch him with a knowing smile as her telekinesis put his cell back in order and reassembled anything that had been broken. He curiously observed all that was happening around him. Her mind unlocked the cell door and opened it. She stepped inside. The door closed and locked behind her before she set her bag down. Adaline sifted through it as he growled at her. She shot him a scathing look with her illuminated gaze to remind him who he was aggravating. He quieted.

That's right, she thought.

Adaline knew being both doctor and nurse to her deranged patient would be more like a veterinarian tackling a wild animal. She lifted him a few inches off the ground and refilled the water basin. She poured in some of the oil Ena had given her for her own bubble bath experience from her previous visit to Theris. The king might end up smelling a little bit like a floral arrangement, but Adaline decided it was better than him smelling like his dirty feet. She blew another light ball into her hand and lifted it to his face. His inhale caught it and absorbed it, and his eyes cleared as he tried to shake the light away.

"What is happening?" the king asked, uneasy about the nature of his sobriety.

"I've got you restrained for a bit," she said. "Are you comfortable enough?" Aureon surveyed his body and noticed he wasn't standing on the ground. "Don't panic," she said. "I have never dropped anyone. I won't start today." His eyes scattered as she sensed his anxiety. "I need you to focus, Aureon."

The use of his name without his title triggered his attention, and his eyes narrowed at her. She smiled.

"Where is the warden?" he asked.

"He was asked to step away."

"Why?"

"Doctor-patient confidentiality," she explained. "Your treatment is your business and for no one else to witness unless you choose it."

Aureon thought for a moment. "Even from my son?"

"Even from Theo, if that's what you want," Adaline nodded.

A beat went by before the king nodded.

"There are a few things I get to help you with today," she said. "You are still a bit dangerous, and your sobriety will recede soon. Before it does, I need to ask your permission on a few things."

"Go on."

"You need a bath, fresh clothes, and a little extra healing work," she said. "Is it all right with you for me to handle this for you today?"

"What extra healing work?"

"I was going to extract another piece of what you are carrying," she explained. "Not a whole lot, like last time, but a piece each day, so we can expedite your recovery, as well as make this a less stressful experience for you."

His eyes shifted. "You will not be hurt?"

Her heart softened, and her eyes smiled as she attempted to remain clinically detached. "No."

He finally nodded. "There is no need for the bath and clothing," he said to limit her output in his process.

"Nice try," she said. "But your feet alone smell pretty gnarly. I won't touch you without you being clean."

Aureon stared at her for a moment as he thought about her hands on his body, slowly divesting him of his clothes. He shook the thought and conceded. "Fine."

Adaline nodded while approaching him. "Good. Beyond that, how does your body feel?" Her hand hovered inches from him, glowing as it scanned his vitals. His irises swirled, a sign of the madness returning. "Speak quickly."

"Physically weak, hollow in the chest, generally depleted," he said before his lips started to curl back over his teeth, and a growl broke free.

"Last question," she asked. "Do elves wear underwear?" She was about to strip him down, and she'd rather have a warning.

"I do not," he said before snapping his teeth at her.

"Okay," she said with a sarcastic smile. "*So* excited to get started."

CHAPTER 29

H ours later, Theodon was up to his pointed ears in requests that his father would typically handle. Elders were starting to question the king's absence, and he did his best at evading them. It wasn't easy to fool elders who were at least 7,000 years old.

Flavial detected that something was off when he interacted with Theodon, but Theodon's temperament didn't give away any indication that something was genuinely wrong. Still, Flavial offered the prince his assistance, should he need it. Theodon thanked Flavial for his offer, but he did not utilize it. As honorable as he knew Flavial to be, and even though Flavial was his father's friend, the Usleons were not family. And it wasn't yet clear to Theodon who was against him and his father, so he thought it best to curb anyone who tried to get closer to him while the king recovered. He wasn't surprised that he also ran into Talia, who also wanted to question him about the king's absence. She masked her inquiries by suggesting it an opportunity for the prince to throw a big party without consequences.

He'd still know, Talia, Theodon thought as he entertained Talia's conversation for a bit before excusing himself to attend to his excessive duties.

Talia let Theodon go, but she didn't leave the palace. Pretending to wander, she made her way down the long hallway to her destination. Once the king's suite was in her sights, she raced for it. Stopping in front of the large doorknobs long enough to marvel at the intricate carving that fed into the design on the doors, Talia seethed. This was supposed to be hers. Her knobs. Her suite. Her life. Her lips curled over one sharp canine. She grasped a knob and turned it.

"How interesting," a voice startled her from behind.

Talia gasped and spun around to find Adaline's face inches from hers, staring at her through the void of her dark eyes. Judgment filled them, and Talia could swear she saw them flicker with light. The human doctor was suspended in the air. Her toes barely touched the ground.

"Adaline!" Talia gasped. "You startled me."

Adaline's head was canted. "Did I?"

Talia's eyes shot around the hallway, searching for physical evidence of why she didn't hear the human approach her. "Where did you come from?"

"That's not what's interesting at the moment," Adaline said, her eyes never wavering from Talia's. Adaline stepped closer, and Talia scrambled back but was stopped by the large door. Stuck and rattled, the she-elf searched for an exit plan as it seemed that the doctor was peering through her as if all of Talia's secrets were laid bare. No thought was more terrifying. But the doctor cut her off.

"W-what's so interesting?" Talia finally sputtered.

"You knew exactly where the king's suite was located," Adaline said with a slight smile. "You didn't even hesitate. You went right for it. What would you have done had I not come along? Gone inside? Laid in his bed? After he rejected you because he was in love with someone else?" Talia's countenance turned cross as Adaline's words struck a chord. "Or," Adaline said as she stayed in Talia's face, "is it to set up the king to die by poison like you and your father did to the queen?"

Talia's eyes widened. She felt the vial of poison she had tucked in her pocket move until it floated in the inch of space between her and Adaline. Adaline's thumb and forefinger grasped the vial.

"Hmm," Adaline said as she surveyed the vial. "What do I have here? An old dog using an old trick." Adaline's glare turned knowing. "Don't worry... I know everything you've done."

"So do I," Theodon's voice boomed behind Adaline.

Adaline didn't flinch. She kept her face an inch away from Talia's as a victorious smile spread across her face only for the she-elf to see.

"Theodon!" Talia screeched. "She lies! I would never do any such thing!"

Seconds later, Theodon was at Adaline's side.

"Show me," he said to Adaline.

"Are you sure you want to see this?" Adaline's gazed softened. It was, after all, the memory of the death of his mother. A mother he never got the chance to know.

"Yes," he said as he glared at Talia as Adaline handed him the vial of poison. "I have the evidence needed to arrest her for attempting to murder the king. I need evidence of her carrying out poisoning my mother."

"All right." Adaline sighed before placing her hand on Talia's head, who flinched. "I won't do worse to you yet," Adaline told the she-elf.

With Adaline's free hand on Theodon's temple, the memories passed from Talia to Theodon. As both elves' eyes sealed, Talia started to tremble as Theodon's anger grew. Talia's memories showed her boiling the toxins from the faranti flower, a blossom that could only be found on the other side of the kingdom's northern border. Theodon witnessed Talia pour the toxins into a vial that she later added to a drink she took to his mother, who laid exhausted in bed after giving birth to him.

"Steady, Theo," Adaline whispered to the prince as he fumed.

Theodon refocused on breathing evenly as he saw the memories of Talia and her father plotting to kill the queen and weakening the king in their attempt to take the throne. Adaline sped forward in Talia's memories to reveal her making another batch of the poison yesterday, once she heard the king had left the palace for mysterious reasons. She was eager to move along with her father's plan, marking the downfall of the Sleones.

"Enough," Theodon said finally. Adaline removed her hands, and everyone's eyes snapped open. Theodon's angry glare bore through Talia. "Captain!"

"Yes, My Lord!" Iventuil, the captain of the guard, appeared in the hallway and hurried toward them.

"Arrest Talia Miathan," he said, without his eyes leaving his mother's killer. "She's charged with the murder of Queen Aravae and with the attempted murder of our king."

"No!" she said as Iventuil bound her wrists. "It wasn't me, Theodon! I beg you! I had nothing to do with it!"

Adaline's eyebrows lifted in surprise as a small smile spread on her face as pride for Theodon's swift leadership welled within her. Talia sobbed, knowing she would face harsh punishment that her high-society temperament couldn't bear.

"Silence!" Theodon shouted before he addressed the captain. "Her father is guilty of the same charges. Find him and arrest him as well."

"First things first, friend," Adaline said to Theodon as she looked at Talia. Adaline delivered a mean right-hook to Talia, knocking her unconscious. Adaline stepped back, tucked her hands behind her as her knuckles began to heal, and smiled at Theodon and the captain.

"Why did you do that?" Theodon asked her.

"Elves are telepathic between families, yes?" Adaline asked.

"Yes," Theodon answered.

"You don't want her father to know you are coming for him, do you?"

The human has a point, both elves thought as they glanced at each other.

Iventuil, knowing full well that Talia's father, Graydon, was an elder on the king's counsel, said, "My Lord, are you certain you wish to have him arrested?"

Theodon's lip curled in disgust at Talia as he stared at her. "I don't wish it. I want it done. *Now*."

"My Lord," Iventuil pressed, "He's a powerful elder. The guards cannot wrangle him alone."

The fury from Theodon's vision cleared. "Then Dr. Adaline and I will accompany you." Adaline smiled, impressed at Theodon's levelheaded decision-making. She knew he would be a great king one day. Theodon faced Adaline, who nodded in agreement with his instructions. Within minutes, Talia Miathan was locked away to rot in the dungeon until sentencing, and the three of them, along with a half dozen guards, made their way to the house Miathan to arrest its patriarch.

CHAPTER 30

When they arrived at the Miathan's home, Adaline learned that their homes had wings for each family member. As a result, the homes of nobility were sprawling monstrosities. As she walked up the front steps with Theodon, he signaled Adaline to be silent. His ear twitched at the sound of an old, strong, steady heartbeat inside, along with a few others.

Theodon lifted his chin at Adaline before whispering to her, "Last resort."

Adaline nodded, having no problem staying out of elfin matters unless her interference was necessary. She was trying to respect the rules of Theris and not exert her powerful will over everyone because she believed the elves must choose for themselves. However, she wouldn't hesitate to step in for Theodon's benefit. As she predicted, the moment Theodon walked through the front door, a tall elf with honey-blonde hair lunged at him with a sword.

Graydon.

Theodon ducked out of the way as the elder landed with a force that cracked the stone floor, then drew his own sword and shifted into a fighting stance. Again, the elder attacked Theodon, and Adaline stood back to watch how Graydon's many years over Theodon gave him more strength and power in every move he executed. Yet, Theodon did well at keeping up with the traitor.

"You have no power over me, youngling!" Graydon snarled at Theodon as the elder's blade clashed with the prince's.

"You are misinformed," Theodon said evenly as he pushed the elder back.

"Your *father* didn't even know," Graydon hissed.

"He knew," Adaline chimed in. The elder's focus swung to her when she did, giving Theodon a chance to gain the upper hand with a hard kick to the chest that sent Graydon flying into a wall. "He just didn't have all necessary evidence until today," Adaline muttered to no one in particular.

The elder sprang to his feet. "Lies!"

Adaline cocked her head at the elder. "Try me."

Graydon charged for Adaline, but Theodon crashed into him before the elder could reach her. Their hand-to-hand combat lasted for a while, destroying the house in their wake. Adaline found herself leaning against a wall in the foyer, checking her manicure as the guards remained outside.

Adaline sighed with boredom.

Then Graydon body slammed Theodon, and a second later, held a blade against Adaline's throat. She let him grab her and put her between him and Theodon. "I will gut your family's little pet right here if you continue to test me, boy!" he snarled.

Adaline's heart rate didn't speed up, nor did the bored look on her face evaporate. She thought it sweet that Theodon stared at the blade at her neck in horror.

Graydon moved to dig the blade into her neck a little, cutting a faint line in her flesh as Adaline winked at Theodon and froze the elder's momentum. She pushed the edge away from her neck effortlessly and stepped away from Graydon. The elder's shocked facial expression was the only movement Adaline permitted.

"You evil, old bastard," Adaline said smugly with her arms crossed over her chest. "I bet you didn't see that coming, nor could you have predicted this…" Adaline reached forward and placed her palm against the elder's temple, and his eyes snapped shut. She waved Theodon forward, who rushed to her side with his brows drawn, focused on the line of blood on her neck.

"I'm okay," she told Theodon. She rested her palm against the prince's temple, and together they witnessed the elder's original plot; him including his daughter into his plans and his daughter carrying out the poisoning of the queen's drink. "There's more," Adaline prompted Theodon before showing him the other memories she found. Memories of the elder waging conflict, purposely, with enemies of Theris to get them to turn on the elves and breach the border so it would start a war. A war Graydon hoped would be fought in Theris, for once, killing as many civilians as possible, so he could hold Aureon responsible in the eyes of the elders.

After Adaline dropped her hands, she peered at the elder in disgust. "All of this because a marriage contract was canceled." She shook her head as she thought *he had no problem weakening his king and leaving his prince without a mother!* Adaline squared her shoulders to Graydon as he remained frozen in place. She glanced over her shoulder at Theodon. "I need two minutes." She proceeded to use the elder's face as a punching bag. Two minutes later, Theodon's gentle touch grasped her shoulders. She tucked her fists and growled as her nostrils flared while her eyes blazed with white light. "I have more rage, Theo." Her voice changed to the otherworldly, powerful tone she had when she embodied her true form.

"I know," Theodon replied. "I'll put him somewhere where you can continue your 'conversation' with elder Graydon, should you be inspired to do so."

Adaline turned an evil eye and a knowing smile on the frozen elder. "I look forward to seeing you again."

Adaline kept the elder suspended as they took him to the dungeon. They imprisoned him in a similar cell to the kings. Graydon was too strong for anything less. The rest of the Miathan family was placed under house arrest, with guards at every door, for the king to deal with as he saw fit once recovered. Adaline and Theodon ensured that Graydon was adequately locked away, with Adaline adding a few reinforcements of her own.

Afterward, they decided to check on the king. While standing in front of Aureon's cell, the king focused on them with an angry, preying stare, just like he had that morning when Adaline first visited. Adaline was glad to see that he was still clean, and he kept his shoes on so far.

"Father," Theodon said to the king.

The king stormed toward the bars but stopped right in front of them. Adaline launched a light ball at him. He sneezed at the contact.

"Bless you," she said.

The king tried to shake the residual light away as the haze of the madness subsided. He sighed at the relief. "That is better."

"Good evening," Adaline said to the king.

The king surveyed them thoroughly. His gaze narrowed on the scars on his son's face and on Adaline's neck that were healing but hadn't vanished yet. And he noticed Adaline's knuckles on both hands were swollen.

"What happened?" Aureon asked. His mind entertained all possibilities of trouble the two of them could have gotten into while he'd been detained only one day. They looked away and hid their hands behind their backs, like children trying to avoid punishment. "What? Happened?" his annoyance growing with his annunciation.

"So," Adaline started cheerfully, "today was an eventful

day."

"Why are your knuckles busted?" the king asked Adaline. "Fess up, now."

Theodon and Adaline glanced at each other.

"Go ahead, Theo." Adaline pushed the prince.

"No, you first," Theodon said.

"He's your father," Adaline argued.

"He's your patient," Theodon threw back.

"I think family ties trump professional affiliation," Adaline snapped.

Thunder rumbled outside before a bolt of lightning struck above the dungeon. Adaline and Theodon froze, knowing that nature was responding to the king's mood.

"*Now*," the king breathed.

"All right," Theodon said. "Father, today we were able to collect a substantial amount of evidence against the Graydon and Talia Miathan for—"

"The murder of your mother," the king interjected.

Silence.

"So, you *did* know?" Theodon asked.

The king nodded. "Your grandfather and I could not gather any solid evidence, so I could never make a strike against Graydon without conflict from the other elders and their families. I was forced to wait indefinitely for it to surface." The king's clear gaze focused on Adaline. "I am assuming it is you who collected this evidence?"

Adaline noticed the madness was beginning to swirl over his eyes. She quickly produced a new light ball and let it float through the slats to the king. He inhaled it and shook his head at the tingly sensation in his nostrils.

"Better," the king said.

"Good," Adaline said. "And yes to your question."

He could tell she was happy she could help Theodon but not boisterous in admitting heroics. Instead, she was confidently rooted in her abilities that produced successful results. It was normal for her to achieve her goals.

"Show me," the king said to her as he stepped closer to the slats of the cell. She nodded while the king brought his face close to an opening between the slats. She masked her hand in her force field and reached through the slats to touch his temple. She transferred everything she and Theodon saw of Graydon and Talia's memories.

"Enough," the king said, signaling that he'd seen all he needed.

Adaline retracted her hand as the king addressed Theodon. "What did you do with them?"

Theodon pointed at the ceiling. "You are neighbors at the moment."

The king nodded. A pause floated between them before he noted, "You did well today."

Theodon averted his eyes and nodded at his father's acknowledgment. The prince radiated joy, but he didn't let it show. Adaline was happy for Theodon, for them both. They were already showing progress in reinforcing their family bond.

"Why are your knuckles busted, Dr. Adaline?" the king asked again. She was excellent at deflection, but he was too sharp to let it pass from his attention.

Adaline examined the backs of her hands. Her knuckles were rapidly healing but still bruised. "Would you settle for me saying that I contributed to an elder's good, old-fashioned ass-whoopin'?" she asked.

Silence.

A smirk tugged at the king's lips. "Do you heal quickly?"

"Yes," she responded immediately. Aureon's eyes were still on her. "Can we discuss your recovery now?" He nodded. "How are you feeling compared to this morning?"

Aureon took a moment to review his health. "Significantly better. It feels like the madness had roots in my psyche before, and now it does not. Overall, I am stronger."

She nodded at his response with a faint smile. *Progress. Lots of progress today.* That made her happy.

"If you had to rate yourself on a scale from one to one hundred with one hundred being perfect condition," Adaline said, "what number would you rate your mental and physical states?"

He thought about it for a moment before answering, "Seventy for mental, eighty-five for physical."

Adaline nodded again. "Good."

"Good?" Theodon asked her.

"Good," she confirmed for the prince.

"What does that mean?"

"Considering his review, and how long he's able to maintain his sanity while speaking to us, which is already significantly better since this morning," Adaline stated, "and provided that his healing rate doesn't slow down, he should be out of the woods in the next three to four days."

Theodon exhaled in relief as the king nodded, accepting her conclusion.

"I don't know if I can act as a ruler longer than that," Theodon admitted as he glanced at his father. "I don't know how you handle all you do to keep everyone happy."

The king shrugged. "In time, I learned to juggle."

Adaline smiled as the joke settled between the three of them.

"We should let you sleep," Adaline said gently. The king nodded.

"Good night, Father," Theodon said to the king.

"Good night," the king replied.

Adaline nodded at him and smiled before following Theodon out of the dungeon. She could feel his gaze burn into her as she exited his cell area.

"I could not have handled today without you," Theodon said to Adaline as they walked back to the palace.

Adaline smiled at him. "Yes, you could have."

"I am trying to thank you."

"I know." He nudged her shoulder with his. Adaline

chuckled. "I mean, your arrest of Graydon might've taken you a little longer had I not been there."

Theodon laughed. "The look on his face when you froze him in the air."

"Priceless."

"Yes!"

A moment of silence passed before Adaline wrapped her arm around his shoulders. "You're welcome, Theo."

CHAPTER 31

S ounds of pleasure were muffled at the far property wall of house Aetrune. Landon Elacan's shaft was buried deep inside Roserie as she clutched the fence post for leverage. One of Landon's hands kept her skirt out of the way as he thrust into her from behind, while his other hand reached around to stroke the sensitive bud between her thighs. Roserie gasped at the contact, wanting to cry out, but swallowed the reaction to remain undiscovered. It was minutes after dawn, and Roserie was already craving Landon's touch. She could not get enough of the known womanizer, who thrust hard into her, causing his pants to fall to his ankles. A moan almost escaped her as her features strained from the pleasure, but Landon caught her slip.

"No sounds, my dear," he hissed in her ear with a thrust. "Or Mommy and Daddy will hear."

Roserie secretly desired her parents to find them because they would persuade Landon to make an honest female out of her, but she knew she'd never see him again if they were discovered.

"Roserie, honey, breakfast is ready," her mother, Celu, spoke into her mind when she was a breath away from orgasm. "I'm coming." Thrust. "Mother."

Landon felt her wet walls clench his shaft tightly as her body released. A grunt later, he joined her. They frantically righted their clothing before resuming the façade of not interacting in their everyday lives, only for their charade to repeat the following morning.

Roserie hastened through the rear entrance of the main house of her family's estate, praying that the flush had gone from her cheeks. "In here, Roserie," her father called from the other end of the house. She focused on breathing normally then checked her skirt before she entered the dining room.

Ensatus Aetrune sat at the head of the dinner table with his wife, Celu. His hand clasped Celu's while the food was brought to the table, and their children, Roserie and Bole, filed in for family mealtime. As they settled into their meals, gossip was tossed around the table.

"I saw that there were guards posted at the Miathan's home last night," Celu mentioned as she picked up her flatware.

"Really?" Ensatus said curiously. "I wonder what happened."

"I don't understand what could have happened," Roserie feigned innocence.

"I know what happened," Bole said into his sister's mind. "It's what's going to happen to us if you keep letting Landon fuck you instead of Theodon!"

Roserie's eyes shot across the table to her brother before she replied telepathically, "Good things take time and patience, brother." The truth was Roserie's obsession with Landon was the obstacle she allowed to keep her from dedicating herself to her brother's scheme. However, the idea of being queen piqued her interest enough to try, but she could never manage to let Theodon near like she did Landon.

Bole tore into his bread before shooting back, "Considering how long you have teased him and forced him to wait, I wouldn't be surprised if he's fucking someone else, too."

Roserie's eyes went wide. "How dare you say!"

Bole smirked at her. "I bet it's that human. The doctor."

"The one who beat you at arm wrestling?" Roserie reminded him as their parents continued to chatter about the Miathans.

Bole's scalding gaze narrowed on Roserie. "We are not supposed to be in servitude to the crown and never reap any power from the alliance, like the Miathans. They enslaved themselves to the Sleone's for thousands of years only to remain slaves," Bole sneered. "If the crown has figured out what Graydon's done, then it won't be long before they find out about our plans. If this fails, I'm holding you responsible for fucking around where you shouldn't have been." Roserie gasped. Her parents asked her what was wrong.

"Nothing," she said aloud. "The food is a little hot." She settled back into eating as she devised a contingency plan then shared in her brother's mind, "Well then, we are going to have to speed up our faux-fondness for them all, won't we?" Bole took a bite of his breakfast and nodded at his sister. It was time they set themselves up to win.

CHAPTER 32

Adaline was wide-awake at dawn. Staring past the intricately carved ceiling over her bed with her arms folded behind her head, she reviewed the changes in the king's symptoms from the previous evening. *He is progressing nicely*. Perhaps today, she could test his boundaries. She recalled her conversations with Dr. Meza, the physician down the hall in her practice who would conduct psychological reviews with her own patients after dramatic changes had occurred in their lives due to healing.

Adaline devised elf equivalents of reflex tests, fitness tests, analytical reasoning tests, anger management tests, and so on. Today would not be boring, she knew, as she rose to put on her athletic clothing, grabbed her bag, and left her room. She was happy to run into Ena at such an early hour.

"Does the king have clothing that he can wear if he were required to do a significant amount of physical activity and still have a full range of motion of all of his major joints?" Adaline asked Ena.

Ena took a moment to think before smiling and nodding. "I

know what will work."

"Great!" Adaline said. "Show me."

Adaline took the clothes that Ena pulled from the king's wardrobe and set out for the dungeon. She noticed that the sun was peeking through the overcast sky, and she smiled. *Progress!* Pounding down the steps of the dungeon, she passed Theodon along the way.

"What are you doing?" Theodon asked as she zoomed past him.

"Testing!" she called behind her as she kept her pace. "Lots of testing!" He chuckled and shook his head before exiting. She made it to the king's cell and moved so fast that when she braked, her shoes skidded. The king's eyebrows lifted at the sound.

"Good morning," Adaline said to the king.

"Good morning, Dr. Adaline," Aureon said.

Her attention shot to his face. "You're coherent this morning."

"The episodes seem to come and go less frequently than yesterday."

"Excellent," she said as she set down all she carried. Aureon eyed the stack of clothing. "We're going to do some mental health tests to see where you are at today."

"Mental health tests?"

Her attention lifted from her notes. "I'm going to test your analytical skills, your anger management, and test how you argue." He thought about her ideas for a moment and nodded. "And depending on how you do with those tests, I'll know if I can take you outside to get some fresh air," she slipped in, "and do some physical activity tests." His head snapped around to her. Adaline smiled as his excitement at the possibility of getting outside of the cell washed over her. "Do I have your attention, Your Majesty?"

"Undivided, Dr. Adaline," he annunciated perfectly.

Aureon proved to be a master strategist, leader, and above all, fair in his reasoning. For the next two hours, she took him through the analytical test before testing his arguing style, which he passed without effort. Adaline clocked the madness, resurfacing for about five minutes every forty minutes, so she adjusted the testing to occur around the interferences. Finally, Adaline floated the change of clothes through the parted slats in the cell to Aureon.

"Change into these while I go speak to the warden," she said before leaving the room.

When Adaline returned, he was changed into the outfit she brought, and he was fixing one of his cuffs. "Do you know of a place that is secluded from the public where you could get some exercise?" she asked, smiling because she could feel his eagerness.

Aureon's eyes shifted. "Yes."

Adaline's telekinesis opened the door to his cell, and she entered. Aureon immediately reached for her offered hand, intrigued at her allowance for contact. Their touch sparked a sensation that always made her skin break out in goosebumps while his awareness of her amplified. As their auras overlapped when they stood close, the energy between them was a reminder of their connection, regardless if they acknowledged it or not.

"Close your eyes and think of that place," Adaline said. Aureon did as instructed and immediately felt a shift. "Now open them."

Aureon heard a bird twitter before opening his eyes to see that he was in precisely the place he'd imagined. They stood in an open meadow that stretched to the end of a cliff, miles away from the capital. An easy smile spread across his face as he lifted his face to the sun and inhaled deeply. He let go of a loud exhale from his mouth then looked at Adaline.

"Thank you," Aureon said.

"Oh, don't thank me yet," she said. "You may not like me after this."

Aureon tried to be serious by narrowing his eyes at her, but he couldn't manage it. He chuckled at his failure. "Are you to beat me into submission with manual labor, Dr. Adaline?"

"I would never beat you, Your Majesty," she said before adding, "Except at cards. I would totally beat you at cards." The corner of his mouth lifted. "Before we get started," she said as she reached one glowing hand into his chest and pulled out another stubborn piece of the mist that lingered. She flicked it to the ground, and it began to dissolve immediately. *A good sign.* She noticed his breathing quickened. "Are you in pain?"

Aureon shook his head. "My lungs are limited."

"Ah, let's fix that." With her palms on his chest, Adaline flooded him with white light. His lungs adjusted from heaving for breath to their normal function. Her hands dropped. "And now?"

Aureon took a measured breath, then another. He nodded. "Better."

"Good," she said before surveying the scene. She pointed at a large branch overhead. "There." His gaze lifted. "Can you jump that high?"

"Without effort," Aureon said with a hint of arrogance.

"Great!" She cheered before saying, "Jump up and hang for a moment."

Aureon focused on the branch, leaped swiftly into the air, and grabbed onto it. He didn't notice Adaline floated off the ground until she stepped out from the air and onto the branch.

His eyes widened. "How did you do that?"

She waved her hand dismissively. "That's not important, right now. Now, pull-ups. Count 'em off. Ready? Go!"

Adaline eventually stopped him at two hundred twenty-five as it became painfully evident that he didn't tire quickly. She searched for something more challenging. She smirked when she found her next test: throwing a large boulder that looked approximately five tons. He squatted, lifted with his legs, grunted through lifting the boulder a little higher, then curled his arms and chucked it. Adaline's eyes widened as the boulder must have traveled the length of two football fields.

"Impressive," she muttered.

Aureon smirked as his chest rose with pride. "What else?"

"Long jump," she said before pointing at the cliff behind them. "All the way across and back."

His eyes smiled before he took off to the edge of the cliff. Aureon sailed through the air effortlessly and landed softly on the other side. He faced her.

Knowing he could hear her without raising her voice, she said, "Now on your way back, land at full impact."

Adaline watched him take a few steps back before taking off again, but he rocketed through the air this time. He hit his landing hard, shaking the cliff and causing the ground he landed on to crack under his feet. He casually stepped forward, missing the edge of the cliff sliding down the side of the mountain.

"Good," Adaline said before lowering her feet back to the ground.

Aureon lifted his chin at her feet. "You were taking precautions of my landing?"

"Yes," she said without hesitation. "Human knees are a pain to heal whether evolved or not."

"Anything else for me to try, Dr. Adaline?" he asked her, obviously enjoying himself.

"Two more," she said as she scanned his eyes, which were starting to swirl. "But we will begin again in five minutes." She froze him in place as he succumbed to the madness. Five minutes later, he shook his head as his mind cleared and his vision focused. Adaline was shining a small flashlight in his eyes. "Welcome back," she said while using her glowing finger as a flashlight to shine in his eyes.

"How bad was it this time?" he asked.

"You've been much worse," she said, referring to the first night of his healing process. "It means you are getting better."

Aureon felt terrible about what happened. "About that…"

Adaline gave him her full attention.

"I…" he attempted before backtracking over his thoughts. "Thank you for what you did for me, and I am sorry for hurting you."

A soft smile crossed her face. "You're welcome. And it's okay." She nodded to confirm her statement.

"How bad was it after I… withdrew?"

Adaline shook her head. "I'm not going to let you beat yourself up over the past. I'm fine, and we are here for your recovery." Aureon didn't like that statement. He wanted to know. At the same time, he felt it best not to press her. "I will tell you that you have nothing to worry about because you raised a good son who made sure I was all right."

Aureon nodded to himself while his eyes were downcast. "He is a good son."

"Yes, he is." A moment of silence passed between them before she asked, "Are you ready for your last two tests?"

He nodded as a smile grew on his face.

"Okay," she said before she dropped her clipboard and instructed him, "I need you to run at me full speed."

Aureon looked at her like she must have lost her mind. "Pardon?"

"You heard me," she said as she walked backward and checked to make sure there wasn't anything obstructing the path behind her. She crossed her forearms in front of her and leaned into them. "Gimme your best shot. Push until my feet dig into the ground." Alarms went off in his mind. This wasn't a good idea. "What?" she asked before she switched to trash talk. "You can't do it, can you? King Aureon is a pansy." She threw up her hands. "Look, he can't do it. This is too much for you." She checked the time on a watch she wasn't wearing. "We should just go home now and call it a day."

Her taunting caused him to collide with her. He was shocked to find that her feet didn't move an inch as his hands clutched her forearms and pushed.

"Harder!" Adaline yelled.

Aureon pushed harder, but her feet remained still. His lip started to curl, and a growl left his throat.

"C'mon! Let's go!" she yelled. "Show me all you've got!"

Aureon hooked his shoulder across her forearms and pushed with all he had. Suddenly, her feet started to move, skidding along the ground slowly.

"More!" she yelled.

He grunted as he pushed harder, testing his limits.

"Almost there!" she yelled as she gauged how far he'd pushed her.

He moved her another three feet before she shouted, "Done!"

Aureon fell to his knees as his chest heaved for air. *Excellent!* She noted it only took his body ten seconds to recover.

"Never ask me to do that again," Aureon said. He didn't like the feeling of charging at Adaline, no matter her strength.

Adaline eyed him thoughtfully. "You don't like violence against females." He shook his head. "Does this have anything to do with–"

"–No, this has nothing to do with what my father did to me after returning from war," he stated.

Adaline's eyebrows lifted. "Okay."

He dusted off his pants. "No male likes seeing females suffer."

"You obviously have never been to Earth," Adaline mused aloud.

Her gaze was guarded as he tried to assess her. Had there been any indication that a male caused her harm, he'd head straight for the portal and allow his madness to consume him, leaving behind no threats and no bystanders, but her body language gave away no clues. His little human was a strong one.

His.

Adaline noticed his energy started to feel less defensive, so she moved on. "Are you ready for the last test?"

Aureon's eyes widened. "Is it similar to the last one?"

"No." She chuckled. "Some people even like it. It's an ancient game in my world." Adaline pulled a hacky sack from her pocket and held it between them. She let her mind take over and floated it in front of him. "Now, follow it with only your eyes." She moved the hacky sack to the left, to the right, up, and down, then started to do some quick maneuvers with it, and she was glad to see he could keep up just fine. "This time, try to catch it." Aureon only missed it the first time and snatched the sack out of the air every chance afterward. She smirked because she thought he looked like Cailu trying to swat a feather.

"What is so amusing, Dr. Adaline?" he asked as he handed her back the toy.

Adaline failed to swallow a giggle. "Nothing, Your Majesty." His gaze narrowed on her, unconvinced. "Now for the game," she said before she tossed the hacky sack above her. She caught it at the top of her chest, let it slide down her body until it dropped off her knee, ending by catching it on the toe of her shoe. As much as this was going to be fun, it was a sneaky way to further test his reflexes, balance, and agility. Aureon was stunned that she let it roll through her cleavage and the hacky sack still made it to her foot without falling to the ground.

"Focus," Adaline said.

Aureon's eyes snapped to hers.

"The point of the game is to catch the footbag and make a creative move with it that consists of three contacts with the bag before passing it. It cannot touch the ground or your hands at any time." She demonstrated a basic trick. "See?" Aureon nodded. "Ready to catch?"

"Yes."

She tossed it high. Aureon followed it, then let it hit his chest and roll down to his foot like she did. He played copycat for the first few moves before he started to get creative.

"Good!" she said as he nailed a challenging maneuver.

They played for a while before it was time to take him back before the madness set in again. Aureon handed her the footbag.

"Keep it," she said while looking over her notes on the clipboard. "I have a feeling you will be able to do more with it than I can." Aureon regarded the hacky sack thoughtfully.

"Are you ready?" Adaline asked as she offered her hand.

"Yes," he said as he reached for it.

In the blink of an eye, they were back in his cell. Adaline surrendered his hand, but he held onto hers. She searched his gaze for direction. He held her attention as he brought the back of her hand to his lips and kissed it.

Her gaze softened as she became flustered by his touch and proximity, along with his large eyes that noticed everything. "Thank you." The silence between them filled with all he wanted to say to her, but she kept their conversation on track for a moment longer.

"You have about five minutes before you relapse," Adaline said. "I brought you a new change of clothes for you if you wish to bathe before it takes over."

"Must I bathe myself this time?" Aureon whispered in the shallow distance between them. He longed for a repeat of yesterday morning, even if she didn't exactly lay a hand on him, nor did he remember much of it. His little human was clever when it came to maintaining boundaries when he wanted none between them. *Why such boldness?* He pondered his actions. He was never so direct when it came to wooing a female. In the past, he was gentler, more romantic, but something in her called to him to act quickly.

Adaline blushed. "You seem of sound mind, Your Majesty, and therefore capable of bathing yourself."

"The former option is far more appealing." The words rumbled in his chest as he crowded.

"Are you hitting on me?"

He moved closer. "I like you near, Dr. Adaline."

She backed toward the slats of the cell as he heard her heartbeat race. Adaline's goosebumps signaled she was harboring feelings of anxiety, fear, attraction, and maybe arousal. The last emotion made him stop in his tracks and draw in a deep breath. Yes, arousal, he confirmed. Aureon's eyes narrowed on her, feeling clearer than they ever had in his long life. His nostrils flared at her enslaving scent as he crowded her in the corner near the door. He needed to touch her, but he also didn't want to be burned by her force field.

"There is no room for fear here, Dr. Adaline," Aureon said as he leaned in to smell her hair, allowing the tip of his nose to touch the shell of her ear, hoping his light contact would draw her to him.

"It's more than that," Adaline said, shivering at his touch before her body shifted its molecular structure through the slats before her form reassembled on the other side. Aureon's anger stirred, but he curbed expressing it. He didn't want to add ammunition against him in her mind because he was playing to win.

Adaline handed the fresh change of clothes to him through the slot in the door. "I am your doctor first, and I am here to ensure your full recovery." Aureon snatched her hand through the slot, brought it to his nose to smell her skin then kissed each of her knuckles. "And when you are no longer my doctor?" His eyes pinned hers before the tip of his tongue touched the pad of her index finger.

"Then we'll have to address it accordingly... after you've made a full recovery," she said, unable to swallow her breath that was hitching at the contact.

Aureon's emotions warred within him. "Fine. In the meantime, you will know who wants you." He set the fresh clothes aside, and he released her hand before he blurred to undress. Seconds later, he stood before her naked as his chest heaved as his desire for her grew before her eyes, straining to reach her.

Adaline stumbled back a step, her gaze affixed to his powerful form.

"Yes," Aureon hissed as his eyes slid closed for a moment at the feeling of her gaze on him. "Now you see who wants you, Dr. Adaline."

Her eyes drank him in, but her feet retreated. *At least one part of me is acting professional,* she thought as she scrambled for her bag by the entrance before leaving the cell area.

Aureon approached the basin in his cell that contained freshwater. *It better be cold,* he thought, before he picked up the basin and dumped the water on his head.

CHAPTER 33

"**I**s there such thing as Reverse Nightingale Syndrome?" Adaline telepathically reached out to her brother as she hurried back to the palace from the dungeon. Alarmed by the king's blatant come-on, she recalled the first and only bath she gave him without her laying a hand on him. *Clinical detachment at its finest*, she thought. However, that didn't seem to stall the momentum of his growing... interest.

"Huh?" Asher replied a moment later. He'd been buried in studying the new plant samples he had brought back from Theris. He was amazed at what the plants could do, what they could cure. The samples had impressive regenerative properties, and one plant could fully restore dead cells. He tested the plant on a case of Multiple Sclerosis. The compound made from the plant immediately bonded to the parts of live human tissue that were beginning to fail and restored the tissue to an optimal state.

"You heard me," Adaline shot back.

"Why would you think that?" Asher asked as he sliced a tiny piece of cellulose from another new specimen, layered it on a slide, and positioned it under his microscope.

"I'm not saying I'm not awesome," Adaline confessed. "You and I both know I'm awesome. However, considering recent events, I think the king may dig me for unrealistic reasons."

Asher burst into laughter at her ridiculous rhetoric, which Adaline could not hear. "What constitutes as an unrealistic reason?"

"I think he thinks he has feelings for me because I healed him," Adaline admitted. She didn't want to go there, but it was a red flag in her mind, and she never disregarded red flags.

Ah, Asher thought. This was a legitimate concern for Adaline because it had happened to her with male patients in the past. They became a bit clingy and turned into creepy stalkers after they made a full recovery. As easily as Adaline could get rid of someone, she really didn't want this part of the past to repeat itself.

"I really don't think that's the case here, Addy," Asher stated. "Think about your interactions before you healed him. Is there anything that could indicate a false attraction?"

Adaline thought about her first meeting the king with his cold stare but deep curiosity. The observation that Theodon shared about his father having a chance at happiness with her before she first left Theris surfaced in her thoughts, along with the king's apology upon returning. His playfulness during her first projection into his dreams spoke volumes, as well as his protection and helpfulness during Nÿla's labor.

"Can't think of anything, can you?" Asher interjected.

"Shut up," Adaline shot back as she tried to find some sort of evidence that would bring any feelings she might be developing in return to a screeching halt.

Asher chuckled. "Sis, I think the possibility of something being real with him is spooking you, so you are trying to sabotage it before anything has a chance to start."

"How do you know?" Adaline's attitude peeked through her words.

"Because you are my sister, and I know you," Asher argued lightheartedly. "Addy, if there's a chance that you can build a life with him, you should explore it. We both thought we wouldn't have the option to love a mate during this lifetime, until now. So, don't squander it because you're afraid."

"I'm not afraid of anything!"

"Yes, you are!" Asher exclaimed with a smile on his face. "You have always been afraid to love, and before you found Theris, you had good reason not to choose it. But Addy, you don't have a reason anymore. You're finally free."

Adaline's feet stopped dead in their tracks, along with her thoughts at Asher's declaration. She didn't realize that she had already made it back to the palace and was standing in the throne room, completely unaware of her surroundings. *Free?* She knew if she and Asher could permanently leave Earth for Theris, they would finally be free of their world and their role in its end. But it hadn't occurred to her that more than her life purpose would be freed when she left. Her heart would be free, too. She would have the choice to love.

"I'm taking your silence as meaning you had an epiphany?" Asher chimed in.

Adaline's focus snapped back to their conversation. "You have a point."

"I know I do. I'm the brilliant twin," Asher said smugly. "You and I both deserve a chance at a real life, Addy. Not just serving some apocalyptic purpose. We aren't machines. We have souls — souls that have walked this planet many times. I don't think the prophets can be mad at us for wanting something for ourselves after we do what we were made for, since the primary function of the divine is to love."

Wow, Adaline thought. She forgot how profound her twin could be because he was usually caught up in a couple dozen surgeries each day, or he was locked in his lab searching for cures under a microscope. In all their lifetimes together, Asher remained the same when it came to his studious behavior and relentless curiosity for the sake of science... until it was time to party.

"Dr. Adaline?" Theodon inquired from the hallway entrance. He noticed her standing still in the middle of the throne room for a few minutes while she seemed to be focusing on something. Adaline held up her index finger to Theodon to pause his interruption.

"Okay, you win," Adaline said in Asher's mind. "I will give it serious consideration." It was only fair since her thoughts of the king were evolving from clinically detached to passionately inappropriate.

"Don't make it sound like a business deal, Addy," Asher said. "Just listen to your instincts and maybe your heart once in a while, versus your clinical logic."

"Fine."

Asher chuckled. "Don't sound too excited."

"I just need to let this percolate in my brain," Adaline admitted, "This is... something I'd never thought I'd get to consider."

"I know."

"I love you."

"Love you too, Addy," Asher reciprocated before their connection ended.

Adaline focused on Theodon and smiled. "Sorry, I was making a long-distance call."

Theodon smiled. "Not a problem. You seemed a bit panicked when I first saw you. Is everything all right?"

"It will be."

"Do you have a big decision on your mind?"

"I do," Adaline admitted. "It deserves careful consideration."

"Well, allow me to distract you for a moment for the purpose of necessity." Theodon smirked before asking her, "Are you hungry?"

"Famished," she blurted as Theodon gestured for her to enter the dining room.

They took their usual places across from each other at the dining room table, leaving the king's seat at the head of the table empty. A moment later, plates of food were set in front of them. While Theodon quietly settled into his meal, Adaline only managed to pick up her fork loosely in one hand while she stared off into the emptiness of the king's chair. Her mind pondered the choice she believed she was still in the process of making.

"Was it easy for you to choose to love?" Adaline asked Theodon.

The prince focused on her question as he dabbed his napkin at the corner of his mouth. After giving it some thought and reflecting on his latest discovery of another male's stench attached to Roserie, he tried to tell himself that they had made no formal arrangement to be together. Because of that, her behavior was acceptable for now.

"Yes," Theodon revealed. Adaline stayed quiet, giving the prince space to share his thoughts. "It was easy."

"You are a braver person than I am, friend."

He chuckled as he glanced down at his plate to spear another piece of his dinner. His gaze lifted to Adaline before taking a bite, understanding why she asked the question in the first place. He told her, "It's okay to love him, Dr. Adaline."

Adaline's gaze froze on him. It was the first time he'd ever witnessed shock on her face. He smirked. Her attention returned to her plate, more lost in her thoughts than ever. He decided to share a story with her.

"When I was very young," Theodon started, "I was a restless little youngling. I tried to sneak out of classes my father set for me that I thought were boring. I decided to go hunting on my own."

Adaline's eyes brightened, clearly amused. "You would cut class, Theo?"

The prince chuckled and nodded. "I would never get very far, let alone for very long because my grandfather would always have an eye on me while my father was busy ruling the kingdom. However, there was one day where I went a little too far and for too long." Adaline canted her head in curiosity as she waited for the rest of the story. She finally started eating her dinner. "I wandered to the top of a hill near the Ieobu River. It turned out it wasn't a hill I was standing on, as falling through a hole in the top of it solved that mystery." Theodon chuckled before continuing, "I'd found what seemed to be a place of dark magic."

Adaline's eyebrows lifted high on her forehead. "Did you scramble out of there?"

"Worse! I explored the place," Theodon admitted. Adaline's eyes widened. Theodon nodded at his foolish behavior. "I was drawn by a light I saw down a hallway. I followed it into a cavern that contained three ponds that very few of my people know exists. They are called the Eternity Ponds, and at the time, I had never heard of them. Naturally, my curiosity got the best of me, and I wandered too close. I fell in." Adaline stilled then set down her flatware to listen to the rest of the story. "The pond swirled, showing me scenes from my future." Theodon's eyes smiled as he looked at Adaline. A moment passed as he took a bite of his dinner, chewed, and swallowed. "The last scene I was shown was of my father's happiness."

"As in the source of his happiness?" Adaline asked.

Theodon nodded. "It's you."

Adaline had no words. All she could manage was to stare at Theodon from across the table. Her inner skeptic kicked in, fighting the scene young Theodon witnessed with logic, no matter how much her heartbeat picked up at the possibility of the foretelling being true. "Are these ponds accurate?" She asked.

Theodon nodded. "The reason their whereabouts are known by so few is that there was a time when people would seek them out to know their lives instead of living their lives.

Because they hung on the pond's every proffered image, they did nothing to help facilitate the result, so the outcome wouldn't happen. It caused a lot of suffering, so during my grandfather's reign, he had the ponds hidden and banned anyone from seeking them out."

Adaline's gaze turned playfully suspicious. "And who pulled little Theo from the water?"

Theodon looked down at his plate, trying to hide his blushing cheeks now that the conversation returned to his original misbehavior. "My father," Theodon admitted. "He was furious with me."

"I'm sure now that you are an adult, you understand his fury was actually fear for your safety."

Theodon's eyes narrowed on Adaline. "You are always so clever."

Adaline chuckled. "It's true. He loves you very much."

Theodon was silent for a moment while his attention fell to his plate. "I know that, now." He snuck a glance at Adaline, who was smiling as she chewed her food. "Why are you smiling?"

"Because it looks like we both know something about each other that was worth sharing, whether it was easy to digest or not."

Another moment of silence passed.

"I know there's a possibility that you may not believe in fate, Dr. Adaline," Theodon stated. "I also believe that we get to make choices that contribute to the outcome of our lives." Adaline nodded as she listened. "I say this to you because of the scene I was shown," Theodon admitted. "I saw him express happiness I've never seen in my lifetime. I don't wish you to be frightened at the thought that you do not have a choice in this matter because you do. However, as your friend and son, I should tell you that what I saw between the two of you looked unlike any bond I'd ever seen in a couple. It seemed... transcendent."

Adaline's eyes filled with yearning for what he described.

Did such a bond exist?

"Again, it is all your choice," Theodon reminded her. "Just don't allow yourself to fear. You would be robbing the both of you of a chance at something great."

They finished their meals in silence as their thoughts swirled from their conversation. Finally, Adaline sat back in her seat and rested her elbow on the beautifully sculpted arm of the chair. While appraising Theodon as he finished his meal, he felt her eyes on him and met her gaze. He lifted his chin at her as he chewed.

"She doesn't deserve you," Adaline admitted.

CHAPTER 34

A cloudless, sunshine-filled sky beamed down on Theris the following day. King Aureon stood like a statue in the middle of his cell with his eyes closed and his ears searching. He found sounds of nature, of peace. Then he searched for the little human who was becoming important to him. He relaxed at the sound of her heartbeat. It wasn't as slow as it was a few minutes ago, proving she was now awake.

Would she visit him this morning after the spectacle he made yesterday?

Since dawn, he had been reviewing the memories Adaline had shown him, and he strategized his next step. Once he devised a necessary course of action, he needed sounds of peace to calm his soul. Aureon swallowed his unease, making peace that the path forward would be rooted in deception to discover who else associated with Graydon and his queen's murder. He searched for sounds to ease his anxiety about what would come, what he had to do. *History must repeat itself.* It was the only way to force the crown's enemies into action that would cause them to reveal themselves.

Dr. Adaline entered the cell area with determined steps. She was adamant about making the third day of his recovery effective, even after his blatant confession at the end of their time together yesterday.

Aureon didn't precisely regret his actions, but after understanding what had happened to capture the crown's enemies, it was indeed poor timing. His attraction for the human would have to be suspended for everything to unfold as planned. He hoped such a notion was possible.

"Good morning," he heard her say, tearing him away from listening to the sounds of the nature that thrived beyond the walls of his cell.

"Good morning," rumbled from his chest before he opened his eyes. It was the first time he'd spoken aloud since waking up from a sleep filled with dreams of Adaline. She didn't project into them, although he wished she had. Aureon didn't move from his position since she entered the area, allowing only his eyes to follow her. He enjoyed watching her. Her simplest actions were graceful and strong. He could tell she was well-practiced in conducting herself as an average human, even though she was far from it. He was confident that as she continued to visit Theris, the human façade would fade to where she could always be her powerful self. Adaline's body shifted at a molecular level, allowing her to step through the slats of his cell and solidify once inside.

Beautiful, he thought.

"How are you feeling today?" she asked while surveying him. Aureon was hard to gauge because he stood motionless while his stare remained wild.

Apprehensive, protective, on fire for you at every second, and so sorry regarding what I am about to put you through, he thought. He signaled to Adaline's hand, hands that brought forth great power. She lifted one. He took it and placed it against his temple, then nodded. She assessed his expression for a moment, searching for something revealing, only to find him staring back at her. She nodded and searched his thoughts and memories.

What does he want me to see?

Adaline saw him watching her force field activate when she slept. She noticed his concern when it happened because he wasn't sure of what it was and how he clenched his fists. After all, he couldn't touch her. He tried to speak to her, but she didn't awaken.

Because she couldn't hear him.

Oh, she thought, as she opened her eyes and took her hand away.

Theodon rounded the corner from the stairs into the cell area. He nodded at his father, who nodded in return. Aureon gestured to Adaline to allow him inside the cell. She glanced at Theodon and smiled, then her telekinesis unlocked the cell and opened the door. Theodon strode through before the door closed and locked behind him. Once the three of them stood close, Aureon finally spoke.

"Test it," he told Adaline.

Theodon was receiving telepathic messages from his father, who turned to Adaline and gestured. "Me and you."

This is getting odd, Adaline thought. She humored them and draped her force field over her and Theodon. Theodon spoke out loud from the inside to his father, who heard nothing.

"Now, all of us," Aureon spoke in his son's mind.

"Can you contain all three of us?" Theodon asked Adaline.

She shot Theodon a look. "This better be good." She extended the field around Aureon, and the two royals examined the field then each other.

"Okay, spill it," Adaline said.

"We must draw out any remaining enemies that helped Graydon and Talia murder Aravae and any others who have plotted crimes against our family." Aureon's statement shocked Theodon because it was the only time in his life that he heard his father say his mother's name.

"We?" Adaline asked.

"Yes," Aureon confirmed. "The elders have been cross with me for some time because I haven't arranged a marriage for Theodon."

Uh oh, Adaline thought as she recalled Sorsacha revealing the story of Aureon's arranged marriage.

Aureon faced Theodon. "After I broke my arranged marriage contract to be with your mother, I knew I would never force my own child to marry anyone they didn't choose for themselves." Adaline heard a "but" at the end of his statement. "After we complete this task, you will be free to marry whomever you choose." A pregnant pause hung between them. "Right now, you must be engaged to Dr. Adaline."

Adaline's eyes widened. "Wait, what?" Her thoughts raced. *Engaged? I've never wanted to be engaged. How does someone act when they're engaged? Doesn't an engagement last for a year? Can I lie for that long?*

Well, you've been lying about yourself for your whole human life. Ouch, she thought of her self-burn. *That's different, though, right? That's for survival until the end of the world.*

"Yes, Father," Theodon said obediently.

"Engaged?" Adaline spat out. The elves watched her as she ranted, "I can't be engaged. I've never been engaged."

"All the more evidence to show how idiotic the males of your species are, Dr. Adaline," Aureon snapped back. Theodon smirked.

"You don't understand," she explained. "I can't do this. I can't be in Theris for the length of time for the dedication a role like this would require. And furthermore, how is us being engaged going to find Graydon's accomplices?"

The corner of the king's mouth lifted. "Graydon's plan was set into motion once I denied the arranged marriage my father agreed to take place between Talia and me. Graydon wanted a path to the crown. And I suspect he's not the only one." Aureon's face remained on Adaline while his eyes shifted to Theodon.

"Making it look like my only son, the future king, is to marry a human, who would be viewed as 'less' by an elder–"

"Gee, thanks," Adaline huffed.

"–Would cause such a stir that the remaining accomplices would strike. Just like the Miathan's did because they viewed Aravae as less, also," Aureon stated.

Theodon's brow furrowed. "They did?"

Aureon nodded as he placed his hand on his son's shoulder. "They did. And she was effortlessly more." Adaline's heart clenched as she felt Aureon's emotions during that nostalgic moment. He was finally finishing working through his grief. "The difference is," Aureon explained, "Dr. Adaline is capable of protecting herself at all times and won't be in a vulnerable state like Aravae was after childbirth."

Ah, there's the rub, Adaline thought. "How long would we have to keep this up?"

"Two weeks," Aureon stated.

"Why must it be a quick betrothal?" Theodon asked.

"Because the elders have been asking me to arrange a marriage for you for more than a century," Aureon said. "Therefore, I predict their reaction to the news will be to push for a quick engagement." Aureon addressed Adaline, "And you will not have to be in Theris for all of this. You can resume your life as before and visit us on your weekends. That way, Theodon and I will deal with most of the theatrics."

Adaline nodded in understanding before glancing at Theodon. She thought for a moment before she asked, "Do elf couples engage in public displays of affection?" Adaline couldn't remember witnessing any.

"It's limited," Theodon answered her. "Our mate connections are so deep that they are felt without touching, so most displays of affection occur behind closed doors. You may see a couple hold hands or give a kiss on the forehead, but it is mostly in the way they look at each other."

"And because you are human, you get a reprieve. So, your performance does not have to be perfect, just convincing enough," Aureon chimed in.

"Speaking of closed doors," she pointed out.

"No, you will not have to cohabitate with Theodon for the next two weekends," Aureon said without missing a beat. "Only the wedding night after the reception."

Adaline felt every nerve ending in her body turn cold as his words hit her. Her thoughts raced with possible outcomes of friendships destroyed, unrequited feelings that could bloom, and any other damages that could unfold between the three of them during the execution of such a plan. Everything could change, and not necessarily for the better. Theodon put his hand on her shoulder to comfort her. "My suite is large. We can divide the space and still have privacy." Adaline nodded as her thoughts continued to fan the flames of worry in her mind.

"You have a choice in this, Dr. Adaline," Aureon said, bringing her attention back to him.

"I know," Adaline said, adding yet another choice to her plate. She knew she always had a choice, regardless of what anyone tried to make her do. Initially, Adaline thought finding out about Graydon and Talia would be enough, but having real-time evidence of the others helped build a solid case. She couldn't deny that the thought of catching everyone involved all at once was appealing.

"I'll do it," she said after a long pause. She found Aureon donning a slight smile, and he carried emotions of gratitude and concern.

Concern? *Worry.*

"When will this be announced, and what's required of me while I am in Theris once it is?" Adaline asked.

A beautiful strategist, Aureon thought. "You will be in the public eye during this time," he noted. "All proper attire will be provided for you. You are required to touch and gaze lovingly at your betrothed until this is over."

Adaline sighed before stating, "I will do this as long as you understand that should anyone strike against me during this time, I will immediately retaliate."

A pause hung between them.

"I would have it no other way," Aureon rumbled, clearly not liking the idea of anyone harming her. He stared at her for a moment, allowing his gaze to drown in her dark eyes. She lured him in without effort. He would have to be mindful of how he conducted himself around her for the next two weekends.

Then maybe we could talk about her and me, he pondered. The possibility gave him hope, as Aureon needed another goal in which to look forward. A happy one. Not only one to finally put to rest, but one that would carry him forward once their plan was over and peace could thrive.

"My recovery ends tomorrow at midnight," Aureon stated before sounding-off orders. "Theodon will bring me back to the palace. Tomorrow morning, Dr. Adaline will return to Earth and resume her normal schedule of returning to Theris on weekends, two days later. Upon her return, the announcement will already have been made, and the celebrations will begin." Adaline and Theodon glanced at each other. "Your wedding ceremony," Aureon annunciated clearly for emphasis, "will be scheduled to take place the following weekend."

So fast, Adaline thought. The elves of the kingdom would need evidence of action taken against the crown before they would believe in the odd abilities of a human outsider. She tried to re-hash the scheme in her mind by using her abilities, so the royals wouldn't have to get involved and came up short. She rubbed her temples in small circular motions as she fumed about doing things the long way.

"They will strike at Dr. Adaline before they would ever strike against me," Theodon thought aloud. "No one would be foolish enough to attack their future king."

"But they have no problem murdering a lowly human," Adaline blurted out.

Silence fell.

Aureon leveled his gaze on her. "The only reason we can do this is because of you, Dr. Adaline. You are the only female strong enough to handle it."

"I know," Adaline whispered. "What happens when this is all over, and the bad guys are caught?"

"They will be arrested, charged, and their sentences will be immediately carried out," Aureon said.

"I meant for the three of us," she interjected while pinching the bridge of her nose.

"I will be forthcoming regarding the engagement being a setup to lure in those who have committed crimes against the crown," Aureon said. "And your arrangement will be voided."

Adaline focused on Theodon. Simply looking at him made her smile. He was the spitting image of his father, yet he still maintained his kindness to a humbling degree. He smiled back at her. "When I first met you," she told him as she reached for his hand, "I knew you were going to be one of the greatest friends I would ever have in my life."

Theodon grasped her hand and squeezed it. "I knew it, too." He knew far more than that. He knew exactly what she would be to his father. And he would protect her at all costs to ensure his father's happiness.

"What we're about to do can impact our friendship," she said to him honestly. "So, I need to tell you that if that happens, whether it's a positive or negative influence, know that you will always be my friend."

Theodon kissed the back of her hand and said, "You will always be mine, too." They nodded in agreement.

Powerlessness gripped Aureon at their honest admission, but he buried it deep and neutralized his expression. At first, he had no doubt that the three of them would exit this scheme un-scathed once it was over. But after seeing the exchange of fondness between his son and Adaline, he was no longer sure.

But he knew he couldn't allow his thoughts to waver now, or this opportunity would prove unsuccessful.

"Is that all?" Adaline asked Aureon.

"No," he said as he reached for her face and cupped her features gently. He gave the soft skin of her cheekbones a reverent caress with his thumbs. She peered at him with her doe-eyed gaze as her eyes flickered with white light. Her reaction to his touch buoyed his confidence, so he lifted her face to his then kissed her. As juvenile as it seemed, he'd never forgive himself if his son got to kiss this beautiful creature before he did. Adaline's eyes fluttered closed as they both slipped into a state of bliss as their mouths melded together. Aureon's head swam at the taste of her giving lips until Theodon cleared his throat to bring them out of their heady exchange. Aureon watched Adaline, whose eyes were still closed as she savored the sensations that were taking over her rational mind. His gaze returned to her delectable mouth with his brows drawn as he attempted to navigate his passionate thoughts of her.

Before she could open her eyes, Aureon leaned in and touched his forehead to hers. His energy radiated through her, making every cell in her body tingle. The longer he lingered, the more his natural magic circulated through her. Their eyes opened on each other as they both thought, *Wow*. Adaline could hear the word in his mind and smiled. She couldn't read minds, technically, but if someone thought something passionately enough, she could sometimes hear a word or two. She smiled in relief to know he felt the same.

"It's about time that happened," Theodon muttered.

Adaline's attention snapped to Theodon, who chuckled at her response.

"From this point forward," Aureon said to Adaline, as he slowly let go of her, "this will be an indicator to you to bring up your shield for a private discussion." He tapped his temple twice. Adaline nodded. "Aside from that, we are to assume our roles starting now," he instructed, already regretting his order as he watched his remaining hand fall away from holding her face. He wasn't ready for the coldness of disconnection from her.

"Yes, Father," Theodon said.

"You may take the force field away," Aureon told Adaline.

The force field dissolved, and the three of them shifted awkwardly as their safety net was gone.

"I will see you tomorrow night," Aureon said to Theodon. Theodon nodded and turned to exit the cell as Adaline's telekinesis opened the door. "Be careful, Theodon," Aureon spoke in his mind. The prince's ear twitched before he glanced over his shoulder at his father. Wonder lit the king's face as he gazed at Adaline, who was facing Theodon. "She is easy to fall for." There was a pause between them as Theodon glanced at Adaline and smiled.

"I will not disappoint you, Father," Theodon replied telepathically as he exited the cell area.

Aureon was relieved that at least one of the three of them was utterly confident in the plan that he hatched. His focus shifted to Adaline, who observed him thoughtfully.

"To keep to the schedule you specified," Adaline said, "We must finish your healing process, now." Aureon's brow furrowed as he recalled what happened when he had first interrupted his healing process. Before he could answer, she had already sunk her glowing hand into his chest. His teeth gritted at the harsh sensation, and his body went rigid. She pulled out some of the mist that was left in his chest and flicked it away before diving her hand back in for the rest. "Almost done." A moment later, she pulled out the last of it then held his wrists as she gauged his steadiness. "The last step," she said before laying both of her palms over his chest and allowed her white light to flood his entire body. Noting that her power was absorbed at a cellular level, she watched the light traveled through his veins until his eyes lit up. Finally, she stepped back.

Aureon's eyes remained closed while he took stock in how his mind and body felt. A few deep breaths later, he stretched his arms overhead. Finally, his eyes flashed open, appearing highly defined and endless. His known powers became stronger. He examined his hands and noticed his skin radiated waves of energy. To Adaline, the waves gave off brighter colors than before. Aureon's age, known abilities, and diligent practicing of those abilities were cemented in his being at that moment, no longer in hibernation due to his grief. A wide, knowing smile stretched across his face as his confidence in his strategy solidified in his mind.

"Welcome back, Your Majesty," Adaline said with a pleased smile.

Aureon's endless gaze found her and was amazed he was now able to see the details of the energy she emanated. Adaline's aura was a bright white light, exactly as it appeared when he witnessed her healing ability. Then he noticed the shadows under her eyes. He cupped her face in his hands, worried as his thumbs swept under her eyes even as the shadows faded.

Adaline placed her hand over his. "I'm okay." He wasn't convinced, but a moment later, she finished healing before his eyes. They regarded each other until he heard her heart rate sped up, and her gaze softened on him. She rubbed her cheek against one of his hands that cupped her face and softly kissed the pad of his thumb.

"You really wanted…." Aureon realized.

Adaline nodded with a small smile. She'd made her choice, the choice to love. She was terrified to take the plunge, and she still did it.

She wants me too, he thought to himself. Adaline wasn't simply playing along. She was finally willing, and he wanted to roar with pride, but his emotions hit a wall. Aureon's shoulders fell as his new reality surfaced. He'd just handed her over to his son to marry. It was a fallacy, but it would appear authentic. And here he was, minutes after his discussion, as covetous as ever. He slowly released her, but she didn't get upset. She saddened, briefly, but then her countenance neutralized. As he noticed that, he understood how good she would be at their theatrics for the next two weeks. It made him wonder how she got so good at it. That's when it became clear to him that there was still a lot about his little human that he should make an effort to know. After all, she will become his daughter-in-law.

CHAPTER 35

Two mornings later, Aureon returned to the palace. Had anyone believed him less than a god before his return, all lingering doubt was now gone. Before his healing, his power was evident and a vaguely threatening addition to his appearance. Now, his power broadcasted the evolution of his soul. Aureon overlooked the attention when longtime servants stopped and stared upon seeing him, baffled by the change. Many of them were startled out of their staring and immediately bowed.

Aureon set to work on his plan and announced to the kingdom of his son's engagement to Dr. Adaline. After he reported the coming festivities, gifts spilled into the throne room for the betrothed couple.

Aureon remembered when his father had made the same announcement for him and Aravae. A mountain of gifts accumulated as well, and subjects would congratulate him and offer well-wishes. It was a happy time, and for the next two weeks, the engaged couple would get to enjoy it.

Then everything would change.

Would it? As doubt crept its way into his brilliant mind, Aureon replayed Adaline's response to the kiss they shared. He used it as his point of focus, his endgame. Finally tucking away thoughts of her, he returned to making all arrangements for the coming weekend, when Adaline would return. The art festival, the engagement banquet, and the Ileotil Symphony performance were all scheduled for the two days she would be in Theris. He called Ena to his study and dictated all attire Adaline would need. Options were made for Theodon as well. Aureon submerged himself in the task at hand because each time he stopped, he thought of Adaline and how she looked at him. A relieved sigh left him. *Finally.*

Aureon's stride down the long hallway mirrored the confidence he had in his plans as he headed into an elder's meeting. He successfully dodged questions about his absence for the past four days and those regarding his appearance changes. He made the official announcement to the elders about Theodon's engagement.

A few elders met him with quizzical expressions, as they were unimpressed that their king was allowing his son to marry a human. Others rejoiced and were happy for the prince and glad to see the ceremony on an accelerated schedule.

"If he's found the right one, there's no reason to wait," Flavial said to Aureon as he grasped his ruler on the shoulder. "Forb will be delighted to celebrate with Theodon." Flavial was 2,000 years older than Aureon and always meant well, so the king allowed the elder's casual touch.

"Congratulations on your growing family, My Lord," Helious, a Tearuine elder, said to the king with a tuck of his chin.

Aureon nodded in return. "I am looking forward to the happiness their union will bring to the palace and the kingdom.

"Absolutely!" Flavial cheered. "And with their love willing, they will produce a royal grandchild for you, My Lord."

All the thoughts circulating in Aureon's mind froze at Flavial's comment as he visualized Theodon holding a child in his arms and Aureon embracing them both. Aureon blinked faster once he detected his eyes watering.

"This is a happy time," Helious said, bringing Aureon out of his daydream.

Exactly as I predicted, Aureon thought as he analyzed their reactions.

For one elder present, the announcement of the prince's pending nuptials was sobering. Mouriel Olostuil was usually an indifferent elf. He saw no point in opinion regarding someone else's business, aside from the kingdom's security. This made him a bit of a wild card in the discussions that took place in the elder's meetings until he realized at that moment that his lack of action during a similar situation long ago was the wrong decision, after all.

Perhaps I should resolve my former indecision, he thought, as his heart grew heavy as he reflected on losing his youngest daughter, Sorsacha. His eyes circulated the room from one elder to another, evaluating their responses to the king's announcement. Mouriel concluded that he must have a private audience with the king to divulge what he knew, and he must gather the courage to do it soon.

CHAPTER 36

When Adaline arrived in her world, her movements were slow, and her heart was heavy. Her solemn expression lingered as she replayed all Aureon endured while he was locked away in a cell. Relief filled her lungs when she noticed clarity resurfaced in Aureon, giving him space to hatch his new plan.

The next couple of days will go well for him.

The scheme that Aureon devised was an unpredictable plot on its own, even though he didn't see it that way, and she was relieved not to have to be in Theris for most of it.

While unpacking her bag, she thought about Aureon's reaction to the final part of his healing process versus her original attempt to heal him. He maintained strength and focus both times, and even when it became difficult for him to bear the first time, he chose to save her at his own expense. *It was sweet.* She couldn't remember the last time she used the word, as her mind started to wander to the foot massage he gave her.

And his show-and-tell.

And his kiss.

Adaline found comfort in knowing there was no longer a gray area between them. Although strong attraction was clear, it would have to remain hidden for a while longer. *It's for the best.* She'd rather keep the chemistry between them at bay, for now, so they could learn about each other. And given the boundaries in store for them for the next two weekends, there was no better opportunity to explore.

After Adaline finished unpacking, she wandered out to her usual spot on her patio and folded her legs under herself. Behind closed eyes, she sank deep into the meditation that guided her to an ability-upgrade. Once Adaline received it and uploaded it into her heart, her body integrated it within minutes. Upon hearing footsteps coming up the stairway from the beach, her eyes opened to see Tessa with a ping-pong paddle in one hand. Adaline smiled at the sight of her friend.

"I didn't want to interrupt," Tessa said. "I was going to wait until you finished."

"Oh, I'm done," Adaline said. "What's going on?"

Tessa's head was canted. "What's going on? It's Thursday. Gameday. You were supposed to be our fourth player this morning, remember?" Tessa waved the paddle at her friend. Tessa, Adaline, Asher, and their friend, Scott, got together once every week to play ping-pong in Asher's game room.

"Ah." Adaline realized that she had forgotten entirely. "Yes. Give me a few minutes to change, and I'll meet you at Asher's."

Tessa noticed Adaline's eyes spiral with energy as her body integrated new abilities. "Is everything all right?"

"I'm fine," Adaline said with a convincing smile.

A moment passed before Tessa nodded in return. Before she walked back to Asher's house, she remembered something. "Oh, hey! I forgot to ask: did you ever figure out what's going on between you and that guy we talked about last time?"

Adaline chuckled. "I was given a clear indicator that he digs me, too."

"Oh, nice!" Tessa chirped. "I'm glad the truth came out. I'll see you over there. Asher and Scott are ready to play." Tessa hurried back down the steps.

Adaline thumbed through her closet for fresh clothes. She came across the tiny bikini she wore during her shenanigans in the king's pool, and she smiled. His world felt so far away right now, like a dream. She quickly changed clothes and headed to Asher's house.

"There she is!" Asher called to his twin as Adaline hurried to the far side of Asher's enormous game room. Any lingering thoughts or concerns Adaline had melted away upon hearing the playful tone of her twin. "Partner?" Asher asked his twin. He noticed the far-away look in her eyes.

"Oh, no!" Tessa said. "You two aren't allowed to be partners." The twins looked at each other with exaggerated hurtful expressions before turning back to Tessa.

"Why not?" Adaline asked.

"Because you always beat us when you team up together," Scott said before tossing a ping-pong ball at Adaline. "You're my partner, Addy. Your serve." Scott was an old friend of Asher's and a happily married one. His wife knew Asher was a big partier, and she didn't like her husband socializing with Asher in a reckless capacity. Scott had to argue that Thursday morning ping-pong was a perfectly acceptable interaction with his lively friend. So far, it was the only argument Scott won in his marriage.

As Adaline crossed to the other side of the table to be Scott's partner, she heard Asher in her mind, "You're looking a little drug-trippy this morning, sis." Adaline's eyes widened in surprise before she looked at her brother. "Did you upgrade?"

"Right before Tessa showed up," Adaline admitted.

"Ah," Asher understood. If Adaline had more time to absorb the upgrade of her abilities, she'd appear normal. "So, a lot has happened since you disappear every weekend and power through your work week like you are counting down to board the stripper flight to Vegas."

"Stripper flight? Seriously, Ash?" Adaline replied in his mind as she crooked an eyebrow at him.

"Tessa is now living with me," Asher said, avoiding her questions. He saw Adaline's eyes widen, so he continued, "in my guest room! Relax, Addy." Adaline let out a sigh before taking her serving position.

"Anything else?" Adaline asked Asher in his mind.

"The QC tried to use her and threatened her life," Asher said. "She came to the office, terrified, saying they were about to kill her because she'd only given them insignificant information due to knowing so little about us because we always act human." Adaline's eyes shifted to Tessa on the other side of the table, then back to Asher.

"She's the first," Adaline said in Asher's mind. Asher nodded as he prepared himself to receive her serve. "The first to tell us."

"Go ahead, Addy," Tessa said, encouraging her friend to start the game.

Adaline served the ball.

Tessa's confession floored Adaline. All their friends or lovers were snatched up by the QC and threatened. They were to bring back information that would help catch the Everlys, but none of them had any information to give the QC, so they all died. This new information gave Adaline hope. Maybe more friends would speak up when approached so the twins could defend them, instead of their friends ending up dead in the streets as their parents did.

CHAPTER 37

Theodon ran into Darius again on his way out of the palace. He already knew what the guard wanted. "Tell everyone lining up that Dr. Adaline will return in two days. Have them schedule only life-threatening appointments with you now, so there's no chaos in the palace when she returns."

"My Lord," Darius said, "the Allorallas-"

"Can wait," Theodon snapped.

"My Lord," Darius bowed because he knew his relentlessness might anger the prince. "She cannot."

Theodon stopped and turned back to the guard. "What do you mean?"

Darius slowly rose to his feet upon hearing the prince's annoyed tone. "My Prince," Darius stated, "Brer Alloralla visited this morning, but neither you nor your father was around. He said his wife is struggling with her pregnancy. She's carrying twins, My Lord."

The news shocked Theodon. Twins were impossible for elves to carry to term. If, by chance, the mother made it to term, the best outcome was birthing one live baby and one stillborn. As a result, such pregnancies were monitored by the king's healers because they were so rare. Even so, they always had a tragic outcome.

"How far along is she?" Theodon asked as his father joined them.

"Approximately seven months, Your Grace," Darius reported. "But she's already experiencing difficulties."

Theodon shot his father a worried glance before the king told Darius, "Tell Brer that Dr. Adaline will see his mate this weekend."

"Yes, Your Majesty," Darius said. Before the guard carried out his duty, he side-stepped and asked, "So it is true, then, Your Majesties? Your Grace is getting married?" Darius looked at Theodon for an indication of happiness, and he was convinced when the king wrapped his arm around his son. It was a sign of affection no one had ever witnessed Aureon express in public.

"Yes, he is!" Aureon said, elated. Theodon hardly bought his father's cheerfulness, but it sold Darius, whose expression matched the excitement.

"My Lord!" Darius chirped. "Congratulations! Dr. Adaline is a wonderful female."

"She certainly is," Aureon agreed.

"She has stolen my heart, I-" Theodon shot his father a look before returning to Darius, "I hardly have the words to... describe my happiness."

"Then I will move all of her appointments until well after your ceremony, except for the Alloralla's," Darius said happily. "There's no need for her to rush back to work after getting married to our prince."

"No need at all." Theodon smiled through Darius' sexist remark. That sort of thinking always bothered Theodon.

"There is much to be done," Darius said before excusing himself from the room.

The royals eyed each other before they switched to telepathy to continue their conversation.

"Enthusiasm would help, Theodon," Aureon chided.

Theodon rolled his eyes. "You overdid it! How is anyone ever that happy?"

Aureon smiled as he squeezed his son's shoulder affectionately. "When love hits you, and you want nothing more than to marry the female who has run away with your heart, there will be no faking that level of happiness. It will consume your body and soul. Her voice will bring you out of any haze, and her touch will electrify you. You will be constantly joyous and defensive. You will never want the feeling to end."

"Defensive?" Theodon questioned.

His father nodded. "You will do anything to protect her and what you have together."

Theodon imagined how his father must have been once he fell in love with his mother. The intensity of the mate bond, and the emotions tied to it, were apparent to Theodon. Or, so he thought. But he had yet to grasp its depth. Understanding it meant experiencing it, and the lack of it made Theodon sad for a moment. *Maybe this attraction to Roserie is a charade*, he thought. As much as he didn't like the thought, he tucked it away for later review.

"I understand, Father," Theodon said.

The king's eyes smiled. "You cannot. Not fully, anyway, until it happens to you. That day will be unlike any other day." The royal's gazes remained on each other as another guard approached.

"My Lord, Theodon," said the guard.

"Yes?" Theodon replied before disconnecting his attention from his father.

"Miss Roserie Aetrune is here and has requested to speak with you privately, Your Majesty," the guard informed him.

The royals shot each other a knowing look. Theodon

nodded to his father.

"Where is she?" Theodon asked the guard.

"She's waiting in the throne room. Alone, Your Majesty," the guard reported.

"Thank you," Theodon said as he headed for the throne room.

The prince's mind buzzed with anxious thoughts of how he should handle the coming conversation with Roserie. She was a female that had held his interest for some time but had never really let him near. He decided to let her lead the conversation and see where she took it, given the default of being a royal and not ever having to explain himself to anyone. The prince let out an audible exhale as he turned the corner and saw Roserie.

She stood with her back to him, with her long, wavy, strawberry-blonde hair cascading past her hipline. Theodon moved closer but was mindful to keep space between them.

"Hello, Roserie," he said in the most neutral tone he could muster. He was now discovering how difficult it was to hide feelings for her and to fake feelings for someone else. Such a facade went against his nature, but he stuck with it. She faced him with tears pooled in her reddened, amber-colored eyes. Theodon's stride slowed when he saw she was upset before he hurried to her.

"Why, Theodon?" Roserie's voice cracked. "Why?" Tears streamed down her face.

"Shh," Theodon said as he grabbed her hands and put them against his heart. As he consoled her, he noticed she was icy to the touch. He brought her against his chest, where she continued to cry for a few minutes before leaning back to look him in the eye.

"Why are you marrying her, Theodon?" Roserie pressed. "I thought we…?"

Theodon thought about the few times he caught his father looking at Adaline in such an enchanted and besotted manner that he started to smile at how beautiful it was to witness such a pure moment.

Roserie grew angry at his smiling face. "Theodon!"

"I… I," he started as he let the feeling surface. "I fell in love, Roserie." Her eyes widened as her jaw dropped, and she retreated from his embrace. That was the last answer she suspected. "I did," he said while raising his hands in surrender. He thought about the look on his father's face when he finally got to kiss Adaline and let it fuel his inspiration. "I regret none of it. She makes me happy."

"Happy? Happy!" Roserie erupted. "How can a human make an elfin prince happy?"

"Easy, Roserie," Theodon warned. "This isn't about her. It's between you and me. Or rather, whatever idea you had about you and me." An idea that became clearer each minute into the exchange.

"What's that supposed to mean?" Roserie's voice was low and vicious.

"It means we need to admit the truth, Roserie," Theodon said. "Nothing beyond friendship developed between us because you kept me at a distance for whatever reason."

"How dare you say that!" Roserie raged.

"And!" Theodon continued, "I need more than a cold distance in my partner if we are going to share our lives."

"And this human gives you that?" Roserie asked.

He thought for a moment before nodding. "Yes. And infinitely more." Theodon caught himself thinking about what he desired in a mate, and he was surprised to find that Roserie didn't fit much of the criteria. The more he thought about it, the more he wanted to put space between them because of his newfound clarity regarding his needs.

"You never truly wanted me, Roserie," Theodon said with a knowing stare. "Admit it."

"What are you saying?" Roserie acted taken aback by his

comments. Her theatrics wore thin in Theodon's eyes as his disinterest in her grew.

"What's left to say?" Theodon asked. "You've led me on for the past decade. All my advances, no matter how gentle and considerate, were rejected – some almost cruelly. And you are going to stand there and try and make me believe you truly wanted me and not the crown?" Roserie's mouth dropped in shock. She couldn't believe he was standing up for himself, let alone against her. "You are only jealous that a human played the game the right way instead of your way, and she won while you were off fornicating with other males waiting on me to elevate your title."

Roserie gasped, reached out, and slapped Theodon across the face, sending the prince's cheek jerking to one side. Theodon's kind nature evaporated as rage ignited, marked by a scathing stare. A low, vicious growl ripped from Theodon's throat, and Roserie staggered back.

"Get out," Theodon snarled low.

Roserie's turned on her heel and hurried from the throne room. When she made it to the front steps of the palace, she noticed Sorsacha was sitting on a bench carved out of the base of a tree, peeling fruit to eat with a small blade. Sorsacha noticed the flustered Roserie and asked her what had happened, even though Sorsacha overheard the exchange.

"Are you all right?" Sorsacha asked her, sounding concerned. An exaggeration on her part because the only thing the two of them genuinely shared was the same blonde, wavy hair.

"I... I," Roserie stuttered while mustering up more fake tears. "I can't believe he just growled at me and yelled at me to leave. That's not like Theodon."

"Really?" Sorsacha said in sarcasm-drenched surprise. "Let's explore this, shall we?"

SMACK!

Roserie stumbled back, holding her cheek in shock.

"How'd that feel?" Sorsacha asked with a satisfied grin.

"Why did you?" Roserie fell back a few steps. "How dare you!"

Sorsacha's eyebrows lifted as she inched toward Roserie. "The last thing you want to do right now is dare me."

Roserie scrambled away from Sorsacha and hastened toward her family's home. Sorsacha snickered at the sight of her retreat. A moment later, a powerful energy hovered behind her. She only knew of one being in the kingdom that felt borderline omnipotent.

"Sorsacha," King Aureon said from behind her.

Sorsacha turned to give the king her attention before executing a precise formal bow. "My Lord."

"Was that necessary?" the king asked.

She looked at him like his question was ridiculous and its answer obvious. "Um, Yes."

He raised a quizzical brow at her, but she held her space. "Truly?" he inquired, understanding the original action but not the amount of might behind it.

Honestly, I wanted to hit her harder, was what Sorsacha wanted to say. Instead, she offered a simple, "Yes." His eyes narrowed at her defiant tone. "I'm guessing, since Adaline wasn't around to do that, because we both know that she would have, means she's away?"

"Correct," the king annunciated precisely. He now understood why his little human was friends with Sacha. The two of them were cut from the same cloth, regarding their firm conviction and prominent personalities.

"When is she due back?"

"In two days."

"Is it true she's engaged to Theodon?"

"Yes," he exaggerated his annunciation, causing him to hiss his Ss.

Huh, Sorsacha thought to herself for a moment. "Didn't see that coming." A beat of silence passed between them before her demeanor changed to sweeter than earlier. "Would you please let her know I came by to see her once she returns, Your Majesty?"

"Yes," he said, one final time.

"Thank you," she said before turning to walk away. She spun around abruptly after a few steps. "Oh! And you're welcome," she said with a cocky grin.

Cut from the same cloth, indeed, Aureon thought.

CHAPTER 38

"So," Adaline breathed as she stood back to back with her twin, ready for another fight. It was Friday afternoon, and twenty bodies of QC agents lay scattered on the ground, all of which were either unconscious or dead.

"So," Asher said, as he relaxed his stance before scanning the area for anyone else that was inbound to their location.

"I'm engaged." Adaline dropped the bomb. Asher's eyebrows lifted. "Fake-engaged," she corrected. One of Asher's eyebrows remained arched. "It's a long story. The short version is: this fake engagement is supposed to reveal those involved in the murder of the previous queen."

"That's heavy," Asher commented. He didn't expect to hear something more dramatic than their typical day-to-day sweeping the streets of evil and saving lives in the operating room.

"Yeah, so," she continued, "I may need you to go back with me the weekend after this one."

"Bachelorette party?" he joked.

"No," she said with a chuckle, "It would look weird if I did-n't have any family there to support me at my wedding." Asher smiled at the idea. "Fake-wedding," she corrected again.

"What will we do with Tessa, Jim, and Tony?" Asher asked.

Adaline thought for a moment, then shrugged. "We'll bring them, too?"

"Whoa, whoa, whoa," Asher said. "First, Theris was this big secret. Now you're going to take us all with you?"

"It's a special occasion," Adaline argued. "Tessa would be pissed if I got married-"

"Fake-married," Asher cut in.

"Yes," Adaline continued, "and she didn't get to participate in some way. Tessa is still creepily anchored to the old ways when it comes to people pairing off for the rest of their lives."

Asher cringed at the memory. "The money dance at Scott and Ella's wedding."

"Ugh, yes!" Adaline remembered. "Remember how she got that murderous look when she tackled the bouquet?"

Asher laughed. "That was pretty funny."

Adaline glanced to her right. "Someone's here."

A slight blur rushed by Asher, whose arm shot out to snatch it up. A small body spun around Asher's arm until it slowed with Asher's help. Asher saw that it was a child, a little speedster boy.

"Hey, buddy," Asher said playfully. "What are you doing here?" The boy didn't answer and looked at the twins shyly be-fore Adaline read his soul record.

"He's been watching us because he thinks we're like him," Adaline said.

"You're like us?" Asher said to the boy, who still didn't answer.

Adaline read why then faced the boy so he could see both of her hands. She signed, "What's your name?"

A moment passed before the boy signed back, "Tobey."

Adaline signed, "Hi, Tobey. I'm Adaline." She pointed to her twin.

"This is Asher. Are you like us?"

Tobey signed, "Yes."

Adaline signed, "Can you show us?"

Tobey nodded, and Asher set him on the ground. The little boy ran circles around Asher until his form faded into a blur and the air smelled of burned rubber from his little sneakers rubbing fast against the pavement.

"Whoa!" Asher said. "Slow down, Tobey."

Tobey responded to Asher's command and stopped. Tobey smiled because he got the chance to show off to the twins. He'd wanted to do that for weeks. Adaline concluded the boy could hear and speak, but he chose not to speak.

Adaline signed to the boy, "Where are your parents?" The boy's face fell. He stared at his feet for a minute while Adaline searched his soul record and saw his parents. She kneeled to be at eye level with Tobey. "Tobey, would you like to come home with us?"

"Wait, what?" Asher asked in surprise. He was starting to collect extra people in his home like stray cats. Tobey smiled and nodded.

"Okay, take my hand." The little boy put his hand in hers before Adaline faced Asher. She smiled wide.

"What are you doing?" Asher said in her head.

"His parents were murdered in front of him, Ash," Adaline replied. "He doesn't have someone else to depend on like we did."

Not this shit again, Asher thought with a defeated sigh. He couldn't argue with Tobey's situation. However, they both had to figure out their next steps in caring for Tessa and now Tobey. Asher touched his sister's shoulder, who teleported them to her house.

"We need to discuss our endgame," Asher said to her as he took off his gloves and set them on the kitchen counter.

Adaline nodded. "Tonight?"

"I have that party tonight at my house."

Ah, yes, Adaline thought. "How about when I return from Theris after this weekend?"

"That works," Asher said. "How are we going to watch both Tessa and Tobey?"

"Easy," Adaline said, "Tessa will watch Tobey. Jim and Tony will watch Tessa. We will watch Jim and Tony." Adaline's hand was on the boy's shoulder as she winked at him. Tobey smiled.

"He can stay overnight with me since you're gone on the weekends," Asher said. "I have more rooms than I know what to do with."

"There are no truer words, Ash," Adaline said with a smile.

Hours later, Adaline walked into Asher's house before sunset. Hovering robotic caterers rushed around to finish setting up for Asher's party that started in an hour. Asher took all the precautions when it came to allowing strangers in his home. All staff must be robotic. The only humans allowed over the threshold were friends. Adaline had no problem admitting that her brother loved to party. Even though they were always supposed to maintain a low profile, he loved it so much that he would host but outsource all the hard work it took to prepare for a party. She passed no judgment, as she found his habit amusing. She knew he deserved to have a fun night occasionally because he worked harder at their surgical practice than she did. He was the faster of the two of them and always took on more patients. Most patients she took on were the ones who seldom needed to be near a scalpel.

Adaline wandered into Asher's master suite and found her twin flipping through his v-neck sweater options. He saw her reflection in the mirror and turned to her. Tobey was zooming around the room, hopefully burning his restless energy so he would fall asleep soon.

"Hey," Asher said, as he leaned over to plant a kiss on her cheek, "you look nice."

"Thank you," she said with a smile. She surveyed the sweaters laid out on the bed before choosing. "This one."

"Thank you," he said. "You know I take forever deciding on the right color."

"Well, if the sweater were a sports car, you would be impressively decisive," Adaline jested.

"Black on black," he said without hesitation while he pulled on the sweater. "There's no other choice." Adaline chuckled. Asher took a moment to observe his twin in the mirror's reflection before saying, "Are you feeling better about this weekend?" Her expression changed to contemplative as his question threw her. "I noticed you'd been lost in your thoughts since you got back," he admitted. "I know you aren't ill because that's impossible...."

Adaline chuckled. "Mulling over a matter of the heart, I guess."

"About the king who digs you? And how Tessa is going to be mad because she doesn't know every detail about him yet?" Asher asked.

Adaline smirked. "The former."

"What's your concern?" Asher asked as he tugged at the cuffs on his sweater. Tobey zoomed by, and Asher caught him, only to playfully toss him on the bed. The little boy squealed with laughter.

"I was fearful about admitting any feelings for the king to myself," Adaline said. "Because of experience and all." Asher nodded while he listened. "And now that I've finally admitted it to myself, and the opportunity was about to present itself for this to be something we could explore, this scheme happens, and I can't say no to it. It's too significant of a damn-near guaranteed win to pass up."

"So, you're frustrated that you got a taste of the good things to come between the two of you, then had to shelve it soon after," Asher reiterated.

"Yes," Adaline said. "I've never met a potential partner who is powerful like me, who I don't need to worry about the QC killing, and who likes me for all that he's seen me do outside of being a regular human."

A smile grew on Asher's face. "You really like him."

Her brow furrowed. "Yes." The feeling was foreign to her. "Now that I have to continue with clinical detachment around him," Adaline said, "it makes for the ideal opportunity to discuss our endgame options with him."

"Moving off-world," Asher concluded.

"Yes," Adaline confirmed. "Considering what's happened with Tessa and Tony, I think we should move them off-world before we carry out our purpose. It would give them time to be established there, and-"

"They would no longer be a liability for the QC to target," Asher finished her sentence. The twins stared at each other.

"Our friends don't have to die because of us anymore," Adaline said hopefully. Asher nodded. "I will begin the conversation with the king, now, to understand parameters so we can plan their exit before ours."

"I agree," said Asher.

"And if we don't survive, they will have a chance at a happy fifty to one hundred and fifty years in a peaceful place before they pass on," Adaline concluded. The twin's chins dropped for a quiet moment as they gathered themselves. Their glassy gazes finally met, and they managed to nod at each other while blinking back tears. Tobey was zooming around the room again, knocking the twins from their emotional exchange. It was also time for the twins to go out into the living area to greet guests arriving soon. Asher caught the Tobey mid-dash and set him on his feet. Adaline reached out her hand to Tobey. He automatically slid his hand into hers, and Adaline led him down to one of the guest rooms that Asher had organized for him.

"Have you brushed your teeth?" Adaline asked Tobey.

The boy nodded as he watched Adaline turn down the bed for him. He was mesmerized by her because she looked like an angel. He could see waves of white light ripple off her when she made sudden movements.

"Time for bed," she said to him as she held open the covers. He hurried over and crawled under the blankets. Adaline pulled them up to his shoulders. "Are you warm enough?" she asked. He nodded. "Okay, I'm going to be downstairs with Asher," Adaline explained. "He's having a party for grown-ups. If you want to get up and play in your room, you can do that, but try to fall asleep, okay? You're safe, and one of us will always be around to protect you." Tobey nodded. "Okay," she said before playfully mussing up his hair. "Sweet dreams, Tobey."

Time flew by, and Asher's beach house filled with friends, colleagues, and celebrities who stayed until the late hours of the night. Trays handled by white-gloved robotic hands floated by regularly, conversation among everyone was thick, and laughter filled the room with music playing in the background.

"Hey, Addy," Tessa said while tapping her friend's shoulder. "Who's the hunk with the long black hair?" Adaline's eyes widened in surprise as she only knew two males that possessed that striking feature. She turned to see Theodon standing among the crowd of guests, curiously observing the human festivities. Their eyes met. A smile stretched across his lips, and he nodded in her direction.

"You know that guy?" Tessa asked.

"Yes. Excuse me for a moment." Adaline shrugged away from her friend. She dodged through the crowd of people before she ended up standing in front of the prince. She smiled. "Hey, Theo."

"Hello," Theodon said before glancing around again. "Is this how humans celebrate?"

"It is," Adaline confirmed as her attention landed on his loose hair that masked his pointed ears, and a sigh of relief left her as she was unprepared if people started asking questions. What fortified her resolve was the fact everyone at the party was drunk. So, Theodon may go entirely unnoticed.

"Theodon!" Asher shouted as he made his way across the room. The two males embraced each other and slapped each other on the back in welcome.

"Wait," Adaline said, stunned, "you two know each other?"

"Yes," Asher said while pointing at the prince. "He's going to be your fake-fiancé, right?"

"Yes," Adaline quietly confirmed as they discussed elves around a bunch of drunken humans.

"Wait, she gets to call you Theo?" Asher asked Theodon, now that his buzz was beginning to show.

"Yes," the prince confirmed, eyeing her knowingly.

"So, the ice king's plot begins today, huh?" Asher blurted before he said to Theodon, "No offense." Adaline's eyes narrowed at Asher.

"Not at all," Theodon said to Asher. "Actually," Theodon eyed Adaline as he told them both, "he's quite different now." Theodon was impressed with his father's recovery but knew the king needed something else to help the process. The king needed his little human nearby, even if she was fake-engaged to the prince. Of course, the king didn't know what he needed yet, but it was apparent to his son. So here Theodon was retrieving her in her wasteland of a human world.

Asher's hand was on the prince's shoulder. "So, are you here to party with us, buddy?"

Theodon's gaze bore through Adaline. "I'm not here to indulge, but to take Dr. Adaline back to Theris with me, tonight." Goosebumps traveled over her skin at the exciting notion of seeing the king. Her thoughts snapped back to reality, and she noticed the prince smiling at her. Adaline's cheeks flushed, and she looked away.

"Well, you heard Theodon, sis. Prince's orders," Asher exaggerated.

All Adaline could bring herself to do was nod and spin on her heel to leave Asher's house for her own, with the prince following her. When they arrived at her home, Theodon slowly stepped inside and took his time noticing the details of her home.

"You live in this large house all by yourself?" Theodon asked her as he browsed.

Adaline chuckled. "I could ask you the same question about the palace."

A fair point, he thought; however, he had his father there, too. Until recently, the palace in Ividia didn't provide a feeling of refuge, or home, to Theodon. It was simply where his rank required him to live. Now, Theodon was very aware that he shared the palace with his father, whose emotional state had been a roller coaster ride – up until the minute he stepped through the portal to retrieve Adaline. All the pain his father experienced seemed to have subsided, and his father was livelier than ever.

That morning, Theodon decided, without inquiring about his father's wishes, that he would retrieve Adaline and bring her back to Ividia that evening instead of returning the following morning. Theodon was happy to hand the reins back over to his father to rule Theris and would admit without hesitation that he was not yet comfortable making decisions for the kingdom.

Earlier that evening, Theodon stepped through the portal and landed in the sand under Adaline's beach-bound staircase. The soft impact made him chuckle. He leaped from Adaline's large balcony over to Asher's driveway in a single bound because time was short. His father needed him back at the palace immediately, but Theodon required emotional reinforcements and support. He hoped to share that responsibility with Adaline from now on. He watched Adaline buzz around her house nervously as she asked questions to help her narrow what to pack in her small bag.

"How is he?" she asked.

"He's the strongest I've ever seen him," Theodon admitted. "He radiates a substantial amount of energy."

"More than before?" He nodded. "Do you see the colors?"

"The colors?"

"You see the waves of energy that ripple off him. I also see the colors in each ripple," Adaline revealed. Theodon's eyebrows lifted. "It's stunning." Theodon smiled at the wondrous tone in her voice. "Is he planning the wedding of the century?"

Theodon chuckled. "Of the millennium."

"That's better than him tearing the palace apart," Adaline admitted.

Theodon smiled. "I agree."

Adaline changed into casual clothes, grabbed her bag, and headed to the staircase that descended from her large patio with Theodon.

Theodon noticed the look in her eyes. "Don't be nervous."

"What would you suggest I be, Theo?"

"Prepared for anything," Theodon stated. He straightened his shoulders before holding his hand out to her so that she could step through the portal first.

CHAPTER 39

As Theodon walked alongside Adaline on their way to the palace, he failed to stifle a smile at her reaction. Adaline gawked at the endless greenery of Theris, now thickly layered with vibrant blooms! Flowers flourished all around them, and some buds were as big as beach balls.

Adaline tapped Theodon on the shoulder because she could only find one word at first. "Theo."

The prince's smile warmed. "Yes, Dr. Adaline?"

Adaline pointed at the flowers. "When did this…?"

"This," he gestured at the lush landscape with a turn, "happened over the past two days."

Adaline's eyes widened as her words remained elusive. She faced him and stopped. "Theo…"

Theodon laughed. "Yes, Dr. Adaline?"

"This is…" while her words escaped, Theodon waited. "Extraordinary." Adaline finally exhaled. She was difficult to impress, but this change was truly breathtaking. "Then it's true. Your father has a direct connection to the natural world."

Theodon nodded with a close-lipped smile. A faint blur tried to zoom past them, but Theodon's reflexes were faster. He grabbed whoever was trying to race by him.

"Tobey!" Adaline shouted as Theodon's swift reaction to catching Tobey paired with the boy's speed resulted in him orbiting the prince's arm until he lost momentum, leaving him hanging upside down. Tobey's expression was equally as excited as Adaline's until her eyes narrowed. "You are supposed to be asleep."

Tobey signed, "I couldn't sleep, so I tried to find you."

Adaline sighed before she signed back, "You are safer at Asher's house while I am gone. You need to go back and stay with him."

Tobey's lip quivered before he signed, "But I want to stay with you."

"Who is this?" Theodon finally asked.

"This is Tobey," Adaline told him. "He came to live with Asher and me earlier today, and he snuck out of the house to follow me."

"And he doesn't talk," Theodon observed.

"Correct," Adaline said before asking Theodon, "Would it be all right if he came along? He'd stay in my suite with me."

"That would be fine," Theodon smiled at the boy, who smiled back before he set Tobey on his feet.

Adaline knelt to be eye level with Tobey as she signed, "This is Theodon. He's a friend and safe to be around. Do you understand?" Tobey was still staring up at Theodon, wondering why he had pointed ears. "Tobey," Adaline said aloud to get the boy's attention.

Tobey's eyes snapped back to Adaline before he signed, "I understand. He is a friend."

Adaline nodded before signing, "We will be spending time with Theodon and his father for the next two days, so I need you to stay close, all right?" Tobey nodded. "Okay," Adaline said as she stood. "Give me your hand."

Tobey slid his hand into Adaline's without hesitation.

Theodon offered his elbow to Adaline and asked, "Are you ready?"

"Yes," she said, taking his arm without turning her focus away from the landscape for a few more minutes. The three of them finally turned the corner in front of the palace and walked through the front entrance.

"Understand that this weekend may not be the poolside fun of last weekend," Theodon said to her.

"Oh, I dismissed that possibility days ago," she admitted.

Theodon nodded in agreement knowing the decision was best for all involved. "Considering the events you must endure this weekend," Theodon said, "you will come into contact with elders, all of whom are from noble houses, as well as their descendants. Many of which possess the gift of being condescending while still managing to sound polite."

"Yay! Can't wait!" Adaline pumped her fist in the air, and Theodon chuckled. "Thanks for the warning."

"You are most welcome," Theodon said. "My father will want to see you immediately."

"That reminds me, I have something to discuss with him when he's available to speak," she admitted.

"I am available, now, Dr. Adaline," King Aureon's voice boomed from the throne room as Theodon and Adaline entered with Tobey in tow.

Adaline straightened upon facing Aureon. She couldn't stifle a smile as she recognized more physical changes in him since a few days ago. His green eyes were brighter still, while the whites of his eyes were stark white instead of foggy gray. His authoritative stance made him appear taller. He still possessed his penetrating gaze, but it was no longer a cold stare but a keen awareness. Adaline could feel his emotions, something his energy broadcasted without defense. She sympathized with his high awareness of her and his uncertainty about interacting with her. He was attracted to her and alarmed by that truth. As rooted as he was in his decision-making, he felt ungrounded in his freshly healed form and needed something to tether himself to as he found his way. Adaline knew it was what emotionally drained Theodon while she was on Earth. Now, she must take her turn in playing anchor for Aureon.

The three of them approached the king, who stood with both hands tucked behind his back. The king's eyes narrowed on Tobey, his mind deliberating the possible connection he had to Adaline, who'd never mentioned having a son. The boy stared back at the king in consuming awe.

"Who is this?" Aureon asked as his countenance remained neutral.

"This," Adaline said, before looking down at the boy, "is Tobey. He's my new friend who is under my protection." Aureon's eyebrow lifted. Once again, Adaline became more interesting the longer he knew her.

"And why does he need your protection?" Aureon asked.

"Because he's special." Adaline peered at Tobey and smiled, who smiled back. "He followed me instead of staying home. Is it all right if he stays?"

"Yes." The king gauged the boy for signs of troublemaking. *How much chaos can one tiny human boy create?*

"Thank you," Adaline said to him before kneeling to sign to Tobey. "This is Aureon. He is Theodon's father. He is safe to be around while you are here. If you and I get separated, stay with one of them until you find me. Understand?"

Tobey signed, "I understand." He stared at Aureon and signed to Adaline again.

She giggled. "I can see the colors too. Isn't it neat?" The boy nodded.

"I only see the energy waves," Theodon muttered.

"You're missing out," Adaline joked, then leaned over to put her hand to Theodon's temple. She showed him her recent memory of the king's energy flow ten seconds prior.

"Wow," Theodon commented before Adaline let her hand

drop. Theodon searched his father's appearance, who shifted in discomfort for being scrutinized.

"I will have clothes delivered to your suite for the boy," the king said, refocusing the conversation.

"Thank you," she said before turning to Theodon. "Would you mind taking him to get some food while I speak to your father?"

"Of course," Theodon said as he reached out his hand for Tobey's. Tobey hesitated for a second before he glanced at Adaline for a clue.

She signed, "I'll see you after you eat."

Tobey nodded and went with Theodon. Once they were alone, Adaline brought up her force field around her and Aureon.

"Are you well?" the king asked as he inspected her appearance. He noticed her shoulders were tense.

Adaline chuckled. "You're asking me?" He still waited for an answer. "I have a lot going on right now," she admitted. "And I need to speak with you about something important."

"Go on." He gestured to the balcony off the throne room, and she followed. He hovered on his feet, waiting for her to sit before he took a seat across from her.

"My world will come to an end in thirty-seven years or less," she stated plainly.

"What makes you certain?" The last humans who visited Theris in 1999 CE thought their world was going to end, too.

"Because my brother and I are supposed to end it," Adaline admitted. The king's eyes blinked wide as if she had spontaneously grown an extra head. "Asher and I are the diviners," Adaline explained. "Our coming was prophesized centuries ago. Our purpose is to sweep the earth of evil before ending it."

"When is that?" the king asked.

"Soon," Adaline said. "With what Asher and I continue to encounter, I think the process will start earlier than we originally expected." The king nodded as she shared, not surprised that Adaline and her brother possessed the power to end their world but alarmed that she was chosen for the task.

"Continue," he encouraged.

"Asher and I have been talking about our plans for after we finish," Adaline said. "We were wondering if it would be all right with you if we came to live in Theris with Tony, Jim, Tobey, and our friend, Tessa."

The king's brow arched. "You would take them away from their fate?"

"Fate has a way of rearranging itself when choice becomes a variable," Adaline stated. "When the time comes, I will tell them their options. I'll honor their decisions. As for Asher and myself, we have had a hard life while waiting to do our job and deserve-"

"Freedom." The king understood. He noticed Adaline felt that way while in Theris because she seemed to relax when away from Earth.

"Yes."

"Do you wish to establish a human colony?" the king asked with his tone still neutral, even though this conversation was amusing to him. He would undoubtedly let her live in Theris. He hoped she would live even closer still.

"Hmm," she thought aloud. "That's more your decision than mine. Asher and I are the only humans who know about this conversation happening. Even so, I suspect it's better for us to assimilate than to separate ourselves from Theris."

Intelligent human, he thought. The humans would incur hardship as a species if they tried to settle outside of the border.

"So, I wanted to pose this scenario to you, now, to allow you sufficient time to think about it," she said. "And so Asher and I can plan the rest of our lives."

Her statement was sobering to him—*the rest of our lives.*

In one scenario, it could turn out to be the end of her life.

That will not do, he thought. "Will you miss your home?"

Adaline considered his question while pursing her lips to

one side before shaking her head. "We were never able to live real lives in a world that was already desolate. And Asher and I learned a long time ago that home isn't a place."

He nodded in understanding. "How much time do I have to make a decision, Dr. Adaline?"

Adaline casually flipped her hair off her shoulder as she thought for a moment. The gesture stirred up her enticing scent. His expression neutralized as he inhaled deeply, savoring the fragrance that matched her enticing form. He savored the moment, knowing it was the most he'd get to enjoy of her for the next two weeks.

"Would one week be sufficient?" she asked. She would like to offer more time, but her world was becoming more violent, and she knew she'd have to move her friends soon or else risk losing them.

"Yes," he replied. *More than sufficient.*

"Thank you," she said, then her gaze turned thoughtful.

"For?"

"Considering it."

He waved off her praise as the conversation ended. Their gazes settled on each other as they enjoyed the silence between them, reveling in each other's presence. It was soothing and exciting at the same time. Sadly, further exploration of it had to be set aside for now.

"I must inform you that you have a new patient," the king finally said to her. She kept quiet while he shared. "Farryn's mother is pregnant with twins. It is dangerous for our females to endure anything but a single birth if they live through it." Adaline was intrigued. "Elfin females cannot carry twins to term," the king explained. "It is rare for it to happen, and if it does, one baby might be born alive, but never both." Adaline winced as she processed that tragic statement. "She is approximately seven months along and is already having difficulties."

"Already?" Adaline asked.

"Yes," the king stated. "An elf's gestation period lasts approximately twenty-two months, so to have complications this early is alarming."

Adaline's eyebrows lifted. Her clinical brain raced with details and ideas. *That means that she got pregnant, again, approximately thirteen months after Farryn was born*, she thought.

"It takes time to make an immortal," the king said.

"No kidding," Adaline said as she hopped to her feet. "Picture her," she commanded and reached for his hand. Aureon didn't hesitate to do as she instructed. The second their hands touched, they teleported to the front entrance of the Alloralla's home. Adaline's eyed Aureon as she raised her knuckles to knock on the front door, but it swung open. An exhausted Brer Alloralla opened the door. Adaline sympathized with the elf's struggle to maintain his resolve as weariness etched into his features. She understood how draining complicated pregnancies could be for both partners. And yet, he still took a moment to address the king formally. Afterward, he waved Adaline inside.

Aureon followed close and almost collided with her when Brer asked them to wait in the hallway while he helped his wife gather herself for company. Aureon's body thrummed in anticipation, hungry to touch her since he first laid eyes on her that evening. His fingertips landed tentatively on Adaline's upper arms, and she tensed for a moment. She wasn't used to being touched, even though it was the form of affection she needed most. She relaxed, prompting him to slid his hands up to her shoulders as he remembered the stress she was carrying. He kneaded her muscles. A faint whimper left her throat as her head fell forward in surrender.

"This is where you carry stress?" he whispered.

She lifted her head back until she looked straight up at him and nodded. White light flickered in her eyes, and he bent down and planted a kiss on her forehead. His ear twitched when he noticed her heartbeat quicken and her gaze hooded.

The door of the Alloralla's bedroom opened, and Brer poked his head into the hallway and waved them inside. The king's hands slid from her shoulders and down her back, steadying her before relinquishing contact. Adaline eased into the room to find a miserable Mrs. Alloralla doing her best to sit up in bed.

"Easy," Adaline said as she put up her hands to signal her to stop moving while rushing to her side. "Stay in a comfortable position. Don't worry about keeping up appearances." A winded Mrs. Alloralla could only nod. Every slight movement the mother made caused significant stress to her body. *Yeesh*, Adaline thought. The king wasn't exaggerating at the inability of elves to carry twins to term.

"Were you trying to fall asleep?" Adaline asked her.

The mother nodded before huffing out, "Yes."

Adaline turned to the males in the room and donned her best smile. "I need you both to step outside, please." Brer looked at the king for direction, who gave a stiff nod to Adaline's orders before leaving the room. Brer followed Aureon and the door closed behind them. Adaline faced Mrs. Alloralla.

"Let's get started," she said to the struggling mother as she neared her bedside. "I'm going to help you fall asleep, all right?"

"All right," the mother said, unaware of how that could happen since she'd been failing at it for weeks.

Adaline pointed. "Is that position comfortable for you?"

"No."

"Okay, I'm going to help you scoot down and turn you onto your side," Adaline told her. "But I need to make something, first." She looked around the room and didn't see what she needed. "Where can I find three extra pillows and an extra bed sheet?"

"In the hallway," the mother said. "Brer will get it."

"Great," Adaline said as she opened the bedroom door and poked her head into the hallway. Brer already had what she needed and handed it to her.

"See, had I never been to Theris before, I'd swear you were

a mind reader." Adaline smiled and winked at Brer before closing the door on him.

"One moment while I make something," Adaline said to Mrs. Alloralla.

"Okay," Mrs. Alloralla replied.

Adaline attempted conversation to get the mother's mind off the task at hand. "How is little Farryn doing?"

"She's livelier than ever, thanks to you."

"Oh, good, I'm glad to hear that." Adaline quickly finished her project, managing to jury-rig a body pillow to support Mrs. Alloralla's ample belly. "Now, Mrs. Alloralla."

"Sana," the mother corrected.

"Sana," Adaline said with a smile, "I'm going to reset you into a comfortable position. You are not to exert yourself in any way as I work on you, all right?" Sana had no idea what that meant. She just nodded. She'd consent to anything to no longer be uncomfortable and exhausted. "Okay." Adaline exhaled as she turned her hand palm up and made a lifting gesture. Sana's body slowly lifted off the bed. The mother's eyes widened with shock. "I've got you." Adaline smiled. "Don't worry. I've never dropped anyone."

Adaline's latter statement didn't calm Sana. The mother remained tense for the first few minutes before she understood that this was a regular practice for Dr. Adaline. Finally, she started to trust and relax. She watched Dr. Adaline rearrange the bed underneath her and placed the new pillow vertically toward the middle of the bed.

"All right, Sana," Adaline prompted, "I'm going to rotate you and set you down slowly."

"Okay," Sana nodded, anticipating relief.

Adaline lowered Sana onto her back, focusing on making her belly weightless, taking the weight off her spine. Adaline rotated Sana to face the middle of the bed then lowered her onto her right side. Adaline made sure to set Sana's large belly on the body pillow before releasing her hold. Once nestled on her side, Adaline moved around to wrap Sana's outside leg on the body pillow to stack her hips while she slept. She heard Sana sigh.

"Better?" Adaline asked.

"Much better," Sana whimpered in relief.

"Almost done," Adaline informed her as she moved to Sana's back and placed her hand on her belly. Adaline scanned the babies and drew a few conclusions. One is that Sana could bring both babies to term. She wasn't going to state that because she didn't know all the details about the process and biology of pregnant elves. Still, she knew there was a good chance, especially if either she, or Asher, were around to help monitor her progress and delivery.

"Okay, Sana, let me tell you what's going on," Adaline said. "Both babies are alive. The boy is a bit weaker than the girl, so I'm going to speak with your husband on how he will help you get stronger, so your boy has a better chance."

"A boy and a girl?" Sana said with her eyes filling with tears.

"Yes," Adaline said with a smile, "You have one of each. And we are going to try to get them both to term. To do this, I need you to eat every plate of food that is put in front of you until you go into labor, all right?" Sana nodded as a tear of joy slid down her cheek. "I need you to use most of the time in your day to rest and eat," Adaline told her. "I will visit each week to reset your energy levels and to monitor the babies until it's time for you to deliver."

Sana nodded again before whispering, "Thank you."

"Oh, I'm not done yet." Adaline grinned before her hands glowed before placing one on Sana's belly and the other on her back. "This might feel funny." The light poured into Sana's body. Her twins moved at the surprise.

"I can feel them!" Sana cried happily. "I can feel both of them."

Adaline focused on directing the light to burn away the

stress in Sana's lower back and allowed it to travel up her spine into her shoulders before it reached her brain. Her body went lax, and the babies settled. Sana sank into a deep sleep, and Adaline grabbed the sheet at the end of the bed and tucked it over her. Adaline released a satisfied sigh and quietly opened the bedroom door. She held her finger to her lips to warn both males standing in the hallway. The king stepped away from leaning against the wall as Brer paced until he saw Adaline come out of the room. He rushed to her.

"Mr. Alloralla," she whispered to him.

"Brer," he said.

"Brer," Adaline kept her voice low, "your wife is in a deep sleep. I suggest we allow her to rest while you show me your kitchen."

Brer thought her statement was odd, but he humored her. He led the doctor and the king to the kitchen at the far end of the hall. Adaline glanced around and helped herself to check the contents of all the cupboards. She found meats, vegetables, fruits, rice, and other fresh foods. After a few minutes of building a strategy, she faced Brer. "I have instructions for you. It would be a good idea to write them down." Brer rushed to a nearby drawer, grabbed writing tools, and sat down at the kitchen table, awaiting instructions. The king settled to standing in the far corner, watching them both intently. "All right," Adaline began as she assembled a large portion of a mock dinner in front of Brer on the kitchen table. "This is the amount of food your wife needs to consume at every meal." Brer's eyebrows lifted in surprise at the amount of food in front of him. "And her meals need to be every three hours during the daytime."

Brer's face fell into his hands. "That's so much."

"She's carrying two babies, and their development is sucking the life out of her," Adaline said bluntly. "She needs to consume more whole foods." She turned to point at the drying meats. "She can't eat the two types of meat on the left. The one on the right is okay, and no fish."

Brer hurried to write down all the information. She gave him time to catch up as she paced in the kitchen to gather the rest of her thoughts regarding Sana's care. "She needs to eat mostly the fruits, nuts, vegetables, and whole grains," Adaline sounded off before addressing Aureon. "Can he reach you, telepathically, if something happens with her?"

Aureon enjoyed that she wandered close to him when she asked the question and took a moment before replying, "Yes." Aureon's gaze shifted to Brer, who understood its privilege to be allowed to contact the king directly.

"Great, thank you," she said, before spinning on her heel to face Brer, again. "Should she struggle like she did when we first got here, or should she get worse, contact him so I can get to her immediately."

"Yes, of course," Brer said, as he scribbled more notes before nodding at Aureon. "Thank you, Your Majesty."

Aureon briefly tucked his chin in reply without a word. The king's neutral countenance didn't give away that he enjoyed tagging along on Adaline's medical adventures, first with Nÿla, now with Sana's twins. He enjoyed watching her succeed as she fearlessly responded to challenging situations. Adaline was intelligent, giving when it came to her power, and no-nonsense about the drama of the situation she entered as if it were just another day. Aureon enjoyed witnessing it, and even more so when he got to play a part in it.

Adaline gauged from the Alloralla's home that they appeared to be a steady, middle-class family. Going through that much food every few hours would probably wear thin on their funds. And Brer likely had a job to keep. Adaline turned to face Aureon, again, with her hands crossed over her chest as she looked at him intently.

"Brer, will it be difficult to maintain this care for Sana until she goes into labor?" Adaline asked.

Brer sighed in defeat before he finally admitted, "It will be a challenge."

Adaline's head tilted as she continued to stare at Aureon.

"I will take care of it," the king said from his corner.

The stress released from Brer's chest as tears fell from the corners of his eyes. The exhausted father was grateful beyond measure, and up until that moment, he had no idea how to help his wife. He was living in fear that he might lose Sana and the babies in this risky process. Adaline walked over and rested her hand on his shoulder.

"Finish your notes," Adaline instructed. "Then I'm going to help you fall asleep."

Minutes later, Adaline followed Brer back to their bedroom while Aureon remained posted in the doorway. Brer was amazed at how his wife seemed to be sleeping peacefully.

"Go ahead," Adaline whispered.

Brer kept his eyes on his wife, causing his demeanor to soften as he quickly removed his shoes. He pulled back the sheets on his side of the bed and scooted under the covers before he softly enveloped his wife's extended hand in his own.

Aw, Adaline thought at his tender gesture. She moved closer before she whispered, "Close your eyes."

Brer did as instructed then he felt her hand on his head, growing warm and tingly. Finally, his body purged his stress before his limbs went lax, and he sank into a restful oblivion. He gave off a quiet snore. Adaline smiled and pulled the covers a little higher over him. She walked over to Aureon, who already had his hand extended for hers. She noticed her relief in what it symbolized: going home.

A moment later, they were back on the balcony off the throne room. Adaline's shoulders sank as Aureon observed her closely. She needed more time for self-care, but with everything she was handling, there wasn't much space in her life to do that right now. He decided to make it mandatory for her, knowing just what to plan. He'd have to be strategic about it and make sure she wouldn't be bothered by anyone.

"I should check on Tobey," Adaline said before stepping away from him. He immediately moved with her, not wanting her to leave yet, but understanding her priorities.

"Is there anything else the boy needs?" he asked.

"A change of clothes or two should be enough," she said. "Whatever Tobey needs so he can come along with me tomorrow and the day after that."

"What makes him so special?" the king asked as he lost focus in her dark eyes.

A mischievous grin spread across Adaline's face. "You'll see." There was a pause between them. "Have a good night, Your Majesty."

"Sweet dreams, Dr. Adaline," he returned. She winked at him before turning on her heel and heading to the kitchen to retrieve Tobey for bedtime.

Ena set up a small bed in Adaline's suite for Tobey. It was surprisingly easy to get the boy into bed and to sleep. Adaline suspected it had something to do with being satisfied that he was in an exciting new world, far from the danger he knew. Adaline finally slipped under the covers of her bed and found her focus lost in the details of the intricately carved ceiling. She pondered how she had to act over the next two days – In young love.

Eh, she thought. She wasn't a young human anymore. Young love was so fleeting, as did anything else that existed in her world. Women were coveted on Earth because they were scarce, and the men who knew them protected them at all costs. Because of all the turmoil in the world, very few women wanted to have families, given the expiration date of the planet. Therefore, it was infrequent for Adaline to see a pregnant woman even in her practice. Those who did choose to have families went through a different kind of mate selection process. Women searched for men who could physically protect them and their children, and provide food and shelter, versus choosing a mate who made them laugh or had a flashy corporate job. Hence, performing as a doe-eyed, love-struck female for the next two weekends was a stretch for Adaline.

What could help me hone this? Adaline wondered, then smiled as she concluded that the answer wasn't what but who. She closed her eyes, thought of Aureon, and stepped into his dream. Before the scene could come into focus, his voice reached her.

"You are late," Aureon chided.

"Am I?" she asked as the scene materialized. She glanced around but didn't see Aureon yet. Her attention returned to the patio view that sprawled out onto a secluded beach. She didn't hesitate to hop over the railing of the patio before running for the shoreline. The sand was cool under her feet as she sped toward the water. She slowed as she discovered a spot that granted a premium view of the sunset, bent her knees, plopped back on the sand, and let out a huff on impact.

Staring off into a sunset of colors she'd never seen on Earth, she cuffed the hem of her pants to her calves. She stared in awe at the midnight-blue waves crashing on the shore, making purple foam on impact. The bold colors that animated the paradise around her had no end to their splendor. The water possessed an original, energetic sound as the waves pulled away from shore and rolled back. It compelled her to connect to it.

She sat up straight, folded her legs under her, rested her palms face up on her thighs, took a deep breath, and closed her eyes. With each crash of the waves, the vibration given off by the element passed through Adaline's body, refreshing her senses before exiting her cells. She let out an open-mouthed exhale. She'd never managed to recharge by connecting with nature on Earth. As she allowed the vibrations of the water to cleanse her aura, Aureon's energy enveloped her in his warmth as he moved closer. The familiarity of their auras sizzling as they overlapped calmed her further. A moment later, his chest pressed against her back, and his bent knees caged in her folded legs. She felt his breath on the back of her neck as his hand swept her hair over one shoulder. Her skin broke out in goosebumps as her eyes opened.

"Dr. Adaline," he whispered.

She shivered. "Your Majesty."

"You should be resting," he said as he buried his nose in her hair and inhaled deeply. "You have a busy weekend ahead of you." His affectionate actions implored her to remain with him while his words spoke sound logic.

"I could say the same to you," she said as his bottom lip brushed against the shell of her ear. Her eyes slid closed as she savored the contact. Adaline turned her cheek toward him and was met by him rubbing his against hers. He inhaled her scent where her jaw met her neck and nuzzled her skin down to her clavicle.

"I need minimal sleep," he confessed before he planted a hot kiss on the curve of her neck. He clutched her waist with both hands and pulled her back against his chest. His brows drew tight in concern when he noticed her wince. "You are hurting." His hands trailed up her arms to her shoulders, just as he had at the Alloralla's. He kneaded her shoulder muscles.

"It's a headache that will pass on its own," she shared, as her head dropped forward, granting him access. She noticed previously that an expansion upgrade could come with a headache that lasted a couple of days and acknowledged the temporary discomfort as normal.

Aureon took advantage of the avenue she gave him and worked on her muscles from her shoulders and up her neck. He coaxed her desire when he moved from her neck to her scalp. The massaging made her purr as she relaxed against him. She touched her tongue to the tip of his finger that passed her face, and he stilled. He reclined her against him so he could meet her eyes. Her dark gazed was hooded, and she wore a contented smile before her gaze dropped to his mouth. She bit her lip. His mouth dove for hers, and her arm slid around the back of his neck to pull him closer. His kiss was firm and slow before he stopped and took his time watching her, a mere inch from her face. *Beautiful at every angle.*

"I wanted to do that when I first saw you tonight," he admitted, as he continued to pay close attention to the changes in her body when she showed signs of contentment growing into desire.

"So did I," she confirmed as she ran her fingers up the back of his neck and into his hair. She had been hungry for his touch ever since in the Alloralla's hallway earlier that evening.

"What kept you?" he asked with a quizzical brow, then he kissed her forehead. He scooted her against him so her head could rest against his shoulder. He wrapped one arm around her to secure her in place.

"I... I," she fumbled her train of thought as his other hand found her curves, and his fingertips explored her skin with tender touches. Her eyes fluttered as her thoughts jumbled in her mind before she blurted, "Someone was hunting us."

Aureon snatched her chin, and her eyes met his bold, green fury staring back. His voice was eerily low, "Someone was hunting you?"

She exhaled hard as the desire evaporated.

"You never mentioned that before," he rasped while stroking her cheek as he held her face.

"You never asked," she whispered honestly. Her violent, chaotic life on Earth was typical. However, now that she has experienced Theris, she knows the freedom her life was missing. She understood it further when he had his hands on her, coaxing her senses to feel him, to remain present. His imposing energy demanded that she feel all of him, that his protection surrounded her. Her eyes watered as his worry passed through her. She covered one of his hands with hers and leaned into his touch, relieved he didn't mask his actions.

"For how long?" he demanded.

A tear left the outside corner of her eye. "Forever."

A silent moment passed between them as he wrestled with wanting to leap into action for her. All Aureon could do was gently wipe the falling tear from her cheek. His brow drew tight as his mind assembled a strategy rooted in the purpose of protecting her. The fact that this has been the reality of her life shook his core. *She deserves peace.* He covered her mouth with a hard kiss, wishing her tears to cease. He didn't want her to be conscious of her survival. She moaned in response, and the tip of her tongue flicked against his lip. He froze and pulled her away, creating a soft smacking sound as their lips separated. He stared down at her with an expression Adaline didn't understand at first. Then she felt his apprehension and titillation as he stared at her, entranced.

"Oh." she understood. "Elves don't...."

Aureon shook his head tightly, but she sensed he was fighting a decision as if he was ashamed of his curiosity. Adaline recalled her conversation with Sorsacha by the pool about the guarded sexuality of elfin males. *I have to show him where the line is,* she thought. Adaline turned in his lap to face him, avoiding a disconnect between them. Her eyes remained on his mouth as she slowly licked her lips as her face hovered close to his.

"Do you want to try it?" She trailed soft, tender kisses from the top of his sharp cheekbone, down its slope, until she ended at the corner of his mouth. He waited to see what she'd do while his indecision receded as she enticed the lust that boiled within him. She placed another kiss at the corner of his mouth before she flicked the tip of her tongue across it. An open-mouthed sigh left Aureon as his heart thundered in his chest. She cupped the side of his face as she adjusted in his lap. He pulled her closer, his eyes never straying from her mouth. The light caress on the edge of his jaw undid him as she whispered in his ear, "Aureon... I need to know what you taste like."

The burning lust within him boiled over, and his eyes dilated at her words. Adaline pulled away to gauge him before she cupped his face, so glad that he didn't retreat. She smiled wide, pleased when he gave a slight nod.

"If you don't like it, we'll stop," she said, noticing his focus never left her mouth. She brought his lips down on hers, slanting hers over his as she tasted him. Her cautious exploration of him was gentle as she swiped the tip of her tongue over his teeth, encouraging him to part his mouth. She could feel his need for precision, and she softened at the notion as he opened. She pushed past his lips to tease the tip of his tongue, gingerly dancing hers over his. Her actions stirred a groan within him, and he hungrily squeezed her to his chest as he reciprocated. His intensity grew, wringing a moan from her as she melted for him while he matched her fervor. Her hands tangled in his long hair, needing something to anchor to as his kiss became demanding. The deep breath he drew through his nose caught the hint of the sweet smell of her arousal. A growl stirred in his chest before he separated from her. He didn't let go of her, and he wouldn't dare think of it when she was gazing at him with her flushed cheeks and kiss-swollen lips.

"Is something wrong?" she asked in a throaty whisper.

He leaned in slowly and planted a soft kiss on her lips. "You are well-versed in cleverness, Dr. Adaline. I have never encountered someone who can effectively change the subject as you."

She chuckled. "Contrary to what you may believe, it wasn't in my plan to share burdensome information tonight."

"And what was in your plan to share, Dr. Adaline?" his voice grew husky.

"I just shared it," she flirted as she glanced at his mouth. "Did you like it?"

He nodded. "Is there a name for it?"

She smiled. "There are two. Some humans call it a French kiss, while others call it a soul kiss."

"Hmm," he said as his lips neared hers. "I know nothing of French." His brows drew tight as he contemplated the passion that she awakened in him. "Soul kiss is fitting."

She roused the depths of his desire he wasn't aware existed until this exchange, causing him to crave her beyond logic. Old ideas about sex and intimacy faded as he brought his hungry mouth down on hers. Determined to know if there was more to this kiss with her, he lashed his tongue against hers, thoroughly exploring her mouth. The moan that escaped her riled him, stirring a low growl in his chest. She scooted closer to him, teasing his growing erection against her bottom. She gripped his shoulders as she lifted her body, and he helped her swing her leg over his lap to straddle him without breaking contact. He held onto her hips and squeezed her curves, prompting her to grind against him. Their kiss broke with his groan that grew into a guttural growl at the friction between their bodies.

Adaline locked eyes with the lusty male she held in her arms. Her fingertips slid over his shoulder blades then trailed up his neck before tangling in his hair. She wondered if it was this soft in his waking state. "Mmm," she purred, teasing him by bringing her lips close to his then pulling back. "You taste good." Her lips melted into his as he wrapped his arms around her, feeling her hardened nipples against his chest. His lips tore away from hers to trail his affections down her neck to her cleavage. She pushed on his chest, so he leaned back, bringing her with him as his back rested against the sand. She shifted in his lap, and her gaze turned soft as she surveyed every detail of his satisfaction and smiled. She reached for the hem of his shirt but was distracted. Her gaze lifted to the enormous house that sprawled on the beach. She recognized the balcony as the one she leaped over to get to the sand.

"Nice place," her voice turned sultry as her fingertips teased the skin under the hem of his shirt. She searched for the defining lines of his torso.

He squeezed her hips again, resetting her attention. She looked to find his unamused expression. She smiled innocently. Fine, he'd retaliate. He leaned up on his forearms and imagined what he wanted to see. It was, after all, his dream. Her long-sleeved v-neck tee and pants morphed into the tiny bikini she wore to swim in his pool. An outfit he remembered in vivid detail. She glanced down when she felt the shift and gasped, but she didn't scramble to cover herself. She was confident in her body, but that wouldn't stop him from showing her how mouthwatering she was to him.

"This is my summer palace, Dr. Adaline." He leaned up to kiss her skin above the top corner of one of the triangles of her bikini top. She whimpered when he pulled away.

"Again," she demanded, breathless.

"Mmm," he hummed near her skin. "Tell me, Dr. Adaline. How can someone as strong as you be soft to the touch?"

His white-hot kiss seared her skin, frying her nerve endings. Her eyes blinked wide as they glowed with her white light. The blatant indication of her arousal inspired him to climb to his feet and toss her over his shoulder before he hiked back to the palace. He rubbed the side of his cheek against the side of her pert bottom, then playfully bit it. She yelped and kicked before giggling. He chuckled then kissed her skin. She tried to bait him with playful, flirty arguments as to why he should put her down. However, nothing convinced him to alter his plan. He entered a circular garden that had an open ceiling in the middle of the house. He leaped from the ground floor and landed on a high branch without out a sound, then he slid into a hammock hung between two large trees. The hammock had a three-hundred-sixty-degree view of the world around it.

"Wow," he heard her whisper at her outstanding yet upside-down view.

Aureon slid her over his shoulder, cradling her on his chest, but her attention remained on the view. She pushed up from his body and straddled him, absorbed in the scenery as he was by her, and he grasped her hips as he growled at the softness of her exposed skin. Her large breasts enticed him, and he leaned into them, but she caught him before he could make contact. His upturned gazed was veiled with innocence. She didn't believe that look for one minute.

She smiled. "You like curves."

He squeezed her. "I like your curves."

She leaned down to kiss his covered chest before she said, "Thank you." He waited for her to finish. "For showing me this place."

He gave a slight nod before confessing, "I have not been here in a long time."

"Why not?" she asked. "It's so beautiful." She reached for the hem of his shirt.

"The last time I was here, I was happy with my life," he said, getting caught up in a memory. "I would rotate from the main palace to this place for four months out of the year when the seasons changed in Ividia." What brought him back to the present was the gliding of her palms up his chest, pushing the hem of his shirt to his shoulders.

Her fingertips traced the lines of his muscular form, and his muscles danced under her touch. "And now?" she asked, realizing that the last dream she walked in on also had to do with a place that was rooted in past happiness. Did he believe it impossible to find, again? Her mind spun with questions, but she focused on listening as she lowered her lips to his bare chest.

"I never thought to return," he admitted, as he realized all his memories of the summer palace were good ones, yet they seemed so far away. *It was another lifetime.* Adaline planted a kiss on his chest, and he hissed at the contact. "And now I've put you in the worst situation," he admitted, as he continued touching her while she explored him.

"I wouldn't have let you if I thought your plan had any chance of failure," she admitted. She left a kiss next to his nipple that hardened under her breath. "We'll get through it and find out the truth about everyone involved. Then you and Theodon can move on with your lives."

"That is the intent, yes," he said as his grip on her tightened. "But to achieve that, I have to put you in harm's way."

Adaline rested her chin against his chest while holding his gaze. "You made the right decision." He peered at her in silence as his fingers combed through her soft hair. "It's easy for me to protect myself," she said. "Even from you, if you recall." She gave him a coy smile before she returned to her teasing. "Trust me with this," she said as her finger drew circles on his chest.

"I do," Aureon admitted the truth that scared him. He trusted her with his life, his crown, and his son's future. She slid up his chest to touch the tip of her nose to his before she leaned in to kiss him.

"I just need your help with one part," she said, and her expression turned hungry.

"Anything," he rumbled.

"The acting like an adoring fiancé part of my role," she said. Her smile was inches from his lips. "The inspiration for that feeling was quite foreign to me until recently."

"And now?" he asked as their breaths mingled.

"I could use more inspiration for later. You know, to hold me over," Adaline admitted, as her gaze on his mouth turned hooded. "Kiss me like you did before I interrupted you, and you unjustly punished me by putting me in a bikini." Aureon chuckled, squeezed her bottom, and lifted her higher on his chest, making her mouth collide with his. Their open mouth kiss grew ravenous until something pulled at Adaline. Adaline's eyes shot wide as she felt her grip on him loosen against her will. Her lips separated from his with a smack. "Uh oh." He tried to clutch her tighter, but she slipped right through his fingers and out of his dream.

His head fell back against the hammock as he let out a defeated sigh that turned into a growl as his hands fisted.

Adaline's spirit landed in her body, and her eyes shot open. She saw Tobey standing at the side of her bed, waving at her through her force field with terror clinging to his features. The force field disappeared, and Adaline sat up.

"Tobey," the name rushed out of her. "What's wrong?" The boy started to sign at her frantically, "I heard noises and got scared. I couldn't get to you."

Adaline's shoulder slumped as she realized the poor kid freaked out at the sight of her force field. *He isn't the first and won't be the last.* She patted the other side of the bed. "Crawl in," she said. Tobey hurried around to the other side of the bed and slid under the comforter. "If you touch my hand, it will protect you, too, while you sleep," she told him. "Do you understand?" He nodded quickly. "Okay, try to get some rest," she said as she scooted down on her side of the bed, letting her hand rest halfway between them. Tobey slid closer and tucked his hand under hers. As they sank into sleep, the force field slowly expanded to cover them.

CHAPTER 40

T heodon knocked on Adaline's suite door the following
morning, and Tobey cracked the door then peeked at the
prince. Theodon's smile grew with amusement. "Good morning,
Tobey." Tobey nodded at the prince, but he would not open the
door wider. "Is Dr. Adaline awake?" Tobey nodded then closed
the door on him. The prince heard the boy hurry into the other
room. A moment later, Adaline answered the door. Her smile
always coaxed the same reaction from him.

"Good morning," she said, her voice still a bit throaty for
the early hour. She noticed Theodon's clothes were of a similar
leisurely design, like hers.

"Good morning," he said. "Are you ready for breakfast?"
Adaline glanced over her shoulder. Theodon guessed she was
searching for Tobey.

"I'm almost ready, but he needs to eat now," Adaline said.
"Would you mind taking him with you to breakfast, and I will be
along shortly?"

"Of course," Theodon said as Tobey peeked out from

behind Adaline.

Adaline knelt to sign to the boy. "I need you to go with Theodon so you can eat breakfast. I'll be along in a few minutes. We have a big day ahead. Do you understand?"

Tobey nodded and reached for Theodon's hand. Theodon smiled and grasped it. "We will see you soon."

"Thank you," she said and closed the door. She approached the blush, floor-length slip dress that hung in the open wardrobe of her suite before sighing aloud to the empty room. "When was the last time I wore a day dress?" Ena delivered a dainty, fresh flower wreath for her hair before Tobey woke up that morning, along with sandals in her size. Adaline assumed by the long straps that she had to wrap them around her ankles. Once Adaline finished styling her hair into long waves, she pulled on the dress over her head, laced up her sandals, and walked around the room to test them for comfort. Finally, she carefully placed the wreath on her head and looked in the mirror. Surprised at how much the flowers softened her appearance, she smiled at her reflection and left for breakfast.

Rounding the corner into the dining room, she saw the king sitting at the head of the table. Theodon sat on his left, as always, and Tobey was seated on his right, which was usually her spot.

That's right, she thought. *Today is the day we show everyone a different reality.* All elfin eyes followed her to her new seat next to Theodon. The prince immediately rose from his seat and pulled out the chair for her.

"Thank you," Adaline said as he slid the chair in behind her as she sat down.

"You are welcome," he said quietly and retook his seat.

Adaline greeted the king, "Good morning, Your Majesty."

"Good morning, Dr. Adaline," he greeted her with a warm tone, yet his body language was everything of a refined aristocrat. Although he didn't smile, he said the right things and did it without focusing on her. Adaline smiled to herself, not taking what seemed like the cold shoulder personally. She watched Tobey scarf down his meal, whereas the royals had barely begun enjoying theirs.

"He's got a healthy appetite," Theodon commented as he dug into his breakfast.

Adaline signed to Tobey as breakfast was sent in front of her, "Slow down, so you don't get sick." He stopped and looked at his plate, wondering how the food that tasted so good could make him sick. Adaline chuckled before she signed, "It's not going to hurt you. Just slow down." Tobey then cautiously picked at his food. Adaline smiled as his behavior changed from one extreme to another. She hoped he would find a happy medium.

"What are those gestures that you are doing to communicate with him, Dr. Adaline?" the king asked her.

"It's called sign language," she said. "It's used by those who cannot speak, are deaf, or both."

"I have never seen anything like it off the battlefield," Theodon commented. "It appears advantageous."

Adaline's eyes narrowed at Tobey until the boy began to giggle. She smiled.

"Are there more sign languages in your world, Dr. Adaline?" the king asked as properly as ever.

Adaline settled into her breakfast before she said, "Unfortunately, no. Our world is down to six languages. Only one of them is sign language."

Theodon set his flatware down. "What happened to the others?"

Adaline gave him a knowing look. "Are you sure you want to hear such sad history on this lovely morning?" The royals nodded. "All right, then." She looked at Tobey before she explained, "There was a time when our world was full of billions of people. Those billions shared over 6,000 languages." She noticed Theodon's eyes widened, and both royals stopped eating to listen. "Earth had a few prophetic events and natural disasters, which tanked the population down to a few million people. Some humans escaped through portals to other worlds – very few being nice places." She winked at the king. "The whole ordeal left the earth skimmed down to a sad reminder of the great infrastructure it once was. As a result, there are only six languages left."

The king was intrigued by the story. *This must relate to her directly*, he thought, as he reviewed their previous conversations regarding her purpose. "Do these cataclysmic events have anything to do with you being a diviner, as you called it?"

She nodded before swallowing her food. "The arrival of the three prophets that occurred about 850 years ago came with foretellings humans were meant to heed." Adaline chuckled. "My ancestor was a trusted follower of the one who foretold of the coming of the diviners. Because she was loyal, the prophet told her that her lineage would produce the diviners in the form of twins. They would sweep the evil from the earth before its end."

The royals sat in stunned silence.

"So, you and Asher will actually–" Theodon started.

"End our world," she said softly.

"And the two of you are powerful enough to do that?" Theodon asked as he kept eating.

Adaline smirked and nodded before she glanced at Tobey. "Tobey had been following me for over a week or so. He knew what I was when he saw me."

Tobey nodded happily before signing as Adaline interpreted, "Heavy energy ripples off them both when they move. No one is a match to their power."

Adaline chuckled. "Thanks, kid."

He continued to sign, and Adaline kept interpreting. "It looks like an electric current coming off him and heat waves coming off her. It's cool."

Theodon smiled at Tobey's use of the colloquial phrase. It reminded him of the last humans that visited Theris.

"While on the subject," the king said, "did your powers relate to when you mentioned your father was able to keep you safe for a time?"

Adaline leaned back in her chair as her mind spun through memories that were over sixty-five years old. She was ready to share her history with them because she knew the information would be safe.

"My dad was able to keep us safe for a long time," Adaline said. "But then a slip-up happened. An evil organization tried to get me to hand over information about gifted kids that attended my school. They didn't know what I could do because Asher and I had become well-practiced in acting ordinarily human. Asher found out I was taken and tore through several walls of concrete to get to me. I destroyed my captors. He got us out of there."

The royals and Tobey sat in silence. Theodon measured Adaline's story to what little he knew of Asher, and he had to admit, it seemed fitting. Asher showed genuine interest in Adaline's safety but knew she was powerful enough to handle herself. Yet, Asher left room for the possibility that he may need to retrieve her from the palace to get her away from Aureon, had the king chosen to continue with his original motives.

"A week later, both of our parents turned up dead in a car accident when neither of them drove a car." She eyed Tobey before saying, "Similar to what happened to Tobey's parents."

The royals' attention leveled on the boy before Theodon asked Adaline, "How old were you?"

"We had just turned seventeen," Adaline said on an exhale. "We achieved exemplary marks in school, so we graduated early and moved far away to go to medical school, which started us on the path of becoming doctors."

The king nodded in understanding that the twins did what was necessary to survive. It was something his little human excelled at, but it bothered him that she didn't have a carefree childhood.

"Asher and I fight evil every other night or so," she admitted. "However, our purpose is highly destructive."

"Will you survive it?" the king asked.

She considered his question. "Honestly, we're not sure. Asher and I have made a point of practicing our abilities to make them stronger, and we have learned to develop new ones. I believe we have put ourselves in a position to survive. However, it's impossible to know what will become of us."

An alarm grew in the king's mind, but he didn't show it. "And when does this phase take place?"

"Anytime over the next thirty-seven years," she said as she cut into her food.

"Then what?" Theodon asked her.

"Then we either find a new place to live, should we survive, or perish with the earth," she said with nonchalance.

Theodon's attention shot to his father as he switched to telepathy. "We can't let them die."

"We won't," his father replied just as quickly. "We must get through these next two weeks first, and then we will determine how to help them." Theodon relaxed before he nodded as he took another bite of his food.

Adaline signed to Tobey, "If you're good while we are here, I'll ask Asher to teach you how to run faster." Tobey's eyes widened in surprise before he quickly nodded. Adaline chuckled before signing, "Do you remember what I told you about Aureon and Theodon?"

Tobey sat back to sign, "They are our friends."

She signed in return and spoke aloud, "Yes, they are our friends. So, if you get lost, who do you look for?"

"You three," Tobey signed as he pointed everyone out.

"That's correct," Adaline signed and smiled before addressing Theodon. "We are attending an art festival today, correct?"

"Yes," Theodon said. "It's a casual opportunity to get out among the people so they can see us together after the announcement."

Adaline nodded. "What sort of medium do elves use for their artwork?"

"It varies," Theodon said. "However, there are a select few artists that have an affinity for sculpting of almost any substance they can find."

"Some of which were selected to construct many of the sculptures you might have seen while wandering around the palace," the king offered.

"Impressive," Adaline commented. "I'm looking forward to seeing everything." Adaline glanced at Tobey when she heard him patting the table to get her attention.

He signed to her, "What is...?" He gestured at her.

Adaline's heart hurt for Tobey. She signed in reply and spoke, "Art is a form of creative expression. Artists find ways to bring creative ideas into a physical form so they can share them with the world." Tobey thought about what she said for a long moment before nodding. "You will see a lot of different kinds of art today," she said. "It might inspire you to make your own." Tobey smiled.

"Are you ready?" Theodon asked her as he rose from his chair.

"Yes," she said. She stood and waved for Tobey to join her.

In a blur, Tobey was at Adaline's side, sliding his hand into hers, while her free hand grasped the crook of Theodon's elbow. They exited the palace together, with the king watching after them long after they faded from his view. There was something lonesome about seeing his son take part in his own (although fake) family dynamic where he got to enjoy both Adaline and Tobey. The king did not get to experience such precious moments after Theodon was born. At the same time, Aureon became sentimental and happy that Theodon would get a glimpse of what it would be like to have a family of his own. The idea of a new couple in the palace with a little one running around amused Aureon. He pictured Theodon chasing after the little one, just as Aureon and Cerus had done when Theodon was

Tobey's age.

A precious time, Aureon thought. As he exited the dining room, another truth struck him. He had previously wondered how to provide for and protect Adaline, who has been fine taking care of herself. Their conversation over breakfast gave him insight into how he could play a part in her life. He recalled how at ease she was as she entered the dining room for breakfast, which was a far cry from the defensiveness she exuded when they first met. He could provide a new life for her, one where she could be herself, and he would protect her. She wouldn't have to pretend to act human anymore when she was much more. She'd be free.

CHAPTER 41

A daline was bombarded with the feelings of every passerby as she, Theodon, and Tobey eased through the crowd of elves that attended the art festival. As much as she sensed their stares, their excitement, disapproval, or contentment, her expression remained neutral as she searched for specific feelings: jealousy, contempt, and hatred. Her focus to find the enemies of the royal family remained steadfast.

"Good morning, Your Majesty," a familiar female voice cut through the crowd. Adaline noticed Theodon's subtle recoil when the greeting touched his ears. *Roserie.*

Roserie went rigid at the sight of Adaline, who looked refreshed and lovely, triggering the she-elf to seethe with jealousy. Roserie's attention dropped to the boy holding Adaline's hand, and confusion rippled from her as she wondered his origin.

"Roserie," Theodon said coldly.

"I came to apologize–" Roserie blurted.

"–Enough," Theodon cut her off. Adaline noticed how he reminded her of his father just then. Roserie's gaze fell to the ground. Elves stared.

"What's going on?" Adaline whispered to Theodon as she casually wrapped her arm around him, tucking herself close to his side.

"This broad," Adaline heard a familiar voice over her shoulder before she turned to see Sorsacha and smiled upon seeing her friend, "was dumb enough to think she could get away with striking a royal."

Adaline's eyes shot wide. "Is that true, Roserie?" A moment passed before Roserie nodded while still focused on the ground. A few elves gasped upon hearing that someone would dare strike a member of the royal family.

"It's okay," Sorsacha nudged her human friend. "I handled it while you were away."

Adaline smirked. "And how did you do that?"

Sorsacha crossed her arms over her chest, widened her stance then lifted her chin. "I slapped the taste out of her mouth."

Adaline beamed at Sorsacha. *This is why we are friends.* She noticed Roserie's feelings of jealousy remained while her distaste for Adaline grew, but pure hatred for Sorsacha blazed within her. Theodon shot Sorsacha a knowing look since he did hear her deliver the retaliating blow. She grinned and winked at him.

"Roserie," Theodon said as he reciprocated Adaline's gesture by snaking his arm around her, pulling her tightly against his side. Adaline immediately responded by adjusting her fit into the crook of his arm. Roserie's jealousy boiled at the fond exchange, but it wasn't because she loved Theodon.

That's my place, Roserie thought. *That's my crown, and this human is getting away with it all!*

"You are to give us a wide berth from this point forward," Theodon instructed Roserie. "Do you understand?"

"Y... yes," Roserie fumbled. "Yes, Your Majesty."

"Off with you, now," Sacha shooed.

After Roserie left them, Adaline shot Sacha a wowed expression. "Slapped the taste out of her mouth? Really Sacha?" Sacha grinned and nodded. "Nicely done."

"I thought you'd approve," Sacha said with pride.

"I do," Adaline admitted before addressing Theodon. "If she comes near you again, I'm going to do more than slap her."

Theodon chuckled. "There will be no need for that, I'm sure."

Adaline wasn't so sure. Given the feelings Roserie carried, even though she had no love for Theodon, indicated that she was a part of the whole sham that involved the desire for the crown. Adaline hoped that Roserie would wander back soon so she could verify the truth for herself.

"Who's the kid?" Sacha asked, looking down at the boy who was clinging to Adaline's leg. He didn't like Roserie from the moment he heard her voice.

"This is Tobey," Adaline said as she peered at the boy who was finding Sorsacha to be quite amusing.

"Is he your son?" Sacha asked.

"No." Adaline chuckled. "He's my friend that I'm keeping a close watch over."

"Vague yet interesting," Sacha commented with a nod. "I like it."

"Would you like to join us, Sorsacha?" Theodon asked her.

"Sure," she replied.

After walking past a few more displays, Adaline's curiosity finally got the best of her. "So, Theo," Theodon's ear tilted toward her. "Do elves have a mating season?"

Theodon chuckled. "Notice many pregnant females, did you?"

Adaline's focus followed another one that walked by. "I couldn't avoid it if I tried." Her mind ran the numbers as she observed females that appeared to be approximately seven to eight months along, considering it was mid-August. Others she decided must be around nineteen to twenty months along given how full their bellies appeared. *So, most elves must have November and December birthdays*, she thought.

Sorsacha laughed.

"Yes, we do," Theodon confirmed. "Females are most fertile during the winter months."

"Ah," Adaline said. "So that's how elves keep warm in the winter."

"Wah! Waaaah!" Sorsacha blundered.

"What? That was funny," Adaline said, unable to stifle a grin at her silliness.

The four of them wandered through the displays from different artists until Tobey saw something he liked, and he yanked on Adaline's hand and pointed. "Okay, let's go see," she said as she detached from Theodon's side.

The two of them walked over to a sculptor's arrangement of artworks, with Theodon and Sacha following. The sculptor stood tall and lean, and his eyes never left the look of wonder on little Tobey's face as the boy circled a giant statue.

The statue was of a female elf, whose features were carved flawlessly out of a large piece of light blue crystal. The entire image of the figure was refined with tiny facets all over, making the artwork glitter in the sunlight.

"How beautiful," Adaline commented. The artist gave a gratuitous bow at her praise.

Tobey signed to Adaline, "Who is she?" Adaline repeated the question aloud.

"She's my mother," Theodon said.

Adaline got lost in the figure. If the artist captured any percentage of Queen Aravae's likeness at all, then the late queen was genuinely stunning. Adaline tucked herself against Theodon's side and squeezed him in a side hug. Tobey was still staring at the statue, unable to look away. Adaline's attention wandered to the other sculptures created by the artist. She saw crystal bookends of what looked like Aureon fighting Cailu.

Adaline chuckled as she pointed at it. "Is this how your father and Cailu came to an understanding?"

Theodon laughed. "Is that what he told you?"

"Yes," she giggled.

Theodon eyed the piece. "It's quite accurate." His father had fought the beast three times in the same year to stop Cailu from killing elves. Theodon remembered how his grandfather carried his father into the palace after their third and final confrontation. Cerus shooed his grandson away before young Theodon could see the blood that dripped on the floor from his father's wounds.

"They have a love-hate relationship," Sorsacha commented.

"I believe it," Adaline confessed.

They continued to make their way from one artist to the next, and Adaline was able to teach Tobey about different kinds of art along the way. The boy seemed enamored by it all, and Adaline had a feeling she would need to help him find a creative outlet after the event. *Maybe an artist teaches classes for younglings.*

"Theodon!" Forb called to the prince. Theodon kept one hand in Adaline's while he reached the other to slap his friend on the back in greeting. Adaline felt Forb's uneasiness toward her, probably for his friend's sudden engagement and his protectiveness over the prince. Adaline didn't have to read his soul record to know that Forb was a true friend to Theodon.

"So, you're engaged?" Forb asked.

"I am," Theodon said as he hugged Adaline to his side. The couple smiled at each other. Forb plastered a smile on his face to look happy for his friend, although he had his reservations since Theodon had rarely mentioned Adaline to him and not in a romantic capacity. "I thought you and Roserie-" Forb began to ask.

"No," Theodon cut him off.

"Well, shows what I know!" Forb said with an exaggerated shrug.

The two males chuckled as they spent a moment catching up. Adaline separated from the prince to wander to another artist's booth with Tobey, who was fascinated by all the sharp tools used to sculpt wood. He watched an artist guide the piece of wood in his hand into form, working with exceptional speed and precision. A moment later, the artist finished a small sculpture of a bird and handed it to Tobey.

"Oh," Adaline said to the artist as Tobey's face lit up. "How much do I owe you?"

"It's a gift," the young artist said with a smile. He winked at Tobey, who smiled back.

Adaline signed to Tobey while speaking, "Say thank you."

Tobey signed to the elf, "Thank you."

"You're welcome," the artist said to Tobey, amused by the boy's hand gesture.

Adaline heard Theodon and Forb's approach.

"Have you seen Talia lately?" Forb asked Theodon. "I haven't seen her in at least a few days."

"Neither have I," Theodon confessed while remaining even-tempered.

Adaline kept her back to Forb and Theodon as she pretended to browse the artworks that ensnared Tobey's attention. She hadn't gone back to the dungeon to see Talia. There was no reason to, but Adaline wondered how the upper-cruster adjusted to her dirt-floored lifestyle. Her gaze settled into a thousand-yard stare as her mind drifted to Talia's memories. Talia showed no signs of remorse for poisoning the queen. She honestly believed she should be queen instead, and she deserved it at whatever cost. Talia didn't love Aureon, let alone care for him beyond his title. When she attempted to console the king for his loss then negotiate her way into his bed, his rage exploded. Aureon made an example of her, which caused the other females who wanted to throw themselves at the king to abandon their selfish plans. Since then, female subjects didn't dare set foot in the palace, except in dire circumstances to ask the king for help.

Adaline smiled to herself as she recalled the first time she met Aureon. His predatory grace paired with his analytical stare was amusing to her now. He didn't explode at Adaline for not being able to control her once he saw the evidence of her abilities in her glowing eyes. Instead, he switched to being observant. She could tell he was analyzing her before devising a new plan, as he didn't allow himself the luxury of being stubborn. Instead, he remained planted in his intelligence and switched tactics with ease. And it didn't hurt her case that he thought her beautiful and intriguing.

Adaline didn't understand the extent of Talia's thirst for a royal title because it came with the lifelong partnership to a male who would likely outlive her, nor would he put up with her schemes. *She wouldn't have made it a week past their wedding night.* Adaline pushed that visual from her mind. Talia would have had to spend a lot of time with Aureon and produce an heir, making her a part of a family versus someone who could revel in personal glory. *So, she was delusional, or becoming queen had been drilled into her from a young age.* The latter seemed possible. Graydon, her father, had gone to great lengths to hurt Aureon when the king chose his future by picking Aravae over Talia. That meant Graydon had been building his strategy for a long time. Talia marrying Aureon and stirring up the enemies of Theris if the king forsook her hand couldn't possibly be the only plans Graydon had. *There must be more.* Adaline focused on reading more soul records to compile the pieces of this awful story.

"That's odd for her to be silent for so long," Forb said to Theodon. "Talia always needs to be seen and heard."

"She certainly does," Theodon agreed before getting Adaline's attention. He tilted his head toward the table of sculptures. "Is there one you want?"

"Oh," Adaline said. "No. I'm just fascinated by it all." It was odd for her to even think about anyone purchasing something for her. She and Asher were exceedingly wealthy in their world, and that fact just ignited another sobering truth: should they leave Earth for Theris, they would have to work their way up from flat broke. She knew the king wouldn't allow her to go without, but she wouldn't tolerate herself to go from extreme usefulness to freeloader. She would need to speak with Asher to discuss how to generate income after moving to Theris.

"Are you sure?" Theodon asked her.

"Yes," she said as she looked at him adoringly. "Thank you."

He smiled while giving a nod that was more of a clipped bow of acknowledgment. He offered his arm, and Adaline took it. His free hand covered hers as they continued to stroll. Tobey relinquished Adaline's hand and sped through the crowd of elves.

"Stay close," she called after him.

For a short time, Forb accompanied the newly engaged couple, along with Sorsacha, before saying his goodbyes. Someone caught Sorsacha's attention, and Adaline turned to read them - it was a family member of hers, and the she-elf also excused herself before disappearing into the crowd.

Gentle applause and a few cheers stirred around them as the prince escorted his beautiful fiancé through the streets. The couple looked at each other and smiled. Theodon held Adaline's gaze long enough to signal that he was going to kiss her. He cupped the side of her face and brought her other cheek to his lips. A moment passed as he skimmed the tip of his nose up her cheekbone before he softly kissed her on the side of her forehead. Cheers erupted at the public display of affection from a royal, something they hadn't seen in over a millennium. Theodon clutched Adaline close, caught Tobey with his free arm, and threw the boy over his shoulder as they walked back to the palace. Adaline laughed at Tobey's surprised expression because the prince had caught him so easily.

After they returned to the palace, Adaline suggested, "We should speak with your father."

Theodon nodded before he telepathically linked to his father. One of his ears twitched. "He's in his study."

CHAPTER 42

A ureon descended the stairs into the dungeon, making his
way to Graydon's cell. Guards' greetings echoed in his ears
as he arrived at a cell similar to the one he inhabited. Graydon's white-blonde hair almost glowed even in the darkness, and
his once deep amber eyes radiated fury.

"Look who's here," Graydon hissed. "The bane of my existence." The elder gave a sinister laugh, all pretenses long gone.
"Please tell me, Your Majesty, how may I continue to serve you
since that seems to be the only thing I'm allowed to do in this
godforsaken lifetime."

"You forsook your honor, Graydon," Aureon said plainly.
"You have only yourself to blame for this outcome."

Graydon charged the bars of his cell, and Aureon seized the
opportunity. The king reached through the slats and wrapped his
hand around the elder's forehead. The electricity from the roots
that wrapped the bars only tingled against Aureon's skin, unlike
before when they burned him. Shock filled Graydon's features
as Aureon's power flowed into his brain. The elder hollered in
pain then fell to the ground before scrambling to his feet.

"What did you do?" Graydon hissed before he raged. "What did you do!"

Aureon shook out his hand before he said, "I blocked your telepathy." Graydon bellowed. Aureon exited Graydon's cell as he muttered, "So much for underestimating me."

"You are nothing, Aureon!" Graydon yelled after him. "You will see my wrath has yet to come down on you, but it will soon! And it will destroy you!"

Aureon gave no weight to the elder's words, but he did not dismiss them. He tucked the warning away in the back of his mind as he continued to gather all evidence for Aravae's murder. Soon, justice would prevail to all involved in the treason. The king would admit to no one that he had a surprise waiting for Graydon that the elder could never predict. Aureon smirked as he imagined the look on Graydon's face when the moment arrived. After Aureon blocked Talia's telepathy, he returned to the palace and headed to his study.

The king reached into Ena's mind. "Meet me in my study."

A moment later, the she-elf replied, "On my way, My Lord."

Aureon barely passed the large chaise in his study when he heard Ena's soft knock on the door. "Enter," he said without turning around. She neared the king while maintaining a noticeable distance. She was never afraid of Aureon, but she had a deep sense of propriety, and she had served his father the same way. He gestured for her to take a seat on the chaise, and she did. Ena took her time to sit up straight and cross her ankles before her chin lifted to Aureon, who fell into his habit of pacing around the chaise while he organized his thoughts.

He spoke into her mind, "We found him." Ena's eyes widened in shock before she looked over her shoulder at him as he circled behind her. "But I need the next two weeks to gather important information about it before I make this public. You will notice odd behavior from myself, my son, and Dr. Adaline until we bring this to a close. Then we can all move on." Ena nodded in understanding. "During that time, I need you to casually dismiss or deny the true motive of our behavior to anyone who asks you or tries to discuss it with you until I make the announcement," Aureon explained. "Am I clear, Ena?"

"Yes, Your Majesty," she replied in his head.

"Good."

"Your Majesty?" He nodded for her to continue as he paced. "Did you really catch him?" she asked as her voice cracked in his mind. Tears fell from the corners of her eyes.

The king stopped pacing and rested his hand on Ena's shoulder. "Yes. He was arrested, and he will pay dearly." Ena let out a quiet sob and just as quickly swallowed it back, then wiped her tears. "This will all be over soon."

Ena nodded. "Yes, My Lord."

Aureon gave Ena a moment to collect herself before he concluded his meeting with her. After she left his study, Theodon, Adaline, and Tobey filed inside. He noticed the boy was pretending the tiny, wooden bird in his hand was flying, and he promptly let go of Adaline's hand to explore the room. The boy's excessive energy amused Adaline.

"How was the festival?" the king asked the newly engaged couple.

"It was nicely done, as usual," Theodon said, having attended the event every year.

"It was incredible," Adaline boasted. The king noticed her eyes light up.

Does the little human like art? He tucked the detail away for later.

"We saw people we knew," Adaline said before she glanced at Theodon. "Some seemed happy to see us."

The king tapped his temple with his index finger, and Adaline immediately brought up her force field around them. The king gestured for the two of them to sit while he took the large armchair across from them. He liked sitting across from Adaline, where he could enjoy the sight of her without consequence. The three of them were delighted to pause their role-playing while they exchanged information.

"Roserie found Theo," Adaline said to the king as she eyed her fiancé. The king tilted his head with curiosity, and his hands steepled in front of him. "She was not happy to see me." Adaline chuckled. "And her jealously turned to pure hatred when Sorsacha joined us."

That made sense, given that the king witnessed the youngest Olostuil slap Roserie, who didn't see the move coming. The king nodded in understanding. "How was it handled?"

"I dismissed her," Theodon replied.

"From what I gathered," Adaline chimed in, "she wanted her apology accepted so she could stay in the running."

"You should let her," the king suggested.

"I agree," Adaline said.

"Not to Theodon, to you, Dr. Adaline," the king clarified.

Adaline thought for a moment. "Why me?"

"Because Roserie will assume she's found another way to Theodon by befriending you," the king stated. He knew Roserie would see the opportunity by becoming close with the next princess of Theris.

"Fair enough," Adaline said. "I'll find a way to smooth things over with her."

The king nodded in satisfaction as a smirk grew on his lips. "What else?"

"Forb caught up to us," Theodon said to his father before glancing at Adaline. "He seemed... off."

Adaline nodded before disclosing to Theodon, "He's your one true friend out of the bunch. He's alarmed you are engaged because you never expressed any fondness about me to him. So, he thinks you are rushing into things." Theodon nodded. The prince was losing many people he thought were dear to him and was relieved to know he had one friend at the end of the charade.

Aureon recognized the opportunity to console his son. "We all go through this when it comes to finding our true friends in life," he admitted to Theodon. "It is not always so heartbreaking, but you still have to take the time to learn people before you give them such a title as a friend."

"Yes, Father," Theodon replied with a slight nod before a silent moment passed between them.

Adaline was thrilled that the bond between them was growing. There was more good coming from their charade than she expected.

"Now, Dr. Adaline," the king said, "Theodon will escort you to the Ieobu House, where you will remain for the next few hours."

Adaline's brow furrowed. "Won't I need the time to get ready for tonight?"

The king shook his head. "Tonight's festivities begin much later in the evening."

"Who will watch Tobey?" she asked.

"I will," the king said as he found himself staring at Tobey. The boy peered up at him, clearly intimidated by the king.

Adaline's eyebrows raised in amusement before she surrendered. "Okay, fine."

Theodon rose from his seat and offered her his elbow as he assured her, "You will like this place. It's very peaceful."

She took his arm and smiled. "Good. I could use peaceful." Peaceful settings did not exist on Earth, and the only peaceful state of being was accessible through meditation, which was short-lived.

"I'll see you before you go to bed, okay?" Adaline said to Tobey. The boy nodded before casting another suspicious glance at the king, who was mirroring him. Adaline giggled as she left the room with Theodon before calling over her shoulder, "If you two survive each other, consider it a personal victory."

CHAPTER 43

A daline carefully tied the belt of her robe before she stepped out of her private room at the Ieobu House. Her skin had been exfoliated, scrubbed, wrapped, and massaged. Even though a small amount of stress lingered within her, she was grateful for how relaxed her physical body grew the longer she remained there.

Initially, she had no idea what she was walking into when Theodon had escorted her inside the Ieobu House. A gracious staff met them, and no one spoke aloud. Theodon took her hand from his elbow and sandwiched it between both of his until an ethereal Ileotil she-elf approached them with wild pink hair and violet eyes. She made a formal bow to Theodon, who nodded in acceptance. She then looked at Adaline and smiled wide before she opened her hands to accept an offering. Theodon placed Adaline's hand in the she-elf's and closed both of his hands over theirs. Adaline figured that Theodon must have telepathic abilities like his father because he looked at the she-elf with authority before removing his hands and backing away. A moment later, he was gone, and the she-elf led Adaline through an enclosed paradise that had randomly placed rooms built into the existing terrain. No two rooms shared a common wall.

"When did *you* get here?" a familiar voice said behind her.

Adaline finished tying her intricate robe closed before noticing Sorsacha, also robe-wrapped and walking toward her. "Hey Sacha," Adaline whispered, "Theodon brought me here a couple of hours ago."

Sorsacha's eyebrows raised in intrigue. "He's quite the attentive fiancé, isn't he?"

Adaline smiled. "He is."

"What's the next treatment on your schedule?"

"I'm not sure," Adaline's brow furrowed. "No one has said a word to me since I arrived, and I keep getting retrieved and escorted to the next room." Adaline chuckled as she glanced around to see if anyone was coming to lead her to where she should go next.

"Well, given how relaxed you seem, I think I know what's next," Sorsacha said. "Come with me."

Adaline followed her friend down a narrow pathway and read Sorsacha's soul record in detail. As much as she liked the she-elf, she couldn't take any chances with everything at stake. After a few minutes of reading, she wasn't shocked to find out why her father had kicked her out of their family home. Sorsacha was more inclined to do what was right versus her father, who preferred not to get involved in anyone else's business. But that wasn't the surprise: Sorsacha wasn't banished from her family home. She left. Sacha felt that Adaline's engagement was a bit hasty, but she knew more was going on for a reason, and she had a few guesses. So, the she-elf decided to play along to support her friend. Adaline's heart fluttered at the trust her new friend gave her. The most shocking part was that Adaline saw Sacha's crush on Theodon.

And she hasn't torn my head off yet, Adaline thought. *That's impressive.* It told Adaline that Sorsacha truly believed more in this engagement than the royals allowed people to know. Sacha knew firsthand about keeping information quiet until the time came to reveal it.

The females' path changed from smooth stones, under their sandaled feet, to an intricately carved path of wooden planks that extended over a large pond. Six giant stone bathtubs formed a circle in the middle. Adaline turned away from the tubs to take in the view. Lush vegetation seemed to stretch on forever.

"Everything has been prepared for two," Sorsacha said while surveying two stone tubs filled with a thick white substance.

Adaline walked over to one of the tubs. "Is there anything I should know before I get in?"

Sorsacha pursed her lips for a moment. "It's warm, not hot... and cover as much of your skin with it as you can."

"Got it," Adaline said as she untied her robe and let it drop to the floor before she slowly sank into the tub.

"Humans aren't shy, huh?" Sorsacha jested at Adaline's comfort in her nudity.

Adaline wrapped her hair into a bun before leaning back against the end of the tub. She closed her eyes as she swept the white mixture over her shoulders, up her neck, and on her face. She sighed. "This human is far from shy."

Sorsacha chuckled and shook her head as she followed Adaline's lead. Quiet relaxation fell over them. Adaline noticed time could not be measured in the Ieobu House, and it simply stretched on in its infinite availability.

"This is amazing," Adaline finally whispered. The mixture made every cell in her body hum at a vibration level contingent on the natural world.

"Mmm-hmm," was all her friend replied.

They sank into the tubs, cocooning themselves in the mixture. Sacha slid down until her hair was submerged in it, and only her face floated above the surface. Adaline took longer to immerse herself because she was still reveling in how her body felt.

Content. Serene.

When Adaline sank further, a blade pressed against her throat. She froze.

"What the–" she heard Sorsacha exclaim.

Adaline's eyes shot open, bright with light as she froze her assailant. She pushed the blade away from her neck and rose from the tub. She saw Sorsacha had already jumped up to crouching position, ready to launch into action. The horror that lit Sacha's features was on Bole, who was frozen in place over Adaline's tub with the dagger in hand. Adaline's appearance morphed to otherworldly and mildly terrifying, with her skin covered in stark white sandy goo as her eyes blazed. Her face was inches from Bole's, and his eyes widened in alarm.

Adaline smirked. "I bet you're thinking something like, 'Fuck! I didn't expect that!' Aren't you?" Adaline laughed. Bole said nothing because Adaline kept him frozen in place.

"It gets better," Adaline smiled mischievously as she touched his temple. His eyes snapped shut as he saw all his memories she sorted through to find what she needed: his darkest secrets. She saw his strategy with Roserie, his sister. Roserie was to wed Theodon then kill him, so a new family could be installed as the new royal house since Graydon and Talia's attempt to do the same to Aureon had failed. Talia had planted the seed of evil in Bole centuries ago when she promised him that once she was queen and killed Aureon, she would marry him. Then the Aetrune and Miathan families would build the next royal dynasty together. He blindly devoted himself to her cause, but Roserie had no idea that Theodon's death was part of the scheme. Bole intended to end Theodon himself, so his sister's emotions and selfishness couldn't get in the way of his plans.

"Treason," Adaline whispered vehemently as she lowered her hand. Sorsacha's eyes widened as her jaw slackened. Adaline's shoulders rose and fell with a stirring fury as her eyes glowed brighter as Bole's filled with terror. Adaline wanted nothing more than to eviscerate him where he stood, but she remembered the plan. Like Aureon and Theodon, she had to commit to playing the long game for these two weekends, and she knew Bole could potentially lead her to uncover more treachery if she let him go. Adaline lifted the blade from Bole's hand with the flick of her fingers and floated it toward her. She rotated it in the air between them as she examined it.

"What a shitty blade," Adaline said to Bole. "I'm insulted that you would choose this to kill me." Sorsacha watched in wonder at her human friend's power. Adaline focused on the blade, disassembling it at a molecular level, maintaining a centrifugal force for the matter until it reassembled into something worthy of her. The blade was elongated, and the hilt and grip wrapped in an intricately detailed vine design. Adaline finished the transformation with a large red stone embedded in the butt of the knife. Adaline smirked at her handiwork before she took the blade in hand.

"Now that is a blade worth dying by," she whispered as she waved it in his face.

"I want one," Sorsacha blurted.

Adaline looked over her shoulder to see her friend staring at the blade. Adaline addressed Bole again, "I think we should test its sharpness, don't you?" Before anyone could respond, Adaline sank the blade in Bole's gut. A howl immediately escaped from within him as he could still not move, let alone defend himself. Adaline turned back to Sorsacha with a victorious grin. "It works!" Adaline pulled the blade from Bole's body and unfroze him. The elf folded to the ground with blood spilling from his wound. He scrambled away from Adaline before he managed to run from the females with his hands clutching his lower abdomen.

Sorsacha rose from her tub to stand alongside Adaline as they watched Bole run away. "I thought you'd do much worse to him."

Adaline smiled to herself. "I wanted to, but there's a plan in store for that one." Adaline turned to her friend. "Do you understand?"

Sacha gave a slight nod. "So… I'll play along for as long as you need me to and won't ask questions until it's over. Wait, there's going to be an over, right?"

Adaline chuckled. "I will share it with you soon. Until then, play along."

Sorsacha finally nodded. "All right. I'm in. Is there anything you need help with tonight?"

Adaline thought for a moment. "That depends. What usually happens at a royal engagement party?"

"The usual as any other party, except it's far more luxurious: eating, drinking, socializing, and dancing," Sorsacha rambled.

"Hmm," Adaline thought aloud. "How do elves dance?"

Sorsacha rolled her eyes and muttered, "Figures." They grabbed their robes before Sorsacha led Adaline back toward the main house, hand in hand. Adaline couldn't help but giggle while being towed.

CHAPTER 44

"**C**ome in," Adaline instructed at the light knock at the door of her suite. The relaxing afternoon at the Ieobu House that climaxed with Bole's interruption catalyzed Adaline's enthusiasm to start the next part of Aureon's plan: a successful engagement party.

"It's me, Dr. Adaline," Ena greeted as she stepped over the threshold with trinkets encased in delicate little boxes. "I have brought you options to go with your dress for tonight."

Adaline spun in her vanity chair to face Ena, and her eyes lit up at the sight of the little boxes. Little boxes meant one thing: jewelry. Adaline hardly ever wore any and was excited to have the chance to show off tonight. "Lemme see!"

Ena opened each box and placed them on the vanity for Adaline to peruse. Adaline was surprised that the jewelry wasn't more minimalist in design. Each piece was encrusted with gems she'd never seen before, enhancing the intricate settings. Most boxes contained complete sets of jewelry, while smaller ones held luxurious hair combs or rings. The pieces hinted at an elfin aesthetic by incorporating natural designs, but they were out-shined by the gems that adorned them. Adaline was wowed to silence as she carefully examined one set at a time. She hesitated to touch them.

"Go ahead," Ena encouraged her.

Adaline pulled one of the boxes closer and carefully touched the stones of the wreath necklace inside. Saturated with red stones that reflected an iridescence of orange and fuchsia, Adaline unlatched the necklace from the box and carefully lifted it. She approached her dress resting on a mannequin in the corner of her bedroom, and she draped the necklace around its neck.

Perfect, she thought before turning to Ena and said, "These are very beautiful, Ena, thank you."

"Don't thank me, Dr. Adaline," Ena replied. "The king chose the assortment himself so that you would have plenty of options."

Adaline smiled to herself before she remembered that Tobey was with Aureon. "He managed to select jewelry while keeping an eye on a little speedster boy?"

Ena smiled. "Just barely, Dr. Adaline," Ena recalled hearing a scuffle in the king's study that afternoon, and she went to address the noise. She opened the door to find the king glaring at Tobey, who was swinging from the chandelier made of antlers. Tobey's attention turned to Ena, while Aureon's did not. The king unhooked the boy's caught waistband from the antlers and set him on the floor. Ena tried to swallow a smile as she quietly backed out of the room and closed the door.

Adaline chuckled before she turned back to the dress and considered the design. "Ena, are there any rules of dress for an event like tonight's that would be best for me to consider?"

Ena thought for a moment as she closed the lids of the un-chosen jewelry boxes. "None come to mind."

"So, I wouldn't be harming any rules of etiquette if I altered my dress to be a little more... bare-shouldered?" Adaline clarified.

Ena moved to Adaline's side, surveying the dress on the mannequin. "That sounds quite lovely." Ena reached for the dress.

Adaline stopped her. "What are you doing?"

"I was going to make the alterations you wanted," the she-elf was confused by Adaline's interruption.

Adaline put her hand on Ena's shoulder and smiled. "I've got this." Adaline focused on the dress, and it began to shift and change on the form. Ena's eyes widened as she saw the straps disappear and the neckline change to a sweetheart shape.

"That's incredible!" Ena sputtered.

"Thanks," Adaline said with a smug grin.

An hour went by, and Ena had gone. Adaline continued to prepare for the evening. She swept up her long dark hair into a smooth, elegant style and decided against wearing the encrusted comb that matched the jewelry set she chose. Adaline surveyed her appearance in the mirror, then added the earrings and bracelet to her ensemble.

The idea of having enough came to mind. As independently wealthy as Adaline was in her world, she never changed her mindset to simply having enough versus having more because she could. She didn't live in excess, aside from her beachfront home, and Adaline didn't throw parties every other weekend like Asher. She came from a blue-collar family and always figured that meeting one's basic needs was simply enough.

Adaline found herself mesmerized by the wreath necklace as the realization settled in: she could do more than enough tonight. Tonight, she could indulge, and it would be all right because she was attending a large celebration. She carefully picked up the necklace at the moment there was a knock on her door.

"It's open," Adaline said as she felt anxiety and a wave of power coming from the other side of the door. It opened slowly, but no one entered. Adaline approached to see who was there while attempting to secure the necklace around her neck. She watched Aureon posted on the other side of the threshold in his evening attire as he peered down at Tobey. Adaline smiled at the sight of the two of them.

"I see you both survived the day together," Adaline joked while looking back and forth between the two of them.

"He is quite fast, but not too fast for me." Aureon's eyes narrowed on the boy, and Tobey had the decency to look sheepish.

Adaline addressed Tobey, "Did you have a good day?"

Tobey barely looked away from Aureon long enough to sign, "Yes."

Adaline narrowed her gaze on Aureon, knowing that some sort of discipline had happened while Tobey was out of her sight. She couldn't criticize the king, even jokingly, because of how he was looking at her.

"Tobey, go get ready for bed," Adaline said as her attention remained on Aureon. The boy ran to his bed, relieved to be out of the king's sight. Adaline's breathing changed as she studied Aureon's outfit. His robes were the same green as his eyes, with accents of black and gold in the embroidered design that wrapped around his chest. In a daze, Adaline touched the design with the tip of her finger. The slight contact changed her innocent exploration into a charged interaction.

Aureon's body heated as his heartbeat raced, and he couldn't take his eyes off her. He liked her body wrapped in the boldest of reds. His hand covered hers against his chest, ceasing her exploration. She met his dilated gaze while his racing heart thundered under her palm. Her eyelids hooded, and she moved closer. He reached for her with his other hand, but reality interrupted the moment, and he fisted his hand at his side. He cleared his throat, bringing her out of her blissful haze.

He noticed the necklace in her hand. "May I?"

Adaline nodded and carefully placed the necklace in his hand. She turned her back to him, and he sighed hard. His breath sent goosebumps down her neck and shoulders as he hesitated to follow through with his assistance. Finally, he carefully lifted the necklace over her head and wrapped it around her neck. He took his time securing it, knowing that this was as close he would be to her all night.

Once he finished, she faced him and smiled. "Thank you."

"My pleasure," he admitted, as his gaze remained locked on hers. "Did you enjoy your time at the Ieobu House today?"

She smiled to herself. "Yes, it was what I needed." Her gaze fell to her feet as she decided now was not the time to share the exchange with Bole.

He gave her a side-eyed glance. "Was there something not to your liking?"

Adaline maintained her smile as she thought of Bole's dagger that she transformed into something beautiful. "There was, but I fixed it." She winked. "Can I share with you later?" She was still wrapping her mind around everyone she would be introduced to at the engagement party that evening and whose soul records were left to read. Aureon nodded. In an attempt to turn the interaction back to a platonic exchange, she asked, "Is there anything about the formalities of this evening that I should know?"

Aureon's head tilted as he thought about her question without removing his eyes from her. Finally, he answered, "You will be standing for much of the evening, and I encourage you to be mindful of the shoes you wear." A moment passed before he added, "Otherwise, Theodon will be there to lead you through everything." She detected the disappointment in his voice. His son was more than capable of keeping her safe through the party. However, the physical and emotional distance between Aureon and his little human was becoming frustrating. Elves bonded deeply, and the fact that he was staring down at his mate with whom he could not be with was unnatural. He reverted to his emotionless countenance, and Adaline noticed the change in him as it occurred. She took it as her cue to do the same.

"Thank you for your assistance, Your Majesty," she said formally.

The king gave his usual clipped nod before stepping away from her door. "You are welcome, Dr. Adaline."

Adaline closed the door to her suite and was jolted from her dreamy thoughts of Aureon by the rustling of Tobey trying to get comfortable in his bed. She smiled to herself and made her way to his bedside, and she moved a chair close to him.

"Having trouble?" Adaline asked as she sat down.

He nodded with the side of his face nestled against his pillow. He lifted his hands and signed to Adaline, "Can you tell me a story, please?"

Adaline searched her thoughts before she remembered an old story that Asher had loved as a child. "Okay," Adaline said before shifting in her seat to get comfortable. "There was a young man who lived in a busy city with his aunt, and he lost his parents when he was a boy."

Tobey interrupted her to sign, "Just like me?"

"Yes!" Adaline said with a smile. "Just like you. He was a brilliant young man, and during a field trip to a fancy laboratory, he was bitten by a spider, and it gave him superpowers...."

Twenty minutes into the story, Tobey's look of wonder changed to a snoring, sprawling boy. Adaline chuckled, knowing that it wasn't because of her story but because Tobey had two modes: on and off, as he had no middle ground.

Another knock on the door of her suite echoed in the foyer. Adaline finished tucking Tobey in and made her way to the door. She slowly opened it to find Theodon, who smiled when he saw her. He was wearing red in his ensemble to match her dress.

"You look enchanting," he said to her.

She grinned. "So, do you."

"May I come in?"

"Of course," she stepped out of the doorway. Once the door closed behind Theodon, Adaline brought up her force field to contain their private conversation.

"I think you should know a few things about the noble houses because members of each one, except the Miathans, will be attending the party tonight," Theodon shared. Adaline nodded, ready as ever to receive the information. Theodon proceeded to share the highs and lows of the noble houses and where they currently stood in the king's eyes. The Miathan house was one of the oldest houses to serve the crown and the Wrocan house. Helious Wrocan's sons would not be present at the party, as they were in the middle of a long journey back from the Braorix Mountains with their mother. Landon from the Elacan house would be present, and Adaline cringed at the thought of having to interact with him again. The Aetrunes would be present, along with their children, Roserie and Bole. Adaline smirked at the thought of running into Bole. Flavial Usleon would attend with his son, Forb. Adaline wasn't worried about ulterior motives from either of the Usleons after reading Forb's soul record. She would check Flavial, just to be sure. Loose ends were not something she could afford to leave untied tonight. Finally, Mouriel Olostuil would be present and arrive separately from his daughter, Sorsacha. Adaline's brow furrowed at the thought of her friend coming on her own when she had a father who was probably trying to connect with her. She was sure she'd learn more about their relationship tonight once she saw them in the same room together.

"Are you ready?" Theodon asked her.

Adaline snapped out of her thoughts and nodded. "The party is starting now?"

Theodon grinned as he offered her his elbow. "The party started an hour ago, and we are the last to arrive."

"The perks of being a royal," Adaline joked as she took Theodon's elbow. "Shall we wow them all, my adoring fiancé?"

Theodon chuckled before he mimicked her exaggeration. "We shall, my bride."

CHAPTER 45

"Where is Graydon?" Helious Wrocan asked Flavial. Before the engaged prince and his bride entered the banquet hall, the elders stood together, socializing with drinks in hand.

Flavial gave the slightest shrug. "I haven't seen or heard from him in days. Maybe four or five. Has anyone else laid eyes on him?" The others shook their heads.

"It seems odd for him to miss such an occasion, given how much he enjoys being seen," Helious commented before taking a sip of his beverage.

Mouriel Olostuil shot Flavial a knowing look before returning to his drink. Mouriel was hoping he would see his daughter at the party and maybe have the chance to speak with her. *How was that conversation going to start?* He wondered. *Hello, darling. I have missed you at home, even though it is my fault you haven't been there. That should go well.*

Whether he saw Sorsacha or not, he must speak with the king. Many years of his knowledge of specific past events wore on him. He'd never felt his old age before until he thought of Sorsacha and what caused him to forsake his youngest daughter. Mouriel was distracted from his thoughts at the sound of the royal band switching from a soft background tune to the music that signaled a royal entrance.

The king was already sitting at the head of the banquet table, waiting for his son and the human doctor's arrival. The guards reached for the double doors at the far end of the banquet hall as the music crescendoed to indicate a big reveal. The doors opened to unveil the Prince Theodon beaming at his bride with a genuine grin on his face. The only image that surpassed Theodon's joy was the equally large smile on Adaline's face. All conversation in the banquet hall quieted at the sight of them. Adaline looked at the prince lovingly, and she used both hands to clutch his elbow as he escorted her across the floor. They seemed to be in their own little world of laughter and jokes, as neither of them looked away from each other until Theodon noticed they were crossing the dance floor.

"Would you like to dance?" he asked her. It wasn't standard practice to dance before dinner, but Adaline brought out his playful side when she got him laughing.

Adaline's eyes lit up as she squeezed his elbow. "I would love to dance."

Theodon brought her close to his body, becoming her frame before nodding to the band to play the next song. He hovered with her in his arms for a moment before leading her across the dance floor. As much of a warrior as Theodon was, he possessed his father's precision along with the natural grace of an elf. Adaline noticed the room fill with emotions of love and romance as they moved across the floor, all the while secretly thanked Sorsacha for teaching her how to dance. As the two of them were having fun, the king was mesmerized by how she moved across the floor.

"Aren't they beautiful, My Lord?" Sorsacha said in his mind as she approached his side.

"They truly are," the king replied as he watched his son have a happy moment. He could tell Adaline was carrying a little anxiety in her face as she hoped to get the steps right.

"I taught her this afternoon," Sorsacha commented. The king gave a slight nod without taking his eyes off them. "It's almost difficult to watch, isn't it, My Lord? At the same time, it's so beautiful you can't bring yourself to look away." A moment later, Sorsacha was gone. The king remained faced forward as his eyes shot to his side where Sorsacha had been standing. Her words echoed in his head, then his eyes cleared in realization: Sorsacha had feelings for Theodon. While he kept his expression at his normal even stare, he thought about whom else's heart they might be hurting due to their scheme, besides his own. Would his plan cultivate new enemies through new heartbreak instead of serving its true purpose?

Aureon swallowed his paranoia and turned his focus back to the engaged couple, who finished dancing. He reset his focus back to his priorities: healing his family and bringing the crown's enemies to justice. Theodon escorted Adaline to the royal banquet table, and Aureon rose from his seat to greet them.

"Father," Theodon acknowledged him with a contented smile on his face. Aureon delivered his usual clipped, silent nod in return before he addressed Adaline.

Adaline gave him a genuine smile. "Your Majesty," she said before executing the perfect formal bow. Aureon's heart clenched in his chest, and his breathing raced in a panic as his thoughts spun. *This is wrong. She should never bow to anyone.* Keeping up appearances was taking its toll on him more than he realized, but he was put at ease when Adaline's attention raised to his once she finished, and her smile widened. Every cell in his body went lax as her actions reaffirmed the truth: she was a good little actress because she was a survivor. None of this charade was getting to her heart.

Theodon passed his father with Adaline still on his arm and pulled out her seat at the banquet table. Everyone present was still silent; their yearning for more visibly romantic moments was apparent to Adaline. The king cleared his throat before commanding everyone to take their seats so that dinner could be served.

The food and drinks flowed for the next two hours. Eventually, everyone was back on their feet, shifting from standing around their tables to standing around the band. Dance music started, and a few couples swayed across the floor while onlookers whispered among themselves. They kept their eyes on those who had enough courage to dance in front of the crowd. Adaline noticed that there was one male elf that cautiously approached a female and offered himself to her. The gesture was specific in that he made sure to stop directly in front of her, close his eyes, extend the frame of his arms, and pushed his chin forward over his toes. The female smiled and set down her drink before she stepped into his personal space. She slowly inserted her hands into his frame and finally touched her cheek to his. A moment passed where Adaline detected relief from the male. He relaxed, adjusted their arms to proper form, and slid his chin back into place. Her cheek followed, nestling her close to his body. They savored the moment of closeness before he led her around the floor.

"What was that?" she whispered to Theodon.

"That was the demonstration of an old custom," Theodon shared.

"Old to an elf is ancient for me," Adaline jested. "Why is he the only one doing it?"

The prince's gaze connected with his father's before he explained, "It's a male offering of himself to a female. It's a form of publicly proposing to one's mate, so to get rejected would bring great despair."

Ah, Adaline thought. It was such a state of vulnerability to enter, making it seem even more precious to her. "What a beautiful gesture," Adaline commented. "Why is it so rarely done?"

Theodon thought for a moment. "There was a time when it often happened because of the example set when my father did it for my mother."

Adaline was stunned. She spun in her seat to look at Aureon, and her heart ached as he avoided her gaze. He acted like he was paying attention to the party guests, who didn't mean nearly as much to him as the two people sitting beside him. Adaline's eyes pooled with tears before she asked Theodon, "And then?"

"And after she died, so did the custom for a long time," Theodon admitted. "It's rare to see it at all anymore." Theodon reached for a spare napkin and dabbed away the tear at the corner of Adaline's eye that was about to fall.

"But it's so beautiful," Adaline's voice cracked in a whisper.

Adaline's emotional statement sank into Aureon's consciousness, embedding itself there forever. He knew she had the capacity for deep emotion, but to show it at such a small gesture surprised him. His little human felt, and she felt a lot.

Could she ever feel all of that for him?

"Your Majesties," a familiar voice broke through his daydream.

Landon.

Aureon noticed Adaline cringe beside him.

"Landon," Aureon replied in a dead tone without giving his direct attention. The king had no respect for Landon because he lacked honor and accountability. Aureon barely tolerated his presence, and only because he was Theodon's uncle since their family was already too small.

"I wanted to come over and personally give my congratulations to my nephew." Landon turned to Theodon.

"Thank you, Uncle," Theodon said graciously before his mood changed. Adaline noticed and slipped her hand between Theodon's jacket and cape to rest behind his heart. Theodon's nostrils flared in anger as he detected a familiar scent, and it was the same one he smelled on Roserie. The realization filled Theodon's eyes as he peered at his uncle as fury rose within him. Adaline let healing light spill from her hand into the back of

Theodon's heart. She sandwiched her other hand over the front of his chest, but she didn't let it ignite to conceal her actions. Theodon's gaze collided with hers, and he noticed her give the slightest shake of her head.

"Breathe," she mouthed to him. Theodon kept his lips sealed as he focused on breathing evenly. His anger disappeared as quickly as it formed.

"Well, I'm glad you chose a female who can't keep her hands off you, Theodon," Landon said shamelessly. "Be careful because her pawing will only last for so long."

Adaline's eyes were still on Theodon, and he saw her irises shift from understanding to glaring rage in the length of a heartbeat. Adaline let go of Theodon and took her time readjusting herself in her chair.

"Would you mind repeating that verbal diarrhea?" Adaline clipped.

A few ears turned in her direction to eavesdrop.

"I'd rather ask you to dance, and we can talk about it privately." He blatantly appraised her while she sat between the two royals. They were growing tenser by the moment, ready to come to her aide. "If you're into that sort of thing." The three males present knew that she would be subject to dancing with Landon if a higher-ranking male did not step in to save her. Little did they know that Adaline was about to change their gender-biased formality.

A smile grew on her face. "No, Landon. I will not dance with you."

"You do not have the power to decline," Landon chuckled at her unfamiliarity with elfin customs.

"I have the greatest power here, you ignorant fool," Adaline said. Her eyes glowed as she rose to her feet. Some elves stepped back because the strength of Adaline's powers was unknown to them, and they didn't want to get caught in the crossfire.

"Females," Landon huffed. "They think they own the world... until I get them under me."

Adaline reached her palm for him and grabbed his throat with her telekinesis. Landon clawed at his throat as she raised him a few inches off the floor. "It seems Uncle Landon needs to learn a lesson in consent." Adaline's grip on his throat tightened, and Landon struggled. Theodon rose from his chair, considering when would be best to intervene. Aureon held up his hand, prompting his son to wait. "When a female tells you no, it doesn't mean we just opened negotiations." Adaline lifted him higher and crushed his throat. "It. Means. NO!"

Aureon gave a slight nod to Theodon, who placed his hand on Adaline's shoulder and squeezed. "I'm almost done," she said to Theodon. Adaline lowered Landon back to eye level and released his throat without releasing her telekinetic hold on his body. "Do we understand each other now, Landon?" Adaline's illuminated gaze blazed. He nodded frantically, unable to answer because his throat was healing. "Good. Unfortunately for you, your presence at this party is not desired."

Elves on the dance floor gasped as they saw Landon floating overhead and out of the entrance doors. Adaline set him on the ground beyond the threshold.

"Close it," the king commanded the guard, who immediately executed his request, shutting the door in the baffled face of Landon Elacan.

Adaline turned to Aureon, who briefly met her gaze. "Thank you." The king returned her thanks with a clipped tuck of his chin before Adaline turned back to Theodon. "Are you all right?"

"Yes," he said. "I discovered some... interesting information."

Adaline's eyes widened. "Should we circulate the party to get your mind off it?"

A moment passed before Theodon nodded. They walked side by side to socialize with the crowd that assembled alongside the dance floor, and Theodon introduced Adaline to each of the elders.

"Dr. Adaline, this is Mouriel Olostuil," Theodon said before someone tapped him on the shoulder from behind. He turned to greet Flavial, who was ecstatic that the prince had found his bride, and they embraced with a few slaps on the back.

"Mouriel Olostuil," Adaline echoed.

"Yes, my dear," the elder canted his head.

"Are you Sorsacha's father?"

The elder rolled his eyes. "What has she done, now?"

Adaline burst with laughter, knowing the elder was unmistakably her friend's father. "We are thinking about the same person." Adaline touched the elder's shoulder. "Sacha's a wonderful person, and I am glad to call her my friend."

The elder's gaze locked onto Adaline, touched by her words. As his eyes searched hers, she took a moment to read his soul record, and it was a long one. As she sped through the endless years of his life, she saw a ruinous fight between Sorsacha and her father, including his warning that she stay out of royal business. The final blow to the elder was his daughter yelling at him, saying he had no honor. Then she threatened to leave. Adaline felt Mouriel's heartbreak, and when he didn't respond due to his pain, Sorsacha left him standing there and never returned.

Sorsacha wasn't cast out of her family home; she left. Adaline reconfirmed. Although Mouriel felt it had been that way. Adaline's eyes widened at the discovery, and Mouriel noticed her surprise when she looked at him. She stopped reading his soul record and attempted to pry, "Have you seen her tonight?"

The elder's face fell. "Unfortunately, I have not."

"I'm sure she's around here somewhere," Adaline assured him with a smile. "If I see her, I will tell her you are looking for her." She said that last part for her friend to hear. Adaline didn't care what had happened previously between the two of them. Mouriel loved his daughter unconditionally, and that didn't deserve to go unnoticed.

"Dr. Adaline," Theodon's voice cut through her moment with Mouriel, and she faced the prince. "This is Flavial Usleon."

"Hello," Adaline said with a wide smile to the elder. Flavial held out both of his hands for one of hers, and she offered her hand, and he clasped his around it.

"It is lovely to meet you, Dr. Adaline," Flavial said with an enchanted grin. "I'm so happy that Theodon has found such a wonderful partner."

"Oh, thank you," she said. "And it's very nice to meet you too. Wait... Usleon? Are you Forb's father?"

"Yes," the elder gave a gracious nod.

Adaline's face illuminated. "Mr. Usleon, you have a wonderful son." The elder almost blushed from the compliment as Forb approached Theodon's side.

"Keep going," Forb jested while waving her on. The four of them laughed as Forb clutched Theodon by the shoulder before hugging him.

Flavial pulled Adaline closer so he could whisper, "Theodon is dear to Forb, just like his father is dear to me."

Adaline met his honest gaze. "They are dear to me, too." They exchanged a moment of knowing before Flavial squeezed her hand fondly and smiled. "How long have you shared friendship with the king?"

"Long before you were born, my dear," Flavial exaggerated.

Adaline smiled. "It seems everything began long before I was born."

Flavial chuckled. "I've known the king since he was a youngling."

"So, you knew his father, too?"

"Not as I know the king," Flavial said quickly. "However, I was a soldier in Cerus' army for some time."

Adaline got a wild idea. "Would you... mind sharing your memories of that time with me?"

Flavial's brow furrowed. "I'm not sure what you mean."

"I have a gift," Adaline began.

"Is it anything like when you floated Landon out of the

room?" Forb chimed in.

"Which was quite clever," Flavial admitted with an open laugh. "I don't think a female has ever put him in his place like that."

Adaline grinned. "No, it's not a gift that affects your mobility." She moved closer. "If you let me touch you, you can show me your memories." She didn't need to touch him to see, but the connection was a little clearer.

Flavial's eyebrows lifted, a rare occurrence for him as very little surprised him. "Why not? I'm intrigued. Let's try it."

"Thank you for humoring me," she said, then she touched him.

Flavial's eyes slid closed, and he dug back through the lengthy timeline of his even longer existence. He showed Adaline his first interactions with Aureon, who looked even younger than Theodon did at that moment. Even at so young an age, Aureon didn't stumble, fall, or fail in public. He was relentless in his desire to learn all he could, so he practiced and studied privately. His father didn't sugarcoat what was expected of him, so he worked tirelessly.

Flavial fast-forwarded thousands of years later to the war of the Hexaborgs in the northern mountains of the kingdom. Flavial fought by Aureon's side on the battlefield, his loyalty to serve his king was unflinching. Aureon would eat with his soldiers, but Flavial and Helious were the only two that would dare be near the new king. Flavial kept encouraging Aureon that his time for a break was coming because Aravae was due to bear Theodon at any time. Adaline's eyes watered from witnessing the memory. Then Flavial showed her what changed in the king when Aureon returned to war from home.

The rage within Aureon was unsettling, even more so when he unleashed it on their enemies. Flavial could not have predicted the king's capacity for such brutality. Flavial stayed close to the king as Aureon's ferocity rippled over the battlefield, making sure his king wouldn't make a reckless move that would cost him his life. Flavial didn't want to lose his king, one he believed truly deserved the crown. More importantly, he didn't want to lose his friend. Flavial heard Adaline sniff back tears, and he covered her hand on his temple with his own.

"One more," he said with his eyes still closed. "I'll make it a good one."

"Okay," she whispered.

Flavial reached forward in his memories and showed one of Flavial escorting his son, a little youngling, to the palace's gardens. An equally little Theodon jumped down from a small tree, his bow pulled back, with an arrow knocked and aimed at the two of them.

"Your Majesty," Flavial said to young prince Theodon. "I would like to introduce you to my son, Forb."

Theodon surveyed Forb skeptically. Forb clung to his father's robe while Flavial's hand rested behind his son's head, encouraging him to step forward.

"My Lord," little Forb greeted the prince.

Theodon kept staring at them, unsure what to say.

"I thought the two of you would play well together," Flavial said to them both as he kept encouraging his son forward, who was digging in his heels.

Forb spun around to address his father, "But why father? Can't I go play at home?"

"You can, my son, but what fun is that?" Flavial crouched down to be eye level with Forb. Flavial could tell his boy didn't understand what he was missing. "You have a chance to befriend a special youngling."

Forb glanced at little Theodon over his shoulder and didn't see what was so special about the prince because he just looked sad. What fun was that?

"Prince Theodon has lost his mother and is still hurting," Flavial explained to his son. "And just like I watched over his father when he was hurting, you must do the same for Theodon." Forb listened closely to his father. "You come from an honorable family, my son. Just like Theodon comes from an honorable family. And when honorable people become friends, the true friendship lasts a lifetime."

Little Forb's eyes widened in wonder. "A whole lifetime, Father?" It was such a long time for an elf.

Flavial chuckled. "Yes, my son. If you remain an honorable and true friend, it can last your whole lifetime."

Little Forb grinned at the idea and turned to Theodon, who was uncomfortable at being the subject of their discussion. Forb looked up at his father, who returned to standing over him. "I'll do it." Then he took off running after Theodon.

A tear ran down Adaline's cheek as she slowly pulled her hand away from Flavial's temple. She opened her eyes to see an ancient, loving gaze staring back at her.

"As I said, very dear," Flavial reiterated. All Adaline could manage was nod and smile, and Flavial kissed her knuckles before he released her hand. "And now you, too."

"Thank you," she whispered.

"My pleasure."

"Is that Bole?" Forb asked the group. Everyone turned to see where Forb's attention had fallen. Bole was shuffling around the room. His body was stiff, and he wasn't letting anyone touch him.

"He looks injured," Flavial commented.

Adaline shot Theodon a knowing look. Theodon's eyes widened.

"Dr. Adaline, I've heard some remarkable stories of your healing abilities," Flavial buttered her up. "It looks like Bole may require your talents."

Adaline smirked. *He got one heck of a preview earlier.*

"Yes, he does," Adaline admitted aloud. "I'll see what I can do."

As Adaline made a beeline for Bole, she heard Forb say to Theodon, "At first, I thought you were rushing into things, but now I see why you picked her."

Aw, she thought, before turning her sights back on Bole, the evil, murderous, dishonorable coward. Her countenance blanked as she approached him. Once he saw her coming, he froze.

"Bole," Adaline addressed the traitor.

"Dr. Adaline," he managed to get out.

"What happened?" Adaline asked. "You look like you got your ass kicked." Her eyes narrowed on him as a deafening beat of silence passed between them. "Here, let me help you." She reached forward before Bole could jump back and rested a glowing hand against his torso. His body jerked as he felt his wound seal up and his tissues heal. Adaline's cold stare was locked on him the entire time. She wanted to slaughter him where he stood. Instead, she dropped her hand when she finished. Everyone around her was in awe as Bole pulled up the hem of his shirt to see that his knife wound was gone – no trace of it left behind.

"That is incredible," Adaline heard a female voice behind her.

"Indeed," a male voice replied.

Adaline didn't look to see who made the comments until both elves finished approaching. They were an older couple who looked genuinely intrigued, with kindness in their eyes.

"Hello," the female said to Adaline.

"Hi," Adaline replied, as she curiously looked the couple over, noticing a resemblance of Bole in the male.

"I'm Celu Aetrune," the she-elf stated.

Realization hit Adaline with a slight nod. "Bole's mother."

"Yes," Celu said with a proud smile.

"And I'm his father, Ensatus Aetrune," the male offered.

Adaline nodded again. "It's nice to meet you both." She was confused because the Aetrunes were so… nice. Yet, their children were so vile. She read their soul records as they thanked her for coming to their son's aide. She was saddened to find that the Aetrunes had nothing but love and good intentions for their children and had no idea that Graydon had lured them into treacherous territory. Adaline knew the inevitable arrest of their children would come as a shock.

"It's nothing, especially when it only takes a moment," Adaline admitted to them.

"Nevertheless, we appreciate it all the same," Celu told her.

"I'm impressed as well." A tall figure walked up next to Adaline. His dark hair and green eyes had her peg him for a Tearuine elf, like Aureon, Theodon, and Helious. He appeared much older than the three elves combined, however. Adaline noticed that Bole had disappeared from the social circle.

"Qelon, I haven't seen you in ages!" Bole's father embraced the tall elf.

"How are you, old friend?" Qelon asked Ensatus as Adaline quietly witnessed their interaction.

"I'm well, thank you," Ensatus replied. "Have you met Dr. Adaline?"

Qelon looked Adaline over intently. "I have not yet had the pleasure. I just know she's taken a lot of work off my desk." The elf smiled at her.

Adaline did not apologize, if that's what Qelon was expecting, so she continued to hold her space in silence with a smile.

"I heard the little Alloralla girl is going to be just fine," Qelon commented.

Adaline nodded. "Little Farryn has made a full recovery."

"And I hear her mother is carrying twins under your care," he disclosed.

"That is correct," Adaline confirmed with a smile. She was still finding her footing with Qelon, trying to be polite while not giving away details about her patients, no matter if they were human or elf.

"That's a hard time for our females," Qelon divulged. "It is rough on their bodies, let alone coping with the loss when it inevitably comes."

Adaline pursed her lips. "I'm optimistic about Sana's case."

Qelon features lifted in surprise. "You don't seriously think that she can bring both twins to term?"

Theodon joined Adaline and slipped his arm around her before pulling her against his side. Her hand rested against his chest as she smiled at him.

"I will give no false hope, Qelon," Adaline said. "But I've put a practice in place that gives Sana a solid chance. At what outcome? I don't know yet. However, I am certain it won't be a complete failure."

Judging by Qelon's rigid straightening of his posture, Adaline could tell the healer didn't like her optimism over his years of experience, let alone her lack of sharing the details. Adaline had no use for bragging when it came to her medical work since it spoke for itself, which was why Qelon had heard of it in the first place. Instead of trying to spar with her intellectually, Qelon greeted Theodon.

"Good evening to you, too, Qelon," Theodon said as he glanced at Adaline. "I see you have met my betrothed."

"Yes, I have had the pleasure just now, My Lord," Qelon tried to make up for his earlier rudeness.

"Good," Theodon said. "I hope you will be open to her methods, as she has done a great deal for my father and me."

Shock radiated from Qelon. "My Lord, had you or your father experienced any difficulty, I would have come to your aide."

"That's just it, Qelon," Theodon said, as he locked eyes with Adaline, "it was pain we could no longer see or feel because it had become a part of us. She could see it because of her objective perspective… and her amazing gifts." Theodon kissed Adaline on the forehead and squeezed her against his side.

Adaline enjoyed not having to argue for herself even though she could manage it. Aside from her work speaking for itself, she knew it was best for Theodon, or Aureon, to handle the discontentment of elves, just as she would handle the same with humans had the royals visited her world. The thought made her shudder. Her world was getting worse, and the possibility of something happening to one of the royals while they were in her world bothered her.

"I'm sorry he was so ornery with you," a she-elf said as she approached. Adaline snapped back to reality to notice a young female Tearuine elf joining the conversation. Theodon's grip on Adaline loosened as she saw that Qelon was gone, along with the Aetrunes.

"Dr. Adaline, this is Iliana Drolon, Qelon's niece and apprentice royal healer," Theodon said.

"Your Majesty," Iliana gave the prince a formal bow before addressing Adaline. "Don't worry about my uncle. He gets like that when someone talks about something new and revolutionary." Iliana winked at her. "I think he's afraid of becoming obsolete."

"I'm sure he's a force to reckon with in his own right to become the king's healer," Adaline offered.

Iliana nodded. "He is but only practicing the old ways has also made him stubborn in his old ways." She smiled.

Adaline liked Iliana and read her soul record. Iliana knew how to use the old methods and the new ones she was developing herself. This will make her a great healer one day.

"I'm very interested in learning about your methods, Dr. Adaline," Iliana admitted. "I've heard only positive reviews regarding your technique. Is it easily teachable?"

Adaline thought about her response for a moment because she could not reveal every detail about her gifts. "It's an innate gift, I'm afraid. If you are looking into the science aspect of it, you should meet my brother as he is a master chemist and can synthesize remedies easily."

Iliana nodded, pleased by the information. "That sounds wonderful. When will I have the pleasure of meeting him?"

"He will be here for the ceremony next week," Adaline offered. "I'm sure you two will meet then. He enjoys talking about his discoveries."

"I like him already," Iliana admitted before extracting herself from the conversation. "Have a lovely evening, the both of you."

"Thank you," Theodon and Adaline echoed as Iliana faded into the crowd. He faced Adaline, and they let out a heavy sigh as they locked eyes.

"We got through that," Theodon said.

Adaline smiled. "We did."

"Dessert?"

"Yes, please," Adaline said as she tucked her hand in his elbow.

After more drinking, dancing, desserting, and socializing, Adaline was escorted to her suite by her loving fake-fiancé. She quietly closed the door behind her so that she wouldn't wake Tobey. Adaline slipped out of her shoes and quietly padded to her bathroom, where she took a long, hot shower. She emerged in her sleepwear and wrapped the beautiful dark-pink robe around her that she found in her wardrobe.

Adaline wandered onto the large, half-circle balcony that extended from her suite and stretched out onto the soft cushions of one of the lounge chairs. She folded her hands over her waist as her gaze got lost in the night sky. Thick with stars, whether static or shooting, Adaline was in awe of the activity visible in Theris' night sky. Two stars were so large she figured they were planets, and she reminded herself that she would need to learn a whole new universe after their charade was over. *Maybe Aureon has a library I can get lost in.*

Adaline dismissed any lingering thoughts, and she sat up to meditate. She didn't hum to the sound of the universe, and she didn't visualize an intended goal. She quieted her mind and focused on remaining present. Her effort benefitted her immediately, as her muscles went lax, and the tension in her neck and shoulders gave way. Her concept of time vanished as the natural vibration of Theris hummed through her cells. Once she finally finished, she opened her eyes and noticed her body had reset, and no stress was present.

Yet, sadness remained.

Odd, she thought. She searched her thoughts to find the root, and her eyes widened when her mind landed on the memories Flavial shared with her. She replayed them once more and couldn't help but get emotional all over again. She saw the memories of how Aureon was when he was rooted in severe emotional pain due to losing Aravae. Yet, he went back to the battlefield to fight with Flavial at his side. She couldn't imagine seeing his pain from his perspective. The thought made her cringe. From Flavial's perspective, he seemed consumed, wild, and so deeply rooted in despair that it was scary to witness. She felt Flavial's loyalty of staying at the king's side on the war front and was wary of his actions, outbursts, and rage.

Adaline teleported into Aureon's suite. She tip-toed into his bedroom from the balcony and found him tucked under the covers facing the opposite direction. His breathing was deep, and even before it changed to shallow due to his awareness of her presence. Their auras overlapped and sizzled together as she moved closer to the bed. Adaline took her time assessing him and was content to find he carried tranquility within him.

Finally!

Even though Aureon wore no crown, no opulent robes, and even if she disregarded seeing the colorful energy waves that rippled off his body, it was evident that he was still someone of importance. Seeing him in such peaceful disarray made her heart skip. His long, jet-black hair reflected blue in the moonlight that peeked through a gap in the curtains. She noticed the muscular definition of his shoulders, arms, and upper back was more defined than how he presented himself in his dreams. However, she wasn't here for the eye candy. She neared the bed, carrying the need to comfort him. His heart rate accelerated as she moved closer, but she didn't pick up on his heartbeat, only his anxiety.

Anxiety?

Adaline stopped to read him. He was anxious to have her near. She softened and slid onto the bed. She laid next to him and wrapped her arm around his chest. She used his weight as an anchor to pull herself closer and stacked her cheek against his. The softness of her skin made him rub against her cheek like an animal as he awoke.

"Is this a dream?" he whispered.

"No," she replied.

His eyes flashed open, and he quickly turned onto his back, cupped her bottom then pulled her onto his chest.

"I didn't mean to wake you," she admitted as she rested her chin on his chest.

Aureon liked having her sprawled on top of him, as demonstrated by his squeezing of her lower back. He tried to keep his hand in that one spot. If he started to explore, the night would surely escalate.

"Then what did you mean to do, little human?" he asked her playfully.

She gave a soft smile. "I felt compelled to comfort you...." Her gaze softened as her words dropped off. He saw her sadness for him. He swiped a loose strand of hair off her face and tucked it behind her ear.

"What did Flavial show you?" he asked gently. He wouldn't force information out of her, but he wanted to understand what point in his painful history she witnessed.

Adaline sighed as she chose her words carefully. Her gaze remained unwavering. "I saw Flavial introducing Forb to Theo, part of the war, and your pain."

Understanding struck the king. "It's most likely an exaggeration-"

"Aureon," she cut him off with a stare that warned him not to test her intelligence.

Aureon's hand slid down to her bottom and clutched her firmly, and his nostrils flared at the sound of his name on her lips. Her eyes widened at his bold move.

"Say it again," he commanded.

Adaline whispered his name in the darkness. His grip on her tightened, and he pulled her up his body until her lips hovered over his. She tucked her elbows underneath herself, so she could push to sit up. He wrapped his arm around her, blocking her from putting any more space between them. When she looked at him in confusion, he was shaking his head. Then his lips reached up for hers. She softened at his gesture, and she kissed him. He was entranced as her actions were soft but hungry. He groaned underneath her, and his lips continued to reach for her soft kiss, ravenous for her. He finally managed to gently part from her. They looked at each other in wonder for a moment while their breaths meshed, noticing the difference in their kiss from his dreams versus waking life.

It was more. Better. Addictive.

"This is unfair," Aureon said, breaking their blissful haze with logic. His eyes were still closed as his brow furrowed at the sensations that traveled through him while he could not remain more than a breath away from her.

"What do you mean?" Adaline asked, confused and still a little dazed as she leaned in to touch the tip of her nose to his. Their eyes opened to meet again.

"You have seen a traumatic part of my past, but I have not seen one of yours," he said, trying to stay focused, but he couldn't pry his attention from her delicious lips.

Adaline wanted to dive back in, to kiss him thoroughly, but she settled for tucking her face into the crook of his neck. She inhaled his scent deeply, exhaled slowly, then placed a soft kiss against his neck. He let out a low growl that made her smile.

"What do you suggest we do about it?" she whispered.

We. Adaline thought to include him, and he liked that. He wanted to take advantage of this opportunity to increase their bond; to build more trust between them. However, it was challenging to focus on relationship strategy when she kissed his neck and nibbled on his ear.

"I think it would be fair for you to share a memory that is of equal emotional impact," he said. Before he could finish the statement, Adaline's head popped up from where it rested to meet his gaze. There was fear there, fear to share with him. He had to win this exchange to build their relationship. A relationship that didn't get to exist just yet. "It will give us both the chance to know each other better."

Adaline was astonished by his admission. "You want that?"

He nodded, then planted a firm kiss on her lips. "Show me."

Show him a war memory of her own? She was sure he would lose his cool, so she raised her force field around them. He eyed the shield, then her. "You may find yourself raising your voice after witnessing this particular memory," she said honestly.

"Which memory?" he asked.

"It's the first war Asher and I fought in," she said nervously. He searched her eyes, trying to find a reason for her tone. "We... fought when we were much younger than you," she said without further detail while raising her hand to his temple. "Are you ready?"

Aureon kept his eyes on her as he nodded, then they snapped shut when she touched his forehead. Aureon saw the reflection of two twin children in a mirror. They must have been around seven or eight years old, and adults fitted them with body armor. Both children had the same dark chocolate eyes, thick lashes, and dark hair. The little boy had short, wavy hair, while his sister's hair was straight.

His sister.

Adaline. Aureon's heart sank in his chest as he recognized his little human when she was, in fact, very little. Too little. And she was being outfitted for war? Rage started to boil the Aureon's blood.

"You are just babies," he seethed.

"Easy," he heard Adaline's voice in the distance as she held him down from leaping into action. "Tell me if you want me to stop."

"No," he hissed. As upset as it was making him, he wanted to see it through the end.

The scene changed from the twins hugging their mother, an inconsolable wreck, to them walking along with their father, who held their hands tightly. Another man approached their father and gazed down at both children uneasily.

"Are you sure you want to do this, Michael?" a younger Jim Monroe asked their father. "They're just kids."

Colonel Michael Everly looked at his friend deliberately, even though fear was rooted in his heart. "They are far more than children, Jim. This is what they were born to do." Michael watched his children before adding, "They will end this war in minutes." Jim looked from one twin to the next. Both nodded at their father's words.

"All right then," Jim consented, even though he was shaking his head after he walked away.

Michael got down on one knee to speak to his children. "I know what you can do, but only the two of you know what you are truly capable of. So, when you go out there today, protect each other first. Protect those who are good. And don't hesitate to get rid of those who are evil. Do you understand?" The twins quickly nodded. Their unafraid eyes never left their father. "Good," Michael said as he pulled both children in for a tight hug. His stern countenance cracked.

A younger Tony Harper approached Michael to take the children to the front line with the rest of the Marines. Tony was smiling at the twins.

"Hey, kids," Tony said.

"Hi Tony," they echoed.

Tony nodded to his friend and superior officer. "I'll protect them," Tony said while reaching for their hands. Michael's grip on his children tightened. "It's okay, Mike."

Slowly, Michael's grip eased, and his children walked away from him with their hands tucked in Tony's. Seeing his children walk away from him to go to the front line of war was crippling, especially when little Adaline turned back to mouth, "I love you." Adaline saw her father's gaze drop to his feet before he sniffed back tears.

The memory changed to the twins standing in the trenches with live fire overhead. They spoke to each other telepathically.

"This won't end if we stay down here," Adaline admitted to her twin.

"You want to go out there?" Asher asked.

Adaline shrugged. "They can't hurt us, Ash. And good people are dying all around us."

Asher nodded and reached for her hand. "I'll protect you."

Little Adaline smiled at her brother. "And I'll protect you."

A moment later, the twins charged from the trenches in a blur. Tony popped up from the hole, yelling their names as terror filled his face. He reached for the kids, but they were too fast for him. The two ran side by side, with Adaline using her force field as a shield. Asher struck down the enemy with his electric current, using anything they wielded with metal against them, while Adaline disarmed their soldiers with her telekinesis. Any weapons pointed at the twins disintegrated in enemy hands. Tanks turned into giant piles of sand. Adaline threw light balls. Some caught bombs before they struck their intended targets, encasing the blast before it folded into itself. Some she brought to her lips and whispered, "Boom!" inside of it, before she threw it, turning them into bombs.

"We're doing it!" Adaline cheered to her brother, who was having the time of his life moving at his normal, fast pace.

A short time passed, and the field was clear. No ammunition against them remained, and anyone on the firing end of the catastrophe was disarmed or dead. The twins walked back to the trenches with dirt smudged on their faces and clothes. Tony grabbed them, pulled them down into the trench, and examined them to ensure they weren't injured. He gave a loud sigh of relief when he found they were unharmed and hugged them.

"We're okay, Tony," little Adaline said, patting the Marine's arm.

Tony chuckled. "You two scared the hell outta me." He took them back to their father, who cried at the sight of them, thankful they had returned unharmed.

"You need to shower and change before your mother sees you," Michael said to them as he hurried them along to find a place for them to wash up.

Adaline took her hand away from Aureon's temple, and his eyes popped open. She was shocked to silence at the sight of tears in his eyes. Instead of using words, she slowly reached for his cheek and caressed him. He grabbed her wrist and moved her palm to his lips, where he kissed her without breaking his stare.

"How old were you?" Aureon asked. His eyes narrowed on her as he waited for the truth.

"We were about seven years old," she said softly.

A loud growl left his chest as he pulled her down onto the bed and pinned her under his body. "Too young," he snarled as he pressed his lips against the side of her neck. He channeled his anger into his hunger for her.

"If it helps," she said, as she braced for how sensitive his kiss felt on her neck, "I wasn't ready to see your war memory, either."

Adaline's statement broadsided his expectations and forced him to recall both memories objectively. He initially thought the war memory she saw was nothing significant, when in fact, it was one of the darkest moments of his life.

"I didn't mean-" he started.

"I know."

Silence hung between them.

"Understand that if you want to see my memories, there are very few happy ones," she admitted. "And if this is something you no longer want to do, I understand."

Aureon growled at her last statement and shook his head hard. "No, I want to see them." His brows drew tight as he switched tactics. He gathered her hands in his and kissed her knuckles. "I don't want you to hide any part of yourself from me." Her desire for him grew upon hearing his admission. "And you can look at my memories whenever you want to if it does not bother you."

"Bother me?" she asked.

"I don't want you to see anything that will keep you up at night," he admitted. "You sleep with a force field protecting you as it is. I have no desire for you to lose any more sleep, especially if it has to do with me."

She slowly outlined his perfect cupid's bow with the tip of her finger. His mouth opened, and he nibbled on it.

"How about if I have any problems sleeping, I just come snuggle with you until I fall asleep?" she whispered as she found her segue.

Aureon's eyes narrowed, realizing her ploy. He gently nipped at her thumb, and she giggled. "You should be sleeping now," he said as he pulled her over before he pressed his bare chest into her back, curling his body around hers. He pulled her robe down off her shoulder and kissed her skin, and then he pulled up the covers. He kissed her skin until she shivered, then replaced the robe and squeezed her to his chest. "Sleep. I'll make sure to return you before Tobey awakens."

Adaline wiggled to get comfortable. As she did, she heard a low rumble escape his chest as his hand dropped to squeeze her hip. She turned to find his lips and kissed him. She grabbed his hand off her hip and pulled it to her front, tucking his palm against her breast.

"Is this okay?" she asked him, with their noses close to touching. She didn't want to be unfair to him, pushing his senses over the edge just to make her comfortable. He gave a slight nod as his hand greedily latched onto her curves. "Thank you," she whispered as she snuggled against him.

Aureon planted another kiss on her neck before he rested his cheek against her ear. "Whatever you need, little human."

CHAPTER 46

T he following day, Tobey sprawled next to Adaline in the garden while she was lost in thought, staring at the tree branches overhead. Tobey couldn't see the natural magic that Adaline could, so he assumed she was daydreaming. But then she snatched something out of the air and examined it. She gently held the mystery substance between her fingers. She filled it with her healing light, and the combination of her ability and the natural magic that existed in Theris triggered a rippling of different colors in that space. Tobey sat up and stared in awe.

Adaline smiled. "Can you see it, now?"

Tobey nodded as he scooted closer, watching the pink light change to green, then blue. Tobey's finger moved toward the colors.

"Careful," Adaline warned him.

Tobey hesitated before continuing with his plan. He pushed his finger into the space, and the colors rippled from his finger. The space felt thick, even though he couldn't see where it started or ended because the color faded before it reached the edges. Adaline stretched her fingers further apart, and the colors in the space grew.

"I have an idea," Adaline said, and she stood while cradling the colors with both hands. She played with it for a moment then concluded she could manipulate it. She stretched the ball from the size of a baseball to the size of a grapefruit. Tobey's eyebrows lifted at the sight of the glowing colors. She approached a small sapling to test her idea. She placed the ball on top of the tree, and she pushed down on the ball until the colors enveloped the sapling. The colors rotated around the plant as the tree slowly absorbed the magic. A moment later, the colors were gone, and the tree returned to normal. Adaline remained focused on her experiment, unconvinced that the show was over. Tobey wandered to her side to watch with her.

The tree burst from the ground, shooting eight feet into the air. The ground tremor threw Adaline and Tobey off their feet, and Adaline's telekinesis caught them in mid-air.

"Are you all right?" she asked Tobey. The boy nodded before Adaline set them on their feet. They appraised the tree, which was now ten feet tall and in full bloom, remaining in silent awe of the successful result.

"So… that worked," Adaline admitted with a shrug. She revisited the old tree that covered them with shade and reached above her again. She grasped onto more of the natural magic the tree generated, and without filling it with her light, she repeated her experiment with another sapling. A similar effect happened to the second plant, but it didn't make the second sapling as tall as the first one. Adaline's arms folded over her chest as she studied them before glancing at Tobey and giving another shrug.

"Dr. Adaline?" a female voice said behind them.

Tobey and Adaline turned to see Roserie standing behind them. Tobey noticed that Adaline wasn't overjoyed to see Roserie, but she still smiled and wished her a good morning. Tobey was confused by her behavior because he thought they were supposed to hate Roserie. Instead of dwelling on it, he kept his original instructions in the forefront of his mind: only the Everlys and the royal elves were friends. Tobey's mind got lost in a tangent as Roserie tried to make light conversation with Adaline before attempting to apologize to her. Tobey's focus snapped back when he heard the she-elf explain herself, not believing a word she said. He'd never listened to a more selfish tone of voice in his short life. After a few more minutes of conversation, Roserie said her goodbyes and left Adaline and Tobey alone. Adaline still had her arms crossed over her chest, and she rocked her weight from one foot to the other. Her attention dropped to Tobey.

Tobey signed, "She's lying."

Adaline gave a slight nod. "I know."

They heard movement and turned back to the two trees, which were growing another few feet. Both stared wide-eyed as the trees topped off around sixteen feet.

"Lunch is served, Dr. Adaline," Ena called from the walking path that returned to the palace.

"We'll be right there. Thank you, Ena," Adaline replied. Adaline's attention shifted to Tobey. "Hungry?" He nodded and smiled. She chuckled. "Okay, let's go."

They headed toward the dining room's double doors, and Tobey hustled to get the door for Adaline. He held it open and smiled wide when she thanked him. Tobey felt larger than life to know he could help someone as powerful as her. He raced over to his chair then slowly pulled it out to climb up in it. He noticed that the king and the prince were already eating, and Theodon paused to pull out the chair next to him for Adaline.

"Thank you," she said sweetly.

"You are welcome," Theodon said.

Everyone settled into their meals in silence for the first few minutes before the king cleared his throat. "Dr. Adaline," he addressed her. "Could you explain to me why I now have two sixteen-foot saplings in my garden?"

Adaline was mid-chew when her eyes connected with

Tobey's across the table. They stared at each other wide-eyed, realizing their experiment was discovered as soon as it was hatched. Tobey grinned.

Adaline tried to swallow a grin and her food before explaining, "Your Majesty, this morning, I was able to focus on the natural magic produced by an ancient tree you have in your garden. I tested its capabilities on a very young plant for comparison. The results were overly positive." Adaline shot a look at Tobey and winked. The boy grinned. Only the sounds of flatware cutting food floated in the air for a moment before she thought to ask, "Were there negative side effects I didn't catch?"

The king finished chewing his food and didn't bother looking up from his plate as he shared, "One spooked gardener."

Adaline's eyes widened before her expression turned amused. "Are they okay?"

Before the king could answer, Theodon stepped in to say, "He won't be going near those trees for a few days."

Adaline snickered.

"You are not sorry?" the king asked her, already knowing her answer.

"No, not at all," Adaline admitted. "That's pretty hilarious."

Theodon chuckled before changing the subject, "We have the Ileoton Symphony event in a couple of hours."

"Oh yes," Adaline said as she shoveled her food with her fork. "I'm looking forward to that."

"You enjoy live music?" Theodon asked.

Adaline nodded. "Live music was an art form that died out a long time ago on Earth. Unfortunately, we only have recordings of songs now. I remember reading about venues that were specifically designed with proper acoustics to enrich the live experience."

The royals knew she would enjoy the symphony today. The sound was round and rich, in a venue carved into their environment and surrounded by tall trees that helped sustain the sound.

"How long is the event?" Adaline asked.

"Two hours," the king answered as he finished his meal and rose from his seat. "But if you have an interest in live music, as you stated, then the time will fly."

Adaline turned to Tobey. "Do you want to go?" The boy nodded. "No running during the performance, all right? It's against the rules." Adaline told Tobey.

Tobey signed to her, "I'll be good."

"Good," she said. "Now go get dressed."

Tobey took off from his seat in a flash. He moved so fast that his momentum pushed at the vase of flowers on the table, sending it toppling before Theodon caught it.

"His power is growing," Theodon noticed while replacing the vase.

"I think it's the environment," Adaline commented.

"Based on your tree experiment today?" Theodon inquired, and Adaline nodded. "Is that good?"

"As long as he learns his strength along the way," Adaline said before glancing at the king. He nodded at her before excusing himself. Theodon and Adaline were alone for a moment. "We are almost halfway done."

Theodon nodded as he chewed his last bite. "Yes, I'm going to be glad when the celebration happens so we can enjoy it."

"Me, too."

"I know you are going to enjoy the symphony," he admitted. "There isn't anything like it in the kingdom."

She rose from her seat. "Then I'd better go get ready."

"I'll be by to escort you and Tobey in two hours."

"Perfect," Adaline said before she left the room. Two hours would barely be enough time to get Tobey and herself ready for a royal event.

CHAPTER 47

"**M**y Lord," Flavial said upon executing a rushed bow before the king. "I must request a private audience with you at your earliest convenience."

Aureon's attention lifted with intrigue to his longtime friend's request since he's never asked for such a thing. The king sat back in his oversized chair and glanced around his private box in the auditorium before returning Flavial's attention. Everyone below was almost finished finding their seats and waited for the symphony to begin. Theodon and Adaline would be arriving at any moment, and Flavial saw the opportunity to get the king's attention before they did.

"The world must be ending if you require a private audience, old friend," Aureon jested, although his stoic countenance never changed.

Flavial smirked. "It may not be the ending of the world, Your Majesty, but perhaps the ending of a father's world."

Aureon nodded. "After the symphony in my study."

Flavial tucked his chin. "Thank you, My Lord." He exited the booth as quietly as he arrived.

The king clutched the arms of his chair as he pondered the potential reasons behind Flavial's request. A moment later, Theodon slid into the chair on his left.

"Your seat is right there," the king heard Adaline say to Tobey. The boy rushed around the booth to the tiny chair in front of the king. The boy smiled up at him before taking his seat. His happiness to witness live music was palpable compared to earlier. Adaline cautiously side-stepped her way to her seat in the small space. She was doing her best to maneuver in her dress with a long train. The king caught himself looking her over and averted his gaze. The off-the-shoulder lavender gown did her glowing skin justice. She swept the train of the gown to one side and sat down. The royals' attention turned to her when they heard her sigh.

"Comfy chair," she whispered as she relaxed.

Theodon smirked while his father observed the room. A series of skylights lighted the space. When the performance began, shutters adjusted over the open ceiling to "dim" the lighting on the crowd and redirect it to the symphony. Adaline and Tobey scooted to the edges of their seats as the musicians filled the space with the sweetest sound that kept them entranced from the first note through the finale. A singer accompanied the symphony for a few songs during the performance, and it stirred emotions in Adaline that filled her eyes with tears. Helplessness washed over Aureon as he watched his son reach across him to hand Adaline his handkerchief.

Aureon wanted to do that for her. It was such a small gesture, but he felt robbed of a special moment. Other than special occasions, the symphony only played two concerts a year. Before frustration rose in him, he masked his expression. Never had he knowingly added to a female's joy without being allowed to fully participate in providing everything she needed in the experience, no matter how small. He was only allowed to offer her the opportunity, which she took graciously, but he could only watch from a distance as she enjoyed it. He wanted to touch her, to ask her what she thought about it—everything that had taken place over the weekend he had wanted to do with her. Instead of getting more frustrated, he decided he would do all those things with her: dance, escort her and kiss her in public. He would ensure all these delightful opportunities would come back around for them.

Aureon allowed his focus to remain in the direction of the symphony as his mind went to work on new plans for him and Adaline. Then the off-the-shoulder strap of her dress slipped further down her arm. He fixated on that strap as it became the only object in the room worth watching. Adaline slid it back into place, but not before the king's stare caught her attention. They locked eyes for a moment, and her gaze softened under his heated stare. Theodon's clearing of his throat snapped them out of it. Adaline adjusted her dress and returned her focus to the symphony. Aureon glanced at his son, who had one eyebrow lifted at him.

Later, when the performance finished, the king excused himself from the venue. He left Theodon, Adaline, and Tobey to interact with the crowd as they slowly exited the forum. They ran into Sorsacha along the way.

"So?" Adaline asked her friend.

"What?" Sorsacha asked.

"Did you have a chance to speak to your father last night?" Adaline inquired.

Sorsacha gave her human friend the evil eye. "Yes, okay? What is it to you?"

"Nothing," Adaline admitted. "I just know a sad parent when I see one."

"Cheap shot, human," Sorsacha muttered.

Adaline smiled. "Perhaps."

"Speaking of parents," Sorsacha commented as she scanned the crowd, "I don't see him anywhere."

"I saw him leave with Flavial rather quickly," Theodon mentioned.

"Hmm, I wonder why," Sorsacha thought aloud.

Theodon's expression changed, and he hurried to take Adaline's hand and placed it in the crook of his elbow. "My father needs to speak with us."

"All right," Adaline said as she stuck out her other hand for Tobey to take. The three of them returned to the palace, and Tobey managed to trip over the train on Adaline's dress a few times along the way.

"He needs us in his study," Theodon informed her as they walked through the throne room.

"Ena?" Adaline spoke in the hallway.

A moment later, the she-elf appeared. "Yes, Dr. Adaline?"

"I'm going to be in a meeting," Adaline explained to her. "Would you mind taking Tobey to get a snack, please?"

"Of course." Ena smiled down at the boy before offering her hand to him.

Tobey threw Adaline a skeptical look.

"I'll be a while, and I know you will get hungry," Adaline said to him. "You should eat, now." The boy shrugged his indifference and slipped his hand out of Adaline's and into Ena's.

A moment later, Theodon held open the door for Adaline to enter his father's study. She entered and heard whispering voices quickly turn silent upon their arrival. The king stood on the far side of the large chaise, flanked by Flavial and Mouriel, who looked at Adaline as if she had interrupted a covert exchange. The king extended his hand out to her, and she didn't hesitate to move closer to him as she felt his magnetism pulling her near. His usual emotionless demeanor hinted at wonder as he looked at her, which Flavial noticed. She gave the king her hand, who gently pulled her closer. He tapped his temple twice, and she covered herself and the king in her force field.

Aureon's eyes never wavered. "Show me what I need to know," he said to her in their protected shield. The simplicity of his statement didn't cover up its imperative nature. Adaline extended her force field to cover everyone. Her eyes moved from Flavial then to Mouriel before she approached Flavial and smiled.

"I'm going to have to touch you again," Adaline said to Flavial.

"Like last night?" he asked.

Adaline nodded. "But this time, I will search your memories at will." Flavial's calm demeanor didn't change, which didn't surprise Adaline, since she was confident that Flavial was the king's true friend.

"Go on," Flavial encouraged her.

Adaline placed her palm over his temple and sorted through his memories. Searching for intentions of deception, murder, traitorous behavior, Adaline came up short, but her search wasn't over. She sifted through memories originating around Theodon's birth but witnessed only war memories of being alongside Aureon on the battlefield. It was clear that Flavial did not know of Graydon's deception. When Aureon returned to the battlefield after a brief visit to the palace to hold his newborn son, Flavial was happy for the king and asked him about Theodon. He was confused as to why the king seemed glum with rage brewing just below the surface. He was in pain, and Flavial didn't know how to help him. So, he did all he could do: he remained at the king's side through every minute of the war for all the years it lasted.

Adaline dropped her hand from Flavial before repeating the process with Mouriel. She saw the climactic exchange between Mouriel and Sorsacha that had happened around the war. His daughter was pressing him to ask for a private audience with the king because of information she'd overheard. Mouriel argued with her, thinking her overly dramatic and trying to draw attention for attention's sake since that was her habit as a youngling. The argument escalated to Sorsacha's ultimatum. The terms hung in the air between father and daughter in silence before Mouriel shook his head. Sorsacha stormed out of their family home and never returned. Adaline's focus on Mouriel's memories searched through his knowledge of the death of Aravae. She found nothing but the despair of losing his daughter. Adaline dropped her hand from Mouriel's face as she opened her eyes. She focused on the elder in front of her and noticed the old pain lingering in his eyes.

"That's why you're here, now," Adaline stated. Mouriel was shocked by her gift and hesitated before nodding. Adaline grasped his hands and gave him a grave smile. "Good luck." She turned to the king to say, "This," her hand on Flavial's shoulder, "is your most trustworthy friend." Then she placed her other hand on Mouriel's shoulder. "This is a father in suffering. You need to listen to him."

"Show me," Aureon commanded while grabbing her wrists and bringing them to his face.

"It's a lot," she whispered to him. He nodded before she let the images flow into his mind. A minute later, he tugged at her wrists, and she released him. He closed his hands over hers as he lowered them but didn't let go.

"Is it best if I go?" she asked.

"No," he said as he finally let go of her hands. The king weighed and measured whether he would bring the two elders in on his scheme, but first things first. "Speak freely, Mouriel."

The elder's shoulders sagged in relief where he stood, now understanding he was out of harm's way. At the same time, Flavial gave Adaline a knowing look. He knew Adaline was significant to both royals, but he noticed the connection between her and his king. Meanwhile, Mouriel took time divulging the entire story of the confrontation with Sorsacha and its result. Silence filled the space between them before the king gripped Mouriel's shoulder.

"Release yourself from this guilt, Mouriel," Aureon urged him. "And do not fear consequences from me."

The elder's shock was undeniable while Flavial smirked,

knowing his friend would behave rationally. After everything the king has endured, Aureon always remained level-headed when it came to his rule. This was the sole reason why Flavial encouraged Mouriel to speak to the king when the elder first approached Flavial.

"Thank you, My Lord." Mouriel's words shook with emotion.

"The mysteries behind Aravae's death are coming to light," the king told the elders as his gaze locked onto Adaline. "We," he emphasized to Adaline and Theodon, "have taken steps to make sure we know of everyone tied to her murder."

Astonishment overtook Flavial. "Murder?"

Aureon nodded. "We are close to apprehending everyone who was involved."

A beat passed.

"What do you need from us, My Lord?" Flavial asked, still reeling.

"Continue to be naturally convincing in your joy about all that I have publicly announced and report to me, Theodon, or Dr. Adaline, any suspicious behavior you see during this engagement and wedding," Aureon stated.

The elders looked at each other in shock, then nodded before echoing, "Yes, Your Majesty."

"You will share knowledge of this information with no one, including family," the king specified.

"Yes, My Lord," they repeated.

"You are dismissed," Aureon said to the elders, who immediately bowed before exiting the room.

Theodon wandered closer to Adaline and his father as Adaline adjusted her force field to enclose only the three of them. Aureon offered his hand to her and led her to the chaise to sit. Theodon sat next to her, as Aureon sat across from them.

"Okay," Adaline exhaled. "It seems we all have new information to share...."

CHAPTER 48

A few days later, the Everlys were juggling their successful practice and preparing their friends for a significant conversation over dinner that evening. Jim and Tony shot each other a knowing look, while Tessa had many questions.

"Hold them all for dinner tonight," Adaline urged her friend as she hurried out of the house earlier that morning. "There's a lot of information that we will be sharing."

One of Asher's surgeries made a turn for the worst, and he called Adaline in to help him stabilize his patient. Adaline stepped out of her surgery consult, scrubbed in, and joined Asher. A minute later, his patient stabilized. The twins high-fived and Adaline returned to her consult. The workday continued with this leap-frogging of critical moments. When the twins reached the top of the stairs to go to their vehicles, they shot each other a defeated expression.

"I can't," Asher confessed about their daily game.

"Me neither," Adaline confirmed before she touched his arm, teleporting them to their vehicles.

After they returned to their homes, Asher reached for her mind, "Tony and Tessa have been preparing dinner. They said they'd finish in ten minutes. Come on over when you're ready."

As Adaline took a hot shower, her mind reflected on the meaningless conversations she overheard while at the symphony with Theodon and Aureon.

"Is she entirely human?" one attendee asked another as they passed Adaline in the crowd.

"She couldn't be if she healed the Alloralla's daughter," the other attendee replied.

An elf asked Adaline while Theodon was escorting her out of the venue, "Won't you miss your world if you stay here?"

Oh, Adaline thought for a moment. "My world isn't a nice place anymore. I'm not leaving much behind."

Adaline took her time drying off after her shower before she slipped on leisure clothes. She shuffled over to Asher's house and greeted Jim with a kiss on the cheek and a hug. Her actions repeated with Tony and Tessa before she grabbed Tobey's face and kissed his forehead.

"Did you wash your hands?" Adaline asked the boy. Tobey shook his head and darted to the nearest sink. Then everyone took their seats at the dinner table. As they dug into the meal, a heavy silence hovered over them.

"How far back should we start?" Asher asked Adaline telepathically.

Adaline thought for a moment. "Let's put all the cards on the table." Asher's brows lifted in surprise. "Our timeline of ending the earth has accelerated, Ash," Adaline spoke in her brother's mind. "It would be best to get them off-world as soon as possible."

"But you are still waiting to hear back on the king's answer?"

"Yes," Adaline replied before she amended her answer. "Let's get Tessa up to speed on what we are and our purpose, along with the wedding this weekend. I will know if we can move to Theris at some point this coming weekend, and we can have another conversation with them about relocating once that's finalized."

Asher nodded in agreement. "I'll follow your lead."

"Tessa," Adaline said to her friend sitting across the table, "we'd like to talk about why the QC tried to use you against us in exchange for your life."

Tessa stilled in her chair, listening to every word Adaline shared.

Diviners.

Sweeping the world of evil.

Killing QC agents.

The truth hit Tessa with an impact, keeping her silent through the end of Adaline's story. Jim, Tony, and Tobey continued to eat during the explanation.

"Do you have any questions?" Adaline asked.

Tessa's thoughts spun with dozens of questions, and she had no clue as to which to say aloud until she blurted, "So, the helicopter explosion...."

Asher waved his fork in the air. "That was me."

"And Tony's weird recovery from gunshot wounds...."

"That was me," Adaline admitted, not taking her eyes off her friend. It was a lot to absorb, and the Everlys were ready to share whatever information she needed to feel secure. Another moment passed with only the sounds of chewing and forks against plates filled the room.

"When is the end of the world?" Tessa asked.

Jim, Tony, and Tobey's eyes lifted from their plates to Adaline, waiting for her answer.

"The QC has been getting more aggressive," Asher jumped in. "And because of that, we would like to end the planet sooner than originally planned."

"And what?" Tessa exclaimed. "We all just lie down and die on the day you choose?"

"No," Adaline said calmly. "We're working on relocating

you all somewhere safe."

"And if that falls through?" Tessa asked.

"It won't," Asher said with a shake of his head. "Adaline is figuring out how to relocate us all without annoying the indigenous population, and she has already begun negotiations with their ruler about the arrangement."

"Well done, Ash," Adaline blurted in her brother's mind for sharing the information without confirmation from Aureon. Asher grinned.

"Because the QC is getting more aggressive, Addy and I think it's best to move you all off-world soon. This way, you can establish yourselves in your new home before we end this one," Asher explained.

"Why move us?" Tessa asked.

"If we don't, the QC will target you more than before, using your tie of friendship to us as leverage," Adaline admitted.

Tessa slumped forward in her chair, staring past the food sitting on her plate.

"And before all of that happens, we get to visit this new world this coming weekend for Addy's fake wedding," Asher chimed in.

Jim and Tony's eyes widened as they blurted, "What?"

"Yes, minor detail," Adaline said. "Thank you, Asher, for leading up to that conversation so delicately."

"Anytime, sis," Asher grinned, then he forked another piece of food into his mouth.

"The short version of the story is: I met the royal family of the place we are going to live soon," Adaline explained. "The king had a lot of deep-rooted pain because he never dealt with his queen's killer. An opportunity presented itself to repeat history to draw out the bad guys, and it's working. I'm posing as his son's fiancé, and this Saturday is the fake wedding ceremony. I would like for you all to attend to add authenticity to the festivities and to give you a chance to see your new home."

"You're marrying Theo?" Tony asked. Adaline nodded as she nibbled on her food.

"That's a ruse," Jim commented. Tony looked at his friend questioningly. "You saw how Theo's father looked at her." Tony took a moment to recall before he nodded.

Tessa softened. "So, the king likes you?"

"That's not important right now," Adaline said before asking, "Are you all coming with me, or not?"

"I'm there," Asher said immediately.

Tobey signed, "Me too."

"We're in," Jim said for him and Tony.

"I'll go too," Tessa confirmed.

Adaline nodded as she finished chewing and swallowing her food. "All right then."

A beat passed.

"You're really getting married?" Tessa said, finally beginning to smile.

"Fake-married," Asher corrected her.

"Yes, fake-married," Adaline said. Adaline knew Tessa would enjoy the festivities, fake or not.

"How is fake-engaged going so far, Addy?" Tony asked her.

Adaline let out a weary sigh. "It's tiring."

"How is the king handling you pairing off with his son?" Jim asked pointedly. Jim didn't know the king personally, but it was clear how he looked at Addy. It was enough to indicate that the scheme may not have the smoothest unfolding.

"You've seen his sustained emotionless visage, right?" Adaline asked.

Jim nodded as he forked down more food. "It's the only expression he wears."

"Exactly," Adaline said.

"That doesn't answer my question, Addy," Jim said with a wink.

"Touché," Adaline muttered. The thought came to her

mind that maybe she should check in with Aureon tonight in his dreams to make sure he was all right.

After everyone finished dinner and Tobey was put to bed, the adults wandered to Asher's living room that opened onto the patio with drinks in hand. Adaline and Tessa were outside, sitting on the ledge of the deck.

"I'm glad you told me," Tessa admitted to her. "Even though the QC showed me that video footage of you and Asher when you were teens, I felt like I was going crazy. I thought they had to have doctored the footage. You two never shared anything with me, so I assumed you didn't have abilities. And now to hear from you what the two of you are is surreal."

"Hold out your hand," Adaline said to her friend while blowing a light ball into her own.

Tessa's eyes widened at the glowing ball of light Adaline held. Adaline handed it to Tessa.

"What is it?" Tessa asked as she examined it.

"It's a holy fireball," Adaline explained. "I can manipulate it into whatever you need it to be. The question is: what do you need?"

"Sleep," Tessa blurted. "I haven't slept a wink in weeks."

"Whisper the word into the ball, then press it into your heart," Adaline instructed.

Tessa whispered the word and glanced at Adaline before she slowly pushed the ball into her chest. The light circulated throughout her body, and Tessa grew happy-drowsy. Adaline caught her friend with her telekinesis before Tessa fell out of her seat as she sank into a deep sleep. Adaline smiled to herself before sipping her drink. She stood and moved into the living room, floating the sleeping Tessa over to the couch and gently setting her down.

"How long will she be out for?" Tony asked.

"It varies - around thirty-six hours," Adaline admitted.

"She has been terrified from the moment I found her in

your driveway," Tony said.

"Poor girl," Jim said.

"No one deserves to live like that," Tony said.

"It's why we are getting all of you out of here," Adaline said before taking another sip of her drink.

"I'm not sure if we should go with you," Jim admitted to Adaline.

"What do you mean?" she asked.

"To move off-world, permanently," Jim clarified.

"What are you going to do, old man?" Asher cut in. "Die in a world of agents that want you dead, or die on your terms in a new world?"

"I'm old, Asher," Jim said. "When I go doesn't bother me anymore."

"How about where and how you go?" Adaline asked. Jim thought about it for a moment, then leaned back in his chair with a thoughtful expression. "Just think about it, Jim," Adaline said. "You and Tony have done so much for us, and we want you to have the choice to pass on due to natural causes in a peaceful world."

Jim let her words sink in before he nodded. "All right, Addy. We'll go with you." The old Marine liked the sound of peace at the end of his life, but he hadn't bought into it just yet. He knew conflict was not something that could be eradicated but ebbed and flowed over generations. There was no happily ever after for a Marine because there was always something worth protecting.

"Speaking of thinking about it, Ash," Adaline said, turning to her brother. "We need to come to terms with something."

"What's that?" Asher inquired while plopping into the chair across from her.

"We will be penniless in the early part of our new lives," Adaline said, leveling with him.

Asher's body went rigid. Asher didn't do broke. He had gadgets, cars, and illegal artwork his sister didn't know he possessed. There was no room for poverty in his life.

"And I think I know a way around it," Adaline shared.

Asher sighed in relief. "Are you referring to your pointy-eared-sugar-daddy-boyfriend?"

Adaline burst into laughter. "No, not at all."

"I'm listening," Asher said as he stretched in his chair.

Adaline explained the healing she had been doing for the elves in Theris and the neo-natal issues she discovered with Sana.

"So, there's a market for a medical practice," Asher concluded.

Adaline nodded. "We'll have to take some time to study the biology of elves and find a way to cut down or eliminate waste, but yes, I think we can make it work." She didn't care if their new endeavor upset Qelon, and Adaline wouldn't allow anyone else to finance her existence outside of herself.

"Eliminate waste?" Asher was confused.

"There are no landfills in Theris," Adaline specified. "There's almost no trash because everything is recycled and re-used. We cannot change this and build their world like ours was because look how well that turned out."

"How do you expect me to manage that, Addy? It's impossible!" Asher exclaimed.

"I know someone who is a master chemist and surgeon, and he is going to figure it out for us." Adaline eyed her brother. "Within the next two weeks."

"Two weeks!" Asher blurted out. "How can I possibly do that when I have patients?"

"Why are we bothering with patients anymore, Ash?"

Asher sighed. He hadn't thought of that. In his mind, Asher just worked all day and fought the QC at night, and he hadn't considered a paradigm shift. "So, we close down the practice and start working on transitioning."

"Next week," Adaline suggested.

Asher's mind spun. "That should give us enough time to go through our offices and gather anything worth taking with us.

Maybe I should get a solar-powered generator? What machinery am I taking with me?"

"Don't," Adaline warned him.

"What?"

"Don't pack in excess," Adaline said to Asher. "Simplify. Condense whatever your brain is running away with right now."

She knows me too well, he thought, as he stared off into the fireplace. Asher was a man who had to have the answers, and now, so he could break down the process of their transition long before it happened. Sorting out the mess in his mind was going to take him all night.

CHAPTER 49

"We must have words about this, Theodon," Aureon spoke in his son's mind. Theodon was in his suite, processing all the information he now knew about Roserie. The more he thought about it, the angrier he grew.

"Another time, Father." Theodon tried to curb his father, who was in the king's suite.

"Now, Theodon."

Theodon closed the chest he had opened and threw his head back in a dramatic sigh as if he already had enough of their conversation that hadn't started. He entered his father's suite and stood quietly at the far corner of the room with his arms tightly crossing his chest.

Aureon noticed that his son had trouble looking him in the eye. *This will not do.* Aureon remembered the first time he had a crush on a female. It caused him to deny all the warning signs about her, resulting in the heartache he experienced after finally acknowledging the truth. Aureon understood this was an experience everyone endured in their younger years, but he was bothered that denial was deeply rooted in his son. And he knew they were going to leave this conversation more frustrated than when they entered it.

"I need you to listen, my son," Aureon said, although he knew his warning was futile. "The first female a male has a strong attraction for is one of two kinds of people: she brings out the best in him, which helps him become a better male, or she brings out the worst in him and uses it to control him. If a male makes it back to his sanity after experiencing the latter, he becomes a better male. But you must make it back, son."

"You are so certain that she is the latter!" Theodon shot back.

"She struck you!" Aureon spat.

"She was upset!"

"She mates with your uncle every chance she gets!"

The low blow caused Theodon to snap and take a swing at his father. Aureon effortlessly caught Theodon's fist, inches from his face. Theodon struggled against his father's might. The king's nostrils flared as he battled against knee-jerk reactions of defending himself. A moment passed before he breathed evenly.

"You have all the evidence in the world against her, much of which you have personally witnessed, and she shows no remorse for her actions," the king said in a fed-up whisper. "Yet, you dismiss it for the sake of feelings based on a lie. Take the time to look within, my son, and see what she is doing to you."

Theodon dropped his fist as his father's words sank in.

Aureon squeezed his son's shoulder. "You deserve better, Theodon." Theodon was stunned at his father's show of support, unable to choose what to do next until there was a knock at the door. "Enter," the king said before his attention left Theodon.

Ena quietly stepped into the room with an intricately carved wooden box in her hand. "Your order was delivered, Your Majesty," Ena said, offering the box to him. "The artist said he is available should you need anything else."

"Thank you, Ena," Aureon said as he glanced at his son. He told Theodon, "Take time to consider my words."

"Yes, Father," Theodon said obediently before turning on his heel and leaving the room.

Once the door to his suite closed, Aureon's shoulders fell as he let out a sigh of frustrated defeat. There was no winning that conversation, he knew. Theodon had to choose for himself. But Aureon had to show him his options because of what would soon happen to Roserie once his plan ended after the coming weekend. Aureon waved Ena forward, and she immediately complied and offered him the box. He lifted the lid and peered inside.

"I think she's going to like it very much, My Lord," Ena offered after waiting in silence.

Aureon stared at the intricately embellished piece of jewelry, content with the results of his request. "Hopefully, she will," he said as he closed the lid and took the box from Ena, and he set it on his side table.

"Will that be all, My Lord?" Ena asked.

Aureon thought about the details of the coming weekend while his back was to Ena. "Make sure the dress is strapless and that the train on it is shorter than the one on the dress she wore to the symphony."

"Did she have difficulty with it, My Lord?"

Difficulty isn't the right word, Aureon thought. Adaline could maneuver in anything, but she didn't need the excess of a long train to add to her radiance. She was more than enough. "No, it is simply unnecessary."

"I'll take care of it, My Lord," Ena said with a bow before she turned and left the room.

Finally, after some time lost in thought, Aureon turned to his bed. He noticed its size and how empty it was with only him sleeping in it. He remembered the contentment that came over him with Adaline snuggled beside him. He adjusted the shutters over the skylights, casting darkness throughout the room. His large eyes blinked, instantly adjusting to the darkness as he shuffled to bed. He gave a weary sigh as he untied his robe and let it fall to the floor. He pulled his tunic over his head but left his pants on before he slid between the sheets. He leisurely spread out on his back with his hands tucked behind his head.

As he tried to settle his thoughts, his mind rebelled and brought forth memories of the original history his scheme was causing him to repeat. Aureon remembered when he had received news from his father that Aravae had given birth to Theodon. The joy of the information brought him out of his bloodthirsty haze that fighting alongside the Allo nurtured, and his soldiers cheered for him. He was happy to be going home to see his new family for a few days. Flavial was elated for Aureon and encouraged him to leave immediately to be with them.

Aureon arrived at the palace in record time. He rushed through the back entrance near the stables and ran into his father, who was wandering the halls in silence, holding a sleeping baby Theodon in his arms. Aureon had never seen a look of such contentment in his father's eyes than when Cerus gazed down at his new grandson. But when Cerus eyes lifted to see his son running toward him, his expression turned grave. Aureon came to a stop a few feet from his father, only focused on the baby in his arms. Theodon was so small. Cerus slowly set Theodon in Aureon's arms, and Aureon didn't hesitate to pull the baby close. He gazed at his son in wonder, so happy at his arrival that his eyes watered. Instead of a sob, a laugh left his chest as he sniffed back tears, and he traced his son's nose gently with the tip of his finger.

"What shall his name be, my son?" Cerus asked.

"What did Aravae say?" Aureon asked as he met his father's gaze.

Cerus' sympathetic expression said it all, as he could barely maintain eye contact. "She-" Cerus tried to begin. "She didn't make it, my boy."

The statement collided with Aureon, jolting him from true happiness into shock. Feeling his knees give way, he sank to the ground as he succumbed to tears. One drop fell on baby Theodon's forehead, and he wiped it away. The little one started to squirm in his father's arms. Baby Theodon wriggled one arm free and reached his little hand out of his swaddling clothes. Aureon immediately gave him his finger to grab onto as the king sobbed over the loss of his queen. Cerus stood beside him with his hand covering his son's shoulder.

Aureon shook the memory away and refocused on his bedroom ceiling. He thought of Adaline and how she hadn't been present in his dreams the last four nights. He'd give anything for her to show up tonight. He found himself whispering while he drifted off to sleep, "Please be there."

CHAPTER 50

Adaline sat in quiet meditation at the end of her bed, reveling in the stillness of her mind. An unknown amount of time passed before she thought of Sana. Adaline laid back on the bed and pulled the covers over her before her force field covered her, then her astral form emerged and stepped into Sana's dreams. Adaline found her pregnant patient in a hammock on a beach with a drink in her hand, and it was in the form of a sizeable carved-out fruit filled with juice and a straw.

"How are you doing, Sana?" Adaline walked over with a smile on her face.

The she-elf gave a relieved sigh. "This feels much better than when I'm awake."

Adaline chuckled. "I'm sure it does. How do you feel when you are awake?"

Sana thought about it as she sipped her beverage before confessing, "My joints feel weary from the weight, and I'm tired all the time. And I feel like I have no strength."

"That's because everything you are eating is going to two

other people," Adaline confirmed. "May I touch you?"

"Yes, of course," Sana said as she scooted to a sitting position to be easily accessible to Adaline.

Adaline's left hand settled on Sana's large belly, and she quickly scanned both babies. Adaline was glad to find progress, but she remained clinically detached. "Okay, Sana, it looks like we have some good news."

Sana's features lit up. "We do?"

"Yes. It looks like the boy's energy level has risen, and his development is progressing," Adaline said. "But he hasn't caught up to his sister yet." Sana let out a sigh of relief, thankful for the good news. "So, keep doing what you have been doing," Adaline directed. "And it looks like your boy will have a shot if he continues to catch up." Sana nodded happily. "One last thing," Adaline said and reached around underneath the hammock. She placed her hand on the base of Sana's spine before white light spilled from her palm. The light traveled Sana's spine and branched out through her shoulders and her head. The pregnant she-elf's body sagged in relief in the hammock.

Adaline straightened. "Better?"

"Yes," Sana said. "So much better."

Adaline swallowed a smile. "I will leave you to your paradise and see you in a couple of days."

"Thank you, Dr. Adaline," Sana rushed out the words.

"Any time," she said before she exited Sana's dream.

Adaline was relieved that Sana was showing signs of progress and took her instructions seriously. *What a game-changer it will be to have her bring those twins to term.* The elves' understanding of incubation to birth was a little cloudy and under-researched. Adaline knew she and Asher could help make the process easier on the mothers and the babies.

A minute later, Aureon felt an energy shift. *She's here,* he thought. He opened his eyes in his dream and saw Adaline looking down at him from the straw roof overhead. He was lying on a swinging platform that hung from the floor of a hut that spanned the Ieobu River, and it swayed in the breeze. A moment later, Adaline was snuggling against his side.

This is contentment. Aureon squeezed her to his side and rubbed her back. Her hand rested on his chest, and she let her white light pour into him. The tension around his heart from his earlier conversation with Theodon released, and he sighed.

"Thank you," he whispered.

She planted a kiss on his chest. "You're welcome."

He leaned down to kiss the top of her head, and he took his time smelling her hair. They laid in silence, relishing in their closeness. Adaline's head popped up at the sound of what she thought was a musical note.

"What was that?" she whispered as her eyes darted around to find its origin.

A small smile hinted at the corner of Aureon's mouth. "The fish."

Adaline was confused. "The fish in Theris are musical?"

"These are," he said. "Blora fish travel south from the mountains to mate before swimming upstream to their home environment. They attract their mates through their musical sounds, which can be heard when they breach the surface of the water."

Adaline focused on the sounds, which reminded her of taking a wet fingertip to the rim of a crystal glass. The sound radiated briefly before the fish dove below the surface. Each note played in a natural concert, captivating her attention. Adaline was impressed that something in the natural world could sound so divine.

"As beautiful as it is to hear, one disturbing fact comes to mind," she said as she peered up at him. He eyed her with curiosity as he waited for her to continue. "Those fish are fornicating more than we are."

Aureon burst into laughter which triggered Adaline's giggle.

He regained his breath after a moment before admitting, "You are right." His hand slid down to grasp her bottom, and she gasped. She reached down to move his hand higher to the small of her back, and he gave her an incredulous look.

"I can't allow that right now," she whispered, with her doe eyes locked onto him. "It's getting… frustrating." She'd planned to keep her interaction with him in this dream more innocent than the previous one.

Aureon meant to remove his arm to give her space, but she pulled it back down around her. She wasn't going to give up his touch entirely. He sat up to get a better look at her, to understand what she needed.

"I need to be touched," she admitted. "I just don't think I can handle groping today." She chuckled.

He nodded before scooping her up. "Grab onto me."

She clutched his shoulders as he slung her over his lap and sat up with her. She shifted in his lap and pushed on his chest until she straddled him comfortably. He covered both of her hands on his chest with one of his.

"Tell me about this need of yours… to be touched," he solicited.

"It's…" She trailed off, and her chin dropped as she searched for the words. He gently tucked his curled finger under her chin and lifted her gaze back to him before he sealed the gesture with a light kiss. After he parted from her, he gave her space to talk. "It's one of the main ways I feel affection from my partner."

After a moment, he revealed, "So do I."

Adaline wasn't surprised by his admission since he'd isolated himself from everyone for so long. *Maybe in his mourning, he felt undeserving of being touched.* Or perhaps Aureon was simply in too much pain. She then recalled how he held her hands in his study when he asked her to show him the memories of Flavial and Mouriel. He was gentle but demanding, and he didn't need both of her hands to see the memories. Nor did he need to pull her close to do so. She sat a little taller in his lap and cupped his face. Her thumbs skimmed over his sharp cheekbones, and he leaned into her touch before opening his eyes to return her gaze. He carefully cradled her face the same way. They mirrored each other's touches, allowing the tension of their time together to build to a steady heat between them. Her knees widened, resting her against his erection. His upper lip curled as he let go of a low growl. She gasped and backed off as she realized she was crossing a line.

"I'm sorry," she whispered.

"I am not," he growled as his hands moved to latch onto her waist.

Adaline heard a rustling sound and her attention lifted to the trees overhead, noticing the birds in the trees escaped once they heard Aureon's predatory sound. While she was distracted, he buried his face in her cleavage, pressing his cheeks against her skin, nuzzling her softness. She gasped at the surprise and giggled.

"You like those?" she jested.

"Mmm," he rumbled as he returned to nuzzling her. Then he wrapped his arms around her and squeezed her against his chest.

She giggled at his silliness until he looked up at her with a contented smile. "That's a yes."

Aureon's lips reached her collarbone. "Four days since seeing you in my dreams again were too long, little human." Adaline shivered under his kiss as her toes curled at his words.

"H-how often do you need to see me?" she tried to get out, as his lips traveled up her neck to her jawline.

"I am willing to bargain," he admitted, "because I want you to have your rest." He tipped her chin down and covered her mouth with his for a moment. "Is every third day possible?"

Adaline thought for a moment while her eyes were on his lips before she nodded. "Yes."

He released an easy sigh of relief. "Excellent." He lifted her off him and gently laid her down on the pillows. Then he propped up on his side, gazing down at her. "We have something to discuss." His seriousness doused her desire.

"I'm listening," she said while scooting closer to his chest.

Aureon's fingertip danced circles on the back of her hand that rested on her belly. "I've made space for you and your friends to live in Theris, and I just need to know a finite amount of people."

Adaline's eyes widened. "Y-you're... you're letting us move to Theris?" Her eyes filled with tears as she grasped the shawl collar of his tunic.

Aureon gave a slight smile as he lowered his lips. "It is clear, little human: I want you safe and close, and nowhere is safer than Theris." He kissed her deeply as her tears fell.

"Thank you," she whispered as she failed to sniff back tears.

Aureon caressed her cheek and wiped away her tears. "You are welcome." He slipped his hand around her hand that clutched his collar, and she squeezed it tightly. He kissed the back of her hand. "Now tell me, how many people are coming with you?"

"Six, including me," she blurted out.

He nodded. "When are you planning to move?"

"In less than two weeks," she said, still in disbelief that he was so great about everything.

Aureon's gaze seemed distant as he made calculations. "That is manageable." He gazed at her, accepting a feeling he hadn't allowed himself to experience in a long time: excitement. He was thrilled that she would be near him every day, that there would be no more waiting until weekends to feel her energy on his plane.

"Asher and I have been talking," she shared. "We are considering moving Tony, Jim, Tessa, and Tobey, first. We would come over after our work finishes."

"How long will it take?" Aureon asked. It was a curious thing to know how long it took to end an entire world.

"We have been unable to calculate the timeframe accurately," she admitted. "The situation is unpredictable."

Aureon tensed at the notion of being without her for an indefinite period. "And no one else can be there with you?"

She shook her head. "There's a possibility that whoever stays with us could be struck down or swept away in The Harvest," she explained. When she saw his questioning look, she said, "It's when the heavens open to bring home those who are worthy in the eyes of the divine. It'll happen before we do our part."

"And you are certain you both can escape such a reaping?"

Adaline and Asher had talked about it many times. The truth was, they wouldn't know for sure until they completed their purpose. That's why they took the time to become stronger in their abilities, so at least they would have the sheer might to push back against a powerful entity to stay alive. They hoped their preparation would give them a chance to get back through the portal before it closed.

"We will," she whispered confidently. Adaline felt the tension in Aureon's body grow. She spoke honestly, "As in any battle, a lot can go wrong. But you still go through it for the sake of what's right."

He brainstormed for alternatives. "Is this process avoidable?"

She was already shaking her head. "This is my purpose, Aureon. It's the reason I was born."

Absorbed into her dark gaze, he knew that couldn't be true regardless of what she believed. Although their conversation barely released the tension he carried on the subject, she knew she would be able to calm his worry with proof soon. Adaline decided she would reveal her true form to him. Only Asher had seen it and not at full power. The twins couldn't simply trigger their true forms around each other at the same time because if they did and came into physical contact, the weapons they became to destroy the world would activate.

"I need you not to worry," Adaline plead.

Aureon's brows drew tight, and he gently outlined her cheekbone with the pad of his thumb. She kissed it before he let it fall away.

"You ask much," was all he managed to say.

"Then trust me to show you more of my power over the next couple of weeks, so I can ease your mind," Adaline stated. He nodded and leaned his forehead down to meet hers. She gasped at the contact as the vibration that radiated through their point of contact was more noticeable than before. He lifted her chin then sealed his lips over hers in a hungry kiss.

Before Adaline could melt into him, she huffed in surprise at the tug on her aura. "It looks like it's time to go," she said as she faded.

"What pulls you from a dream?" he asked her. He wanted to prevent it from happening in the future.

"Considering my current circumstances, it's either Tobey or sunrise," she admitted before she was gone.

Aureon almost fell flat on his face when she disappeared but caught himself.

"That boy," he growled.

CHAPTER 51

T he twins hurried to their office early the following day, eager to determine what they would take with them to Theris. They had a few hours until their employees arrived, giving them time to sort through everything. The reality was finally sinking in for Asher that the entire building, along with the rest of the planet, would be dust in a couple of weeks, as would all the people they've met, passed on the street, or referred to as patients. Everyone would be gone. That was a sobering thought for the twins. They always understood the impact of their purpose, and the result wasn't something they had previously dwelled. Now that their purpose was coming to pass, the reality of the process weighed on their minds. By forcing themselves to maintain tunnel vision, they focused on the result to avoid distraction.

Moving through their offices felt odd as if they were intruding in a place that was no longer theirs. *Is this what knowing about Theris has done to my perception of my life?* Adaline thought. She had been moving forward with her life and was simply working on getting her brother and friends to do the same. Adaline caught up to Asher in his office. He was staring at a blank email prompt open on his computer screen that covered a whole wall.

"What are we going to tell everyone, Addy?" Asher asked his twin without looking away from the screen. "Sorry, but everyone is going to die soon anyway, so we're closing?"

"Blunt was always your forte," Adaline joked.

"This isn't funny, Addy."

"I know," Adaline admitted. "But you forget something." Asher's attention shifted to her. "We won't be inflicting pain on the good ones, and they will be immune to an earthly death because they get to ascend and go home." Her gaze turned envious. "They get to go home, Ash. Do you remember it?"

Asher did, without fail. He remembered every detail of every chance at paradise after each of his earthly deaths. It was a reunion Asher always anticipated after another persecuted lifetime on Earth. However, Asher had gotten preoccupied with the damage he and Adaline would inflict upon the world that he disregarded the silver lining for those who had been good people.

Adaline rested her hand on her brother's shoulder. "We've employed a lot of good people, Ash."

"We did," he confirmed and returned his focus to the screen.

"Just make it a simple going out of business email, wishing everyone well," Adaline said. "And let them know they can take whatever they need from this place."

Asher's shoulders sank with a heavy sigh. He set his fingers on the keys and drafted the email to their staff at lightning speed. A second later, he sent the message and rose from his chair.

"Is there anything else we need?" Asher asked his sister.

Adaline glanced around. "Nothing comes to mind."

"All right," Asher said as he closed the front door behind him. "Let's get out of here."

The twins packed up the last few boxes in their cars and headed home. Adaline pulled into her garage, and as the door came down behind her vehicle, a large explosion detonated at the front end of her house. She sighed as her brother's words came rushing into her mind, "Not today, dammit!"

Adaline exited her car and shifted the matter of her home as she walked through the floor plan of the house. She walked through walls that reassembled once she passed by and down hallways that weren't there before the explosion until she arrived at her patio. Her gaze lifted to see a privately-funded, heavily-armed, stealth helicopter staring back at her as it hovered over the water.

"There is a helicopter outside for you," she said in Asher's mind as the chopper released a missile aimed for Tony's house.

"I'll be right there," Asher replied.

"Now, Ash!" Adaline demanded as she took off after the missile. She popped a light ball into her hand, spoke the word "catch" into it, and threw it between the missile and Tony's beachfront porch. The missile entered the ball, bringing it to an abrupt stop. As Adaline approached the ball, Asher appeared at the speed of light.

"What happened?" Asher asked.

Adaline grasped the ball. "I have a delivery for you." She brought the ball to her lips and whispered, "Boom." She handed it to her brother. "Five seconds."

"Easy," Asher smirked and grabbed the ball before jetting in the direction of the helicopter. He ran so fast his feet skimmed the surface of the ocean, and his momentum propelled him upward. The men in the helicopter's shock that he could reach them filled Asher with pride and a cocky grin. Terror filled their faces when Asher dropped the light ball that held the missile onto the floor of the chopper then sped away.

The helicopter exploded in the sky before two fighter jets dropped from above. They shot through the air and turned around to charge the coastline. They dropped their ammo, nailing every beachfront home, except Asher's. Asher leaped up and caught the nose of one aircraft, punched through the glass, and electrocuted the pilots. The jet plummeted from the sky and into the ocean. Asher sped over the surface of the water back to the shore, and he saw Adaline running toward a helicopter that was taking off.

"They captured Tony!" Adaline yelled as she grew another ball in the palm of her hand. She whispered, "Follow," into it and threw it after the aircraft. She turned to Asher. "Follow and retrieve Tony. I'm moving the rest of them off-world, now. I'll be coming in behind you."

"Got it," Asher said and sped after the aircraft, watching for the glow of Adaline's light ball that was attached to the helicopter. Adaline wrangled a terrified Tessa while Tobey stood with Jim's arms wrapped around them both.

"Are your bags packed?" Adaline asked them. Everyone nodded. "Get them, now. We're leaving."

A moment later, Adaline led them through the portal to Theris. Tobey clutched her hand as he trembled. They heard what sounded like the shriek of a bomb diving for a target splitting the air. Yards away, Aureon landed on his feet to see Adaline with her friends and family in tow.

"What happened?" he asked as he scanned everyone for injuries.

"I don't have time to explain," she said to him. "But I need to move them, now. They are being targeted and won't survive if they stay."

He nodded as he signaled a guard. "I will take them from here."

The fear in Tessa's eyes prompted Adaline to embrace her friend. "It's all right. His name is Aureon. He will keep you safe. I'll return soon, okay? Watch Tobey." Tessa nodded with tears in her eyes. Adaline let go of her friend and raced back through the portal.

A moment later, Theodon appeared at his father's side.

"What happened?" he asked the group before noticing Jim. "Jim, what's going on?"

The weary veteran sighed. "They took Tony."

The royals glanced at each other before Aureon addressed the group as he, Theodon, and the guard grabbed their bags, "Follow me."

Adaline stepped onto the beach and analyzed the fallout. The houses down the coastline were decimated, but that didn't phase her. She searched for the aircraft that took Tony.

"Where are you?" she asked Asher telepathically.

"You're not going to like it," Asher replied.

She latched onto his voice and teleported to his side into darkness.

"Where are we?"

"Remember when you blew up the observatory?" Asher asked.

"Yes," Adaline remembered that entertaining afternoon.

"We are underneath it," Asher explained. "Deep in the hillside."

"Ugh! They're like fucking cockroaches," Adaline spat. "Did you find Tony?"

"Yes, and you aren't going to like that either," Asher said before indicating at the light at the far end of the hallway. "They have him in a room at the end of the hallway. His heartbeat was normal until a moment ago, and I think they've changed tactics from questioning to torture."

Asher's last word ignited Adaline's rage, and her eyes glowed. "You rescue. I'll sweep."

Asher nodded and let his sister lead the way. They floated down the hallway, their feet inches from the ground until Adaline turned toward the door that trapped Tony. With a wave of her hand, she ripped it from its hinges. The two QC agents who were standing over Tony looked at Adaline in surprise. They went for their guns, but Adaline flicked her fingers, causing their weapons to disintegrate. The molecules floated toward her, and she twirled her finger through them to make them orbit around her hand. A moment later, she formed a combat bayonet. It reminded her of Tony's. She gripped the hilt of the blade and slashed it out, catching the throat of the closest agent. He grabbed his throat with both hands as his knees hit the floor. The other agent tried to back away from her but ended up hitting the wall behind him. Asher moved in to unbind an unconscious Tony.

"Is he alive?" Adaline asked as her eyes focused on the agent in front of her.

"He's not breathing," Asher said as he sped through the undoing of Tony's bindings.

"Get him out of here."

"What are you going to do?"

"I'm going to make sure these roaches stay dead this time," Adaline sneered, then sank the blade through the agent's heart, and she twisted it for good measure.

Asher saw that Adaline's eyes blazed, and her appearance was changing. She was closer to taking her true form, which meant he needed to be as far away from her as possible.

"We're gone," Asher said before vanishing with Tony in his arms.

Adaline returned to the hallway and allowed her fury to rule her. Her body burned with white fire, and she went room by room through the entire underground facility, incinerating every soul in the building. She eventually came across Commander Nash, who had his back to her. He was staring out his office window that overlooked their classified studies that resulted in countless innocent casualties.

"I knew this day would come," he said to her. "I knew you would be my downfall." He finally turned to face her and was stunned by what he saw. He was expecting the normal, pretty, human-looking doctor he had seen from a distance. But that wasn't who stood in the doorway. A raging fire goddess stared back at him, and she incinerated anything that was within a few feet of her. The fear in his eyes grew as she moved closer. Fear rooted in the realization that he was never a match for her.

"My work will continue after I'm gone," he said in an attempt to dismiss her power.

Adaline smiled at the truth of the situation. Nash would suffer horribly as he died. She lifted him off the ground with her mind and floated him near. "It's amusing that you think your punishment ends with your death. However, you have so much to learn and atone for, Commander Nash."

"Don't tell me you are referring to your false prophets and their heresy?" Commander Nash spat out. "I've been doing nothing but saving this world and creating the best weapons to keep it secure. And the rest of you believe lies from heretics about a false afterlife."

Adaline was intrigued by his ignorance. "So, you think this death is the end for you?" Adaline hatched white fire within his belly, letting it slowly cook his organs from the inside out. His expression changed as he suffered. She turned away from him and swiped at the air in front of her, causing reality to tear open a portal that led to a fiery hell plane. Giant beasts with horns and claws reached through the portal as Adaline stepped out of the way. She floated behind Commander Nash and felt his fear multiply as the beasts came for him.

Adaline's lips were at his ear. "I'm afraid this is only the beginning of your suffering, Commander."

The hell beast's grasped Commander Nash with their claws, whose vocal cords melted away, giving him no means to scream for his life. They eagerly pulled him into their fiery world. Then they looked at Adaline, who gave them a stern, glowing, stare and they backed away from her as she sealed the portal. A moment later, her mind cleared. *Tony!* She teleported to the beach.

Adaline jumped from the sand up to Asher's patio to see Asher doing CPR on Tony. "Come on!" Asher commanded as he pushed on Tony's chest. "Don't you leave now, dammit!" Asher blew into his mouth before trying to jolt Tony's heart back to life with his electricity.

Adaline's heart sank in her chest as she knelt across from Asher. "How long have you been working on him?"

"Fifteen minutes," Asher said, not pausing his rhythm. Adaline's eyes watered. Her brother knew Tony was gone but couldn't accept the truth. "Come on, old man! Don't make me come over there and get you."

Adaline's heart broke as she reached for Asher's hands to make him stop, and he flung her off him. "Asher, stop," Adaline whispered. "Stop!"

Asher finally sank back on his haunches and cried. "He can't be gone. Not Tony. He's stronger than this."

Adaline knelt behind Asher and wrapped her arms around him. "He's the strongest," Adaline agreed. "But he's also old, and he's not built like us, Ash. His body was going to give out at some point, no matter what we are capable of." Asher sobbed as silent tears ran down Adaline's cheeks. A few minutes passed before she rose to her feet. "Stay here with him. I'll get our bags." She approached her house, and with a wave of her hand, she shifted the debris of what was left of it until she found the basement staircase. She grabbed her bags and dropped them on Asher's patio before she went to his bedroom to retrieve his. After she gathered everything in the same place, she surveyed her brother. He sniffed back tears and glanced at her with his red-rimmed eyes.

"We are taking him with us," Asher stated.

Adaline nodded. "Yes, we are." Tony deserved to be laid to rest somewhere beautiful. She floated their bags through the portal then waited until Asher was ready to leave. Finally, her twin rose to his feet with Tony in his arms.

"Ready," he said.

"Okay, let's go," Adaline said, with her hand resting on her brother's shoulder. They stepped through the portal, leaving Earth behind.

"Dr. Adaline?" a familiar voice said.

Adaline turned to see Darius, the guard who had helped her

organize patients during her second visit to Theris. "Darius," Adaline said. She turned back to the portal long enough to mask the opening with her force field.

Darius stopped to look at the man in Asher's arms. The guard's movements slowed as he grew closer, unable to detect Tony's heartbeat. "I'm sorry," Darius said and signaled at the guards behind him to assist. The guard's grasped the handles of a carrier stretcher and waited for Asher to set Tony on it.

Asher shuffled slowly toward the stretcher, reluctant to let go of Tony. Tears formed anew in Adaline's eyes as she witnessed her brother struggle to move away from the stretcher. The guards carefully cradled Tony and marched him to the palace. The twins followed close behind with one arm slung over each other's shoulders, failing to keep quiet as their tears fell. They clutched at each other, trying to walk straight as they bawled.

Darius asked the twins in the throne room, "What sort of man was he in his life?"

Adaline's brows drew tight as Asher sobbed. "He was like a father to us," Adaline admitted. "And a warrior all the days of his life."

Darius nodded. "We have special burials for warriors." The twins nodded in consent before the guards took Tony's body away. "Do you need anything else?"

"We're kinda numb right now, Darius," Adaline confessed. "Thank you for your help."

"Of course," the guard said with a slight bow before he exited the throne room.

Once the guards had left the throne room, the twins collapsed to the floor, hitting their knees as they sobbed uncontrollably. A moment later, Jim knelt in front of them and embraced them both, causing them to cry harder.

"We didn't make it in time," Asher sobbed. "His body had already given out."

"Shh," Jim coaxed. "It's okay."

Aureon stood in the shadow of the hallway, peering in on the family the three of them made. He felt Adaline's broken heart when she arrived in Theris and immediately dispatched more guards to aid Darius. Aureon wouldn't intrude on their moment of suffering, understanding that the twins had all they needed in Jim.

"We could still go get him and bring him back from the other side," Asher breathed the memory of a hard lesson the twins experienced long ago.

"No," Jim said, grasping Asher by the shoulders to look him in the eye. "Tony deserves peace, and you know that as much as I do."

Asher nodded as he continued to cry. Jim mashed their foreheads against his shoulders in a firm embrace. Time passed, and Aureon remained nearby to see to anything else they might need. As much as it bothered him that he felt he couldn't comfort Adaline yet, he kept his focus on the reality of the situation: the twins had just lost someone significant to them.

Jim finally moved to help the twins stand. "C'mon," Jim said to them as he guided them toward the hallway. "Let's try to get some rest."

"Where do I sleep?" Asher asked.

"Second door on the left," Aureon said from behind them.

They all spun around to see the king, still wearing his day robes, looking over Adaline with concern.

"Ash, this is Aureon," Adaline whispered before she sniffled.

Her brother sniffed back the last of his tears and straightened before offering his hand to Aureon. Aureon untucked one of his hands from behind his back and shook Asher's hand without hesitation.

"Good to meet you," was all Asher could manage to say.

"And you," Aureon replied.

Asher turned to his sister and kissed her on the cheek before embracing her tightly. "I love you."

"I love you," she said back, her voice cracking on the last word.

Asher said good night to Jim, who patted him on the shoulder before he retired to his room. Jim followed suit after he glanced at Adaline to make sure she was all right. Adaline and Aureon were left alone in the middle of the quiet hallway.

Aureon's penetrating gaze stripped away at her layers of self-preservation, renewing her tears. He didn't hesitate to wrap her up in his arms. Her cries eventually ebbed into soft weeping, and he finally pulled away to examine her.

"Are you injured?" he asked her. She shook her head as she wiped away a tear that was running down her cheek. "What do you need right now?"

Adaline was so numb that she wasn't sure what she needed. "All I can think of is a hot bath and sleep."

"Ena already drew you a bath," he said. "And Tobey is asleep in your room."

Oh yeah, I should check on Tobey, she thought, switching to emotional autopilot to deflect the rest of the oncoming sorrow. All she could manage was to nod and whisper her thanks before turning toward her room. Aureon's arm snaked around her and pulled her back against his chest, and his lips were at her ear.

"If you need me, say so," he whispered.

Adaline's eyes watered at his offer, at his touch. Her need for physical contact left her hands searching to cup his face. She needed to feel he was real before she nodded up at him as another tear fell. Her lips reached up to meet his, and he covered her mouth with an urgent kiss. He kissed her hard to convey his willingness to comfort her, to ground her. His endless gaze opened when he parted from her, surveying her with intent.

"Anything," he said.

Adaline nodded and noticed she had trouble moving toward her room, so he stepped ahead of her and opened the door. He scooped his hand behind her back and helped usher her inside.

"Thank you," was all she could manage. Aureon gave his

usual chin-tuck bow.

The door to her suite closed behind her, and her shoulders sagged from exhaustion. She tried her best to step lightly through the suite, so she would not disturb Tobey and made it to the bathroom. A hot bath was waiting for her. *Praise you, Ena*, she thought, even though she knew it was Aureon who gave the order. She let her mind dwell on thoughts of him for a while because she needed to tether her focus to happiness if she was going to get any rest tonight.

Wading in the bath helped alleviate the impact of the day's events before Adaline slipped on her robe over her soft pajamas. She reached her bed and stared at it for a moment, but she couldn't bring herself to pull the blankets back and slide between the covers. While glancing over at the patio to her suite, Adaline considered her options. A moment later, she teleported into the king's suite.

Aureon lounged on pillows with his arms folded under his head when Adaline appeared at the foot of his bed. He sat up and waved her forward with concern still filling his features. She crawled to him, and he untied her robe. The dark pink fabric fell away before she curled up on his bare chest. He pulled the covers over them as he clutched her close with his free arm. Her body tensed on top of his then she wept while he rubbed her back. His brows drew tight when her tears fell onto his chest as he wondered what more he could do for her. He used the slack of the sheet to wipe her face until she cried herself to sleep while clutching him close. It bothered him to know how vulnerable she may feel as the last phase of his plan would be executed that coming weekend. His thoughts raced as she finally sank into a deep sleep. *There must be a way to make this easier for her.*

A few hours later, Adaline's eyes flashed open in a panic. She'd forgotten something back on Earth, something important. She teleported from Aureon's side to her room, changed clothes, and returned to the portal. As soon as she left his plane, Aureon jolted awake with his heart racing as he discovered Adaline was gone, not just from his bed but from his world. He tore open his wardrobe and donned clothing and weapons before racing toward the portal so fast his form blurred, spooking the guards on his way out of the palace. Aureon stopped at the portal, taking a moment to gather his thoughts before he stepped through.

"My Lord," a winded guard said from behind him. "Please reconsider."

Aureon glanced at the guard, surprised at his plea. "You exaggerate. I will only be gone a short while." He lifted his foot.

"And if you aren't, My Lord?" the guard interjected.

Aureon's confident gaze landed on the guard. "Then you will have a new king to serve." He stepped through to Earth, landing in the sand underneath a staircase that he quickly climbed and found his little human. Adaline stood on the remaining piece of the patio, once attached to her home, now a large pile of rubble. He scanned the area to find the houses next to hers were in a similar state of decay. Aureon didn't expect to see ruin when he arrived on Earth but more infrastructure, people, more…. life.

Adaline spun at the sound of someone's approach, and her neutral expression filled with surprise when she saw Aureon. "What are you doing here?" she asked. Her hair was tousled, and her eyes were tired, but at least she was done crying, for now.

"I woke when you left," he admitted. "I wanted to make sure no harm had come to you."

Her tired features managed a small smile. "Thank you."

He gave a clipped nod as he kept scanning for intruders as he processed the frenetic energy of her world. It put him on edge as if he couldn't stifle the panic of an imminent enemy strike. *Did she live like this every day?*

"Why did you come back?" he asked her.

"I forgot something," Adaline admitted as she turned back to the pile. She reached her left hand behind her until Aureon enveloped hers with his own, noticing that feeling their fingers interlocked helped her settle. Adaline sighed before she lifted her right hand and flattened it, and she swiped it across her body as if she was wiping a window clean. Aureon witnessed the rubble of her home lift into the air and rotated in orbit as the home reassembled itself. He stared in wonder, surprised at the power she wielded. He lifted their joined hands to his lips to kiss the back of hers, grateful that she felt safe enough to show this gift to him. The sliding glass door to the patio was the last to reassemble. The door opened, and he followed her inside.

Adaline led him down a hallway that led to the bedrooms, with hers at the end. She rushed to her closet in search of what she had left behind. Aureon continued scanning his surroundings, noticing that she lived well. He was glad to see that because he accepted it as something they had in common. *Our worlds are not so far apart.*

"Got it," she called while retrieving a chest from the closet and setting it on her bed. Aureon approached her side as she tore it open. Happy tears fell from her eyes with a relieved laugh as she fumbled through the contents of the chest. She pulled a handful of photos from the disarray and stared at the top one for a long moment.

"What is that?" he asked, focusing on the different faces in the photo.

"It's a photograph," she explained. "It's taken in real-time versus a painting that you'd have to pose for a while."

He nodded. "Is this all you need?"

"Yes," she said as she put the photos back and closed the trunk.

A large explosion shook the foundation of the house. Aureon's shoulders tensed, and his ears twitched.

"It's time to go," Adaline said as she handed him the trunk. "Follow me." She led him from the house, covering them in her force field as they ran to the patio and pounded down the stairs to the portal. They hooked under the staircase to see two QC agents with firearms on them flanking the portal.

"Surrender, witch!" one of the agents yelled.

Aureon snarled viciously behind her, causing the agents to scramble back and refocus their guns on him. Both agents fired one round. The agents stared in shock as the bullets turned into tiny sand particles then dropped to the ground. They retreated further when they saw Adaline's eyes blazing white light. She lifted them off the ground with her mind, and they struggled against her power. A moment later, their necks snapped to one side, and she dropped her hold on their bodies.

"Let's go," she said to Aureon. They stepped through the portal together, and she covered the opening with her force field. Now, no one could come through until the twins returned to Earth to serve their purpose.

Aureon walked alongside her in silence as they returned to the palace with his brows drawn tight. His thoughts raced about what he witnessed, from her power to those who wanted her dead. *Dead*, he thought, again, and the reality chilled his bones.

Adaline felt his unsettled emotions. "Is there something you want to say?"

"I have no indication on where to start," he confessed.

Adaline touched his arm, teleporting them into his suite before retracting her force field. She sighed as he set the chest on the floor near the bed. As vulnerable as she felt by asking, she still needed to know. "Does what you saw change how-"

Aureon grabbed her face and leveled his eyes on hers. "No." He planted a firm kiss on her lips before he rested his forehead against hers.

Relief filled her as her gaze fell to her feet. She reached for Aureon's hand, and he mirrored her movements. Tears welled in her eyes as their fingertips gently touched, and his fingers caressed hers before interlocking with them. A tear fell from the corner of her eye as he pulled her near.

Aureon searched the depths of her dark eyes, now

understanding how hard her life had been and how much she had suffered. *Never again.* Without a word, he kissed her and slowly pulled off her clothes as he backed her toward the bed. Her sweeper gear littered his floor, along with his own, before he scooped her up and pulled back the covers. Slipping them both between the sheets, she curled onto her side, and his body curled around hers. She relaxed at the contact, the feeling of safety.

Aureon placed a kiss on the curve of her neck and wrapped his arm around her before he whispered, "Sleep, little human. You are safe." He felt her body relax in his arms, and she dozed off.

CHAPTER 52

D awn broke on the horizon as Aureon cradled a sleeping
Adaline in his arms as he slipped into her room without a
sound. He gently laid her on her bed and tucked the covers
around her. Unable to mask the wonder on his face, he placed a
soft kiss on her cheek. Her force field didn't activate when she
slept with him last night, and he was prideful in knowing she felt
safe with him.

An hour passed after Aureon left Adaline's room before she
awakened to the sound of familiar music coming from the long
hallway. She threw on fresh clothes and left her hair loose before
she poked her head outside her suite door. She saw Asher standing there holding Tessa's hands, teaching her dance moves while
a small speaker was playing music.

"There she is!" Asher cheered. "Come here, Addy. Let's
show Tessa the right way to salsa."

Adaline was surprised that the two of them were in a decent
mood and opened her suite door a little wider. She didn't say a
word as she continued to watch them.

"Come on, Dr. Adaline," Theodon said with a smile. He stood to the far right, where Adaline didn't notice him at first.

"We were the best at this when we were kids," Asher bragged.

Adaline smirked as she shuffled out into the hallway. "We *are* the best at this." She approached her brother, who held out his hands for hers. The twins focused on each other as Adaline's heart latched onto the happy moment.

"Who taught you this kind of dance?" Theodon asked.

The twins' gaze fell to their joined hands as Asher admitted, "Tony and Elena taught us."

Adaline's mind reached into the past to earlier memories of her current lifetime. She remembered first meeting Tony and Jim and how Asher seemed to take to Tony immediately, whereas she bonded with Jim. Tony's mother, Elena, added much-needed nurturance to the twins' lives after their parents died. She was a beautiful woman from Argentina who had fled to the U.S. before disaster hit South America. She met Tony's father, Wade, after arriving in Austin, Texas.

Elena was a talented dancer, who searched for places to dance ballet professionally, but after meeting Wade, she wanted nothing more than to follow him everywhere. And she did because he was a military man. Wade died during active duty, and Elena made a point of sticking around to help her son. So, when the Everlys moved to Southern California, Elena followed. She made sure they ate, slept, and studied while they were in medical school. She also taught Adaline the proper way to walk and dance in heels, an archaic notion only practiced by the wealthy. The twins' lives were made lighter for brief moments because of her as they danced across her kitchen floor. When she passed away, the twins were inconsolable for days. Tony was their last connection to those moments of happiness.

A moment passed as the music reverberated in the hallway of the palace. The twins tapped their feet to the beat before Asher lifted his chin at her. Adaline nodded, and they danced. They focused on their steps, and their hot moves glided smoothly across the cold stone floor. There were dips, spins, and funny add-ins that made Theodon and Tessa laugh. Finally, the twins were smiling again. Asher spun Adaline, who ended up in Jim's face.

"Good morning, Jim," Adaline said to him as she looked down to see him offering her his hand.

"Morning, Addy," he said as he led her around the floor.

Asher continued to teach Tessa the steps as Theodon observed from the sidelines. Ena poked her head around the corner before rushing to the prince's side.

"Breakfast is ready, Your Majesty," she told him after a formal greeting.

"Thank you, Ena," he said to her before she left. Theodon entered Adaline's room. He roused Tobey, got him dressed, and brought him out to join the others for breakfast. He herded everyone into the dining room as they were all still laughing from dancing. As expected, his father was already seated for breakfast, ready to enjoy his meal. However, he was interrupted by the group when he heard laughter.

"Where should I sit?" Tessa asked Adaline.

"Wherever you want to, Tess," Adaline said.

Asher and Jim slid into seats next to Tobey, who sat in his usual spot next to the king. Tessa sat next to Adaline, who took her seat next to Theodon.

"Good morning," the king said to the group.

"Good morning," echoed from each person at the table.

It took Aureon a while to admit to himself that he liked the feeling of everyone gathered at the table together, versus it just being him and sometimes Theodon. They all chatted as they settled into their meals and discussed what activities they could do that day.

"I was going to head out for a morning hunt," Theodon admitted.

"Mind if I join you?" Jim and Asher blurted at the same time. Both men looked at each other, and Asher smirked.

"Of course," Theodon said genially. "I have plenty of extra gear for you to use."

Jim nodded before he forked more breakfast into his mouth. It had been years since he had a leisure outing, and hunting was his favorite hobby.

"Dr. Adaline, the Ieobu House is sending over their staff for you, Tessa, and Sorsacha," the king said to her as he kept his attention on his plate, never disrupting the consumption of his meal. He noticed the apparent change in her stress level after her last visit to the spa house and thought repeating the strategy would help her through the grief and the stress she may incur over the next couple of days.

Adaline's gaze grew distant as she revisited her memories of the bliss of the Ieobu House until Bole messed it up.

Tessa nudged her friend. "What's the Ieobu House?"

"Quite possibly the most relaxing house in Theris," Adaline confessed.

Tessa's eyebrows lifted. Adaline nodded in return.

"Sorsacha will be along shortly," Aureon told them. He refrained from telling them Sorsacha had orders to keep an eye on both Adaline and Tessa. He was taking precautions in case her mourning may hinder her reaction time should an emergency arise. Aureon believed that she deserved the time to process the loss of Tony uninterrupted, allowing herself to be vulnerable. But since he could not guard her personally, having Sorsacha nearby would not register anyone as odd, considering their new friendship.

When the king had spoken the orders into Sorsacha's mind earlier that morning, the she-elf quickly replied. "Is she all right?"

"Not entirely," the king relayed. "I do not want her to be concerned with anything else. Your job, Sorsacha, is to defend her every step of the way while she is relaxing."

"I will, Your Majesty," she didn't hesitate to reply.

"Good," he said. "Be at the palace in two hours."

"Yes, Your Majesty."

"Oh, Ash," Adaline said across the table to her brother, "we have a high-risk pregnancy patient we need to see."

Asher peered around the table then eyed his sister. "Who's pregnant?"

"No one here," Adaline said quickly. "Her name is Sana, and she's an elf who is carrying twins."

"Still waiting for the high-risk part," Asher commented as he continued to shove food in his mouth.

"Elves cannot carry a multiple-birth pregnancy to term," Adaline said. Intrigued filled Asher's expression before she added, "I've been monitoring her progress, and I am hoping to make it possible to bring both babies to term."

"How did you manage that?" Asher asked.

"By prescribing her to eat half of the food in my kitchen," Aureon muttered in between bites.

Adaline's eyes shifted to the king, and she almost smiled at his admission. "Her food intake has been substantially increased, and I have been using healing to relieve back pain and help the struggling baby." Asher nodded. "I would like for her to meet you in case you need to deliver the twins instead of me."

"Old school C-section?" Asher asked.

"Probably."

Asher's head snapped toward the king when a thought hit him. "Is there a medical library on the premises that would contain detailed documentation on elfin biology and current medical practices?"

Aureon nodded. "It is an entire aisle in my library. You are welcome to use it. Learning to read Tear would help."

Asher threw a confused expression at his sister.

"The king and the prince are Tearuine elves," Adaline explained. "Tearuine elves speak Tear."

"Learning Tear, it is!" Asher feigned excitement before he stood and said to his twin, "Let's go meet with Sana." The twins reached their hands toward each other, and they disappeared.

"I still can't believe they can do things like that," Tessa commented.

"Tip of the iceberg," Jim said as he finished his meal.

CHAPTER 53

L ater that morning, Adaline, Tessa, and Sorsacha entered the garden to find that the Ieobu House staff pitched private tents to cater to the female's every whim. The amount of care and concern that went into each treatment wowed Tessa.

"This is the best!" she moaned as her masseuse kneaded her shoulders.

"Told you!" Adaline called from the next tent.

Sorsacha wasn't giving in to the pampering and instead remained focused on her charge. Her ears twitched as she listened for everyone in the vicinity; the number of elves, their heartbeats, which tents they entered and exited. She was keen on carrying out the king's orders to perfection. She knew he was nearby because his heart beated differently than any other in the kingdom. She also noticed how much his heartbeat changed when he was within proximity of Adaline. She heard Ena enter Adaline's tent to ask her if a memorial service for Tony would be acceptable to have later in the afternoon. Adaline agreed to it.

"So?" Tessa asked through her tent's thin wall, "What are we doing tonight?"

"What do you mean?" Adaline asked.

"I mean, what are we doing for your bachelorette party?" Tessa sounded excited.

"Bachelorette party?" Sorsacha asked.

Adaline groaned before explaining to Sorsacha, "It's an old human ritual where the bride and her friends go party because it's the bride's last night as a single woman."

Sorsacha's head lifted from the massage table and turned in Adaline's direction. "Humans celebrate that?"

"Yes!" Tessa squealed. "And we gotta do it for Addy. One fun night before the big commitment!"

Sorsacha smirked and decided to play along for the sake of embarrassing her human friend. "You're right! We should celebrate, and I know the perfect place." Adaline's head popped up from her massage table and shot a surprised look in Sorsacha's direction. Sacha couldn't tell her friend's expression through the partition, but the sudden movement was enough to make her laugh.

"We don't need to do this," Adaline protested.

"Oh, I think we do," Sorsacha exaggerated.

"Yay! Sacha's in!" Tessa cheered.

"Ugh… I hate you both," Adaline said as her masseuse worked through her muscles as the two plotting females giggled.

Later that day, Tessa wandered the palace until she found the throne room. Aureon was speaking with someone before acknowledging her. He became accustomed to understanding that when Tessa made herself seen, she usually needed something.

"Yes, Miss Hill?" Aureon asked her.

"Please, excuse the interruption," Tessa said to the king's guest before she approached Aureon. "Who can I ask about obtaining supplies to make something for Addy?"

Aureon's brow lifted in curiosity. "Ena."

A moment later, the she-elf poked her head into the throne room. "Yes, My Lord?"

"Would you please help Miss Hill with whatever she needs?" Aureon instructed.

"Absolutely, My Lord." Ena nodded and smiled.

Tessa turned to Aureon. "Thank you."

The king put a little more effort into his bow than his usual clipped nod. Tessa hurried to catch up with Ena and explained what she needed for that evening.

"Who was that?" Flavial asked Aureon.

Aureon faced his friend. "She is-"

"Incredibly beautiful," Flavial interrupted.

"Easy," Aureon jested. "Let us get through my son's wedding first."

That afternoon, everyone gathered in the throne room for Tony's memorial service. The humans were dressed in black and stood on one side of the intricately carved alter where Tony's body rested. Adaline moved closer. Tony looked so peaceful. He was clothed in beautiful blue robes, with his hair brushed off his face. Thick white flowers that possessed a soothing scent surrounded his body. Tears waded in Adaline's eyes, even though she managed a slight smile. Jim stepped up beside her and wrapped his arm around her. The royals stood on the other side of the altar, waiting to take their cues from the humans.

Adaline whispered to Jim. "I think he'd want you to say something." Jim nodded and urged everyone standing behind them to step forward.

"I think we are beyond formalities at this point," Jim said. "Tony would have wanted us to be comfortable." Asher moved to Adaline's side and reached for her hand as Jim began the eulogy. "I met Captain Anthony Harper of the United States Marine Corps over one hundred and thirty years ago during basic training," Jim admitted. "I was his drill instructor under the order of Captain Michael Everly at the time."

Jim glanced at the twins as he mentioned their father in the earlier stages of his military career. "I made a point of making Tony's basic training a living hell solely because he showed up each morning at 05:00 hours with a big smile on his face." The twins chuckled. "Because I didn't know him, yet, I assumed he was a young kid being smug, so I was determined to train it out of him. Well, it turned out that Tony was simply a happy man." Jim let out a sigh. "That's something I always envied about him. No matter how bad things got, Tony actively chose happiness. That takes a mental fortitude I couldn't possibly possess."

Jim acknowledged the elfin soldiers lining both sides of the alter around them before he said to Tony, "I don't have a twenty-one-gun salute for you, buddy. And our fellow Marines know you deserve every shot, but we managed to gather the swords of some mighty fine warriors." At that moment, the elfin soldiers unsheathed their blades and saluted in unison. Adaline wept, and Tessa failed to sniff back tears. Asher let his fall freely without a sound.

"You are already missed, my friend," Jim said as his voice cracked. A moment of silence passed as Jim gathered himself for his final send-off. He reached forward to rest his hand against the side of the alter. "Semper fi." He patted the alter before giving Tony one final salute. Adaline and Asher hugged Jim as the soldiers moved in to carry the wooden altar from the room for burial. Moments of crying, tight hugs, and tears passed before the royals approached, their words delivered in soft, even tones.

"Captain Harper will be buried in the garden mausoleum as you wish," Aureon addressed the group. Another moment of silence passed before he asked, "Is there anything else to arrange for him that is custom?"

Adaline shook her head, parted from Jim and Asher, and wrapped her arms around Aureon. He was shocked at her public demonstration of affection, so there was a delay in his response to reciprocating. Once he did, she whispered, "Thank you."

Adaline's words made him clutch her closer, as he still tried to measure his reactions to her while in front of other people. "Of course."

"I think you girls should go relax, so you have energy for your party tonight," Jim encouraged Tessa and Adaline.

Aureon felt Adaline tense in his arms. "Party?"

"Yeah, about that...." Adaline said as she parted from him to ask Tessa, "Do we have to?"

"No," Tessa admitted. "But this may be your only chance."

"I'm okay with that," Adaline admitted.

"Addy," Asher said. "It will put you in a better mood for tomorrow."

Adaline sighed. "Fine," she huffed with disdain, then turned on her heel and left the throne room. Tessa smiled and hurried after her.

Aureon was still in the dark. "What party?"

Asher smirked before telling the king, "Tessa has a weird fondness for old human wedding traditions. One of them is a bachelorette party. It's when the bride's girlfriends take her out for a night on the town to celebrate her last night as a single woman." The explanation took a moment to sink into Aureon's mind then his gaze turned distant. "With the shenanigans they will likely get into, it's highly possible they will get arrested," Asher added. Aureon's attention snapped in Asher's direction. Asher chuckled and patted the king's shoulder. "It's all right. I'm fairly certain they won't burn down the kingdom."

"Stop baiting him," Jim warned Asher.

Asher held up his hands in surrender before he and Jim left the throne room together. Jim stopped and turned back to the prince, "I understand elves don't do bachelor parties, Theodon. But we'd like to make a toast in your honor later this evening. If that's all right with you."

"I would be honored, Jim," Theodon smiled warmly. Jim nodded before exiting the room with Asher. "Father?" Theodon said in his father's mind. Aureon's expression was still far away as his thoughts spun on the mysteries of the bachelorette party Tessa mentioned.

What could possibly result in the females getting arrested?

"Everything is going to be fine," Theodon assured him. Aureon gave a slight nod before he came back to the present moment. "We're almost finished."

"Yes," Aureon replied in his son's mind as his thoughts settled. "Almost finished."

CHAPTER 54

"I'm not wearing that," Adaline balked at the parchment and glitter crown that said "Bride" across the front.

"Oh c'mon!" Tessa whined.

"No," Adaline said as she refocused on the mirror to finish putting on her earrings.

Tessa waved the crown at her. "You gotta get used to wearing one, anyway." Adaline's eyes narrowed on her friend in the reflection of the mirror.

Sorsacha exited the bathroom in Adaline's suite, staring down at the tiny dress she wore. "I'm not sure it's wise to go out in public in something so tiny," Sorsacha commented. "I would call it a dress, but I think it's too small to be considered one." Adaline chuckled.

"Yes, it's a party dress," Tessa corrected. "It's what is usually worn on a night out of debauchery."

"Okay, let's get a few things straight, Tess," Adaline leveled with her friend. "This isn't Vegas. We're not going to a strip club, and there will be no lap dances. Everyone we meet tonight who happens to have a penis must keep it in their pants."

Sorsacha's lip curled in disgust. "Is that what happens at bachelorette parties?"

"You are being dramatic," Tessa shot back.

"I am not because I know you," Adaline stated. "Tonight is to be a simple celebration of going out with friends for a few drinks. Maybe dancing if it's available. That's all."

"Oh, there will be dancing," Sorsacha insisted.

Tessa clapped her hands. "Yay!"

"I'm going to regret this," Adaline muttered with a sigh. The females checked their appearances in the mirror and left the room. In the long hallway, they checked the contents of their tiny clutch purses, and they glanced at their stilettos before heading to the front entrance of the palace.

"Ladies!" Asher hollered as he stumbled over to them, carrying full shot glasses.

"Are you drunk already?" Adaline asked.

"Almost," he said to Adaline without missing a beat. "You girls look like you need to catch up." He passed out the shot glasses to them and had an extra for himself, and he held it up to toast to his twin. "To Addy," he said before clinking his glass with all of theirs.

"To Addy," the girls echoed before downing their shots.

Asher finished his shot first, and as intoxicated a state as he was in, he still noticed a beautiful blonde she-elf hurrying past them. She had captivating wide eyes that were the color of the sky, with creamy skin and rosy cheeks. He spun around and watched her walk away, unable to launch a comment that might spark interaction. For once, he was stunned.

"W-who?" Asher pointed after the she-elf, with the shot glass still in his hand.

"No," Adaline said to him.

Asher threw her a skeptical look. "I highly doubt that's her name, Addy."

Sorsacha and Tessa giggled, and Asher took their giggling as encouragement and smiled wide.

"I said no, Ash," Adaline said seriously.

"What?" Asher lifted his hands in surrender. "What would I possibly do?"

"Remember your previous physician's assistant?" Adaline reality-checked him.

"Hey," Asher got defensive. "That was different. She was-"

"A huge liability that could have cost us our practice because you just had to sleep with her," Adaline interrupted.

"You wound me, sis," Asher dramatically placed his hand over his heart. "You wound me with your words and... facts."

Sorsacha and Tessa burst with laughter.

"Leave Ena alone," Adaline warned her brother. "She's one of the royal's favorite members of their staff. Mistreat her, and you will have to deal with Aureon."

"Oooooh!" Asher waved his hands in the air. "I'm so scared!"

"Do not mess this up," Adaline said. "I want her to continue to be around, too."

"She's that good?" Asher asked curiously.

"Yes," Adaline admitted.

"Okay, she's off-limits then," Asher stated, then leaned forward to kiss Adaline on the cheek. "Love you, sis."

"Love you, too," she replied.

His tipsiness caused him to waver on his feet while he made a shooing motion. "Go and have fun."

"Okay," Adaline said. "Pace yourself and remember what I said!"

"Yeah, yeah, I will!" Asher said before he sped back to the dining room.

The three of them stared after Asher for a moment as Adaline contemplated staying behind to keep an eye on him. Asher got into odd situations when he was drunk.

"I'm sure he'll be fine," Sorsacha said. "I mean, he does have the others watching him, too."

"Yeah, he'll be okay," Tessa chimed in. "We should go so we can get started on celebrating."

Adaline turned to Sorsacha. "Where are we going?"

Sorsacha grinned. "There's a skybox at Eleona's, and I reserved it for us."

Adaline's eyebrows lifted. "All right. Close your eyes and picture it."

"Why?" Sorsacha asked.

"Do you really want to walk that far in these shoes?" Adaline asked.

"No," Sorsacha blurted. "Okay." She closed her eyes. "Got it."

Adaline locked hands with Tessa then touched Sorsacha. A moment later, the three females were in the skybox at Eleona's. None of them spoke at first because they were shocked by the view. The skybox was a square platform with a wall a few feet high lined with seating. Thin branches extended up from the platform to keep the shape of the space while allowing the viewers a spectacular 360-degree view of the kingdom and its captivating night sky.

"Did you know it was like this?" Adaline asked Sorsacha as the three of them turned in circles.

"Yes," Sorsacha admitted. "Only a few staff members are allowed to serve this box."

"I can see why," Tessa stated.

Every light in every tree in the kingdom could be seen from the skybox. An active fire pit sat in the middle of it, with fresh foods already grilling for them. Tessa noticed flecks of a glittery substance floating in the air, and she reached out to touch one, and it sparkled at the contact.

"What is this?" she asked Sorsacha.

"It's the pollen from the blossoms in these trees," Sorsacha explained. "They kinda add to the ambiance, don't they?" *And if you inhale enough of it, the night will become even more enjoyable.* Sacha smirked at the thought.

"It's so beautiful," Tessa said.

Adaline smirked as she waved her hand at the floating pollen, causing it to form a sparkling light show that would morph from one shape to another overhead. The three of them found their seats and watched. "This is amazing," Adaline whispered.

"I'm glad you like it," Sorsacha said.

A moment later, a waitress appeared from the only physical entrance to the space. She took everyone's drink orders then disappeared as quietly as she'd arrived. Their night commenced with drinks, food, and funny stories. After a couple of rounds, they headed downstairs to the dance floor and danced the night away. They didn't stumble out of Eleona's until the early hours of the morning and ran into a familiar face.

"Dr. Adaline," Roserie Aetrune greeted.

"Roserie," Adaline said.

"You are looking well."

Adaline smiled. "Thank you, I am."

"Hey, Roserie," Sorsacha said while eyeing the she-elf knowingly.

"Sacha," Roserie said, then turned her nose up at her assailant.

"I wanted to offer my congratulations on your nuptials tomorrow," Roserie readdressed Adaline.

"Thank you very much, Roserie," Adaline said graciously. "I'm so happy to hear you say that."

"I would like to bring a gift for you by the palace tomorrow. If that's all right?" Roserie prodded.

"That would be wonderful," Adaline glowed. "Why not half an hour before the ceremony?"

"That's perfect." Roserie smiled before turning away from the group. "Have a good night."

"Good night, Roserie." Adaline was the only one who had the stomach to wish the traitor a good night, while her friends' faces were stone cold. Adaline faced them. "Home?" They nodded.

A moment later, they appeared in the throne room. The females joked, hugged, and said their thank yous and goodnights, eventually leaving Adaline in the throne room alone. Her high heels clicked on the stone floor, sending an echo of the sound traveling down the hallway as she made her way to her suite. She stopped to reach for the clasp on her shoe to slip them off but was interrupted.

"Allow me," Aureon's voice surprised her before she noticed he stood close by. He moved past her and opened her suite door before gesturing for her to enter. Once she did, he closed the door behind him and stilled as he reveled in their proximity. He moved closer to her.

"Tobey," she thought aloud. The last thing she wanted was for the boy to get an eye full of the two of them in a heated interaction.

Aureon's gaze remained glued to her as he took in every detail of her clothing. He'd never seen a dress so short or heels so high. He turned her to face him. "He's with Asher," Aureon confessed. "I wanted to make sure you returned unharmed."

Adaline's eyes softened with her smile, and her grip on her clutch purse loosened. "I'm fine. I had a fun time. Thank you for checking on me."

Aureon nodded, relieved that no one bothered her on her night out with her friends. He glanced down at her shoes. "May I?"

"Yes," Adaline said before glancing around the foyer for a place to sit.

"Wait," Aureon said, without removing his attention from her shoes. His hands clutched her waist, but as he knelt in front of her, his grip glided over her hips. Then they slid down the outside of her thighs, to her calves, until he reached her shoes. Adaline's body quivered. His eyes witnessed every change in her as goosebumps traveled down her legs after his gliding fingertips.

He took his time examining her shoes, seemingly fascinated by them.

"Does the king like high heels?" Adaline whispered in jest. She knew there was much for him to unbury regarding his sexuality, which included fetishes. She smiled as she watched his curiosity unfold as he discovered one of his own.

"Very much," rumbled from him before he kissed her feet. Surprised by his tenderness, she watched him as his kisses trailed up her leg along with his touch. Her thoughts of him were far from innocent under his heated caresses, causing her to miss the action of his hand slipping back down her leg to undo the tiny buckle on her shoe. When his lips touched above her knee, she gasped, discovering how sensitive she was in such an unobvious place. Then her other shoe was unbuckled and tossed aside. She knew they'd exchange words between them. Naughty words that they couldn't afford anyone to hear. So, she brought up her force field around them, the action taking more concentration than usual. His fingers danced inches away from the hem of her short dress, causing her to tremble under his touch.

"Aureon, you-" Adaline was unable to finish her sentence. The tingly sensation of need running up her legs and into her core made her hiss. If he didn't stop soon, she'd toss his scheme by the wayside and consummate their mutual attraction now. Her breath caught in her throat when he grabbed the backs of her thighs and pulled her toward him, shoving his nose into her thigh gap before he inhaled her scent. A guttural growl left the back of his throat. His grip on her thighs tightened as his senses flooded with the fragrance of her essence. She couldn't recall when she buried her fingers in his hair.

Before Adaline could utter another word, Aureon hauled her over his shoulder, walked into her bathroom, then gently set her down on the counter. As he turned to the bathtub and switched the faucet on, she found herself squeezing her thighs together to douse her arousal. She plucked the pins out of her hair when he returned to her. His attention focused on the subtle, sexy movements of her nighttime regimen to get ready for her bath. He caressed her knee, knowing his little human needed to be touched thoroughly, and he heard her heart race. With his eyes locked on hers, he grabbed the backs of her knees and pulled her toward him. Opening her legs, he put himself between her thighs. His hands slipped down to cup her bottom and scoot her against his body.

"Touch me," he commanded as his grip sank into her thighs. He knew she needed it, and he did, too. Since they could not get away with everything they wanted to do together, he'd find a way to give her what she needed until they could.

Adaline blinked away her surprise to voice her excitement. "Do we really get to touch each other?" She pressed her body against his. "Without interruption?"

Aureon's nostrils flared at her whiskey voice as her breath tickled his throat. "Nothing will interrupt this."

"Good," Adaline said with a slight smile. She wrapped her legs around Aureon's hips and tore open the front of his robe. Grinning at the sight of his bare chest, she leisurely brushed her lips over his skin that she freed from so many layers of fabric. Then she pushed his robes over his shoulders, letting her fingertips trace every line of muscle in his powerful form. He breathed deeper as her kisses grew wetter. Her lips traveled lower until he cupped her chin and lifted her mouth to his. Her legs squeezed his hips to hers, nudging his erection between her thighs as he kissed her hard. He parted from her to find her brown eyes flaring with white light, broadcasting her desire. Each line in her irises glittered shimmery white.

Beautiful, he thought as his unbridled lust ebbed to gentleness.

Adaline noticed the change in him, grabbed his shoulders, and shook her head. "No." His head was canted in confusion. "Gentleness is the last thing I need from you right now." Her eyes flared brighter as her grip tightened.

Aureon's lust reignited, and he leaned into her body,

wrapping his arms around her securely. He touched the tip of his nose with hers marking his last gentle gesture. "Tell me what you need."

"Your lips," she said without hesitation. "Gimme." She pulled him down until his mouth crashed into hers. Her hunger consumed him until she teased his upper lip with her tongue. The action made his head snap back in shock. The two of them stared at each other in silence.

"It's different, now," she whispered in awe. She knew, firsthand, the difference in sensations when experiencing dreams versus reality. The dream usually won, so she was surprised to find that it was the opposite with Aureon. *How romantic*, she thought, as she smiled; to inspire the notion of looking forward to waking versus doing anything to stay in a dream.

"It is better," Aureon rasped, with his brows drawn, marking his effort to tamp his growing hunger. He was ready to pounce on her, to take her for everything she had. However, now was a delicate time, and their intimate exchanges could only go so far. So, he waited for her cue with a wild expression. Like a predator scouting prey he never caught before. Curious and cautious, yet ravenous.

"Better to try again?" Adaline said in a sultry tone.

Aureon nodded as she brought his face to hers before she kissed him. He tilted her head in the opposite direction and slipped his tongue into her mouth a moment later. She moaned as he eagerly explored her, and her legs squeezed his body to hers as her arousal grew. She cupped his face; her thumbs caressed his sharp cheekbones as she responded to his tongue lashing with sensuous strokes of her own. He gripped her hips hard as she teased his mouth, wanting her to give more, but she withheld her fervor in exchange for the slow, ruinous pleasure she doled out to him. He growled low, not liking that she wasn't giving as much as him.

"What is the problem?" he grunted. Adaline blinked once,

then twice, until the passionate haze cleared from her eyes, and she refocused on him. His hands rested on her shoulders as he brought her face close to his again. "Tell me."

"I don't want to get us into trouble," she breathed. "To trip us over the point of no return too soon."

Adaline was thinking logically, like him, even if logic was the last thing he wanted to abide by at that moment. *This is a first*, he thought, and there was one thing he was sure about tonight.

"No matter through kiss or touch, little human, I will make sure you meet release tonight," Aureon said to her, with his mouth a breath away from hers. His words sparked her lust, and she responded by rocking against the pressure of his erection. A low growl escaped him, and he cupped her bottom with one hand and pulled her body against his hardness. He ground against the juncture of her thighs. She gasped at the pleasure the friction electrified within her while he watched every change in her body to navigate her desire. Another deep inhale of her arousal made him groan, and he bent his head down to kiss her as he continued to rub his body where she needed him most. Holding back, as she originally intended, was forgotten. Her tongue ravaged his with the sweetest assault, compelling him to pick up the pace of his hips. His erection grazed over her clitoris, making her moan.

"Yes," she gasped between a break in the kiss. "Like that." She reached out and flicked her hand toward the bathtub, turning off the water. Her arousal took over her body as her legs clenched his hips while she returned his fiery kiss. Even though her body molded deliciously to his, she shifted where she sat, hungering to have him closer. He lifted her off the counter with one hand and continued to grind his growing shaft between her thighs. Pleasure shot through her from her core as he grazed over her clit. She moaned in surprise as her eyes shot open. Their lips parted as he continued his masterful friction.

"Can you?" he asked while keeping momentum.

"Yes," she said while watching the bulge in his pants grind against her.

"Do you need to-"

"*Yes!*"

Aureon wrapped his arm around her, bringing her back against his body before he crushed his mouth against hers. His motions grew faster as he muffled her moans with his kiss. Their arms locked around each other tightly as they held on for their impending release. She reached under his arm to hook around his shoulder so that she could tilt her pelvis. She moaned as she discovered the subtle change that accelerated her orgasm.

"I'm gonna-," was all she was able to say before she bit his shoulder to muffle her cry as her body vibrated through her climax. The surprise of her teeth in his shoulder sent him over the edge a moment later. They gasped for breath as they held onto each other. Their eyes met when they caught their breath, and they chuckled as their foreheads touched. He kissed her on her forehead, then moved so she could close her knees as he pulled down the hem of her dress that had ridden up.

"Way better than a dream," Adaline commented.

Aureon nodded. "I need you, again." He placed her hand over his shaft, which was reawakening. Her eyes widened in surprise, and her grip on him tightened. He looked at her with a contented expression, knowing he would crave her for the rest of his long life. Her touch, her passion, her love would be his undoing. That was a thought he couldn't process until everyone conspiring against him was caught.

Aureon choked back a groan at her touch as his eyes slid closed for a moment. "No ideas, little human." He kissed her. "You are to bathe and to sleep." He made sure he held her gaze for emphasis. "I mean sleep. No dream walking."

Adaline's eyebrows lifted, amused by the term. "Dream walking?"

"You know my meaning," Aureon said, as his hands slid

down the tops of her thighs before dropping off her knees, and he stepped back. Her attention fell to her knees, and her brow furrowed at the loss of his touch. It was too soon for it to be gone. "We are almost finished," he said aloud, as if for himself. When he hatched his plan, he knew that it would require him to sacrifice time with her, and now he wanted their charade to conclude as soon as possible.

"Tomorrow is the last day," Adaline whispered happily while kicking her feet back and forth before sliding off the counter. She stepped past him for the tub, pulling the rest of the pins from her hair and tossing them on the counter. She glanced over her shoulder at him as she reached for the hem of her dress. Aureon was entranced by her, waiting for her next move. "Are you sure it's a good idea for you to watch?"

"A terrible one," he breathed as his nostrils flared. "Go slow."

She grinned as she recalled her earlier thought of him discovering his sexuality. She kept her eyes on him as she slowly pulled the snug dress up her body. She heard his growl build with the rise of her hemline, and when she revealed her bottom and the tiny panties, he groaned. She smiled to herself as she exposed more of her supple skin. "It's probably time for you to go," she teased as she finished pulling the dress over her head and let it drop to the floor. Sensual shock filled her when he pressed his chest into her back and nuzzled her ear.

Aureon didn't dare put his hands on her. Touching that much soft, bare skin would only amplify his need for her, and he would never leave the room. He could already tell he was becoming addicted to her as the pleasure she wrought was unforgettable. However, they still had a game to play for one more day. He kissed her ear then she tilted her head to offer him her neck. He trailed kisses down from her jaw before he slowed his ministrations, stirring her desire again. "You are right, as always, Dr. Adaline. I should go," he whispered in her ear before kissing behind it.

She shivered. "It's for the best."

A sound rumbled in his chest while the tip of his nose glided down her neck. "But soon."

Adaline reached to cup his face and brought it back to hers. "Soon."

He kissed her firmly, and she winced. His lustful gaze turned worried. "What's wrong?"

"It's okay," she said. "Just a headache that hasn't gone away." She knew it wasn't an upgrade headache and had a spiritual root, but she didn't have the time to investigate it yet.

Aureon's expression sobered. "Good night, Dr. Adaline."

She smiled. "Good night, Your Majesty." She turned back to the tub, and a moment later, he was gone. Aureon landed on his balcony afterward, still shocked by Adaline's admission.

Impossible, he thought. Could the mate bond extend to a human? He stormed through his suite to his bathroom and turned on the shower. His eyes shot back and forth, parallel to his spinning thoughts. The mate bond between two elves resulted in one forcing the connection on the other, and it usually occurred without the forcer knowing. It was how couples became telepathic between each other and eventually their future families. It could be painful for some because the brain rearranged itself to make space for the connection. He worried at how much it would hurt her. *She is powerful,* he thought. There was a way to make the pain more manageable, but he'd have to wait until after the wedding to help her with it because of how binding it would feel for them both.

She must accept it, first. If she did not, the headaches would cease, and the bond would not form. His brow furrowed as he thought about the possibility of her rejecting it. The decision would hurt him because it was the most profound way for elves to bond, and he hadn't had that with his queen. Due to Aravae being pregnant and Aureon going to war, they hurried the formalization of the relationship and left the spiritual connection for later. Aureon craved to have it with Aravae while he was away at war, and he looked forward to its end so he could return to her. To come home to the birth of his son and the death of his queen, with an incomplete bond he realized he would never get to experience, broke him. The bond was why elves had no problem waiting millennia for their true mate because it was intimate, everlasting, and intense. So, when Aureon lost the opportunity, the result was devastating for him.

At best, the water in his rain shower ran lukewarm, and Aureon dropped his robes and stepped inside. Under the constant stream of the water, he considered all he had planned for Adaline over the next few days, but he experienced trouble focusing. His gaze dropped to his unrelenting erection, still wanting her. He grasped himself firmly, determined to ease his desire for her for one more night.

CHAPTER 55

"I'm not done with you!" Adaline said while wrestling Tobey on her bedroom floor. She was trying to get the boy into his formal outfit for the wedding ceremony that morning.

"Lemme help," Tessa joined in and secured the boy in his jacket. "There! You look like a little gentleman, Tobey."

The boy scrambled to his feet, glaring at them before he signed, "I hate these clothes."

"We know," the women said.

"But you only have to wear them for an hour," Adaline said. Tobey signed, "Promise?"

"Yes, I promise – one hour," Adaline agreed. Tobey glanced at his pointed shoes before he kicked the rug. He peered up at Adaline and nodded in agreement. "Thank you," she said. "Now run along and find Asher. Stay with him and Jim, okay?" Tobey sped out of the room.

Tessa chuckled before she reached for Adaline's wedding dress. "Let's get you dressed." As Tessa finished securing the last button on the back closure of Adaline's dress, Adaline sensed

Aureon's energy from down the hall as he neared her suite. She sat at her vanity to finish her hair when he quietly knocked on her door.

Tessa hurried to answer it. When she saw who it was, she smiled and opened the door wider. "Please come in. She's almost ready." Tessa approached the threshold to the bedroom and announced, "You have a guest. I'll return in a bit with Jim."

"All right," Adaline said as she concentrated on her appearance in the mirror. She positioned a soft curl into place, turned her head one way, then another to determine if it looked right, before securing it with pins. Suddenly, Aureon's feelings of admiration, desire, and envy slammed through her. Her eyes shifted focus in the mirror to witness his appraising of her. She faced him in silence. His originally intended words died in his throat once he saw the deep v-shape in the back of her dress.

"My son is fortunate," his voice shook before he regained his composure as he took in her curvy figure wrapped in a long, navy gown. "I have a gift for you in celebration of your nuptials," he said while setting the intricately carved box on the table where he stood, far across the room. He tapped his temple twice. She extended her force field to cover them as his gaze was downcast. "I cannot come closer."

"I understand," she whispered with a softened gaze as his emotions flowed through her, discovering that seeing her was significantly affecting him. Her heart sank as she continued to read him, learning that he wasn't satisfied after last night. He struggled to ignore the sensitivity his nerve endings had accumulated, and it was making him feral.

Silence passed between them.

"We're almost done," she echoed their tagline of the past two weekends.

"Yes," he whispered while thinking about all that would come after his plan ended—waking up that morning and needing her when he could not have her went against the nature of the bond. He couldn't take any more days of this beyond the sentencing of the traitors to be with her. After that, he could indulge. But first, loyalty to family and duty to the kingdom. "You look so beautiful," the words burst from his lips as if he couldn't keep them contained.

Adaline's doe-eyed gaze widened before she smiled. "Thank you." Her thoughts turned wicked as she imagined his stride eating up the distance between them so that he could cover her curves with his kneading hands. Her breathing changed, and Aureon's eyes narrowed, following the goosebumps rippling over her bare shoulders. His nostrils flared at the sound of her heart thundering in her chest.

"Soon," he growled as his eyes settled on the floor again.

"Aureon?" she said in a throaty whisper. The use of his name caused his body to tighten in awareness as his attention lifted. "I can't let you leave this room feeling this way." She rose from her vanity and approached him. She moved slowly to refrain from spooking him, like wading into the cage of a wild animal.

Aureon noticed her hips stacked when she walked, which meant she was wearing those high-heeled shoes like last night. He was curious to see which ones she chose.

"Feel this way?" he asked, barely able to get the words out.

"Feel…" she reached for him. He was surprised to see his hips shoot forward for her touch. She grasped his erection behind the first layer of his robes. "This way." Aureon's brows drew, and his head fell back as he reveled in the sensation that came with the firm hold of her soft hand. "Hmm," she hummed as she stroked him through his last layer of clothing. "Leaving you like this is not a good idea."

Aureon's eyes slid closed, and he relished in the lust that stirred within him due to the subtle friction. A moment passed before his eyes snapped open wide, clear, and focused. "We cannot do this now," he said, wrapping his hand around her wrist.

"But you need this now," she purred, not letting go.

He couldn't seem to grasp her wrist hard enough to remove it and found himself backing her into the room as his hands landed on her hips. He spun Adaline and pinned her against the armrest of the oversized chair at the foot of her bed. He pushed on her lower back to bend her over the armrest as he fought for control that he was quickly losing. Nothing else mattered. Not his scheme. Not the roles they played. Not the wedding.

Aureon's hand snaked around the front of her dress, curling his fingers inside the high slit in the front of her skirt. She shivered as he yanked the skirt back around her legs, high enough to reveal her bottom. His hand glided up the outside of her thigh before he found the edge of her panties. His fingertips tucked underneath the edges, as his fingers followed the curve of the fabric as it sloped down her bottom and stopped between her thighs. His breathing in her ear grew heavy as he felt her growing warmth.

"You are going to have me take you right before I send you out that door to marry my son," Aureon snarled in her ear.

"If that's what you need," Adaline said softly as she reached over her shoulder to caress his face. His hungry actions stilled for a moment as he observed her intently. She was ready to give it to him at a moment's notice because she noticed his struggle. He placed a chaste kiss on her lips.

"You do not behave, do you?" Aureon asked. Adaline shook her head. He pushed up her skirt the rest of the way. He groaned when he skimmed her wetness as he moved the crotch of her tiny panties aside.

"So wet," he hissed.

"Quickly, Aureon," she whimpered as she held her skirt out of the way.

The neediness in her voice made him growl as he untied his pants, just as there was a knock on the door. They stilled before their eyes connected.

"Dr. Adaline?" a familiar voice called from the other side of the door.

Adaline wanted to scream in frustration but righted her skirt and faced Aureon. She planted a hungry kiss on his mouth before tearing away from him. Now they were both left to suffer in wanton states until the end of their ruse. "Soon," she said as she pushed at his chest, causing his molecular structure to shift, making him pass through the dividing wall into the next suite before he reassembled. Adaline wasn't going to sabotage their cover after all they had achieved. She lowered her force field and retook her place at her vanity.

"Come in!" she called. Adaline continued placing her large curls and pinning them accordingly when she heard someone enter the room.

"Good morning, Dr. Adaline," Roserie's deceptively cheerful voice rang from the foyer of her suite.

"Hi, Roserie," Adaline said, just as misleading in her tone. "Thank you so much for dropping by!"

"Oh, it's nothing. My family and I wanted to give you a gift." She set a long, shallow box with a bow next to the wooden one Aureon had brought her. "Is there anything you need help with before the ceremony?" Roserie asked as she eyed her gift.

"You're a doll," Adaline said. "Would you mind handing me the little wooden box over there?" She pointed to Aureon's gift.

"Of course," Roserie said as she reached for it.

A moment later, Adaline felt Roserie's rage, hatred, and jealousy before she saw the reflection of a blade raised over her head in her mirror. Adaline smirked before freezing Roserie in place mid-strike.

"Your Majesties," Adaline spoke clearly to reach their elf hearing. "I have another one for you."

Seconds later, Aureon burst through the door to her room with Theodon in tow. Once they saw Adaline continuing to style her hair with Roserie frozen in place with a blade aimed at her neck, their faces filled with shock.

"Roserie!" Theodon shouted. His feelings for her took

another hit as his anger spiked. Roserie's eyes widened in surprise. The king's emotions radiated from him. Adaline could feel his fury at the thought of someone wanting to hurt her as she stood from her chair.

"How do we hinder her from telepathically communicating with her family, again?" Theodon asked, recalling what Adaline had done to Talia.

"Like this," Adaline punched Roserie so hard the she-elf blacked out. Witnessing the action felt gratifying to Theodon, and he felt self-conscious in admitting it to himself. As if the catharsis also meant he felt pleasure in seeing a female suffer. Yet, that wasn't the truth. Roseries broke his heart, and sustained anger wasn't a state of being Theodon found comfortable.

Adaline put her hand on Roserie's temple to search her memories. She waved Theodon closer. "You need to see this." She paused, "This will hurt, Theo." The warning made their eyes connect for a moment.

"Do it," Theodon commanded.

Adaline showed him Roserie's memories, and what he saw shook him: Roserie's conversations with Talia, her knowledge of the Miathan's killing Aravae, and Roserie deciding to become Talia's protégé so she could have a shot at being with Theodon.

Angry tears filled Theodon's eyes. "Enough." Adaline dropped her hand, and Theodon gave her his back to gather himself. After a moment, he faced the unconscious Roserie and called to the guards. When they rushed inside, he instructed, "Put her with the others." Theodon felt his father's hand covering his shoulder in a grounding grip, and Theodon touched his father's hand in return.

Adaline reached for Theodon's hand. "Almost done." His eyes fell to the floor before he could manage to look her in the eye. Once he did, he gave a slight nod.

There was a knock at the door before they heard Jim's voice. "Addy? Everything all right?"

"Yes, Jim," Adaline called. "I'll be right there."

She returned to her vanity to open the little wooden box Aureon had brought for her. She stilled once she saw the gift inside. She lifted a large hair comb encrusted with blue, purple, red, and pink crystals. It was the most intricate gift she'd ever received. Her surprised gaze reflected Aureon's sense of victory, and his chest puffed with pride. She leaned toward the mirror and gently slid the comb into place. She checked her hair in the reflection. "Okay, I'm ready."

The wedding ceremony was tiny but not small enough for either royals or Adaline to squander their performances. Jim took the liberty of walking Adaline down the aisle while Tessa stood in the front row with Asher. Asher was clutching Tobey in a firm grip, so the boy wouldn't take off running or start stripping out of his formalwear. Since Theodon was already the crown prince of Theris, he wore his crown from the beginning of the ceremony. After the couple exchanged vows, Aureon crowned Adaline. A few elders were present, along with a small handful of nobles, including Sorsacha, who smiled at Adaline with a thumbs-up from her seat.

All present softly clapped at Aureon's sermon that closed the ceremony. Adaline let Theodon take the lead on the kiss, and she did her best to picture Aureon in her mind. The newlyweds smiled at each other knowingly as Theodon moved close and dipped her, and she chuckled before he planted a close-lipped kiss on her.

She caressed his cheek to block the view of the kiss as a few elders chuckled at Theodon's theatrics. Theodon set her back on her feet before they faced their small audience, which erupted in cheers. The room's doors flew open, and Theodon and Adaline went straight out to the balcony at the front of the palace. Thousands of subjects gathered outside to see the newlyweds - the first they'd seen in over a millennium. Theodon's arm wrapped around Adaline, and the newlyweds waved to the crowd with smiles plastered on their faces.

"Almost done," Adaline commented through her smile.

"Almost done," he echoed.

The reception began immediately, and the newlyweds managed to play their roles well into the late hours of the night. Finally, Theodon retrieved Adaline to make it look to everyone like they no longer wanted to put off their wedding night. Everyone in the banquet hall cheered for them and said their goodnights as they left the celebration. They quietly walked down the long hallway to Theodon's suite while lost in silly thoughts of all the elves' funny drunken dancing at the reception. Theodon nudged Adaline with his shoulder, sending her stumbling. She burst out in tipsy laughter before returning his action. He stumbled and chuckled before they finally made it to his suite. He pushed the door open for her, but she didn't move.

"What are you waiting for?" he asked.

"For you to carry me," she said.

His brow furrowed. "I don't understand."

She chuckled. "It's a human custom where the groom carries his wife across the threshold."

"What does it mean?" Theodon asked.

"I don't remember," she said as she struggled to recall. "I just know it's an old custom."

Theodon seemed intrigued. "A human custom that's truly old? All right then." He scooped Adaline up in his arms and stepped over the threshold before he kicked the door closed behind him. As soon as he set Adaline down, her force field went up around them.

"Thank you," she said. "I've never gotten to do that, and I never thought I would."

"Why not?" Theodon asked her.

"My life has been pretty hard, Theo," Adaline admitted. "I settled on the possibility that I would never marry a long time ago because it's just not safe."

"Surely, there would be a male who could keep you safe in

your world," Theodon said while slipping off his boots.

"No, friend," Adaline said while stepping out of her heels. "It wouldn't be safe for him." Theodon stilled at the truth-bomb she dropped. Adaline sighed. "Any lover I've ever had has always fallen a casualty to the bad guys who are always after Asher and me."

Theodon's brows lifted. "Well, you no longer have to worry about that here," Theodon said to her as he moved closer. "I do have one question." Adaline waited. "How are we going to make it sound like we're consummating our fake marriage for everyone to hear?"

Adaline smiled wide. "You weren't allowed to jump on the bed as a child, were you?"

Theodon's expression changed to something shy of horrific. "No! That was not allowed."

Adaline laughed as she grabbed his hand and pulled him into his bedroom. "We must make up for lost time, Theo."

Aureon's hearing was dialed-in to all that was happening around him while he sat at the banquet table as everyone continued to celebrate the newly married royals. Most of the elves in attendance were genuinely excited that Theodon had gotten married. Many of them liked Adaline as their new princess, and they spoke of their healing appointments with her as miraculous and life-changing.

Princess doesn't seem like a fitting title for her, Aureon thought. *She is more… far more.*

"What a pair!" many said.

What a pair, indeed. The king shrugged off the statement as he focused his hearing on someone quietly creeping down the long hallway toward Theodon's room. Aureon perked up in his seat, and his ear twitched when he heard the unsheathing of a blade. In one second, the king was gone from his table. In another second, he stood behind the person wielding the blade outside Theodon's suite door. The traitor's ear was tilted toward the door, listening to the fake moaning and mattress movement coming from Theodon's bedroom. Aureon's teeth ground upon hearing the phony ecstasy.

Bole. One of Theodon's oldest friends, Aureon thought as his heart clenched for his son. Theodon was a good person, but Aureon knew well from his life experiences that didn't exempt him from pain and heartbreak. He knew this would bother Theodon as much as Roserie's betrayal.

"Bole Aetrune," Aureon said from behind the traitor. Bole froze at the sound of his name, and he righted himself before facing the king.

"Your Majesty," Bole said in a shaken tone.

The king went from statuesque and cold to instant rage as he flew at Bole. His hand wrapped around Bole's neck while he slammed the elf against the door. Aureon's snarl revealed his sharp canines as he roared, "It was you! You are the last one!"

Silence fell on the other side of the door.

"Wh-what?" Bole replied before the king's grip tightened around his neck, choking him.

A faint knock came from the other side of the door. Aureon could hear Adaline's heartbeat, which helped him regain his composure. He set the elf back on the ground and pulled him away from the door, his hand not leaving Bole's neck.

"Come on out," Aureon said to them. The door opened, and the newlyweds stepped outside barefooted. Theodon's eyes widened as he saw his father gripping the neck of his friend. "His memories, Dr. Adaline," Aureon demanded.

Adaline's grip left Theodon's upper arm, and she gave him a sorrowful look. She didn't like that so many people had betrayed Theodon's friendship when he was so kind. She placed her hand on Bole's temple and the other on the king's, then sifted through Bole's memories.

After a minute of witnessing Bole's connection to Talia, who wanted to kill Aureon and replace him with Bole, Aureon said, "That's enough."

Adaline let her hands drop before the king called for the captain of the guard. "Yes, Your Majesty?" Iventuil asked before looking at Aureon's hand wrapped around Bole's neck. "Shall I put him with the others?"

"Yes," the king said, as his angry gaze bored through Bole. He dropped his hand, and Bole stumbled on his feet. Then, Iventuil arrested him and dragged him away.

"What is happening?" Ensatus Aetrune's voice boomed from the far end of the hall. "What are you doing with my son?"

Aureon pushed past Theodon and Adaline before blurring with speed until his face was inches from Ensatus'. The elf gasped in surprise as Aureon grasped the elder's collar tightly. "I have arrested your children for crimes against the crown, including two attempted murders against the new crown princess and another against my son," Aureon seethed.

"What?" Ensatus said, exasperated. "That's not possible."

"They stand trial in the morning," Aureon continued. "You and your wife are required to attend for a chance to absolve yourselves or admit your guilt."

"I would never do-" Ensatus sputtered.

"Silence!" Aureon roared before he dictated, "Should you make any attempt to flee the kingdom, heed my warning: you better move faster than a god because once I find you, I will kill you. Am I clear?"

"Y-yes, Your Majesty," Ensatus stuttered.

"Now get out!" Aureon barked. Ensatus hurried to the banquet hall to collect his wife and leave the palace. Aureon addressed the nearest guard, "Report their whereabouts to me for the next twelve hours. If they try to flee, kill them."

"Yes, Your Majesty," the guard saluted his king before hurrying after his assignment.

Adaline and Theodon approached Aureon from behind and reached for his shoulders. He tensed in surprise before he faced them. The three of them let out a sigh. Adaline raised her arms to them both and waved them in for a hug. They embraced tightly. "It's done," she whispered. They slowly pulled away from her. Theodon's eyes were rimmed with red, again. Adaline's hand cupped his face as her other settled on Aureon's chest.

"Are you certain?" Aureon asked her.

She nodded. "By the time you conclude questioning their families tomorrow, you will have tied all loose ends."

"Get some rest, Dr. Adaline," Aureon said. "You have aided us greatly these past couple of weeks."

Adaline gave a soft smile and nodded. "See you both at breakfast." Before she left, Theodon rushed forward and wrapped her in a tight hug.

"Thank you," he whispered to her before he kissed her cheek. "You have been the best fake wife I've ever had."

Adaline chuckled. "You're welcome." He released her, and she headed to bed before Aureon's voice interrupted the silence.

"Theodon," Aureon said, while heading into Theodon's room, "there are things we must discuss." He wanted to seize the opportunity to show support to his son during a time of great personal betrayal. It was the opportune moment to have an open discussion with his son about people he'd allow close to him in the future.

"Yes, Father," Theodon said as he followed.

CHAPTER 56

A few hours later, Aureon finally walked the long hallway back to his suite. The celebration was over, the last guests had all gone home, and the night shift servants were already putting the palace back in order. He shared his scheme with the elders then notified them that the trials would begin the following day. He required them to attend, and all the elders rushed their consent to stand by their king.

Considering so much was accomplished in the past two weeks to be joyful about, weariness set in Aureon's bones. The hard part was over, but more was still to come over the next few days. The admissions of betrayal at the trial would be painful for him and Theodon, but with the help of Dr. Adaline, they would accomplish their goals. There was just one more person Aureon needed to notify before he turned in for the night. As he continued to walk the long hallway, his mind reached far beyond his kingdom for the one person Aravae's death affected most.

"I found him," Aureon spoke into his mind.

A moment of silence passed.

"Where?" an old, gruff voice responded.

"Here," Aureon said. "He stands trial tomorrow. Sentencing will be executed the following day."

Another moment of silence passed.

"I will be there for the sentencing," the voice confirmed. And then the connection was gone.

Aureon reached for the doorknob of his suite and slipped inside. He remained lost in his thoughts as he lifted his crown off his head and secured it on its display. He finger-combed his hair, loosening it from being tucked behind his ears. He peeled off his outer robe as he entered his bedroom, then froze when his eyes landed on his bed. In the center of the mattress, tucked under the covers, was a sleeping Dr. Adaline curled onto her side. An ache bloomed in his chest at the sight of her, one that made him want to join her immediately so she would be safe, warm, and protected by him.

What did I do to deserve such a gift? He'd put her through hell to help him lay to rest an old wound, and she went along with it.

Aureon focused on one matter: the bond headaches. He disrobed and slid between the sheets behind her. He was surprised to find her naked and reveled in the sensation of the contact of her bare backside against his front as he pulled her close. Adaline roused until her eyes blinked open, and she glanced over her shoulder to smile up at him. She rolled to her back as he leaned over her while propped up on one arm. He brushed her hair out of the way, unable to mask his concern.

"How are you feeling?" Aureon asked her while tracing her features with the pad of his thumb. If she brought up the headaches, then he would have some explaining to do.

Adaline took stock of how she felt for a moment, then stretched. She moaned into the movement and smiled. "Good. Been waiting for you." She playfully nuzzled his chest as she scooted closer. Her hands started to explore the hard lines of his body with her soft touches. She drew her outer leg around his and looked up at him once she felt his pants. "You're wearing too many clothes."

He chuckled. "And what do you plan to do about it, little human?"

She snaked her arm around him and stroked up his back as she grinned. "Well, it is my wedding night. I'm sure I can think of a few things…" her words trailed off as her lips caressed his chest. His body responded to hers, and he was surprised when she rolled him onto his back. The sheets slipped down to her waist as her large breasts pressed against his chest. Her lips found his while she kept his hands locked in hers on either side of his head. He pushed against her hands. He could feel her strength and was grateful for it. It reminded him that with his strength and her own, she would always be safe.

"Do you think yourself stronger than me, little human?" Aureon teased.

She gripped his hands firmly while her dark eyes absorbed his. A mischievous smile crossed her face. "I am. Would you like a demonstration?" She kissed him hard and leveraged her weight before she rolled her hips against his pulsing erection. His eyes slid closed as his groan turned into a growl at the growing need the friction coaxed in him. His hips shot up off the bed, lifting her into the air. She moved against him again. "Who's the stronger one now?" she purred.

Aureon's eyes flashed open, lit with ecstasy. "You are."

While he set her back down, she reached between them to unlace his pants and felt his body tense to govern his urges. She felt his anxiety and his lust, but the former caged the latter.

"What's the matter?" she asked him.

"I was hoping - no, that's not right," he said, in an attempt to get his thoughts clear as her naked body pressed into his. "I was planning for us to… enjoy this after the trials and sentencing finished."

Ah, he needs a logical plan… order, she thought. Adaline liked how rational Aureon was because they shared a characteristic, but that didn't mean he shouldn't be coaxed from it occasionally. And given all they had endured, they both needed a win and not an emotionally painful one. She wondered if he could put it off so easily because he didn't have a high sex drive, which she disproved as she recalled his reactions to her. *Maybe he hasn't had it in a while, so it is easy to overlook?* She wouldn't admit it, but the notion of him going without it excited her. Because as much experience as he may have had before his abstinence, he still held back from fully embodying his carnal self.

Nothing a little encouragement won't fix, she thought. Nothing about sex was logical to her, but if that were the angle she had to play for him to see reason, she would manage.

"I understand," she said to him, as she danced her fingertip over his chest as she thought for a moment. His muscles rippled under her touch, and she smiled. "What does sex provide for you?"

His eyebrows lifted. "Truly?" She nodded. It took him a moment to review his experiences. She waited as she coiled herself around his body, unable to forego touching him for even a minute. "It relieved stress, helped me to refocus, and connected me with my partner," he said succinctly. She waited to see if he had anything to add. "And it felt amazing."

"I know you have a certain order in your mind about how things should proceed," she said. "But for me, sex isn't something to list last. It helps me to function at my best and happiest, so I make it a greater priority because of what it provides." He considered her answer for a moment. "Do you have stress you need to relieve?"

"Yes."

"Do you need help refocusing, given all that's happening in the next few days?"

"Yes."

"Do you want to connect with me?" Adaline asked as she

swiftly unlaced his pants and pushed them down his legs. She grasped his erection, which pulsed in her hand.

"More than anything." Aureon breathed hard as he rolled them onto their sides to face each other.

"So do I," she purred, as his hand tucked behind her knee that wrapped around him, lifting it higher. The tip of his cock touched her wet folds as he held her open, and he growled as his hips shot forward. She gasped at the contact and tried to roll her hips against him, wanting him inside of her. He grasped his shaft and rubbed the tip of his cock against her wetness. His growl continued through the contact as her brows drew tight, and a moan escaped her.

"How important is foreplay to you?" Aureon growled before nibbling on her jaw.

"*Ah!* Not important today," Adaline admitted as she rolled her hips again to slide his shaft past her entrance. He slowly pushed inside of her—one inch, then two. A small cry left the back of her throat.

"Is there anything I need to know about sex with human females that can help or hinder your pleasure?" he said through gritted teeth as the rest of the muscles in his face froze at the intense sensation of being inside of her. He struggled to govern his urges, putting all the effort he had into making their first time together gentle for her.

"It usually takes a little while for me to orgasm during intercourse," she admitted before her breath hitched as he pushed inside of her more.

"Thankfully, we have all night," he rumbled as he rolled with her, putting her onto her back before he rose onto his forearms and pushed the rest of his length inside her. Her head threw back against the mattress as she called out his name. Her eyes flashed open, revealing a subtle glow as her irises glittered up at him. His body hummed under her illuminated gaze as he tucked a loose strand of her hair behind her ear, waiting for her body to adjust. "My little human is so responsive."

Adaline's legs wrapped around his hips, and her heels dug into his ass. His muscles flexed under where she spurred him as he ground against her. She moaned as he stimulated her most sensitive parts before he slowly pulled out of her halfway before thrusting deep. His muscles in his torso rippled as he restrained his pleasure to cater to her desire. Her heels dug into him harder. He reveled in how her body clutched him close as if she didn't want him to slip from her grasp.

Aureon locked his hands in hers over her head, like what she'd done to him a moment ago. His wide gaze swallowed every detail, every change her body went through as she took pleasure in his every measured thrust. "Like this?" he asked her, as he was gentle in his ministrations.

"Harder," she breathed, as the weight of his big body against hers multiplied her desire. She'd never had a male who focused on her pleasure and whose body felt so delicious to cradle between her thighs.

His eyebrows lifted as he raised himself off her. "Harder?"

"Yes, gimme," she confirmed as she pulled his body against hers as her fingers sank into his hips. He drove into her, quickly discovering the pace that had her moaning in reckless abandon and calling out his name. The pleasure that consumed him while connected to her submerged his senses in a state of euphoria. Sex had never felt this good. It made him wonder...

"Are you using your abilities?" he breathed.

"Not one," she said, as she relished in the same sensations.

Adaline's answer sparked his intensity. He covered her mouth with a deep kiss that caused her knees to fall wide open as he swallowed her cries. He felt her walls hug his length briefly, a preview of the pleasure to come. A growl tore from his chest as he pounded into her hard, his eyes crazy with lust on hers. The sight of her playing with her large breasts almost sent him over the edge. He pushed one of her hands away, replacing her grip on her softness with his greedy hand. He salivated again, but fear didn't consume him this time. Instead, he flicked her nipple with his tongue. She moaned in bliss as her fingers knotted in his hair while his swirling tongue pushed her closer to release.

"Don't stop!" she cried.

"Not stopping," Aureon growled against her breast.

"Don't!"

"*Never.*"

"I'm gonna-," Adaline said before her head fell back, crying out as her orgasm washed over her. Her body clenched down on his, making it impossible for him to hold out any longer. He gave in to his pleasure with a grunt as he released inside of her, yet he couldn't stop thrusting and continued to after her pleasure had subsided. Once his fatigue rushed to the surface, he lowered himself onto her, sinking her deep into the mattress. She giggled as she threaded her arms around him while he buried his face in the crook of her neck. She wrapped her legs around him, too, while she stroked his long hair. His chest heaved for breath for a moment before he had any words.

"To think I was going to put that off for a few more days," Aureon joked.

She laughed.

He leaned up on his forearms and kissed her. "I must be insane."

"Certifiably so," she jested.

"Fortunately, I have you to speak sense into me," he said as his body reignited for another round and gave a shallow thrust within her.

Adaline gasped as she felt his recovery and searched the bed for something.

"What do you need, little human?" he asked her as his thrusts deepened, amazed at how his body reacted to hers and how much she enjoyed the unrestrained version of his desire. He would never get enough of this new way of being. She made him want to roar to the rafters in triumph that he found a powerful female who wanted him to be everything he was without limitations.

Adaline reached for a pillow to slide under her hips, but she got a better idea and rolled him onto his back. "More of this," she said, as she leveraged her weight on her straightened arms with her hands planted firmly on his chest. She rolled her hips with him inside of her, and a low rumble escaped him as his fingers dug into the softness of her thighs then slid up to grasp her hips.

"Your quick recovery makes me very happy," she admitted as she rocked her hips to find her pleasure.

Aureon groaned as his thrust lifted his hips off the mattress. "Does it?" He had no other words as his body hardened at the sight of her taking control.

"Mmm hmm," she purred. "Because we're not done yet."

CHAPTER 57

At dawn, Aureon returned a sleeping Adaline to her room. He tried to slip her underneath the covers without waking her, but she stirred and latched onto him.

"Tobey?" She whispered.

Aureon's ears twitched, searching for the boy until he detected his slumbering heartbeat nearby. "Asleep in Asher's room."

Adaline protested Aureon's leaving, which he subdued by making love to her again.

Upon returning to his suite to dress for the day, Ena arrived to braid his hair. "Good morning, My Lord," she greeted.

"Good morning, Ena," Aureon answered.

The she-elf appraised him, noticing a difference in his appearance. As Ena expertly braided half of the king's long mane, she considered what could have sparked the change. Then Adaline came to mind, and Ena smiled to herself.

"My Lord," Ena pressed.

"Yes, Ena?"

"You seem… settled."

"How do you mean?"

"A lot has happened over these past few weeks," Ena explained. "And given how rattled someone would be in the middle of the circumstances, you seem to have found a way to deal with it." Aureon remained quiet as his eyes bore into Ena's reflection in the mirror. "Whatever you are doing to keep a level head… it's working." Aureon turned in his chair and shot the she-elf a knowing glare. Ena's attention dropped to the floor, and she blushed.

"Then I shall continue not to disappoint you, Ena," Aureon said.

"Yes, My Lord," she said in a whisper as she finished his hair. He didn't always need help with his hair, but sometimes, he'd outsource the task to Ena. She proved to have an exceptional talent for it, given the intricate hairstyles she wore. Ena slid his crown into place. "Done."

"Thank you, Ena," Aureon said as he rose from his seat.

"Of course, My Lord," Ena said with a shallow bow. "Anything else?"

"No, that is all," he said as he adjusted his cuffs on his slate blue and silver robes.

Ena was gone a moment later, and Aureon was still adjusting his clothes. His mind felt clearer than it had after Adaline healed his body, and he carried no stress.

Human - 1. Elf - 0, he thought with a smirk, as he recalled her logical rebuttal to his original plan to hold off on intimacy for a few more nights. He left his suite for the dining room and found that Theodon was the only person seated at the table.

"Good morning, Father," Theodon greeted.

"Good morning, Theodon," Aureon responded. He noticed the staff hadn't yet delivered the food to the table.

"I trust you slept well," Theodon commented with a smirk. "You seem noticeably at ease this morning."

"Stop it, now!" Aureon hissed before he spoke in his son's mind, "Do not make comments for anyone to hear."

"Father?" Theodon replied in his father's mind after a moment. Aureon glanced at his son. "I'm happy for you." A moment of silence passed between them as servants entered the room and delivered their breakfast. After they left, the humans filed into the dining room.

Asher let out a yawn with Tobey in tow. Jim was as even-keeled as he always seemed. Tessa covered her mouth when mid-yawn as her free hand tried to make sense of her curly hair. Adaline walked in with an energetic stride and a big smile on her face. Theodon was drinking his beverage as he saw her and tried not to smile. She saw Theodon, and her smile widened. She winked at him, causing him to choke on his drink. Aureon's unfazed expression was aimed at Theodon as the prince righted himself, and Adaline slid into the seat next to him.

"Good morning, wife," Theodon joked with Adaline.

"Good morning, husband," Adaline threw back. The newlyweds chuckled as they picked up their flatware to dig into their meals. Adaline's attention lifted from her plate to say to Aureon, "Good morning."

"Good morning, Dr. Adaline," the king replied. He was surprised by how much more he wanted to say and ask her, but giving in to the notion would cause many questions too soon. He had work to finish before everyone around them could know about their union.

"So, was everyone successfully reprimanded last night?" Asher asked from the other side of the table.

"Yes," Aureon replied. "All have been arrested, and their trials will take place early this afternoon."

"What kind of punishment awaits those dumb enough to commit murder or treason?" Asher asked.

"It ranges from banishment to death," the king said concisely.

Asher's eyebrows lifted, impressed by the steadfast power of the king. "Would it be intrusive for humans to watch the proceedings?"

"No," Aureon said immediately. "There will be plenty of seating in the room to accommodate any of you who wish to attend."

"You may be underestimating your subjects," Adaline commented as she lifted a fork full of food to her mouth.

Aureon canted his head. "Why do you think so, Dr. Adaline?"

Adaline took a moment to chew and swallow her food before she offered, "This is an unprecedented event. Your subjects are finding out their queen was murdered after accepting that she died due to difficulties during childbirth. If they think of her anything close to how they think of you, you won't likely have enough seating to accommodate everyone."

Asher nodded and pointed his fork at his sister. "Good point, sis."

"Fair point, Dr. Adaline," Aureon formally agreed.

A moment of flatware grazing plates and quiet gulps of beverages filled the room. Tessa smiled to herself as she ate her meal as it was evident to her which royal belonged to Adaline. Tessa always knew that there was a mate out there for Adaline, even though Adaline disagreed. Now that Tessa knew what she and Asher were, she understood why it took a powerful male from another planet to be the best match for her friend.

"So," Adaline nudged Theodon. "Are we officially divorced today?"

Theodon smiled as he chewed his food.

"You both are officially unmarried," the king confirmed. "The announcement will happen at the trials, so everyone understands the point of the setup."

"It was kinda fun in some ways, wasn't it?" Adaline asked Theodon.

"The parties," Theodon interjected.

"The pretty clothes," Adaline agreed.

"The presents," Theodon offered.

"That you must return," Aureon interjected.

"The jumping on the bed," Adaline said excitedly.

"Yes!" Theodon said happily. "That was the best part!"

Aureon rolled his eyes, causing them both to burst into laughter. A moment of giggles passed before they settled back into their meals.

"Good times," Adaline whispered as she stabbed a piece of her breakfast with her fork.

"What happens to those who receive a death sentence?" Asher asked Aureon.

"Those having direct involvement of Aravae's murder will be subject to the Ophidian Pits," Aureon said without hesitation. "In our justice system, when it comes to horrific crimes, it is a system that has proven fair through the ages."

The Ophidian Pits is a stadium built in the southeast region of the kingdom, close to the border. On the other side of the border is a territory known as the Shadow Lands. There, black sand covers most of the ground and is inhabited by giant snakes. The sand was deceptive as it shimmered beautifully in the moonlight. It would draw the attention of younglings, and once they stepped on the sand, giant snakes would shoot up from underneath with their jaws spread wide. The beasts clamped down on their prey and dragged them back below the surface for eating. When Aureon's great grandfather first discovered a small amount of the black sand in Theris, he immediately ordered the stadium erected to contain the snakes. Soon after the stadium was finished, dying by duel in the Ophidian Pits was written into law to handle murderers and traitors.

"When it comes to murderers proven guilty without a doubt," the king said. "The convicted has one chance at life in prison." Adaline's eyes narrowed, and she didn't like the opportunity available to any elves arrested over the past couple of weeks. "It is a bit barbaric, due to its ancient lineage, but effective."

"What happens?" she asked him.

"A fight to the death," Aureon explained. "If they win, they get life in prison... unless they are executed by their challenger or eaten."

Adaline's eyebrows lifted, impressed that a species as evolved as the elves still had this law. She liked this law. "And how large are these snakes, exactly?"

"The smallest one I have ever seen was approximately three hundred feet long. Perhaps six feet wide. They can kill in seconds if they get their jaws around you," Theodon told her. Adaline let out a low whistle.

"When will this take place?" Asher asked.

"Tomorrow," Aureon answered.

The twins glanced at each other as Asher asked in her mind, "Wanna go? Sounds entertaining."

"We should go," Adaline replied.

"But not Tobey," Asher threw in.

"Definitely not Tobey," Adaline agreed.

Asher got an idea and turned to the boy. "If I remember correctly, I'm supposed to teach someone how to run faster." Tobey's eyes lit up with excitement as he nodded. "Okay, buddy, let's go," Asher stood and held out his hand for Tobey's. The boy hopped out of his chair and hurried to Asher's side, happy to take his hand. The two sped out of the dining room. As the adults finished their meals, Tessa, Jim, and Theodon gradually left the room, leaving Adaline and Aureon to finish their meals in unhurried silence.

"What time do the trials start today?" she finally asked.

"Immediately after lunch in the throne room," he said, as their attention remained on their plates.

She gave a subtle nod. "Asher and I will be there."

A moment of silence passed before he said, "Thank you." Her attention lifted from her plate upon hearing a statement he rarely said aloud. "Truly," he said. "None of this could have come to pass without you." The reminder of how lacking his existence was before she set foot in his kingdom barreled through his mind earlier that morning. He couldn't imagine reverting to such an unfulfilling life where he was a lesser version of himself or the father his son needed.

Adaline rose from her seat and rounded the corner of the table. He leaned back against his chair, ready for her to be close. She cupped his face and softly kissed him before resting her forehead against his. "Of course," she whispered. His hand rested on her lower back and pulled her closer. "Ow," she winced. The headache had returned.

Aureon's guilt wouldn't allow another moment to pass without her knowing what was happening to her. "Addy," he said as he clutched her close before kissing her forehead. "We must discuss the reason you are having headaches." She remained quiet and listened. He relinquished any apprehension about potentially being rejected by her because, first and foremost, he didn't want her in pain. "The headaches are contingent with the mate bond that occurs between elves," he started. "It's when an elf finds its mate, and a telepathic bond begins to link them. Sometimes, it can be painful in the form of headaches until the bond is either accepted or rejected by the mate."

"So... that's how elves are telepathic among families," Adaline put two and two together.

"Precisely."

"But I'm not an elf."

"No, you're not," he agreed. "But it seems to be happening all the same."

While lost in her thoughts, silence passed between them.

"What are the outcomes of my choices?" she asked.

"If you accept the bond, your brain will make space for it, which is the reason for the headaches," he said. "Once that happens, the headaches will cease, and we will be linked." His expression changed, almost unrecognizable, but sadness came over him as he explained, "If you reject it, the headaches will also cease, and the bond will not form."

Whoa, Adaline thought. This was a heavy decision to make today. "I know I will have more questions before I make a decision," she said. Many were already swarming through her mind. "Would it bother you if I asked for some time to think about it?"

Aureon nodded. "Yes, of course. Ask anything you want."

"Okay," she said. "I'll consider it while I'm out with Tessa this morning."

He regarded her curiously. "Where are you going?" He didn't want her far from him, especially after what they had shared last night.

"She is coming with me to scout commercial real estate properties," Adaline chuckled. "If you haven't noticed, Asher and I went from being rich to flat broke once we moved here. We are considering opening a medical practice since there seems to be a couple of untapped markets."

"Such as?" Aureon asked, intrigued.

"Well, it seems like the best way to help elves would be part emergency room, part maternity ward, and leave a tiny part for consultations," she said. "Few elves have come to me with longstanding issues because your biology repairs you rather seamlessly. So, unless you are carrying twins or become impaled, you don't need us much beyond that."

The king touched the tip of his nose to hers and chuckled. "That is quite accurate." He would gladly take care of all her material needs if she would let him, but as independent as he knew her to be, he wouldn't tread on her goals.

"So, I thought I should get an idea on how renting space works before Asher, and I set forth a plan of action," she concluded.

"Fair point," he said. He offered a brief overview of how acquiring space in the capital worked and what questions to be sure to ask.

"Thank you," she said before she kissed him again. She eyed him. "I noticed a spectacular rainbow spanning the width of the kingdom from my balcony this morning. Is it needless to ask you how you feel after last night?" She found herself staring at the natural wonder for minutes before leaving her suite for breakfast, failing to count all its colors.

The corner of his mouth lifted. "Words were insufficient."

Adaline giggled. "Does that mean you wouldn't mind if it happened tonight?"

"On the contrary," Aureon's hand slipped down to cup her bottom. "I insist that it happen tonight." He squeezed her as his lips reached for hers. She kissed him firmly, letting the tip of her tongue tease his lower lip. A quiet groan rumbled in his chest before she pulled away. "Especially if it could be my last night alive."

Her eyes shot wide. "What are you talking about?"

"Who did you think fights the traitors in the pits?" Aureon asked her with a slight smile.

"Oh," she said. "I get it. Then, no, I'm not worried."

Surprise lit his features. "No?"

"No," Adaline said, as she placed her hands against the sides of his face as if she readied sage words for him. "I pity the poor bastard who is dumb enough to cross you."

The king laughed at her cockiness then he tickled her. She squirmed and laughed as she tried to dodge his touch with no success. It was the perfect excuse to touch her. He pulled her in against the side of his body and demanded, "Kiss me."

"Mmm, I dunno," she jested. "The king's starting to sound like a dictator."

He tickled her more until she burst into laughter before he hauled her into his lap. He hooked his hand behind her neck and brought her lips down onto his. As their mouths melted together, his hands latched onto her curves. She was surprised to feel his hand shooting under her shirt.

"Right now?" she asked him in between kisses. He groaned at the visual, loving the idea of him riding her in his chair as his grip sank into her hips. The reality of the day set in, and his eyes opened. He pulled away, the parting causing a smack of their lips. "That's a no?" she asked, still holding the back of his head. She wasn't disappointed, just reacting to his actions.

"It is not a no," he said truthfully. *It's never a no.* "I simply need to get through the formalities of today before we can resume…." His gaze was lost on her swollen pout.

Ah, I'm a distraction right now, Adaline thought as she slid off his lap. "I understand," she said. "As long as you understand that sex is not something to be put on hold."

Aureon's brows drew tight. "It would be impossible to allow after last night."

"That is the right answer," she said before she gave him a peck on the lips. Then she spun on her heel and headed out of the dining room. "See you after lunch."

The king sagged back into his chair as he watched her leave. *That human has changed everything and isn't near finished,* he realized.

CHAPTER 58

"This space looks nice," Tessa commented as Adaline kept her thoughts to herself. They were touring their fourth property of the morning.

"Mmm hmm," Adaline finally murmured, as her thoughts kept spinning; with future practice plans, refining what she and Asher could offer the elves, the trials that began in a couple of hours, and this nagging notion that she was missing something.

"That's all you've said for the last three properties, Addy," Tessa commented. "What's going on?" After waiting for her friend to answer with no success, Tessa turned to the landlord. "Would you give us a moment alone, please?" The older elf nodded and excused himself from the room. Tessa turned back to Adaline, narrowed her eyes, and tapped her temple twice. Adaline's eyes widened, forgetting that she had told Tessa about the signal before she pulled up her force field over them. "Spill it."

"A lot is going on in my head right now, Tess," Adaline admitted. "We couldn't possibly go through it all."

"Okay, then what is bothering you the most?" Tessa asked.

Adaline paced for a moment before she faced her friend. "I've guided these royals to find the killer of their queen and his accomplices. I've healed one of his grief and helped the other see an opportunity in rebuilding their familial connection that once was lost. I've managed to expedite all of that in record time...."

"But?" Tessa asked.

Fear swept over Adaline's features as she admitted, "I'm missing something, Tess. I can't put my finger on it, but there's something that I've missed in this whole process. It's not something that negates all that's happened so far, but something that adds to the existing treachery against the royals, and I can't find it."

Tessa enveloped her friend in a hug. Adaline didn't realize how much she needed the embrace. She hugged Tessa tightly.

"Addy," Tessa began. "Your feelings are completely valid."

"Thank you," Adaline exhaled.

"And I know how much it would bother me if I were in your position, given the relationships that have grown between the three of you," Tessa admitted. "The sense of urgency to finish helping them, to make sure you've dotted every 'I' and crossed every 'T,' but as perfect and all-seeing as you are, Addy, life is not. All you can do is focus on the good because a lot of good came from you finding this world." Tessa stood back and squeezed her friend's hands. "I mean, you found love, Addy." Adaline's eyes widened in surprise as the realization hit her. "He responds to you, unlike anything I've ever seen a man do. Before he enters your space, he watches you. Then he influences your environment to either make your task easier or make you happier before he joins you. I've never seen anything like it. It's so beautiful."

Adaline held back tears. "Well, if you're gonna put it that way." She opened her arms for her friend. Tessa didn't hesitate to hug Adaline again.

"And if something else does occur," Tessa whispered to Adaline, "we will deal with it together. You can't live waiting for something bad to happen."

Adaline chuckled. "Asher and I stopped doing that a long time ago."

"See?" Tessa said. "Because you're strong, and they seem to be, too. You will be able to handle conflict together just fine."

"Thank you," Adaline sniffed.

"You're welcome," Tessa said graciously. The girls parted from each other and smiled. Tessa glanced around. "You don't like this place, do you?"

Adaline chuckled. "No, not at all!"

The girls giggled as Adaline let her force field recede. They walked out of the space arm in arm. When they ran into the landlord at the front door, Adaline asked to see his last available space, and he was happy to accommodate them. Before they ventured in their new direction, the girls heard someone clearing his throat behind them. Turning to see Flavial standing a few feet away, the elder appeared captivated as he approached Adaline and Tessa.

"Good morning, ladies," he said to them.

"Good morning, Flavial," Adaline said as she reached out her hand to shake his. He enveloped both of his around hers and smiled. Adaline gestured to Tessa, "Have you met my friend?"

"I have not yet had the pleasure, Dr. Adaline," Flavial admitted with eagerness apparent in his tone.

Adaline smirked. "Allow me, then. Tessa, this is Flavial Usleon. He's a friend of Aureon's."

"It's nice to meet you, Flavial," she offered her hand to shake as Adaline had and was surprised at how quickly he dropped Adaline's hand to shake hers. Tessa heard Adaline chuckle.

"Quite enchanted to meet you, Miss...?" he probed.

"Hill," Tessa said. "Tessa Hill."

"Miss Hill," Flavial said with perfect diction. "Will you be staying in Theris for a while?" A grin grew across Adaline's face as she watched the elder delve into learning more about her friend.

"I'm a permanent transplant, actually," Tessa smiled.

"Oh?" he asked. He still hadn't let go of Tessa's hand. "I would be delighted to show you around when you are available." Tessa glanced at Adaline as if she needed a cue.

"That sounds like a great idea," Adaline chimed in. "Tess will be assimilating as I will be, too. Who better for her to tour the capital than you?" Sure, she laid it on a little thick, but she couldn't help herself.

"You flatter me, Dr. Adaline," Flavial said to her. "I would be honored to show you around, Miss Hill, at your earliest convenience."

His manners wowed Tessa. "All right. Three days from now?"

Flavial's face lit up. "Perfect! I will escort you from the palace in three days."

"Okay," Tessa said as he shook her hand again.

Flavial faced Adaline. "Will I see you at the trials, Dr. Adaline?"

Adaline grinned. "You certainly will."

"See you soon," he said before he regarded Tessa. "Miss Hill, it was a pleasure meeting you." He gave a sharp bow, and then he was gone.

"What just happened?" Tessa asked Adaline, who couldn't stop giggling.

"You are going on a sightseeing date with one of the most honorable elves in the entire kingdom," Adaline explained.

"Really?" Tessa asked, exasperated.

"Yes," Adaline said before she slipped in, "and he's at least a few thousand years old."

"Whoa, what?"

Adaline snickered. "Yep. The nicest male and a close friend to Aureon. So, be nice, okay?"

"I can do that."

"He looked at you like... wow," Adaline admitted with a

smug grin.

"Now you know how Aureon looks at you," Tessa threw back.

"Touché, friend," Adaline admitted. "Are you ready for one more property?"

"Yes," Tessa said. "I have a good feeling about this one."

CHAPTER 59

Tobey sat on a stool in Asher's suite kicking his restless legs back and forth while Asher changed clothes for the trials. "Why can't I go?" Tobey signed to Asher in the reflection of the mirror.

Asher tucked in his shirt as he explained, "Because I don't know what happens at these trials, bud. It might be the most boring thing in the world, and you would have to sit there until the end of it. Ever think of that?"

Tobey hadn't thought of that.

"Tessa is going to keep an eye on you until it's over," Asher told him.

Tobey quickly signed, "Can I stay with Ena?"

Asher paused at the use of the she-elf's name. He turned to Tobey, "Ena has watched you before?" Tobey nodded eagerly. A moment later, there was a knock on the door of Asher's suite. "Come in!" Asher called. The door opened and in walked Ena.

"Good afternoon, Dr. Asher," Ena announced. "I understand Tobey needs looking after?" Ena smiled down at Tobey, who was excited to see her. Ena had abilities because she was an elf, and that made Tobey feel a kinship with her.

Asher approached Ena without thinking, marveling that a female could be more beautiful when he was sober than when he was intoxicated. He was also impressed by her reaction time and hearing ability.

"Yes," Asher finally replied. "We haven't officially met, I'm-"

"Dr. Asher Everly," Ena said with a smile. "I know who you are. You are a speedster, just like Tobey." Ena smiled down at the boy again.

"Yes," Asher replied. He got lost in looking at her because she looked like a pixie, with her tiny upturned nose, rosy cheeks, and glowing smile.

"Tobey," Ena said, keeping her attention on the boy, "I have to handle some work in the garden this afternoon. Will you help me?" She reached out her hand for his. Tobey shot off his stool and eagerly took her hand. Ena walked him toward the door before she called over her shoulder, "I'll keep an eye on him." A moment later, the door to his suite closed, and Ena and Tobey were gone.

"Thank you?" Asher said, confused as to his reaction to her. He found her presence arresting. He always had a one-liner to bait a woman, but he had nothing when Ena entered the room.

Not going to assess that right now, he thought. Priorities, first. He was going to join his sister at the trials in case she needed his support. The ground trembled under Asher's feet, and his instincts rose to high alert. His senses scanned the palace. He smelled sulfur, and his attention shot in the direction of his suite door as he reached for Adaline's mind.

"I felt it, too," she said in his mind.

The twins rushed into the hallway. Their surprised expressions met before they hustled to the throne room. They burst through the double doors to find the congregation of elves and royals had already filled the room, and it was just as Adaline had forewarned. There were elves packed in every free space to witness the trial of the millennium. Everyone's silent attention turned in their direction, and the twins froze.

"Well, this is awkward," Asher spoke into Adaline's mind.

"Yep," was all Adaline could manage to say.

They took the time to straighten and calm themselves to release the tension they carried before moving toward the two chairs left open for them near the royals.

"I have a bad feeling about this, Addy," Asher admitted telepathically. The twins knew the shift in the ground paired with the smell of sulfur: someone struck a dark deal.

"Me, too," Adaline said, as she waved her hand at the chairs, moving one next to Theodon, and the other next to Aureon. Elves in the audience shifted uncomfortably by the telekinetic demonstration as the twins walked toward their seats. Adaline instructed Asher, "Watch over Theo, and I'll keep an eye on Aureon."

"Done," Asher said as he took his seat.

A moment later, Adaline slid into her seat next to Aureon. She noticed Flavial attempting to swallow a smile, and she winked at him before she faced the court. She had the dagger that she snatched from Bole holstered on her thigh.

Many in the congregation had mixed views of the demonstration of power. Some thought the humans were egotistical for assuming a seat next to the royals without asking. Others were misinformed about the humans and feared their power. Then there were those who Adaline had healed and shared their experiences about her. They were glad the twins were present.

The royals noticed the twins were on high alert but continued to proceed with the trials. Aureon announced that the late queen was murdered after childbirth and that she had been discovered by a trusted friend of the crown and King Cerus while Aureon was at war with the Hexaborgs. The room gasped in shock, unprepared for the news. A few elves wept. Aureon explained how evidence against the murderers had been flimsy until recently, when he saw an opportunity to bring them to justice by throwing a fake royal wedding. "We succeeded in catching the culprits behind the murder of Queen Aravae, as well as finding new traitors planning to kill the new princess and betray the prince, in an attempt to take the crown," Aureon stated succinctly. Gossip rippled through the throne room. "As a result," Aureon raised his voice to quiet the audience, "they stand trial today."

The king nodded at the guard, who disappeared for a moment before retrieving Roserie and Bole Aetrune. The siblings were in shackles, barefoot and dirty. The guards pushed down on their shoulders until their knees hit the floor, forcing them to bow. Aureon felt Theodon tense at the sight of them both. "Breathe, my son," Aureon said in Theodon's mind. Theodon did as his father instructed and shifted in his chair.

Ensatus and Celu Aetrune stood off to the side. Celu continuously wiped tears from her cheeks with a small handkerchief. Both parents were still in shock at the accusations against their children. Anger emanated off Ensatus that stemmed from helplessness. He could not protect his children, now, no matter what they'd done. Roserie started to cry as Aureon decreed the charges against her and her brother.

"Roseries Aetrune, we have irrefutable evidence of your attempt to murder the crown princess on the morning of her wedding to my son," the king annunciated the last word.

"No!" Roserie cried. Tears fell down her face as she shook her head. She was ready to do anything to get ahead, but to be held accountable for her actions, was something in which she possessed no spine. Celu sobbed at hearing the first charge against her daughter.

"Silence!" Aureon yelled as a thunderclap ripped through the sky above the palace. The twin's eyes widened at the sound.

"Was that from him?" Asher asked Adaline in her mind.

"Yes," Adaline replied.

"I'm never going near Ena, now."

"Not the right time for this conversation, Ash."

"Sorry."

"You led on my son for the sole purpose of a cast upgrade. When he was finally rid of you, and I announced his engagement to Dr. Adaline, you struck him. Then you attempted to kill Dr. Adaline the morning of their wedding," Aureon sneered. "There are three witnesses to the event, including myself."

More gossip rose among the audience, shocked that Roserie would act so heinously.

"No! It was her!" Roserie cried out as she shot Adaline a scathing glare. "She made me do it with her sorcery! She framed me!"

Another gasp cut through the room from the audience.

"Did she just?" Asher said in his sister's mind.

"Yes," Adaline growled back. "That heifer went there."

"Get her, Addy!" Asher egged his sister on.

Adaline rose from her seat and stood in front of Roserie. "Shall we show them the whole truth then?" Adaline asked the traitor, who gave her a defiant look. Adaline grabbed Roserie by the back of the head and turned the she-elf's head to face the blank adjacent wall. "I will show you all of her memories surrounding the event," Adaline said for everyone to hear.

"No!" Roserie tried to struggle against Adaline's grip, but the diviner held her firmly. Light poured into the back of Roserie's skull, through her ocular nerves, and burst from her eyes. The light projected images on the wall. The room of elves stood in awe at the scene, to witness someone's memories so clearly. In this one gesture, both Aetrune siblings' wrongdoings were laid bare. Cries rang throughout the room when they saw Roserie in the reflection of Adaline's mirror as she raised the dagger over Adaline's head. Celu Aetrune wailed as her husband held her and watched in shock.

"I think that's all the truth we can handle from you," Adaline said to Roserie as she dropped her grip on the she-elf's head and walked back to her seat. Roserie sulked into a puddle on the floor, crying about her uncertain fate. The guards picked her up and put her back in front of the royals, alongside her brother.

As Adaline retook her seat next to Aureon, he continued to dole out charges. "Bole Aetrune," Aureon addressed Theodon's friend, "you have also been charged with attempted murder against Dr. Adaline after I announced her engagement to my son." Bole's head hung in defeat, knowing he had no words to better his circumstances. A moment passed before Aureon continued. "Ensatus and Celu Aetrune," the king addressed the parents, "now is the time to come forward with information that may absolve you of the sins of your children."

"W-we didn't know." Celu wiped the tears from under her eyes.

Aureon turned to Adaline, who was busy reading their soul records. When she finished, her eyes shifted to Aureon before nodding to confirm that Celu was telling the truth.

"Very well," Aureon said. "You are to relocate from the capital immediately. Your title is forfeited, along with your seat at the elder council." Aureon refocused on Roserie and Bole. "Roserie and Bole Aetrune, for your crimes against the crown, I sentence you to be banished to Kheca in the Shadow Lands." The room gasped. "You will be taken there two dawns from now to endure the remainder of your existence among the Crae... however long you can survive them," Aureon specified before he gestured to the guards to take them away. Roserie wailed while dragged from the room. Celu buried her face in her husband's chest as they exited.

"Savage move by your boyfriend, Addy," Asher said to Adaline telepathically.

"Makes you curious about the Crae, huh?" Adaline asked.

"No kidding."

Aureon signaled to the guard to bring in the next person. The guard brought in five elves. One female looked to be older than the other four. "Saida Miathan and her four children," Aureon addressed. "You have been brought here because you are suspected to be accomplices in the murder of the late Queen Aravae Sleone. How do you plead?"

"Innocent, My Lord." Saida begged, "Please, my children are innocent."

"That's a lie," Theodon chimed in, shooting Saida a searing glare. Saida's gaze fell as Adaline read their soul records.

Aureon went down the line of Miathans for their pleas. With each one, he turned to Adaline to confirm. She either nodded or shook her head, depending on their truth or lies. The two Miathans on end, the youngest two, were innocent. Saida released a loud sigh of relief. As tears ran down her face, she rocked back and forth on her knees, hoping for mercy for the lives of her children. The two older children were guilty of knowing what their sister and father had done to the queen, and Aureon banished them along with Bole and Roserie.

"Nooo!" Saida wailed as she reached for her two children, who guards dragged away. She sobbed as the guards held her back, keeping her on her knees in front of the king.

"Saida Miathan," Aureon said. "Choose your words wisely."

"I am innocent," Saida said as her lungs heaved.

Aureon turned to look at Adaline, who was looking at Saida knowingly. "It's not that simple, is it?" Adaline said to Saida. "What did you know about your husband and daughter's doings?"

"I will not testify against my family," Saida said defiantly.

"How could you be testifying against them when you didn't know anything?" Adaline asked her. Saida said nothing. Adaline turned to Aureon and said softly, "She knew that her husband hated you, but she thought Greydon was constructing a political scheme against you to sway subjects into following him and revealing you as a less than able ruler. She never knew about any acts of treason done by her husband or daughter."

Saida's shoulders sagged when Adaline finished.

Aureon nodded and refocused on Saida. "Saida Miathan, you and your two innocent children are banished from the capital and must depart, immediately, to the mountains of Braorix. The Miathan house forfeits its title, wealth, and place among the elder council." Saida nodded at the king's wishes as tears ran down her cheeks. "Mark my words, Saida," Aureon pinned her with a determined stare, "if a Miathan ever sets foot in the capital again, I will execute them on site." The twin's eyes widened. Aureon waved for the guards to remove her from the throne room before he announced, "Next, Talia Miathan."

Everyone winced at the sound of a loud screech due to their sensitive ears. They heard clawing and shouting as it took three guards to drag Talia into the room. The three guards remained stationed around her, giving her no quarter.

"Talia Miathan," Aureon said on an exhale as he remained steady in his seat. He noticed Gesso stationed at the far end of the room. The king nodded at him, and Gesso quickly approached to bring the king a beverage. The king took a swig from his glass.

"Are you sure you want to be drinking from that glass, Your Majesty?" Talia sneered.

The king's nostrils flared as his eyes filled with rage. Only the sound of one voice brought his temper down.

"Wow, you are that stupid," Adaline said to Talia. Adaline looked at the she-elf with her head tilted in appraisal. She was dumb enough to hint at how she killed the queen in front of everyone. Talia's eyes narrowed on Adaline. Adaline stuck out her hand, and the king's glass floated to her palm. She brought the beverage to her nose and took a deep breath. Then Adaline sat back in her seat and lifted the water from the glass with her mind. After a moment of examining it, she put the water back into the glass and took a sip. "Nothing," she said before she handed the glass back to Aureon.

"Taunt me again, Talia, and I will end your life where you kneel," Aureon warned. Talia didn't have a comeback. "You are charged with the murder of the late Queen Aravae Sleone," Aureon stated. "How do you plead?"

Talia smirked as she spat out, "Guilty."

"Tell them why, Talia," Adaline stated. "This is your moment of glory, after all."

"Make me," Talia defied.

Asher hopped up from his chair and shrugged toward his twin. "She asked."

Adaline smiled and nodded at her brother. Aureon glanced at her, not understanding what was happening. "Listen," was all she said to Aureon as she pointed to her brother.

Asher straightened and cleared his throat for the ability he hadn't exercised since he first discovered it as a child. It proved problematic to use at such a young age because it was a potent born gift for him. His was far more powerful than Adaline's strength in the same gift because his energy revolved around frequency, and Adaline's revolved around fire.

"Talia Miathan," Asher's voice boomed with a round sound, ringing with absolute truth, "confess the reasons behind your treachery."

Everyone in the room fell silent as they were overcome with surprise by Asher's voice. It compelled the truth from whoever he addressed. Attempting to lie made the person sick. Talia tried to fight against answering him, but her body trembled and tensed as the delivery of the truth crept up her throat. Her mouth flew open, and she spouted information.

"Father promised me that I would be queen one day," Talia admitted as her chest heaved. "I did not love Aureon, and I planned to kill him and remarry my lover, Bole, so that we could rule Theris together forever."

The room exploded in hysterics. Elves shouted, "Murderer!"

"Then Aureon denied our marriage contract, taking my dream away from me. The canceling sent Father and me into a rage, so we conspired to take what was promised to us. We began by wounding him with the death of his queen," Talia spouted. "We could then show that he was unfit to be king and take the crown from him. We had plans to have him killed, but he continued to become stronger with each passing year. Our only direct hit to the royal family that would still help us achieve our goals was to target Theodon after the announcement of his engagement to her." Talia's eyes landed on Adaline.

Theodon seethed as his father sat quietly listening. It wasn't that Aureon wasn't furious, and he was beyond measure, but to finally hear the truth come out was cathartic after centuries. Shocked faces filled the room.

"Thank you, Dr. Asher," Aureon said. Asher gave him a clipped nod and returned to his seat. Aureon addressed Talia, "Talia Miathan, you are hereby sentenced to death which will be carried out tomorrow in the Ophidian Pits promptly at midday." The audience clapped and cheered at the verdict as the king gestured for the guards to take her away. Talia snarled and clawed at the guards as they dragged her from the room. Talia threw a heated glare at Adaline before she was no longer in view, and Adaline's countenance held no emotion in return.

"Send in the last one," the king said to a guard.

The guard hurried to the king and bowed. "My Lord, we cannot restrain him. Would it be impertinent to ask Dr. Adaline to assist?"

Aureon turned to Adaline, who was already rising from her seat. She smiled. "Not at all. Lead the way."

"Do you need me to go with you?" Asher asked her.

"Yeah, you'll get a kick out of this." Adaline tilted her head toward the direction she was walking.

Asher joined her. Questions swarmed in his mind as the guards led them down into the dungeon before he finally spoke. "This is… intense," he commented, as they kept descending to lower levels of the dungeon that housed Graydon.

"You're not wrong, Ash," Adaline stated as they rounded the corner to Graydon's cell.

The elder rippled with rage, but that's not what stopped the twins in their tracks. It was the black smoke billowing from his nose, encircling his corneas, and flooding the space.

"Shiiiiiiiit!" Asher blurted.

"This is bad," Adaline said.

"The worst," Asher said, not tearing his eyes away from Graydon, who appeared to have sold his soul while captured.

It looks like he bargained with more than what he had, was the thought flooding Adaline's mind.

"Let's get the formalities done, and we'll talk to Aureon about the rest," Adaline said to her brother.

"All right. You maneuver him, and I'll bring up the rear," Asher instructed before he gauged the expression on his twin's face. "Are you okay?"

Adaline gave a slight nod. "I didn't expect this."

"Neither did I," Asher admitted.

Adaline and Asher floated Graydon Miathan into the throne room, where they lowered him to the ground without letting go. Everyone in the room whispered to each other about the dark, threatening appearance of the elder. Aureon's countenance remained unwavering while Theodon's eyes widened at the sight of Graydon's body spewing hell smoke. Aureon noticed the twins held onto Graydon with brows drawn tight. Graydon's eyes glowed red, and he snarled as he launched a ball of dark power at Aureon. It spread in flight and reached for Aureon with a screech as if it were a living thing. The king moved before it could make contact, and it ate through the back of his chair. The audience gasped in shock.

Adaline shoved one of her white-lighted hands into Graydon's chest, wrapping her hand around his heart. The elder gasped at the jarring sensation since the pain was something he never expected to feel anymore.

"Try anything cute, again, and I will end you where you stand, demon," Adaline hissed at Graydon as her eyes blazed white.

A maniacal cackle left Graydon's throat as his gaze fell to Adaline before his expression quieted. He saw her changing before his eyes as she was in the beginning stages of taking her true form, illuminating from within.

"Ah, Aureon," Graydon taunted. "I see you've found yourself a human that's actually of use." Graydon nodded at Adaline. "Bravo, my dear."

Adaline squeezed his heart again, and his body jerked through a coughing fit before she eased her grip. She cast a warning look at Aureon. "Make it quick."

"Graydon Miathan," Aureon addressed the elder, "you are charged with the murder of the late Queen Aravae Sleone, conspiracy to commit murder, and treason of the highest offense. You are sentenced to death, which will be carried out at the Ophidian Pits tomorrow at midday."

A demon laugh came from the elder. "Good luck beating me in the pits, Aureon. Your forest magic is no match for me, now."

"Take him away," Aureon commanded.

It took a while to return Graydon and for the twins to reinforce his cell with their gifts to ensure he wouldn't be going anywhere for the next twenty-four hours. As the twins resurfaced from the dungeon, they ran into Gesso, who let them know that the king wanted them both in his study right away.

"It never ends, does it?" Asher asked, referring to the help they were giving to the royal family.

"Nope," Adaline said. "There is always something to be done and someone to help."

"I kinda like it," Asher said. He was no longer uncertain if he would be of use in an evolved world like Theris.

"Me too," Adaline admitted. Adaline knocked on the door to the king's study, and Theodon immediately opened it.

"Hi," Adaline said with a smile.

"Hello," he said before he stood back and opened the door wider. "Come in."

"Hey, buddy," Asher patted Theodon on the shoulder. Theodon nodded in return.

Aureon and the remaining elders were convened on the far end of the study and fell quiet as they observed the twins. There were two seats left at the table, and Aureon gestured for the twins to join them. "Everyone, this is Dr. Asher, Dr. Adaline's twin brother," Aureon shared with the table. The elders perked up upon hearing the word twin.

"Twins!" Helious raved. "How interesting. We have never seen twins before."

"Glad to be a first for you," Asher said proudly, with his arms crossed over his chest. Adaline smirked at her brother before she turned her attention to Aureon.

"We were going over the details of the trials," Aureon explained to them. "We are curious as to your experiences of the same event."

Adaline nodded at Asher for him to go first.

"We both noticed a dark shift right before you saw us burst into the room," Asher shared. "It's a shift that we feel when a substantial new evil is born into our mortal plane." Aureon gave an understanding nod.

"Graydon has done something undeniably awful," Adaline admitted. "He's sold his soul for dark power, and who knows what else."

"What do you mean, Dr. Adaline?" Flavial asked her.

Adaline sighed. "It was difficult to read him because he's sold himself. Usually, when a being goes dark, they try to sell off something that isn't theirs, so they don't give off as much dark power, but Graydon…."

Her thoughts stretched before she came back to the present moment. "He sold himself for one last shot against you." Her eyes found Aureon. "But the shot he's going to take isn't just at you." Aureon looked at Adaline, remaining silent so she would continue. Her brows drew tight. "I saw Theodon in his mind."

"What is bothering you, Dr. Adaline?" the king asked her.

"At every step of the way, I've known every action of every player in the game we played to get everyone to reveal themselves," she admitted. "But when it's this kind of dark power, it can confuse interpretations. So, when I say I see Theodon in his mind, it could not mean Theodon literally."

"It could mean his children, for example," Asher continued. "And it can be showing Theodon because it will have the greatest impact on him. Or, he could simply be the target."

That statement took the wind out of Adaline.

"Do you have any idea as to what or which it is?" the king asked them. In a defeated gesture, the twins slowly shook their heads. "Do not be distressed," Aureon said. "We aren't going to live lesser existences because we fear what some lunatic has done that might come to pass, or not. If we do that, he wins."

"Here, here!" Helious cheered with a pound of his fist on the table.

"Graydon meets his end tomorrow," Aureon said confidently.

"What about the eastern border?" Mouriel asked the king. The elder had been concerned ever since Aureon had mentioned to him the part of Graydon's strategy to stir up the enemies of Theris. A surprise attack that would result in the elves warring on their home soil would be devastating for civilians. They must implement precautions immediately to locate their enemies and uncover their plans.

"Ah, yes," Aureon said before nodding at his son. "Theodon will lead a small reconnaissance team to the border to scout the situation the dawn after we conclude the sentencing at the pits."

"Yes, Father," Theodon said, and his confidence boosted that his father would give him such a task.

"Is it necessary to put the prince in danger, My Lord?" Helious asked.

"Nonsense," Aureon said while he looked at Theodon. "It is as if I am going myself."

Flavial stood next to the king, with his hand on Aureon's shoulder. "Forb will go with Theodon."

Theodon nodded in acceptance of Flavial's offering.

"I will see you in the training room in half an hour, Theodon," Aureon said, dismissing his son.

"Yes, Father," Theodon said as he rose from his chair and exited the study.

"Is there anything else to cover while we are all here?" Aureon asked the elders. They all rose from their chairs in unison.

"I wish we had known what you were going through, Your Majesty," Mouriel admitted. "As much as your father exhibited coldness during his rule, I know he would not have wanted you to bear this alone." *No father would.*

Aureon's eyes were on Adaline as he admitted, "In the end, I was not alone." Adaline's doe-eyed gaze locked onto him, and she smiled. The elders looked at the two of them knowingly.

"We are glad to hear it," Flavial said, patting the king's shoulder. "We are on our way, My Lord."

A moment after everyone had gone, Asher was starting to feel uncomfortable because Aureon was zeroing in on his sister, and that was gross.

"So, which way to the training room?" Asher asked.

"Straight out the back end of the hallway, past the stables on the left," Aureon directed, not taking his eyes off Adaline.

"Great," Asher said and left the room.

Silence remained as Adaline and Aureon kept looking at each other as their smiles mirrored each other.

"I noticed something about you today," Aureon finally said as he stepped back from her to begin his usual pacing.

"Did you?" Adaline said, mirroring him.

"When you had your hand wrapped around Graydon's heart, you changed."

Her eyes remained downcast as she sheepishly blushed. "Oh. That."

"Little human, tell me what I saw," Aureon prodded when she offered no further explanation.

She tensed for a moment and stopped pacing. Aureon continued to walk until he stood behind her. He gently swept her long hair over one shoulder.

"It was incredible," he whispered. Adaline spun to face him and saw the wonder in his eyes. He inched closer. "Now, tell me." He teased her by lingering close without making contact, a move that was easy bait for her.

"It's the beginning of my true form," she whispered.

His eyebrows lifted. "Your true form?" A moment passed. "What does the rest look like?"

"Um, picture a giant white flame."

"Impressive," he said as he leaned in, his lips a breath away from hers. "I hope to see it someday."

Adaline smiled as she thought, *Oh, you will!* She waited to see if he would bridge the remaining distance between them. He hovered close for a moment longer, which crumbled her discipline altogether. She grabbed his face and covered his mouth with hers.

"Mmm," he rumbled as he matched her intensity.

There was a knock at the door of his study, and they parted from each other. Adaline saw his eyes adjust their focus on her, and his pupils enlargened.

"Come in," Aureon said, without taking his eyes off Adaline.

Gesso poked his head into the room. "Um, Your Majesty?"

"Yes, Gesso," Aureon replied.

"Prince Theodon and Dr. Asher seem to be practicing very hard in the training room, My Lord," Gesso reported.

Aureon faced him. "What of it, Gesso?"

"They're causing the north side of the palace to rattle, My Lord," Gesso said plainly.

Adaline's eyebrows lifted in surprise. "I will sort it out. Thank you, Gesso."

"Certainly, My Lord," Gesso said with a quick bow before closing the door behind him.

"This is your brother's fault, is it not?" Aureon's accusing eyes wrangled her attention.

Adaline squinted one eye as she thought for a moment. "It's probably mostly Asher's fault." Aureon was surprised that she wasn't defending her twin as he expected. "What? I know my twin." Adaline said as she headed for the door. "I'll catch up with you in case he becomes insufferable."

CHAPTER 60

Aureon entered the training room in his sparring clothes and found Theodon and Asher fighting. Aureon could not determine what Gesso's fuss was about, but then Asher's electricity-covered blade came down on Theodon's sword block. A rattling boom shook the training room upon impact.

Ah, there it is, Aureon thought.

"You are scaring the staff and shaking the palace," Aureon said to them.

The two stopped fighting and faced Aureon.

"We will be quieter, Father," Theodon said.

Aureon nodded as he sat nearby and inspected his scabbard before he unsheathed his sword. The swordsmith had taken the liberty of cleaning and sharpening his blade that morning for him. Aureon examined it for a moment and saw that she had done excellent work. *There you are, old friend.* Cerus had it made for Aureon in his thousandth year, and it accompanied him through every battle since.

"Well, that looks nice," he heard Adaline's voice as she walked into the room with Jim at her side. Jim's focus remained on the blade.

"Does it have a name?" Jim asked Aureon.

Aureon gazed at the blade fondly as he thought of the human translation. "War Ender."

Jim nodded in approval before he took a seat to watch Theodon and Asher spar.

"There must be a good story that goes with such a name," Adaline voiced her curiosity. The corner of Aureon's mouth lifted before he nodded. Asher and Theodon stopped using weapons and were now fighting hand-to-hand. Adaline glanced over her shoulder at them before admitting, "That's a bad idea."

"Why?" Aureon asked before he heard two cracking sounds.

They turned to see Asher and Theodon holding their noses while blood rushed down the front of their clothes.

"That's why," Adaline muttered as she walked over to them and set their noses before healing them.

"*Thank you*, Addy," Asher exaggerated.

"Yes," Theodon joined in. "Thank you, Dr. Adaline."

"You two are no longer sparring partners for tonight," Adaline said to them.

"Yes, ma'am," Asher conceded.

"Theodon," Aureon said with his head tilted toward the sparring circle.

"Yes, Father." Theodon got up from the bench, wiped the remaining blood on his sleeve, picked up his sword, and headed back to the center of the training room to spar with his father. The sparring between the royals was part sparring and part teaching from Aureon. The humans sat and watched how elves fought and noticed the elves were swift in delivering a punch or a kick. They were naturally graceful, so their transitions were, too. A while passed before Adaline was tired of watching and not participating.

"I play winner!" she called to them, which distracted Theodon. That opened up Aureon to deliver a killing blow. However, instead of delivering the strike's full impact, Aureon stopped his sword at his son's neck, pricking him enough to get his attention.

"Focus, Theodon," his father said.

"Yes, Father," Theodon said, with his hands raised before Aureon removed his sword.

"Sorry, Theo," Adaline said as the prince walked back to the bench to gather his belongings.

"There is nothing to be sorry about," Theodon said while smiling. "I still have lessons to learn."

"That's right," Jim chimed in. "A warrior knows he always has something to improve on."

"Yes, exactly," Theodon agreed with Jim as he stood. "I'll see you all at dinner."

"Bye, Theo," Asher called after him as he left the training room.

"My turn." Adaline hopped up from the bench and approached the rack of weapons standing near the training circle. It took her a few minutes before she found a weapon that might be adequate.

"You don't like it," Asher commented, knowing his twin well. Adaline glanced in his direction without a word. "If you don't like it, change it, Addy."

Change it, she thought before smiling. *Yes!*

Adaline took a staff from the rack and walked over to stand opposite Aureon. She unsheathed her dagger then separated the molecules at the end of the staff and the hilt of the dagger. Next, she stacked them together and solidified the weapon into a new one.

"That's better," Adaline whispered. Her eyes met Aureon's, and she smirked when she saw his raised brows.

"I think my weapon deserves a name," Adaline said with a

sly smile before striking against Aureon.

Her blade clashed with his. "Indeed. Any thoughts?" He threw her blade off him as they both twirled their weapons and circled each other.

"I'm thinking something like Kernel Reaper, Bringer of Popcorn," Adaline said before her next strike. She heard Asher and Jim chuckling from the bench.

"That sounds murderous against corn kernels, Addy," Asher rebutted.

Aureon blocked her next strike and stole a kiss from her.

"I think that's our cue to leave, Jim," Asher commented.

"It looked pretty clear to me," Jim replied as both men rose from their seats.

"Did you just-?" Adaline's eyes narrowed at Aureon before dropping the arm that held her weapon, and then she kicked him in the chest. Aureon skidded backward a few yards, but he didn't wince or stagger. Instead, he stood tall with his chest puffed with pride at her strength. It was a turn-on, one he wanted to bait. She noticed he became visibly larger as she felt his desire for her. His need to dominate, to be lost in her, grew as the minutes ticked by as they sparred.

"Where did you learn to fight?" Aureon asked her as neither of them let up.

Adaline glanced over Aureon's shoulder to Jim, who stood quietly next to Asher. The old Marine smiled with pride while watching Adaline, who fought beautifully and ferociously. Jim taught her the latter, and she developed the former on her own. Jim's words from long ago echoed in her mind, "You can't hide behind your stethoscope when someone wants you dead."

"It's a long story," Adaline replied as Aureon faced her with his blade raised.

Her blade struck his as their eyes locked. "You have many of those."

Their sparring ebbed and flowed with the renewal of their

energy as time passed. Then in one swift move, Adaline's blade shredded through his tunic, leaving him bare-chested. She tilted her head to one side and smiled. Asher and Jim left the room.

"That was supposed to work *for* me, not against me," Adaline admitted with a grin. "I didn't think that one through."

He grabbed her weapon by the dagger's hilt and threw it at the opposite wall, where the blade stuck firmly.

"Enough," he growled before he tore away her shirt. "On the ground, now."

Okay, she thought, as she turned her back on him and slowly got down on her knees. She could feel his desire rage within him due to the rush from fighting. He needed something to control because he felt out of control. She baited him by putting her palms on the floor before she looked over her shoulder and shimmied her bottom to seduce him closer. He growled at the visual, and he sank to his knees behind her. He tore through her clothes, leaving her in only her panties and her bra on the dirty floor. The sight of her soft skin called to his lust, but not enough to make his ministrations gentle.

She is strong, kept chanting in his mind, as his carnal need for her spiked. Aureon's body lurched over hers, sealing the skin of his chest to her back. His arm threaded between her breasts, and his hand latched onto her neck. She gave no signs of fear or recoil, but his brows drew tight as he felt out of control. He didn't want to hurt her.

"I can't... I need..." His words failed him.

"I know. It's okay," Adaline said sweetly as she cupped his face that rested against hers. "You need to take?"

Aureon nodded. "Hard."

"I'm ready," she whispered in his ear in a sultry tone.

He groaned, then his knee pushed against the inside of hers to widen her stance before he tore her panties away. His grip on her neck tightened as he positioned his cock at her entrance and pushed inside of her.

"*Addy*," Aureon breathed in surprise at how wet she was

already. His body shuddered over hers in response. His thumb tipped her chin up to him, so he could make sure he didn't cause her any harm. He bucked against her once, then repeated until her gaze turned hooded, and a moan escaped her lips. He released a guttural snarl as he rose to his knees. His grip sank into her hips as he bucked against her hard. She moaned his name. Unable to resist the silky touch of her skin, he leaned back down to touch his chest against her back while her body strained for release. He felt her walls tense around his length, almost on the verge of orgasm. He kept his fast, hard pace as he whispered in her ear. "Need to be inside you, Addy," he rasped as he thrust deep. "Cannot stop thinking about it."

"I'm gonna come, Au-," she managed to get out before she cried out in ecstasy as her body shuddered.

"*Yes*," he whispered in her ear before he gently bit her lobe. He groaned as he continued to pump inside of her through her orgasm and barely through his own. She gasped for breath as she realized how much her body reacted to his words. He kissed a trail from her shoulder to the base of her neck before he confessed, "We are missing dinner, little human." He didn't care, but maybe she did. And he discovered she did when she teleported them to his bathroom. She kissed him before teleporting to her own, but he grabbed her forearm before she left and pulled her close.

"I want us to shower together," he admitted.

"If we do, we will never make it to dinner," she said before she winked at him and disappeared.

"Fair point," he said aloud as he turned on his rain shower and stepped under the water.

Dinner turned out to be a rush for them both. Neither of them apologized for their absence or gave a reason why they were late. Everyone was already eating, and the two of them joined in.

"So, Your Majesty," Tessa said to Aureon, as he began

digging into his meal, "how long have you been friends with Flavial?"

"For many human lifetimes, Miss Hill," Aureon replied. "Why do you ask?"

Tessa shied away from responding, so Adaline chimed in, "Because Flavial asked her on a date."

"A date?" Theodon asked.

"When a male wants to begin courting a female or to learn more about her because he likes her, he usually takes her nice places to be alone while making fun memories to establish a connection," Asher explained to the royals. "They're usually pretty horrible, from what Addy has said over the years."

Aureon and Theodon turned to look at Adaline.

"Yeah, well, can't really blame them... much," she said, as she started picking at her food with her fork.

"I don't believe you," Theodon said to Adaline as his eyes narrowed on her. Adaline eyed Theodon while she stacked food on her fork.

Courting, Aureon thought. Something he forgot during all the chaos they'd been dealing with since his healing. He must do that for Adaline after the sentencing concluded, and he already knew where to take her.

"So, how about these pit fights tomorrow, huh?" Adaline said, dodging further interrogation.

"Nice one, Addy," Asher poked fun at her.

She shoved food in her mouth to stop herself from making any snide comments. "What's the protocol behind the custom of dueling at the pits?" She asked Aureon.

"The guilty choose to fight a member of the royal house to the death," Aureon stated plainly.

"Has a guilty person ever challenged a specific member of the royal family?" she asked.

"What are you getting at?" Asher asked in her mind. Adaline waved him off for Aureon's answer.

"They don't have a say, usually, but if the royal is willing to oblige, they can," Aureon informed. Adaline nodded as her eyes remained on her plate.

"Addy," Asher whispered in her mind, "you aren't thinking of challenging, are you?"

"No," Adaline replied in his mind. She kept her focus on her plate so that she wouldn't set off alarms in Asher or Aureon due to one truth: Adaline knew that if she were in Talia's shoes, she'd challenge the person who put her in chains if the opportunity arose. It was another chance to deliver a crippling blow to Aureon by killing the king's mate. Adaline wasn't in fear for her own life, but she feared for Aureon's sanity, should she be challenged.

It's time he saw more of what I can do, she thought. It was the perfect place to show everyone what she was in her true form. And Asher would be there to help the royals understand.

Asher quickly finished his dinner, along with Tobey, who had popped up from his seat to retire to Asher's room for the night. As Asher held Tobey's hand and exited the dining room, he whispered in his sister's mind, "Love you, sis."

"I love you too, Ash," she replied as an awful feeling swarmed in her stomach, as it was the first time she kept the details of her strategy from Asher.

CHAPTER 61

T he next morning, the twins roused at dawn and meditated for new upgrades to their gifts. Asher noticed that it was easier for him to connect to the divine while meditating in Theris versus Earth. He received an increased electric pulse to his speed, making him even faster, while Adaline received a weapon unlike anything she'd ever seen. It was something she'd read about in old texts, and she appreciated the timing of such a gift.

Throughout the morning, Adaline's focus was unwavering on the task at hand; to accept and win all the day's challenges. When it came time to dress for the Ophidian Pits, the twins changed into their sweeper gear. Dressed in black from head to toe, they left their rooms and headed to the pits together to meet the royal family.

"I know what you two are up to." The twins stopped when they heard Jim's voice, who approached them before he said, "You are looking for trouble."

"When have we ever done that, Jim?" Asher asked.

Jim rolled his eyes. "You must think me a senile old fool to think I'd miss a step from you two."

Adaline smiled. "We're going in prepared, Jim." Jim lifted a skeptical eyebrow at her. "Will you join us?"

Jim thought for a moment. "What the hell — It's not like I have a packed schedule anymore."

They headed south of the palace to the Pilia River that flowed east to the Ophidian Pits. It split into a fork around the pits as it exited Theris, isolating the kingdom's one public expression of barbarism. Adaline peered into the water until a platform of the element rose from the river. "Come on," Adaline said while stepping onto it.

"It's almost like surfing," Asher told Jim as Asher stepped out to join his twin. The twin's powers still spooked Jim on occasion, even if Adaline had brought him back from the brink of death when she was a little girl. Jim finally boarded and stood between them.

"Hold onto my shoulder," Adaline instructed Jim. A moment later, the three of them surfed down the river until they made a left at the fork and exited the river on the south side for the stadium.

The stadium consisted of carved stonework that included scenes from ancient elfin lore. Large trees grew up the sides of the arena, intentionally placed to hold up the structure, while their canopies provided shade to those in attendance.

The humans approached the entrance and saw one of the king's guards, who waved them over and escorted them to the king's box. It sat a few rows back from the front row seats, just above the warrior's entrance tunnel into the stadium. On the opposite side was the challenger's tunnel, where those found guilty would enter. A version of the king's throne was present, which Aureon was already perched while dressed in his armor, and Theodon sat at Aureon's side. Two more chairs were available, but once the guard saw Jim, he added another chair.

"Would you mind putting that one next to me, please?"

Adaline asked the guard.

"Of course, Dr. Adaline," he said as he set the chair next to hers at Aureon's left hand.

Aureon turned, expecting to see them in festive clothing, but his gaze turned inquisitive when he saw the twins dressed in black.

"Good morning," Adaline said to him.

"Good morning, Dr. Adaline," Aureon said in return. Theodon popped up from his seat to greet them all.

"Interesting clothes," Theodon marveled. He examined Asher's outfit and pointed at a slim holster. "Does a blade go there?"

"A blade does go there," Asher said with a smug grin as he unsheathed a blade that was camouflaged by the flap that snapped over it.

"Impressive," Theodon said, enamored by the cleverness of the garment's construction.

Aureon swept his free hand around the small of Adaline's back and pulled her in for a kiss. Before his gentle kiss turned hungry, he parted from her, and it reminded her of the urgency in their lovemaking of the previous night. He came to her room with the need to purge emotions that had intensified. Carrying anxiety about the duties he had to perform the following day and fear regarding the vulnerability he and Theodon would face as they delivered death blows to the Miathans. Her hand moved to his heart and poured healing light into him. She did the same to him the night before, as they lay with their legs tangled once they were both sated.

"Thank you," Aureon whispered, with his endless gaze fixed on her. She nodded before she gave him a soft kiss. "Sit with me," he said as he took her hand and escorted her to her seat. He placed her hand on the edge of his armrest, then wrapped his hand over hers. It took a while for all elves in attendance to herd into the stadium and find their seats. After everyone settled,

Aureon released Adaline's hand and stood. As he approached the edge of his box, the crowd fell silent. His voice was clear and strong, and elves heard him for miles.

"Today is a day of reckoning. After centuries of knowing the truth, only to find whispers of evidence, thereby left in unending despair for centuries." He sighed before he glanced at Adaline. "We made new friends who have gifts that showed us the way so that we could deliver justice for our queen." Some in the crowd cheered. "She was extraordinary," he said, lost in thought for a moment. He grasped the edge of the box to hold himself up for his oncoming words, the truth he needed to say. "And she deserves justice!" Aureon looked at the crowd for a moment before he chose his words. "And it is hers today." Pause. "However, justice is not enough for me. I do not possess the same grace or gentle heart as our late queen. Therefore, I demand something more on this day." The crowd hung on the king's every word. Aureon's eyes shifted from one side of the stadium to the other. "Vengeance," he breathed. The crowd erupted with cheer for their king. A moment passed before Aureon lifted his hand, and everyone fell silent. "The first duel is with Graydon Miathan."

The crowd remained silent as everyone's attention turned to the challenger's tunnel on the opposite end of the stadium. Down the center of the stadium was a wide path, with black sand filling the rest of the space on both sides of it. A tremor passed through the ground as the gate on the challenger's tunnel opened.

"What was that?" Asher asked Theodon.

Theodon smirked. "Watch."

The ground trembled again. A moment later, a giant serpent burst through the surface of the sand. It stretched over sixty feet into the air and appeared to be at least five feet wide. It looked down at everyone in the stadium, and its gaze stopped on Aureon. The energy that rippled off the king hypnotized the serpent.

"Away!" Aureon commanded the serpent in Tear, and the beast didn't hesitate to dive below the surface.

"He can command massive anaconda snakes, Addy," Asher said in his sister's mind.

"Mind. Blown." Adaline replied. She heard Asher chuckle.

The gate finished opening, and out stepped Graydon Miathan with a single sword in hand. Dark power still pooled off him, making the twins shift in their seats. Graydon noticed their tension and smirked as he assumed his power was the greatest force present. The elder's gaze turned to Aureon as he finished walking to the center of the path. Anger fumed from Graydon's features as he yelled, "I challenge King Aureon Sleone to a fight to the death!"

The audience turned to gaze upon their king. Aureo's triumphant expression was unmistakable. "I decline your challenge, Graydon," Aureon stated. "And I pass it to someone more worthy of this moment than I." Whispers spread through the crowd. The twins looked at each other, wondering to whom Aureon referred, then a loud thud caught everyone's attention.

Another happened.

Then another.

It was the stride of a large being.

The gate in the warrior tunnel raised as the sound grew closer. Everyone in the king's box rushed to the king's side to see who was entering the stadium. Graydon's expression changed from cockiness to sheer terror at the sight of his opponent.

"I give you your challenger," Aureon announced. "Cristatus Elacan, Lord of House Elacan, father of Queen Aravae Sleone."

The elves in the audience gasped. Anyone who knew anything about Cristatus Elacan knew he fled the kingdom after his daughter's death, filled with inconsolable grief. Even with the long life span elves possessed, it was still considered unnatural for a child to die before a parent. But Lord Elacan's attendance wasn't the most shocking aspect of his arrival. Dark power poured off the lord as well. However, there was a difference between him and Graydon. Lord Elacan's darkness was deep-rooted as if he adjusted to it centuries ago, immediately following his daughter's passing. He's been ready for this moment ever since he left Theris. A giant scythe was gripped in his hand as he stopped opposite Graydon.

Adaline couldn't stop the tears welling in her eyes before her gaze dropped to her feet. Jim put a concerned hand on her shoulder. "What's wrong, Addy?"

"H-he," Adaline started, "he sold his soul after she died because she was haunting him because she died tragically."

"What good did that do?" Jim inquired.

"He traded his soul so hers could pass into the afterlife," Adaline explained. "He did it so she could be at peace." Since that decision, a piece of his soul was anchored in hell, tortured without ceasing as it would be until the day he died and beyond. Jim's expression changed to one of understanding as Adaline sniffed back tears.

I would have done the same for my child, Aureon thought with his eyes fixed on the two elves in the center of the stadium. Then he announced, "The ring is yours, Lord Elacan."

The dark elves assessed each other, attempting to measure the other's power in silence.

"Lord Elacan," Graydon said, upkeeping formalities as he took his fighting stance.

"Miathan," Lord Elacan's voice rumbled in a frightening, demonic tone. The lord's towering height easily cleared seven feet, and he was muscle-thick in body. It appeared the years had not been kind to him, and he was the same in return. The audience remained silent out of fear, and the twins felt the hairs standing on the backs of their necks.

"If we have to intervene on this...." Asher said in his sister's mind.

"Well, we might," Adaline replied. "That's partially why we are here."

Lord Elacan charged Graydon with his scythe. Graydon blocked the staff of the weapon, but the blade was so long that it hooked over Graydon's sword, stabbing him in the shoulder. The elder cried out in pain as Lord Elacan declared, "Your head is *mine*." Graydon's teeth clenched as he yelled to gain momentum and pushed Cristatus off him. Their blades crashed as lightning split the sky.

"That wasn't me," Asher said.

"It was me," Aureon admitted, as he leaned forward in his chair with his eyes glued to the fight. He reached for Adaline's hand and folded their fingers together, and his grip on her hand tightened when blades collided. Graydon managed to get a few good hits against Cristatus, who seethed with rage. Finality settled into Lord Elacan's dark heart. A conceited move on Graydon's part cost the elder a moment too long of no defense. Cristatus brought his scythe down fast over the elder's neck, severing his head from his body.

The stadium fell silent before everyone erupted into triumphant cheers. Lord Elacan peered at Graydon's head that had rolled away from its body. He knew what could happen if the body parts were too close together once a soul was turned over to the darkness: reanimation. Graydon's death must be final, so Cristatus grabbed the head by the roots of Graydon's long golden hair and held it up to the crowd. He basked in his victory and their praise, absorbing all the glory they gave him.

Adaline could see the lord was heaving for breath because his body was purging old pain. Not knowing who killed his daughter had haunted him, and now he was free of that burden. He pushed Graydon's body onto the black sand with his foot. The body sank into the sand before a large set of jaws came up from the sand around the body, gulping it down. Another set of jaws surfaced, and Lord Elacan threw the head in its direction. A large, split tongue shoveled the head into its mouth before snapping closed and sinking below the surface.

"That is both cool and disturbing," Asher commented.

Aureon sat tall, seeming to shed a burden of his own. Absolution filled him, and he squeezed his son's shoulder with his free hand. Lord Elacan finally turned to leave the ring but stopped when he caught sight of Theodon in the king's box. He'd never laid eyes on Theodon after he was born, and Lord Elacan knew if he had, he would have never left Theris. At the time, he thought going was for the best, but now seeing his grandson, he was no longer sure.

A loud screech echoed from the challenger tunnel, and the stadium went silent. The screech happened again–It was Talia. She knew her father was dead and fought against her shackles to escape and avenge him. Lord Elacan exited the stadium through the same tunnel he had entered; his duel swiftly won, and his burden gone. His presence filled the tunnel with black smoke as he passed through it, alarming the guards posted along the tunnel once more.

"You have no reason to fear me," Lord Elacan said to them. He noticed a figure at the end, and as the person came into view, Lord Elacan's steps grew morose. His grandson's curiosity came into focus before they stood opposite each other in silence.

"You look just like your father," Cristatus finally said.

"I have never met you," was the only thought Theodon managed to voice, with his brows drawn in confusion. He had so many questions for the grandfather he never knew was alive.

"I left before I could meet you," Cristatus confessed. He knew that wasn't nearly a sufficient answer, but it would have to do. There was much to talk to him about after the sentencing concluded. Theodon gave a slight nod. Cristatus' hand landed on his grandson's shoulder. "I will tell you everything you want to know. First, let's get your father through today." Theodon straightened and nodded. "Go on," Cristatus urged him to return to the king's box. "I'll be along in a bit."

Theodon made it back to the king's box and froze in the middle of taking his seat when he heard Talia screech, "I challenge Dr. Adaline in a fight to the death!"

Every cell in Aureon's body went cold when she spoke the words. He faced Adaline, whose countenance was neutral as she rose from her seat. She stared down the she-elf for a long moment.

"I accept your challenge," Adaline said.

The crowd gasped, and the royals sat wide-eyed in shock. Aureon grabbed her wrist and pulled her toward the side entrance that led to the weapons tent under the king's box. He burst into the tent behind Adaline with frustration fueling his movements, and Asher followed them. Lord Elacan watched the exchange as he finished removing his armor.

"I have never forbidden you from anything," Aureon started.

"Not that it would have worked if you had," Adaline blurted.

"But this is something I cannot allow," he threw back. Adaline spun around to face him. "I've repeatedly put you in harm's way for weeks," Aureon admitted. "And I never liked the idea. So, understand how much I could hate it now!"

"I do know how much you hate it," she brought her voice down and stepped closer to him. "But I need you to understand that I've got this handled. I knew this was a possibility, and I'm ready for it. I need you to trust me to make this decision and trust that I know it's the right one."

His brows drew tight before he blurted out, "Please do not do this, Addy." That was the first time he'd ever addressed her casually in front of others. She cradled his face in her hands, and he turned and kissed her palm. She leaned up to touch her forehead to his as they remained silent for a moment.

"I need you to support my decision," she whispered. "And to give me the space to show you what I can do, so you can see who I am."

Aureon gripped her wrist tightly as he turned to Asher. "You seem completely calm about this."

"Oh, I am," Asher said as he took his time admiring all the weapons in the room.

"How is that possible?" Aureon spat out.

Asher turned and looked at his sister thoughtfully. "Because I fully understand what she's capable of." Asher walked up to Aureon and looked him dead in the eye. "Let her show you."

Have they gone mad? Aureon thought to himself as he let out a defeated sigh.

A moment later, Theodon joined the room and, therefore, the argument. At one point, he said to Adaline, "The Miathan's come from a long line of warriors."

Adaline's attention snapped in his direction. "So do I."

"Aren't you worried in the slightest?" Theodon asked her.

She eyed Theodon, choosing her words so she wouldn't reveal too much. "There is only one thing I'm worried about regarding the events of today, and winning is not it."

"Everyone out of the room," Aureon said to the males present. After they were gone, he hit his knees as his eyes watered. "My darling," his voice was vulnerable and ragged. "This I cannot bear." She approached him with open arms. He smashed his cheek against her belly as he wrapped his arms around her securely. As she embraced him, she couldn't resist playing with his hair. She cupped his chin, encouraging him to look up at her. Once he did, he saw the light in her eyes. Only this time, it didn't stop at her eyes; it spread to her lids, her forehead, her nose, and it ignited all over her body. She planted a soft kiss on his lips and stepped back from him. He tried reaching for her, but she evaded his touch.

"I can hurt you in my true form," she said, her voice changing. She sounded all-knowing, eternal, and infinitely powerful. "Are you ready to see me?" He nodded as he rose to his feet. She closed her eyes as the holy flame burst through her cells, transmitting a violent white flame from her spirit. Aureon stood staring at her in shock and awe, beside himself that so much power existed in a human. She headed for the tunnel and whispered, "Trust me." His response stopped her.

"Return to me," he implored, and Adaline nodded before walking down the tunnel to the stadium.

Aureon raced back to the king's box as the warrior's tunnel gate opened, and out walked his fiery female. Talia still stood just outside of the challenger gate, and her eyes widened in surprise at the sight of Adaline. The fire within her raged as her focus remained on Talia. She blew a light ball into her hand. When it grew large enough, Adaline flattened the ball into a large disc, split it in two, and attached them to her forearms as armor. Talia watched in shock as Adaline then reached out into the air at her side. She gripped down on a hilt that materialized before it revealed the rest of a blade made of the same fire as her.

Theodon nudged Asher in the king's box. "Did you know she could do that?"

"That Addy could wield a sword of fire?" Asher asked before shrugging. "No, but I'm not surprised, either."

Aureon was silent, his full attention on the duel. He watched Adaline sandwich her hands over the hilt of her blade and split the sword into two. "Now that's impressive," Asher commented before he clapped for his twin.

Adaline twirled both blades in her hands, stretching her wrists as she approached the middle of the path and took her fight stance. Jim was proud because he could tell from her stance that she would do something he'd taught her decades ago. Adaline didn't need weapons to win, but Jim made sure she knew how to handle a blade, anyway.

Talia approached Adaline with her long sword in hand. Her previous fury over her father's death diminished at the sight of Adaline. The she-elf shifted nervously on her feet.

"My Lord?" Gesso whispered to Aureon. Aureon leaned his ear in Gesso's direction but didn't take his eyes off Adaline. "Is she a goddess, Sire?"

Aureon finally rasped, "Yes."

Talia launched a dagger over Adaline meant for Aureon, and Adaline followed it with her focus. The blade disintegrated to nothing before it could reach him. Adaline smirked at the king before his face filled with horror as Talia ran the end of her sword up through Adaline's shoulder from behind. Adaline yelled in pain, and many of the elves winced at what the abrasive sound did to their sensitive ears. Adaline looked up and saw Aureon trying to hold it together as storm clouds formed overhead. Then she saw her twin, her steady pillar of strength if she ever needed one. Asher nodded at her in encouragement and clapped his hands as thunder rolled overhead.

"Finish her, Addy!" Asher yelled.

"Finish me?" Talia laughed haughtily. "She can do no such thing. The human can barely stand. She will die in seconds."

Adaline straightened as she turned to face Talia. She grabbed the end of the sword and yanked it free. Some elves in the stands winced. "Today is not my day to die," Adaline said ominously, while the flames sealed up the hole in her body as if the damage had never occurred.

"Witch!" Talia accused with a pointing finger.

"Words have yet to help you, Talia," Adaline told her. "If I were you, I'd shut up and find a weapon because you don't have much longer."

Talia turned her back on Adaline and sprinted for her fallen sword. Adaline launched herself into the air after Talia as a serpent erupted from the sand and arched over the pathway before diving back below on the other side. Before Talia could grasp her blade, Adaline kicked her in between her shoulders, sending the she-elf flying down the path. Talia collided hard with the ground, the impact disorienting her. Adaline stormed toward her with her blades of fire as another serpent breached the surface and charged at her. Adaline let one sword cut through the beast without effort. It shrieked in pain and immediately retreated to the depths of the black sand. Adaline's gaze never wavered from Talia, who tried to scramble away from her. Adaline's foot came down on Talia's chest, holding the she-elf in place. With her unshakable blazing-white stare, Adaline smiled.

"Congratulations, Talia," Adaline said, with the blades crossed like scissors over Talia's throat. The skin at her neck blistered and burned.

"For what?" Talia hissed.

"For failing to accomplish the oldest trick in the book," Adaline said. "Using a male as a status upgrade."

Talia's gaze on Adaline turned cold. "You have no authority to end me," Talia hissed. "You are no one!"

"I have the greatest authority here," Adaline said with a wry smile. "While you were busy scheming and murdering, you forgot to take the time to find out what I truly am." Talia was trembled, finally aware that she had met her end. "And now you pay for that mistake," Adaline said as she crossed her blades hard, severing Talia's head from her body. The heat cauterized the wound instantly, not leaving behind a single drop of blood. The crowd stood in silence, needing a moment to process all they had witnessed. A moment later, a few claps began, then more, until the crowd roared for Adaline's victory. As Adaline lifted Talia's remains with the flick of her hand, a giant serpent shot up next to where she stood.

"Ugh! You again," Adaline huffed. The serpent tried to charge at her. "I said no!" Adaline put up her force field as a shield and pushed back at the snake, which became confused by the force of such a small person in comparison. "Are ya hungry?" She floated Talia's remains over to the serpent that immediately gulped down Talia's head. The crowd cheered. "That's a good boy!" Adaline praised the beast like it was her pet Doberman. "Look! Look! Where's it going? Go get it!" And she let the body drop down into the sinking sand. The serpent dove after it, causing an uproar of laughter from the crowd. She combined her fire swords into one and let the divine weapon fade into nothingness, then allowed her true form to recede. Adaline walked back to the king's tent and noticed the stone facade of the king peering down at her, the relief on Theodon's face, and the shit-eating grin on Asher's smug mug. Jim was equally prideful.

Adaline was almost at the gate when a scream reverberated behind her, causing her to shift her attention. Roserie had broken from her shackles and was charging at Adaline, moving so fast that she was already halfway across the stadium. Adaline took off running at her head-on, picking up speed with each step. She reached behind her as she thought of a weapon, and she heard the king make a sound of surprise as his sword shot from his scabbard. Roserie launched herself at Adaline as her hand closed over the hilt of War Ender. Adaline brought the sword up to defend against Roserie's powerful blow. Roserie tried to kick Adaline while their blades tangled, but Adaline threw the she-elf off her.

Roserie canted her head at the human. "Well... you're stronger than I thought."

"Well, you're dumber than I thought," Adaline said. She waited for Roserie's next move because she didn't plan on killing the traitor.

Roserie's gaze penetrated like daggers as she charged at Adaline again. When their blades locked once more, Roserie tried her best to sound threatening.

"You should have stayed out of it, human," Roserie sneered.

"You should have stayed chained up," Adaline warned. "Banishment is kinder than what I will do to you." Roserie weighed her options. "Go ahead," Adaline lifted her chin in the direction of the guard that would re-shackle her. "If you return to the guard now, I won't hurt you." Roserie glanced over her shoulder at the guard. She could hear her parents pleading that she return to the guard, but she had stopped listening to them a long time ago. "But if you come at me one more time, I'll feed you to my new pet, just like I did your bestie."

Roserie turned to retreat but simply used the gesture to pivot and bring her blade down on Adaline. Adaline blocked the blow and ran War Ender through Roserie's chest just as quickly. Adaline held the defeated Roserie up by the sword as a shocked expression filled the she-elf's face. Roserie dropped her blade before her eyes fluttered closed as life left her body. Adaline cringed when she heard the cry of Theodon from the king's box as Aureon and Asher held the prince back from climbing over the wall and into the stadium. Tears fell hard and fast down Adaline's cheeks as his pain rippled through her. Her sword hand grew unsteady as she knew the death blow she delivered to Roserie was the same end to her friendship with Theodon. Her knees buckled, and she sank to the ground. She pushed Roserie off Aureon's blade. Adaline stared at the traitor's body as the serpent returned, nonplussed by Adaline's presence. The beast casually swiped its giant split tongue over the pathway, shoveling Roserie's body into its throat before it sank back into the dark oblivion.

Adaline could no longer hold her tears. They weren't just from killing Roserie and losing Theodon but from the pent-up emotions from the past couple of weeks. There were so many she felt she could not express, and others she didn't even know she had repressed. A blur of electricity shot across the stadium before she saw Asher standing over her, and he offered her both hands to help her stand.

"C'mon, Addy," Asher encouraged his twin with an understanding smile.

Adaline released a cathartic sigh before she slapped her palms into Asher's, and he pulled her to her feet. Seeing her red-rimmed eyes and Roserie's blood on her clothes prompted him to shelve his congratulations. He glanced around the stadium before he spoke into her mind, "Whatever you want to do, Addy, I'm with you."

Adaline tried her best to smile and almost succeeded. She sniffed back tears before she replied, "I'd like to go back to the palace and spend some time alone." She peered over Asher's shoulder at Aureon and noticed Theodon wasn't beside his father anymore. "But I need to show him I'm okay, first."

Asher nodded, holding his twin's hands. "All right. Do you need me to come back with you?"

"No," she sniffed. "I'll be fine. I just need space."

Adaline examined War Ender and did her best to wipe the blood off the blade. It was a failed attempt, considering how much blood had already covered her.

"I'll handle that," her twin said, reaching for the blade, and he wiped it off and handed it back to her.

"Thank you," she said before she noticed the crowd was chanting her name. She watched them all, unsure if she felt prideful or if it added to her emotional injury. She asked Asher, "Ready?"

"Yes," he said before she teleported them into the king's box.

Adaline appeared next to Aureon, who released a sigh he was unaware he was holding. Adaline handed him his sword. "Thank you for letting me use it." She glanced around for Theodon.

Aureon disregarded her words as he cupped her face and peered through her biology. He saw emotional damage and searched through all her systems. No problems. He lifted his chin to her shoulder. "Show me." She obliged him by zipping down the side of her shirt, revealing perfect skin with no evidence of being run-through. Still, his brow tightened as he clutched her shoulders.

"I'm okay," she said with a nod while the crowd was still chanting her name. "But I need to go home."

"Home?" Aureon questioned.

"To the palace," she explained.

His shoulders sagged in relief. Aureon thought she meant she wanted to return to her miserable existence of a planet. The fact that she acknowledged the palace as home gave him the strength to let her go.

"I understand."

"I'll see you when you return," she said as she wiped away new tears.

Aureon nodded, not wanting her to leave but understanding she needed time to herself. He noticed she cringed upon hearing Theodon's reaction to Roserie's death. Adaline hugged Jim, then her brother. Before she teleported away, Asher caught her attention.

"Addy," Asher pulled her focus back to him. He waited for a few seconds before he said, "I love you, sis."

Tears spilled over the corners of Adaline's eyes. She spoke in his mind before she teleported away, "I love you, too."

CHAPTER 62

T heodon barricaded himself in the weapons tent as he struggled to get a grasp on his temper. He never really had one, so feelings of rage felt foreign and overly destructive. He went over to one weapon stand, picked it up by the bottom corner, and threw it against the adjacent wall.

"Hey, buddy," Asher joined him a moment later. He glanced around the tent at the weapons that had ricocheted all over the room. "Wanna talk?"

"Leave!" Theodon shouted. "I want no more of you humans."

"Theodon!" Aureon's voice boomed before he entered the tent. His father's gaze was almost menacing because the king was on his last nerve given the events of the day. Just before he entered the tent, he had words with Ensatus Aetrune, whose grief over his children's betrayal quickly turned to anger that manifested into unquenched revenge. Revenge Ensatus desired to exercise. Aureon posed a warning to the lord that if he and his wife did not exit the capital immediately, that Aureon would personally see to their end. Ensatus wavered and backed down, then quickly left the stadium with his wife. Aureon sent guards to escort them home and then out of the capital.

"It has been a trying day, my son," Aureon stated while rubbing his temples with one hand.

Theodon's temper almost subsided, but then Landon Elacan barged into the tent. His attention shot around the space until he found Theodon. Cristatus Elacan wasn't far behind Landon. One look at his uncle tripped Theodon's switch before Landon could raise his hands in surrender and apologize to his nephew. Theodon's fist connected with Landon's jaw hard, sending his uncle to the ground.

"Theodon!" Aureon's voice tore through his son's mind. "Enough!"

"Apologize," Aureon said aloud to his son.

Theodon's lips flattened into a defiant line.

"That is not necessary," Cristatus Elacan said, peering at his son in disappointment. "From what I know of my son, he likely deserved it."

Landon wiped the blood from his lip and stared at the red stain on the cuff of his tunic. Landon knew he was in the wrong, which was why he didn't retaliate against his nephew.

Aureon approached Cristatus. "Do you plan to remain in Theris?"

Cristatus focused on his son. "Yes. It seems that I need to get my house in order." Landon's shoulders fell at his father's statement. House Elacan was not something Landon took seriously while his father was away, hence being knee-deep in his cavalier lifestyle. "It's time for some changes." Cristatus glared at his son before turning to leave. "Come, Landon." Landon rose to his feet and reluctantly followed his father.

Aureon faced Theodon. "You are at your wit's end. I understand this as I am experiencing the same. We have finished the long process to apprehend those who killed your mother. You cannot, I repeat, you cannot take your anger for Roserie's death out on Dr. Adaline. Do you understand?"

"She killed her," Theodon threw back.

"Only after the she-elf was dumb enough to get in the ring with Addy," Asher blurted.

Theodon nailed Asher with a furious stare before he stalked out of the tent. Asher was prepared to go after him but felt Aureon's hand latch onto his shoulder.

"Let him go," Aureon said to him.

"Why is he so insufferable about that traitorous broad?" Asher asked Aureon.

Aureon's head tilted. "Were you not overly forgiving to a blinding degree at the first female to which you possessed a strong attraction?"

Asher pursed his lips to one side as he thought about it. "Mmmmaybe?"

"Imagine making such excuses for the same female for a decade."

"Wow." Asher blinked wide at Theodon's capacity to concentrate on one female for so long. Asher's ability to complete everything at super speed made it difficult for him to focus on one female for a long time, and it was a fact he'd used for his convenience for years.

"Precisely," Aureon stated. "It's difficult to get over someone when you have had plenty of years to adore that person because you are an elf who has nothing but time, Dr. Asher." Asher nodded in understanding. "Perhaps you could answer something for me," Aureon said as he began his habit of pacing.

"Sure."

"What are the two of you, truly?"

Ah, Asher thought. He noticed how enamored Aureon was when he saw Adaline in her true form. "She told you we are diviners, I'm assuming?"

"Yes, and that your purpose is to bring about the end of your world," Aureon said. "But it is apparent to me that is not the entire story."

Asher smirked. "That's true. The term diviner loosely encompassed all that we are."

"Which is?"

"We are two souls who have lived one thousand lifetimes over ten thousand years," Asher explained. "Our sole purpose was to evolve exponentially through the service to others. Over the millennia, we served our fellow humans well." Asher's expression changed to a far-off stare.

Aureon noticed the change. "But they did not serve you well in return."

Asher shook his head. "We were never supposed to be served – We knew that. But we weren't supposed to be brutalized for bringing the divine to Earth as the cost for showing our fellow humans the path." Aureon nodded in understanding. Showing people truth when they have been clinging to pre-existing dogma would have backlash.

"We never faltered in our charge, which is why our souls continued to evolve at a rapid rate versus our fellow humans," Asher explained. "In each lifetime, we had to hide so much of ourselves, yet still carry out our purpose." This current lifetime was no different. "As a result, our purpose changed as our souls evolved. Now, we are simply a pair of divine energies in human form. She is the holy fire, and I am the holy frequency. Together, we can make and unmake worlds."

"You are legitimate extensions of the divine?"

"Yes."

A moment passed as Aureon processed the information. He knew his little human was extraordinary and powerful, but the enormity of her purpose was finally sinking into his mind.

Asher chuckled. "It's a little amusing that you're amazed by this, considering the amount of power you wield."

"To which power are you referring?"

Asher looked him over. "You don't know?" Asher thought

Aureon knew how much he'd elevated his soul, and Aureon's stare didn't change. "With the amount of energy you emit, I would be surprised, nay disappointed, if it didn't pair with additional abilities beyond that which are considered normal for elves."

All things that elves could do, Aureon could do far better; his hearing, the distance he jumped, his strength, his telepathy. All his abilities surpassed those of his subjects centuries ago. Only the ability to see living things at a cellular level and influence over the weather entered his mind as additional. But for there to be more?

"Hmm," Asher said as he observed the energy that rippled off Aureon. "Your power is nature-based, correct?"

"Yes," Aureon admitted.

"Then there's much to uncover," Asher said before admitting, "I'm surprised you haven't explored this."

"What do you suggest?"

"Talk to Addy," Asher admitted. "She's the one who helped me troubleshoot or just plain unlock my abilities."

Hmm, Aureon thought. His little human continued to become more interesting as time passed. Another question entered his mind. "Did you and Adaline know each other in your past lives?"

Asher released a settling sigh as his eyes softened for a moment before he smiled. "My sister has been by my side through every lifetime."

Aureon's interest was piqued. "Do you remember them all?"

"Every—Single—One."

CHAPTER 63

T he sunset as Adaline walked up the steps to the palace. She took her time to be human, to process the day. Her strong desire to return to a wondrous state of mind seemed far away when elfin blood stained her clothes. She finally made it to her suite and left a trail of her bloody clothes on the way to the bathroom. She allowed the hot shower to wash away the blood and emotional wounds the best it could. What images she couldn't get out of her mind were not about the duels.

Every move, every death blow she delivered, she made peace with – She defended herself and annihilated evil. Adaline did as she trained to do since she was born–to deliver justice. It was the horror on Aureon's face when Talia challenged her and the pain in Theodon's cry when she stuck a sword through Roserie's heart that pained her own. She turned off the shower and turned on the faucet to fill the bathtub.

Sinking into the water, Adaline entertained the bigger picture as weariness pulled on her soul. The royals had been through so much since her first visit to Theris. And before she could blame herself for being the cause of it all, she remembered what Asher had told her about giving the royals a chance at happiness. As a result, she developed a fondness for Theodon, always seeing him as a good person in his actions and a little boy in his pain. And she developed deep, passionate feelings for his father.

Maybe we'll get to explore that now, she thought, as she tried to refocus her thoughts while towel drying her hair. She wrapped another towel around her body and wandered into her bedroom. She found her sweeper clothes already clean and folded and her dagger sheathed.

Wow, that's even quick for Ena, Adaline thought, as she glanced around the room to find no one else present. She heard intense arguing down the hallway and quickly threw her robe on before poking her head outside the door.

"Theo, you can't condemn her for this," Asher stated.

"You mistake me for someone who can be told what to do, Dr. Asher," Theodon said while giving Asher his back. Asher wasn't the type to swallow bratty behavior. He was blunt and direct like his twin, and his anger flared at the prince's pettiness. Asher grabbed the prince's shoulder, forcing Theodon to face him.

"You mistake me for someone who gives a shit about your title," Asher said, inches from Theodon's face, as electricity blazed across his eyes. "Understand that I don't care who or what you are, but I do care as to how you treat my sister... who has done nothing but *help* your family."

"Asher," Adaline said gently. Asher didn't back down, nor did he step away, but he finished communicating with words. "Theo," she said to the prince. Theodon moved to put the twins behind him, but her whisper made him stop. "You will always be my friend, Theo...."

Theodon's brows drew together as he thought about when she first said that to him in the dungeon when his father proposed his scheme. It was easy then to believe that he could remain friends with her, but it wasn't so simple once everything unfolded. Theodon left the twins standing in the hallway. Asher strode in the direction of his twin and wrapped his arms around her. A tear ran down her cheek as her twin embraced her.

"I'm gonna go rest," she whispered to Asher.

"I'm gonna go... check on a few things," Asher said. There was mischief in his tone, but Adaline didn't possess the emotional fortitude to issue warnings. She returned to her room and sat on the edge of her bed. There was a knock at the door.

"Come in," Adaline said as she glanced at the stack of clean clothes. Ena entered with Adaline's clean underwear in hand.

Ena smiled at her. "Hello, Dr. Adaline."

"Hello Ena," Adaline said. "You didn't have to clean my gear or anything. I could have done that. You do too much for me." Adaline's words triggered something in the servant because her eyes pooled with tears. Adaline approached Ena and held her by the elbows.

Before Adaline could ask Ena what was wrong, the she-elf blurted, "I couldn't possibly do enough!" Adaline was wide-eyed. "She was my friend!" Ena sobbed. "And those evil, power-hungry elves murdered her!"

Oh, Adaline realized before wrapping her arms around Ena.

Ena cried hard as Adaline did her best to comfort her. Adaline didn't stop to think who else was significantly impacted by the loss of Aravae, but it made sense. In all the memories Adaline saw, the queen's kindness extended to anyone she addressed. Her son was often the same way. Adaline's eyes watered as she thought of how the queen managed to pass that on while Theodon had no memory of his mother. It took a while for Ena to calm down before Adaline let her go. The servant stared at Adaline for a long moment.

"She was my friend," Ena said. "I found her when..." Ena looked away as her eyes watered again. She wiped her tears and turned her back to Adaline. "A second before, she was a happy new mother, and the next…" Adaline's tears slowly fell as she listened to Ena. Ena wiped away more tears as her expression turned cold. "I was so glad that someone could find out the truth. That someone could find out who did this to her, so they could be held responsible." Ena failed to stay cold in her expression as she succumbed to sobbing again.

"You knew," Adaline whispered in understanding. Ena nodded. "You told the king," Adaline reasoned. A sob tore from Ena's chest as she faced Adaline. "Can I see?" Adaline lifted her hand and stepped toward Ena. Ena glanced at Adaline's hand and nodded. Adaline rested her palm against Ena's temple, and the servant's eyes snapped shut. Adaline reached back into her memories and saw Ena coming into Aravae's room to find the queen resting. Ena stilled when she noticed her complexion was gray. Ena rushed to her bedside and put her hand against the queen's face, and all color left Ena's cheeks as she felt the queen's cold skin. A glass half-full of liquid on the nightstand caught Ena's eye.

Ena knew she didn't bring the glass into the room. She picked up the tiny spoon next to it, scooped up the liquid inside of it, and poured it on the wood surface of the nightstand. The liquid began to sizzle and burn through the wood. Ena's jaw dropped in horror. Her eyes shot around the room until her gaze landed on one of the queen's small ribbon boxes. She emptied the box, picked up the cup and spoon, and placed it carefully inside. A moment later, she was carrying it to the king's study, where an older looking Aureon, Adaline guessed it to be Cerus, held his sleeping newborn grandson.

Tears were streaming down Ena's face as she set the box in front of Cerus, opened it while explaining that she had found the queen dead. She demonstrated the toxicity of the contents of the glass as she did on the nightstand. Cerus' gaze on the burning liquid turned cold as the realization surfaced that someone murdered his daughter-in-law. Ena started to cry in front of Cerus, gauging from his discomfort; he wasn't used to handling people who cried. "You will tell no one of this, "Cerus warned, "For the culprit to be caught, we cannot disclose that we know she was murdered. Do you understand, Ena?"

"But Your Majesty-" she started before he cut her off.

"This will not be easy for any of us," he said to her. "It will take time. Patience. Do whatever you need to gather yourself, and don't return to the queen's bedroom. I will handle it from here."

Ena's downcast eyes ran with tears as she tried to sniff them back before nodding. Cerus approached her and covered one of her shoulders with his hand as he held baby Theodon in the other. Adaline could tell that simple gesture was probably the kindest thing Cerus had ever done for anyone outside of his bloodline.

"We will find out who did this, Ena," Cerus promised her. Ena could only manage another nod before she left the room.

Adaline removed her hand from Ena's temple, and both females opened their red-rimmed eyes as their tears continued to fall.

"I'm so sorry you had to go through that, Ena," Adaline whispered to her.

"It doesn't matter anymore," Ena said while wiping her face. "The promise was fulfilled." A pause hung between them. "That's why I said I couldn't possibly do enough." Ena finally managed a small smile for Adaline. Adaline leaned forward, and the two females kissed each other on the cheek.

"I'm glad I could help," was all Adaline could think to say.

Ena nodded before changing the conversation, "So, Dr. Adaline, is there anything I can get for you? Dinner?"

Food, Adaline thought. *What a great idea.*

"Is there any chance I could have dinner under the stars tonight?" Adaline asked, in need of a peaceful experience, and she hoped stargazing would do the trick.

Ena smiled at the idea. "Yes, of course. It'll be ready for you in the garden in about twenty minutes."

"Thank you."

"Thank you, Dr. Adaline."

Twenty minutes later, Adaline found herself laying on a plethora of large pillows neatly arranged for lounging, surrounded by a crisp white tent with the canopy open to the night sky. The staff brought dinner to her shortly after that. As she enjoyed the finger foods arranged for her, she felt Aureon's energy behind her, although she didn't hear his footsteps.

"Good evening," he finally said.

She glanced over her shoulder and smiled. "Hello."

The tension between them changed. Earlier it had been full of vulnerability and fear, but now it was piqued anticipation, playfulness, contentment, and relief. The king closed the flap to the tent's entrance behind him.

"Are you hungry?" she asked.

"Yes," he said.

"Here – have some food," she offered.

"I already ate."

Adaline eyed him curiously before she smiled at his cleverness. Aureon approached the pillows and stretched out across them, folding one arm behind his head. The other lay at his side as he waited for her. He gazed at the night sky while she finished her meal. The space next to him felt cold without her until she finally joined him. She giggled as he pulled her flush against the side of his body. Her hand rested on his chest, and her leg curled over his. They both sighed in unison and chuckled.

"It's finally over," Adaline whispered.

"Mmm," Aureon agreed as he played with her hair. He felt at ease with her tucked into his side, which was a far cry from what he had felt when he heard Talia challenge Adaline at the pits. His heart froze in his chest when he heard her accept the challenge. He couldn't return to the palace fast enough to see her once the duel concluded. He crossed paths with Ena as he headed for

Adaline's room, and he asked the servant if she had seen Adaline.

"Oh yes, Your Majesty," Ena confirmed. "She's finished bathing and is getting ready for dinner."

Aureon's hearing stretched in Adaline's direction, and his thoughts settled at the sound of Adaline thumbing through her wardrobe. Her heartbeat was close to a regular rate for humans.

"Did she request anything?" he asked.

"Dinner under the stars, My Lord," Ena answered.

He nodded. "Thank you, Ena."

"Of course, My Lord," she replied before Aureon headed for his suite. He planned to join Adaline after his dinner to give her space for a while longer. Now here he was, with her at his side, as they watched the stars in silence.

Adaline felt his anxiety dissipate now that they were together. They talked about the day, and Aureon covered her with the train of his robe when she yawned.

They fell asleep in each other's arms. Aureon dreamed of the duels, specifically an exact repeat of the day, refreshing him of all his thoughts and feelings. His emotions swarmed as his countenance remained neutral during Adaline's time in the pits. He feared for her, and the raw emotion prompted him to reach for Adaline in his sleep. He nuzzled her like an animal, desiring to comfort her and possess her to ease his fear. His actions roused her.

"Aureon?" Adaline said sleepily. She tried to reciprocate, but he held her down. It wasn't until he rolled her to her back and pinned her wrists over her head that a light bulb went off in her mind. She saw the faraway look in his eyes. *Lights are on, but no one is home.*

"Aureon," she said evenly. When he didn't wake up, she repeated his name louder. No change. His grip tightened around her wrists. *Okay, time to interfere,* she thought, as she froze his body over her. Adaline launched her spirit into his dream. She was stunned to see Aureon in a replay of the duels. She watched him watch her fighting Talia and heard every thought in his mind.

She shouldn't be fighting.

I cannot watch this.

I feel powerless.

Adaline was saddened, but the thoughts that followed halted her emotions.

I was supposed to keep her safe.

I cannot lose her.

Adaline pulled out of the dream. Her eyes popped open, and she looked at him lovingly. Then, slipping her wrists out of his grip, she smiled when she decided how she would wake him. She leaned up on her elbows and kissed his chin, then trailed her affections up to his ear. She wondered if his pointed ears were sensitive. She slowly kissed his earlobe before softly touching the lower crest of his ear with her tongue. She heard him inhale a gasp as her tongue traveled up to the point of his ear and flicked its tip. A guttural groan rumbled in his chest, and Adaline lowered herself to see his face.

"Are you awake, now?" she whispered playfully.

"Yes…" Aureon released a strong exhale as his eyes locked onto hers and his nostrils flared.

"Good," she said softly with a wide grin. "I'm glad. It was getting a little weird, even for me."

"What was I doing?" he asked uneasily before her latter statement clicked. "What did you say?"

"You were sleepwalking," she giggled, slipping her wrists back into his grip to show him. "After you snuggled me awake, you pinned me here." Horror filled Aureon's features to discover he was unaware of his actions. "Don't flip out," she cautioned.

"How could I not?" Aureon wanted to ramble, but she put her hand over his mouth.

"It's okay." She waited for him to focus on the problem before she took her hand away. "Your dream started to rule you. Do you remember it?"

His eyes shot from left to right. "Yes."

"It was bothering you enough to put you into action," she said as she tucked a stray strand of his hair behind his ear. She touched the tip of it before pulling her hand away. His reaction made her smile. "They're that sensitive?"

"Yes," Aureon rasped.

"Do you want me to do it again?" her voice sultry. She slowly glided her fingertip up the shell of his ear until she reached the tip and circled it with the pad of her finger. He shuddered.

"Let me down," he growled.

"Like this?" she said as she lowered him an inch. Their lips almost touched if they both reached for contact. He growled in frustration before she kissed his upper lip. "I need you to do something for me," she whispered.

"Anything," his chest heaved from a low snarl.

Adaline caressed his cheek with the backs of her fingers. "Please don't worry."

Aureon's appetite for her stilled, and he looked at her intently. "That is asking too much."

"Why?" Her head tilted.

"Because I care," he said as his eyes explored hers. He searched Adaline's gaze for her understanding of his feelings and contemplated revealing more to her. "There was more I wanted to say to you when you changed." She continued to listen in silence. "You were so beautiful," he said, confessing his captivation. He considered all he wanted to tell her when she transformed, but his words died at the sight of her. "I have never seen anything like it in all my years."

Adaline's gaze softened as a smile spread across her face and her eyes watered. She lowered his body until it covered hers. Aureon clutched her against him and kissed her hard while her hands found the ties of his sleep robe. She slipped the robe off his shoulders, causing his black hair to slide to one side, shrouding them from the rest of the kingdom. He slowed his kisses as he lifted the back of her knee and wrapped her leg around him.

"Um, Your Majesty," Adaline whispered. Aureon stilled over her as he steadied himself on one arm. She was distracted by the muscles in his shoulders before she could finish her thought. Instead of speaking, she leaned forward to kiss his chest as her leg squeezed him to her, disregarding verbally acknowledging that he was naked under his robe.

He took her hand, kissed its palm, and placed it flat against his heart. "I like it best when you call me by my name."

"You heard me?"

"Through the haze, yes," he admitted. He leaned down to kiss Adaline. "It was the same as when I experienced the madness. It did not matter what rage I expressed. If you were near, I could navigate what was happening to me objectively and allow myself to feel." She was his anchor, he knew. She was the one person who could physically and emotionally handle him no matter his state of being.

"I'm glad you found comfort in my helping you," she said, admitting, "I wish you would have let me do more..."

His amusement was evident as he kept one hand holding her wrists over her head while he stripped her of her clothes with the other. "You rid me of a fate of dying too early, unmasked the dormant strength of my power, revealed all of my enemies, and you are wishing I let you do more?" His attention was quickly becoming lost on her creamy flesh.

"I mean... when it came to your healing," she said as she lifted her chin, prompting him to focus on her words. "I would have liked for the process to be over for you sooner because I didn't want you suffering for so long."

Aureon kissed her hard as he pressed his body into hers. She reciprocated his enthusiasm until he pulled away. The anchoring embrace of her legs wrapped around his hips showed him she wouldn't let him go far. The thrill caused him to grind against her slowly, and she gasped at the friction.

"Addy," he whispered, not allowing his lips to wander far from hers.

"Aureon," she whispered back before she stole a kiss.

A smile crossed his face. "I need to make you mine, little human."

Adaline's head tilted. "What does that mean?"

Aureon quietly thought about it for a moment, leaving Adaline to listen to the symphony of sounds that occurred at night in the garden. Before she could get carried away in it, he formed his answer.

"You would be my female in all things," he explained.

"And you want to be my male in all things?" she inquired.

"Yes," he said.

"No sharing," she said, needing clarification. Aureon's eyes blazed as those words hit his ears. "Before you erupt," she rushed, "I'm asking for clarification because royals in my world had some philandering kings, and I don't know how elfin ones operate."

"I do not share," Aureon annunciated perfectly. The rage behind his eyes simmered as he waited for her response.

"Neither do I," Adaline whispered. A smile crossed her face before she planted a soft kiss on his lips.

The heaving of his chest subsided, and his temper receded before he said, "Elves mate for life. The mate bond is almost impossible to break."

"And you want this bond between us?"

Aureon nodded firmly. He was glad he had the opportunity to introduce the bond to her earlier because he didn't want to spook her with the gravity of the meaning behind it. He was ready to take the time to show her the benefits of the connection, and he looked forward to witnessing her discover parts of it for herself. It was a miraculous and magical connection that no elf could resist desiring. He was eager to show her and experience it with her but needed this formality clear before they began.

Adaline's doe eyes focused on him as she pondered his words as he waited patiently for any further questions. After all that had happened, he wanted her willing. Whatever would make it so, he was ready to provide – but he would not share her. His eyes searched hers as she seemed decided.

"I have a few questions," she admitted.

Aureon wasn't surprised. "Go on," he said as he rolled onto his back, bringing her with him. She sprawled on his chest then pushed up on her forearms.

"How much does it hurt?"

"Only the first time at the moment you choose to accept the connection."

"Is it permanent?"

"It is meant to be," he answered as his fingers ran through the soft strands of her hair.

She cast him a sidelong glance. "How can you help lessen the pain of the connection?"

He leaned up and kissed her. "By making love to you, slowly."

Her brows lifted. "Slowly?"

"Mmm-hmm," rumbled from his chest as he rubbed her back.

She smiled. "I require a demonstration."

Aureon considered her for a long moment, content with her emotional recovery from the outcome of her duel with Roserie. He rolled her onto her back and raised himself over her. Their eyes locked while he pushed away the rest of her robe, and he lifted her hips with one hand and slid a pillow underneath her with the other. He skimmed the tip of his nose along her cheekbone before his lips sank a kiss into her cheek. His fingertips trailed down from her collarbone to between her breasts, to her belly. His hand ventured lower until his middle finger caressed the seam of her feminine folds before parting them. He groaned at how wet she was and immediately sank his finger inside of her. She gasped and clutched his shoulders as her legs tensed at the pleasure. His chest rumbled at her readiness, and he released his finger. She whimpered at its absence as he reached for her ankle.

"One day, little human," Aureon said to her while placing her heel at his shoulder before reaching for her other ankle. "We will explore foreplay." He rested her other ankle on his opposite shoulder and leveraged some of his weight against her straightened legs.

"But not today," Adaline moaned as the tip of his cock nudged past her entrance.

"Definitely not," he confirmed, as he pushed inside of her in one gliding thrust, anchoring himself in his mate. Their bodies sighed at the tight, hot connection. He clutched her hips. *I could not deny myself of her, not for a single day*, he thought as his shaft pulsed inside of her. He watched her as he thrust. She moaned as her wet walls clenched him, and her legs shook. "So soon?" he asked her as he reveled in her responsiveness. He couldn't help pumping through her body's reaction.

"No, it's… it's different," Adaline moaned. "You're rubbing my G-spot." His head tilted. She quickly explained what it was, and he nodded in understanding as he thrust again. She cried out in pleasure, and he shuddered.

"Can you stand the pleasure?" Aureon asked, his voice growing ragged as he embraced the slow, steady rhythm of his hips.

She moaned. "Barely."

A contented sound stirred in his chest as he watched her body experience sustained ecstasy. Their joining brought him pleasure he yearned to express. And this, seeing her so vulnerable while under his care, inspired him.

Adaline let out a hard exhale as she felt a pressure change that made her purr. "Did you just get bigger?"

"Yes," Aureon hissed as he cupped her bottom in both hands and worked her along his length. His brow drew tight as he concentrated on pumping into her, as he rumbled words in Tear. His head fell back toward the ceiling as his eyes closed, and he let his other senses overtake him. He growled when she arched her back, rotating her hips to where he could grind against her clitoris. Her body tensed in his hands, so he readjusted before moving faster.

"Aureon, I'm-" Adaline cried out again as her legs continued to shake.

His lip curled back over his teeth as he felt her wetness grow. His brows drew tight as he watched where their bodies joined. He was thrusting so hard that he was moving her across the pillows. She latched onto his knees, regaining the leverage of his weight on her. He continued to graze her G-spot with precise repetition, and her eyes widened at the overstimulation he wrought. She needed release, and she needed it now. She grabbed his hand and brought it to her breast. She reached for his other hand and did the same with it. He started to thumb and squeeze her nipples as his weight pushed against her legs.

"Yes," she hissed until a cry escaped her. "Like that – more of that!"

Aureon growled as he played with her soft curves before leaning down far enough to snake his tongue over one tightened bud. She gasped as she reached to grab the pillow over her head as she came. Her body squeezed his over and over as he growled through each thrust of her orgasm. He continued to stimulate her, and her legs continued to shake.

"I can't stop-" Adaline said, powerless.

"Almost there," he grunted as he felt a surge within him at the base of his spine. He called out Adaline's name as his back bowed, causing him to thrust deep as he came. "Not finished," he bit out as he picked up her hips and worked her over his length. She continued to clench his shaft as she cried out in pleasure while he prolonged their ecstasy, setting her off again.

"Aureon," she panted as she released her grip on the pillow she clutched overhead.

"Addy," he groaned, as his brows drew tight while he grappled with his self-control. Sensitivity rocked every cell of his being. When the spasms receded, he sat back on his haunches, still holding her, refusing to withdraw from her body. He peered at her with a sated gaze, realizing that sex with her was so fulfilling that it scared him. He could not stand the thought of being without her, without this consuming magnetism between them.

Must protect this, always, Aureon thought as he leaned down and kissed her lips, then her forehead. He turned them onto their sides, facing each other, as their breathing normalized. He reached for his robe and threw it over them before pulling it high enough to cover her shoulders. He tucked her against his chest and kissed her forehead again. She shivered.

"Sleep, little human," he whispered as his protectiveness enveloped her.

CHAPTER 64

Adaline awakened warm and cozy as dawn approached. Aureon tucked her back against his hard chest, with one arm wrapped around her front. His hand clutched her breast as his body cradled hers. She smiled, and although she didn't move, he could sense her awaken. His hyperawareness of her made him rouse to clutch her closer to him, nuzzle her ear, then bury his face in her hair. As soon as her eyes fluttered closed after he finished adjusting, her eyes shot open when she remembered Theodon was leaving for his reconnaissance mission that morning. Then she noticed they were in Aureon's bed. He must have carried her in after they had fallen asleep in the tent last night. That meant her force field didn't cover her while she slept, she realized. She felt safe, so her ability didn't activate. She smiled to herself.

"Aureon," she whispered while rubbing his arm that was covering her. The gesture earned her a grunt. "Your son is leaving this morning." He stirred, stretched his body, and squeezed on hers. His breath teased her neck, prompting her to offer it up to him. "Kisses," she requested. He didn't hesitate to deliver. He looked like he was going to get up, then pulled her underneath him. She squeaked in surprise then giggled. He nuzzled her neck and her ear before kissing her.

"Good morning," the words stirred sleepily from his throat.

"Good morning." She smiled.

Aureon rested his forehead against hers. Their auras sizzled as the vibration radiated through her body, causing her to shiver. "Your son needs you," she reminded him. "Are you going to say goodbye?" His focus stilled for a moment. "You haven't in the past," she knew. He shook his head, ashamed. She lifted his chin. "Well, you can start today. Do you want me to go with you?" She would be supportive even if Theodon wasn't happy with her right now.

He shook his head. "I will handle it." He leaned down to kiss her on the nose. "Stay here."

"Okay," she said as she snuggled under the covers.

He squeezed her bottom before stepping away from the bed to get dressed. He made it halfway to the other side of the palace in an instant and heard his son and his crew finishing their packing for the journey. Aureon stated, "Wait," at an average volume as they were about to head out.

One of Theodon's pointed ears twitched as he received the information. "Yes, Father."

Aureon strode out the rear entrance to the palace to find his son along with his crew. They froze at attention when they saw the king. Aureon surveyed each of his son's choices, and he concluded they were adequate. They only had one job: to protect their prince. He faced his son and said, "Be safe." He was a little stiff in his delivery, but he meant well. Aureon was still adjusting to showing emotion for his son, especially with others present.

Theodon's surprise was evident. "I will, Father."

The king stepped forward and embraced his son, and Theodon froze. Then the prince realized he should probably respond. Both males slapped each other on the backs, and the king squeezed his son's shoulder before letting him go. Aureon addressed Theodon's crew, "Bring him home safely." He acknowledged Forb with a nod.

"Yes, Your Majesty," they said in unison.

Aureon made a sharp turn on his heel and left. Theodon remained there, stunned.

"Do not look so shocked," Aureon said in Theodon's mind as he strode back to his suite.

Realizing who might have encouraged him to show his feelings hit Theodon, and his face fell. He had been consumed by his anger over Adaline killing Roserie that it had blinded him from seeing the human's consistency of unconditional friendship to him. She made both him and his father better males, and he was punishing her for his thick-headedness. He would apologize to her when he returned from his mission, he decided. "Keep her safe so I can make things right once I return," Theodon replied to his father.

Aureon smirked for no one to see. He slipped back into his room and heard the shower running, and his robe pooled on the floor. He joined Adaline under the water, making love to her for the first time since the night before. Carrying her in his arms to put her in bed next to him last night brought him gratification he hadn't experienced in a long time. She brought forth his emotions with ease. To avoid the feelings would mean to avoid her and that he could not handle.

As much as he wanted to think about a future with her, he didn't let his mind run wild. Because a future with her meant she would accept the mate bond, and that hadn't happened yet. However, that loose end wasn't making him feel vulnerable because he was sure she had more questions for him first. But it didn't mean he yearned for the bond to exist between them any less. He decided he would remain content because she chose his world to live in permanently until she decided. Now, he could do for her all an elf would do once finding his mate; He could begin courting her.

Adaline and Aureon kicked questions and answers back and forth throughout the day when they ran into each other, as he saw to his duties, and she planned her financial future. He finally asked her about the unlocking of his abilities.

Adaline smiled in relief as she'd forgotten about it during her errands. "I'm so glad you asked about that! I've wanted to talk to you about that since you told me you don't need much sleep." Aureon looked at her questioningly. "I do believe you need more sleep, but you carry so much power without spending any of it that it keeps your mind awake, causing you to believe you need only a few hours every night."

For Aureon to sleep only three or four hours each night had been a common practice for him for centuries. He never gave sleeping for a short time a second thought, but if she wanted to test the reason behind it, he was open to it.

"What power are we unveiling?" he asked, glancing down at himself.

She looked him over for a moment. "Your abilities are linked to your natural magic, so you likely have abilities that exist in nature."

"Like my influence over the weather?"

"That's one, yes," Adaline said. "But there's also flying like a bird, moving like the wind, swimming like a fish, and possibly shape-shifting. Should we start with those?" Aureon's eyebrows lifted in surprise before he nodded. They stood facing each other in the garden, and she offered her hands to him. "Place your hands over mine," she instructed. He did so without hesitation. Her gaze turned far away as she scanned his soul to see his abilities and how to bring them to the surface. She nodded.

"All right, close your eyes and picture what I say." His large eyes slid shut as his palms rested against hers. "Take a deep breath in and let it go," she advised. Once he did, she continued. "Picture the largest bird that exists in Theris, the most beautiful one with the largest wingspan." She let a moment pass. "Now, picture yourself as the bird, and imagine standing at the edge of a calm lake, about to take flight." She smirked when she felt his ability kick in, and she lifted against his palms. He floated an inch off the ground. "Your attention turns toward home across the lake. You take a step, and another, while your large wings flap and lift you into the air." She smiled as she looked down to see Aureon's feet about a foot off the ground. She used her hovering ability to float along with him. "Your wide wings spread to their full length, and you begin to soar high into the sky."

Aureon's eyes remained closed as he lifted himself another two feet off the ground. She grinned. "Now, very slowly, open your eyes and look at me." His eyes slid open, and he immediately unsteadied. "Don't look down," she said. He didn't. "You are about three feet off the ground," she said calmly. "You're doing very well." She reached to unhook the clasp of his outer robe and let it fall to the ground, so he didn't have excess fabric that would cause drag in flight. Aureon steadied his thoughts and waited for her guidance.

"Asher," Adaline said in her twin's mind. "You are needed in the garden."

A flash blurred next to them, and Asher appeared. He smiled up at them. "Yes! Flying!" he cheered. It was one of his favorite things to do. Adaline could hover, almost like surfing through the air, but Asher could soar through the sky.

"Join us," Adaline said.

"Sure," Asher said before he effortlessly pushed off the ground and hovered next to Aureon.

"You, too?" Aureon asked.

Asher grinned. "Oh yeah."

"Since I can't fly the same way, I thought Asher could lead you through this next part," Adaline shared.

"Now let go of her hands, big guy," Asher said to Aureon. The king clutched at Adaline's hands as soon as Asher instructed him to let go.

"It's okay," Asher said. "You won't go anywhere." Adaline slipped her hands from his but still hovered in front of him. Aureon stabilized in the air as Asher's hand landed on his shoulder. "Now, we are going to soar. Look up and think the word."

Aureon's chin lifted toward the sky, and the moment he thought to soar, he did. Energy exploded from his feet, and he flew with Asher close behind him, coaching him along the way. Adaline remained on the ground, with her hand shielding the sunlight from her eyes as she watched them. As they dove toward the planet's surface, their speed produced a sonic boom.

Gesso rushed to the garden to inform the king that his lunch with the elders was starting.

"He'll be landing shortly, Gesso," Adaline said, pointing at the sky as the king flew by with Asher in tow. The servant gaped as he watched his king fly, and Adaline chuckled. Asher and Aureon came in for a landing. Asher touched down first, and Aureon perfectly mimicked his landing. Adaline gauged Aureon's energy. The usual amount of energy that rippled off him was lesser than when he began flying. "Now that you have spent some energy, you will sleep better. How did that feel?"

Aureon inhaled deeply and exhaled. "Invigorating." He slapped Asher on the back. "Thanks to this one."

"Anytime," Asher chuckled.

"My Lord?" Gesso asked timidly, afraid to approach his king.

"Yes, Gesso?" Aureon asked.

"Your lunch with the elders has begun, Your Majesty," Gesso offered.

"Ah, yes," Aureon said as he turned to leave but stopped and addressed Adaline. He picked up her hand and kissed the back of it. "Thank you, Dr. Adaline. May I take you out tonight?"

Adaline's eyebrows lifted in surprise. "You're asking me on a date?"

"Absolutely," he said as he pulled on her hand, bringing her closer to him. He waited for her answer.

"Okay," Adaline replied, as she felt the humming vibration that happened when he touched her.

"I will see you in the throne room this evening," Aureon said as he allowed her hand to slip from his before heading to his lunch meeting. He was glad she had no desire to return to Earth, and he couldn't handle his son and his mate leaving him on the same day.

"So that's what it takes," Asher said, with his arms crossed over his chest.

"What are you talking about?" Adaline asked him as her cheek color returned to normal.

"To score a date with the king, a girl's gotta save his life a few times and teach him how to fly," he jested.

"That's nothing," Adaline joked. "You should've seen what it took to use his pool!"

CHAPTER 65

Theodon and his team arrived at the eastern border of the kingdom by sundown. The group peered over the edge through the dense forest that made the strong walls of Theris. Their pointed ears leaned toward the east to listen for skirmishes.

Silence.

Odd, Theodon thought.

"We will take shifts in pairs," Theodon whispered before he named the pairs of elves that would take the first, second, and third watch. Theodon would take the first shift with Forb, even though he knew he'd be wide awake through the third watch, too. No matter the sleep schedule he tried to maintain, he always woke up well before dawn, and his father thought it a good practice and common among younger elves.

His father.

Theodon reflected on their good-bye earlier that day during the ride to the border. As he accepted a shift in his father's behavior, he made a promise to himself that he'd try his best to do the same. His father had always been cold and disconnected from him. Theodon's mother's passing had hit the king hard, as explained to Theodon by his grandfather. As a result, his father's lack of warmth was behavior Theodon knew as usual. Theodon didn't throw a tantrum or become a difficult child as a result. Instead, he accepted it as his reality and did all he could to be the best, including his frustrations. After all, he would be king one day. Of all things, Theodon didn't want his father to have any doubt in his ability to secede him. He wanted his father's confidence in that one thing, and he could live without the rest.

Or, so he thought.

Then guards hauled one human doctor into the palace, and his father began to show signs of change. After all these centuries, Theodon found himself clinging desperately to hope that the change was permanent, and the latter was a phase due to loss and nothing more. It ended up obliterating an old thought in the back of his mind: that his father's disconnect from him was Theodon's fault.

Theodon took first watch with Forb. Forb was excited to go on Theodon's mission, and Theodon was happy to have one true friend once the trials were over. The two of them left the camp to see what they could find in the darkness.

"We are not going over the border," Forb said as he saw Theodon cross into the Shadow Lands.

"Yes, we are," the prince said.

"No," Forb was firm. "We promised your father."

"I cannot get the information he sent me for unless I go," Theodon argued in a whisper. "Would you rather stay behind and have me go alone?"

Forb sighed hard, defeated, then followed Theodon while griping to himself under his breath. "You were the reason I got into so much trouble when we were younglings."

Theodon smirked. "And I take full responsibility."

The two crept into the Vorcat camp quieter than the still night. Forb kept watch while Theodon slipped inside the largest tent. Inside, a large Vorcat was snoring in his sleep against the far wall with his back turned. The tent smelled of decay, a familiar scent found around Vorcats. As evolved as the large, upright felines were, they still embraced their old ways of eating their enemies after a day of fighting. Theodon's nose wrinkled at the stench, and then he moved over to the large table. On it, a map of the lands and figurines marked their battle strategy. The Vorcats planned to march on Theris after defeating the Shadow Dwarves.

This will not do, Theodon thought like his father.

The elves snuck into the Shadow Dwarf camp with the same stealth finesse as they did to the Vorcat camp. Theodon was shocked to find that the Shadow Dwarves had also planned to turn on Theris after annihilating the Vorcats.

Enemies on both sides, Theodon thought.

Theodon and Forb withdrew from the Shadow Dwarf camp, but not unnoticed. The Shadow Dwarf king awakened just in time to see the elves fleeing on the horizon. Instead of waking his camp and calling for his soldiers to be ready to fight, he sat back and concocted a plan. *I will take something precious to Theris*, he thought, as he stared after the elf prince who was fading from view. He thought about how it had been a long time since anyone delivered a lethal blow to King Aureon. *Effective, it was*, he thought, as he recalled the death of the elf queen.

One of Theodon's pointed ears twitched as the realization hit. "Someone saw us leave." He went on high alert when the two of them returned to camp as the second set of elves started their watch. The prince's command silenced the group's whispered argument about the fact that Theodon and Forb had crossed the border. "Prepare for battle."

*****

Adaline was fixing her hair for her date with Aureon as Ena was refreshing her room. "Ena?" Adaline asked, "would you happen to know where the king is taking me this evening?"

Ena stopped what she was doing. "I do know, Dr. Adaline, but I'm not allowed to say."

Adaline pursed her lips, impressed at the loyal vault of information Ena kept secret. "Fair enough, but all I need is an idea as to what is appropriate to wear. Can you help me with that?"

Ena thought for a moment. "An understated gown would be appropriate."

"Okay, I can work with that," she said. "Thank you, Ena."

"Of course, Dr. Adaline," Ena said before she disappeared from the room.

Adaline opened the door to her wardrobe, flipped through a few gowns toward the back, and selected a suitable choice. She styled her hair in an upswept fashion and finished it off by wearing the comb he gave her for her fake wedding. The fuchsia gown shifted on the hanger until the silhouette reflected Adaline's desire for the v-neckline to dip deeper than initially constructed. She buckled her heels and checked her appearance in the mirror, feeling as if something was missing. She opened the shallow drawers of her vanity to find a dainty bracelet that matched her dress and slipped it on.

Aureon waited patiently for Adaline in the throne room. He wore no extravagant robes and instead presented himself as understated yet refined in his clothing. His ear twitched when he heard her walking down the hall toward the throne room, and his interest piqued when he heard the clicking of her heels against the stone floor. When he turned to watch her enter the room, his eyes met hers, then dropped to her mouth, her cleavage, then took in all of her at once. His chest swelled with pride as he moved toward her. He offered his hand, brought hers to his mouth, and kissed it slowly while his eyes absorbed her every detail.

"You look gorgeous," he said.

"You look insatiable," she jested, with a smile hanging on her lips as she felt his attraction for her.

"You bring it out in me, little human," he rasped as he inhaled her scent from her wrist. She giggled and blushed. He placed her hand in the crook of his elbow without taking his eyes off her. "There is quite a night ahead of us."

"Then let's not keep the night waiting." She smiled at him as she squeezed his elbow. The two of them walked out of the palace and into the streets of the capital. Subjects stopped to bow when they recognized the king, and some regarded Adaline with awe.

"They want to approach you," Aureon said, scanning everyone in sight as he led her to their destination.

"Why?"

"Some want to give thanks for helping their queen," he shared. "And others are curious as to what the fire goddess is like without her fire."

Adaline's head snapped in his direction. "Fire goddess?"

"Yes, that rumor is my fault," he admitted as he continued to scan through everyone they passed. Adaline's eyes widened in surprise. "It is also one I will never correct."

She laughed, and he smiled. Everyone around them was captivated by their king doting on a female since it was such a foreign notion to witness. Aureon escorted her down a narrow path flanked by torches. Eventually, they ended up at the entrance to a large tree where a young she-elf stood at a podium in front of the door. Her eyes widened when she saw the king and stepped out from behind the podium to greet him with a bow. She nodded at Adaline and smiled.

"Dinner for two, Your Majesty?" the young she-elf asked in Tear.

"Yes, over the southern branches," he clarified in his native tongue.

"Yes, Your Majesty," she said quickly. "Please, follow me."

Aureon gestured for Adaline to follow the hostess, who led them up a carved staircase inside the tree. Adaline could smell food being prepared and noticed a dish that smelled mouth-watering before being led to a carved-out room high in the tree.

Adaline stopped at the edge of a platform in the center of the space. On top of it were two chairs and a small table, and ropes on pulleys were mounted overhead and secured to each platform corner, carrying it like a basket. Adaline's mind raced before the hostess gestured for her and Aureon to take a seat. Aureon pulled out a chair for her before seating himself. He found Adaline's curious gaze shooting around the space amusing as he committed to his choice to reveal nothing to her, allowing her to be surprised by a new experience. Elves rushed in to arrange food on the table before scattering from the room.

"Are you ready, Your Majesty?" the hostess asked.

"Yes, we are ready," he said in Tear, as his eyes remained on Adaline.

Another elf entered the room and moved to the station where the ropes from every pulley met. The elf chose a line and unknotted it before pulling on it steadily. Adaline gasped in surprise as the platform lifted off the ground and propelled out of the room. The elf kept pulling, sending their platform far out into the night air as the platform hung from the sturdy branch overhead.

"Now I know how you felt when you were learning to fly today," Adaline said. Aureon laughed. Adaline's eyes shot around. "So, dinner for two in a very tall tree?"

"With a three-hundred-sixty-degree view," Aureon pointed out.

Adaline turned in her chair to take in the view, helpless in succumbing to wonder. "What is this place?"

"This is Helious' restaurant called Heartwood," Aureon shared. The elder needed something to occupy his time now that his sons are grown and ventured out along with their mother, and Helious always had an affinity for good food.

"I commend him for his imagination. This is a brilliant setup," Adaline said while still entranced by the view. "It's so beautiful up here."

"It is," he agreed.

They settled into their meal, and Adaline marveled at how the elves curated the food in such detail, like an intricate charcuterie table. As they talked, it didn't take Aureon long to reach for her chair and pull it closer to him. Then they started to feed each other as they laughed, joked, and took in the sights that surrounded them. He pointed out significant landmarks to her.

"What's that one over there?" Adaline pointed to the west, where she saw what appeared to be a giant statue.

Aureon's gaze focused on what she was pointing at and sighed. "It's the statue of everlasting love. It immortalizes the story of Itol and Varassna. They were lovers who met during the war of the Hexaborgs." Their lives ended tragically due to the old magic that once saved them both. After the war, Aureon heard of the couple's tragedy and the baby they had left behind. He made sure to place the youngling with a loving family. It was the only happy ending in the love story.

"I'm guessing from your tone that it's a romantic notion but a sad story," Adaline said.

"Tragic."

"And you don't want to dampen the moment."

"Correct."

"Very well then," Adaline said as she continued to stare off into the horizon, discovering the details of Theris from a bird's-eye view.

Aureon wrapped an arm around her and pulled her even closer. He tipped her chin up to him to dominate her focus. His expression turned thoughtful. "Thank you for today."

"For what?"

"For showing me how to fly."

She was ready to deflect, to bring to his attention that Asher taught him to fly, but she noticed he needed her to receive the compliment he was giving. "You're welcome." Her eyes softened as she smiled. "Did you have fun?" A smile tugged at the corner of his mouth as excitement lit his eyes. He nodded. "Good."

Aureon's mouth covered hers, communicating the emotions behind his words. His kiss turned hungry, and she separated from him abruptly. "Be careful," she breathed with a giggle. "Extreme emotion can bring forward dormant abilities, too."

He blinked in surprise. "Truly?"

Adaline grinned and nodded. "After I bought my first house, I was so happy that I made it disintegrate." His eyes widened. She laughed. "But it was okay because I fixed it."

Aureon smiled and gave her a gentle kiss as they felt the rope tugging their platform back to the tree. Aureon could feel all eyes of the restaurant staff on them as the platform was lowered to the floor, but he didn't part from his little human, who was wrapped up in him as she clutched his collar. He caressed her cheek before parting from her, with his eyes still taking her in. Hers searched the room to see who was present, and she blushed. He turned her chin so she'd face him and leaned in to touch the tip of his nose to hers. He stood up and offered her his hand.

They finally faced everyone in the restaurant, who took the time to bow to the king. Afterward, their eyes remained on Adaline. It wasn't out of fear or suspicion but reverence. Adaline smiled and blew a light ball into her hand, Larger than usual. The light reflected in each surrounding elves' eyes, and their eyes widened in surprise.

"Hold still," she said, then heard Aureon repeat what she said in Tear before she stepped forward and realized he would not let go of her hand. She blew at the top of the ball, and pieces as small as glitter floated from it, landing on the restaurant staff. The top of everyone's heads and shoulders glowed before the light absorbed into their bodies. A few breathed deeply, shocked by the instant difference in their health.

The youngling hostess bound forward and wrapped her

arms around Adaline, who was surprised by the touch. Everyone in the room gasped, but Adaline just chuckled and patted the youngling on the back.

"Pardon the youngling," a familiar voice came from the back of the crowd. The group parted for Helious to step through. "She's still a bit green when it comes to personal space." The youngling finally let go of Adaline and hurried back to her station.

"That's all right," Adaline said.

"You two caused quite a stir by being here." Helious studied them knowingly. Aureon and Adaline glanced at each other as Aureon pulled her against his side, and Adaline barely stifled a smile. Neither of them made excuses or apologies to Helious, and Helious' light green stare moved to Adaline. "They want to celebrate you."

"Pardon?" she asked.

"The elves, not just my staff, want to throw a party in your honor for all you have done for the kingdom," Helious explained.

Adaline's eyebrows lifted. "All right."

"All right." Helious nodded, and the room cheered.

"They want to do it soon but will wait for you to set a date," Helious said to her.

"I will have a date for them within the next few days," Adaline confirmed.

Aureon squeezed her hand as the two of them left the restaurant in silence. Aureon led her along the narrow path to their next destination, and he glanced down to see her heels peeking out from under the hemline of her gown.

"Do your feet hurt?" he asked her.

"No, not yet," she said.

Aureon's lips flattened, then he bent down and swept her up into his arms. "Close your eyes," he said. She did. "Before you teleport us to the place I am thinking of, remember to keep your eyes closed after we arrive."

"I'm intrigued," she whispered.

"Good," he said. "All right, when you are ready."

A moment later, Aureon stood inside the auditorium where Adaline watched her first Ileoton Symphony performance. The skylights remained cracked to let narrow lines of glittering moonlight mark the floor. Adaline could feel Aureon's excitement as he carried her through the space. She patted his chest before interlocking her fingers behind his neck.

"No peeking," he said.

"I'm not."

He set her down on something soft. Goosebumps broke out over her legs when she felt his hand cover her foot and unclasp her shoe.

"What are you doing?" she asked.

"Making you more comfortable," he commented as he took off her other shoe. He sat next to her and tucked her against his side.

"Better?" he asked.

"Mmm, much better."

"Open your eyes."

Adaline slowly opened her eyes. As her gaze shifted around the space, she noted that the big, comfy seats she sank into were from the large couches in the orchestra section of the auditorium where she recently heard the most beautiful live music. *Unforgettable*, she thought, reminiscing as she cozied up next to him in the romantically lit space. "I like this place," she admitted, as her heart thrummed with joy.

"I know," Aureon said, gazing down at her. He didn't take his eyes off her as one elf quietly wandered onto the stage, followed by another, and then more joined. Her eyes widened as she perked up, curious as they all filed in and picked up an instrument. They quietly seated themselves and began to play romantic music that quickly settled into Adaline's heart at the cue of their maestro. Aureon couldn't tear his gaze away from her. To see the wonder on the face of a divine being was something he never wanted to forget for the rest of his life.

Adaline's eyes watered. "You did this for me?"

"Yes," he said as his arm slid around her.

Adaline listened in silence as she clutched onto him, unwilling to soften her grip. A tear threatened to spill from the corner of her eye. Aureon reached into his vest, pulled out his handkerchief, and handed it to Adaline. She took it, whispered her thanks, and used it. The simple exchange meant the world to him. He had the most powerful being in the world sitting next to him, and he was able to find ways to provide for her. He could make this work between them, between the two most unlikely creatures to ever meet. He could add to her happiness as she inspired his own. They could build a life together. As he yearned for the future that he dared to envision, he unknowingly pushed on the mate bond that was trying to form in her mind. She hissed in a wince as her eyes slammed shut.

Concerned, he tilted her face up to his. "I am sorry."

"It's okay," she said as she sniffed back another tear.

Aureon placed a gentle kiss on her forehead. He didn't like that she was in pain, he didn't like being without the bond either, but he would wait until she came to a decision. As much as he wanted it, he also wanted what was best for her. She felt his tension and poured more light into his chest as the symphony entertained her.

Aureon rose to his feet and offered his hand, and she took it. He slowly pulled her close and set her hand on his shoulder as he cradled her other hand while his free hand rested high on her waist. When he brought her closer, his cheek rested against hers as he led her across the small orchestra floor. Lost in their private world as time flew, they continued to sway long after the music stopped and the musicians had gone.

"Let's return home," he whispered. A moment later, they stood in front of the door to his suite.

"I need something from my room," Adaline mentioned as

she turned in the opposite direction, but he remained planted and didn't let go of her hand. Although confused by his resistance, she watched him lead her to the suite that was the last door on the right, just before the king's suite. He gestured for her to enter, and she opened the door to find her room had been relocated.

"You moved my room?" she asked him.

"You were too far away," he said, following close behind her before he closed the door.

Adaline approached the wardrobe to pull her favorite dark pink robe, and a question hit her. "What does it feel like?" A beat passed before it registered that she was referring to the mate bond. He took a moment to form an answer for her.

"It is a feeling of intense connection," he admitted. "But not overbearing. It is a completing feeling as if evolving into something greater. There is…. no other experience that comes close to it."

Adaline could feel his breath on her neck as her thoughts circled his answer. She stopped reaching for the robe and faced him. "And you want this with me?"

Aureon's brows drew tight as he nodded. She cupped his cheek and leaned up to kiss him. Their sweet connection turned hungry, and his clothes disappeared as she backed him onto her balcony. She pushed him down onto one of the long lounge chairs and climbed up into his lap. He grabbed the deep v-neck of the dress and tore it off her. He was surprised she wore no undergarments; his attention was lost on her gorgeous form. She smiled and pushed him onto his back before he could get his hands on her. She grabbed his hands and held them away from her curves, and she smirked before her expression changed to an exaggerated seriousness. "I think it's time we experienced something." She rocked back against his growing erection, and he growled low.

"And what is that?" Aureon asked as his fingers curled,

wanting to sink into her soft curves.

"Foreplay," she waggled her eyebrows. Before Aureon could laugh or protest, she flicked her hand in the air, binding his wrists over his head and his ankles to the lounge chair. His arms flexed. "Don't fight it," she said before leaning down to place a kiss on his chest. "I promise a pleasurable experience for the both of us." The contact of her lips against his skin made him still. The tension left his breathing, and he tried adjusting on the chair. "Agreed?"

"Agreed," thundered in his throat.

"Good," she said. There was something she had discovered many years ago. It wasn't a super-human ability, but she thought it wasn't used properly and deemed this a perfect moment for it. She hovered her hand a couple of inches from Aureon's chest.

"Up," his energy directed.

Adaline floated her hand up toward the side of his neck and felt his energy heat up. She let her fingertips barely caress his skin there and noticed his breathing change.

"What are you doing to me?" he rasped as his nerve endings caught fire.

"Exactly what your body is telling me to do," she whispered before leaning over the same area and planting a soft kiss there, making sure no other part of them touched.

"This is not one of your abilities?" he said hoarsely.

"No, this is just us," she confessed, as her fingertips grazed the shell of his ear as they traveled higher. He sank into the euphoric state that came with being intimate with her, and she noticed the shift in him. "There we go," she whispered in praise as her hand continued to sweep over him. "Just enjoy and show me where to go."

Adaline's fingertips, palm touches, and soft kisses spread all over his skin where his energy directed her. His erection strained against the front of his pants as she moved down his body. As she kissed down his torso, her unoccupied hand unlaced his pants. The freeing of his shaft tripped his switch, and he put pressure against his wrist restraints, needing to touch her. His muscles rippled as the wood in the lounge chair creaked then cracked as she was about to take him in hand. Her attention lifted in surprise as his wrists broke free. He grabbed her waist and pulled her up his body until her hips were against his chest. He moved her legs to make her straddle him. She noticed his brows drew tight with sweat gathered on his forehead. His resolve was wavering, but he wanted them both to share in the intense pleasure. His eyes locked with hers as he cradled her bottom in one hand and grasped his erection in the other as he sat up. He lowered her slowly, even after the tip of his cock pushed past her folds. Adaline moaned at the slow, torturous intrusion. She glanced over her shoulder to watch their bodies connect. He leaned forward to close his mouth over one of her hardened nipples. Her fingers sank into his shoulders as she breathed his name.

"Mmm, yes," He growled at her taste before he leaned back to thrust his hips up off the chair to slide to the hilt. He loved looking up at her in this position, so he could easily nuzzle her big breasts. Her hips shifted in his lap, then swirled, earning her more of the carnal sounds he couldn't stifle. He sank his fingers into her hips to hold on for whatever she did next. She leaned in and kissed him hard as she lifted her hips and sank back down on his length. His upper lip vibrated through a quiet snarl.

"You like that?" she asked before she twisted her hips.

"Yes," he grunted, trying to maintain his composure for the entire duration of her passionate assault of his senses.

Adaline's lips caught his as she continued to ride him. Linking their bodies together at both ends sent him into orgasm, but he wasn't finished, and neither was she. Her fingers tangled in his hair before she pulled his head back, separating their kiss before she turned his head to the side and slowly tongued the shell of his ear. She felt the tension in his chest and his groin as she teased him there. "Mmm," she purred as she continued to lick and nibble on his ear. Before she got to the point of his ear, she stopped, only her breath covering the sensitive point. His hands sank into her waist, holding her up.

"Do it," he demanded.

She waited a moment more before her tongue swiped over the peak. A loud growl tore from Aureon's chest as he pulled her down onto his lap. She cried out at the sensation of her body feeling so full.

"I can play this teasing game too, little human," he growled as he wrapped his arm around her, trapping her arms at her sides as he thrust up into her. He braced his stance wide on the chair as he thrust without cease. She cried out his name. He continued to growl as he sucked on one nipple, then the other as he fucked her. Her wetness grew, arousing him further, and he moved faster. She tried to pull one arm free, but he tightened his grip around hers.

"No, no, Addy. I promise a pleasurable experience for the both of us," he hissed the last syllable, looking at her with a devilish grin before his lips reached up for hers. She kissed him as he pounded inside of her. Their lips parted, but their eyes never did. His gaze turned from lustful to vulnerable. "Need you, Addy," his voice turned hoarse.

Adaline tried to reply, but her orgasm overtook her words. Her body squeezed his as she cried out, and he growled through her release that triggered his own. They collapsed on the wrecked lounge chair, sated and breathless.

"So that is foreplay," Aureon jested. She laughed against his chest. "I like it," he mused. "Let's keep it."

"You're a dork," she said before she giggled.

Aureon scooped her up into his arms and returned to her suite. He drew back the covers on her bed and slipped them both underneath. They snuggled together with her tucked against his side. Before he drifted into his first deep sleep in centuries with his arm wrapped around her possessively and growled, "Mine."

CHAPTER 66

"Father," Theodon's voice spoke into his father's mind, but Aureon did not respond. He was deep in sleep, an occurrence the king could not recall happening before in his long life.

"Father," Theodon spoke firmly.

No response.

"Father!" Theodon shouted in his father's mind.

Aureon's eyes flew open as his body tensed. He sat up in bed and exhaled loud, which roused Adaline. She reached for him as she stirred.

"Yes, Theodon," Aureon replied in his son's mind as he met her touch. He scooted her closer to him and rubbed her back while he listened for Theodon.

Theodon sighed in relief before he quickly explained, "Both the Vorcats and the Dwarves plan to turn on Theris once one side is defeated. I am certain the Shadow Dwarf king saw me leaving his camp."

"Are you sufficiently armed?" Aureon asked as he considered a strategy as the warmth of Adaline's body kept him at ease.

"Yes."

"How long until they strike?"

"It looks like a victor will be clear by the afternoon."

"I will arrive with two battalions before then."

"Thank you, Father."

The connection was gone, and Aureon was left wide awake. He looked at Adaline, who was blinking up at him without a word. He pulled her close, inhaling her scent, and kissing her before he implemented his strategy.

"Iventuil," Aureon spoke into the mind of the captain of the guard as he kissed her.

"Yes, My Lord," the captain responded immediately.

"Ready two battalions to leave in one hour for the eastern border," Aureon instructed.

"Right away, My Lord," Iventuil replied before the connection was gone.

"Gesso," Aureon spoke into the servant's mind.

"Yes, Your Majesty," Gesso said almost cheerfully.

"Ready my armor," Aureon commanded.

"Of course, Your Majesty," Gesso said, then the connection was gone.

Aureon took a moment to focus on Adaline before he had to leave her side. She felt his uneasiness and snuggled against his chest.

"You should be sleeping," she whispered. "Pretty heavily."

"I was," he admitted. "I received an update from Theodon at the border."

"It's time for you to go?"

"Yes."

"Do you need me and Asher to go with you?" she asked. She never assumed their participation in elfin events, but that didn't stop her from offering. She and Asher had already discussed that they could not alter the lives of those in their new home too much unless they were asked to intervene or if the dire need presented itself. The elves had their process for handling their affairs, and the twins would stay out of it unless otherwise specified. That included acts of war.

Aureon studied the features of her face as if he would find the correct answer there. He had put her in harm's way over the past couple of weeks, and he wouldn't knowingly do it again. "No," he finally answered. "I'm taking two battalions with me to meet Theodon. This skirmish should be over soon."

"Okay," she said as she stroked her fingers through his hair. "We'll be around if you need us."

You are what I need, Aureon thought, and he kissed her hard. He rested his forehead against hers before he pulled up the blankets to tuck her in.

"What are you doing?"

"Helping you go back to sleep."

"You think I can sleep once I know my friend is in trouble and my male has to go save him?"

"Your male?" he repeated tenderly.

"Yes," she leaned up and kissed him, then scooted out of bed to get dressed. The captain of the royal guard knocked on the door of Adaline's suite. "Come in," Adaline said before Iventuil burst into her suite.

"My King," he quickly bowed at the site of Aureon.

"We are going into battle, Iventuil," the king addressed his captain informally as he exited Adaline's suite and made way for his own.

"What's happened, Your Majesty?" Iventuil asked, following close behind the king.

Aureon quickly sounded off all the necessary information since the captain would be in charge of protecting the palace while he was gone. Aureon's requests continued, "I need you to double security here at the palace. Send word throughout the kingdom of the conflict so that civilians can move away from the eastern border."

"Yes, My Lord," the captain confirmed. "Anything else?"

The king froze with shock before turning back to Iventuil. "Adaline."

"Your human, Your Majesty?" the captain asked.

My human. Protectiveness settled into Aureon's heart, but he shook it away before addressing Iventuil. "She and her human friends and family will continue to stay at the palace while I'm gone. Make sure two guards trail each human at all times, and two guards are posted outside of each of their suites."

"Yes, My Lord," Iventuil replied.

"It is of the utmost importance that she is protected, that the portal to the human world remains hidden, and that there are no civilian casualties while I retrieve my son," the king clarified. "Should you need to promote from within to avoid spreading yourself thin, do it. I do not have the luxury of possessing the ideal temperament of recovering from fatal mistakes." The captain nodded. "Dismissed." Iventuil turned on his heel and hastened from the king's suite.

Back in her room, Adaline showered and changed into fresh clothes before she wandered the palace as guards rushed past her. Two seemed to be following her. Aureon's doing, she knew. Their presence didn't bother her, even though she didn't need protection. If it soothed his mind to know others were watching over her, then that was fine with her.

"What's going on out there?" Asher spoke into her mind as he shifted in his bed.

"The elves are preparing for battle along the eastern border of the kingdom," Adaline answered.

"Do they need us?"

"No."

"Is it insensitive for me to go back to sleep?"

Adaline smiled. "No."

"Okay," Asher said before he yawned, turned over in his bed, and dozed off.

Adaline wandered to the large balcony that extended off the throne room. She settled into a chair while she sipped the hot tea Ena handed her. The two guards posted behind her chair in silence. She continued to sip her tea through sunrise as she heard more boots hurry down the long hallway. She set her cup aside when she was finished with it and curled her knees into her chest. She closed her eyes for a moment until she felt Aureon's fingertips run through her hair. Her eyes opened to find him crouching in front of her. His brows tightened with the numerous thoughts on his mind.

"You know I would never tell you what to do," he started. Adaline smirked. "But it would help my resolve greatly if you would consider staying inside or near the palace until I return."

"I just need to see Sana, but other than that, I can stick around," she admitted.

Aureon pointed to the guards behind her. "Take them with you when you go."

She nodded in agreement as he leaned in for a kiss. Although she sensed his distress, she still posed the question, "Would it be all right to check on you this evening?" His face was inches from hers as he thought about it, then nodded. He kissed her again before saying goodbye and rising to his feet. It was difficult to walk away from her, knowing he would be gone for an unknown period. But he managed to exit the balcony and head to the armory.

"Ready?" Aureon said in Flavial's mind.

"Yes, I am waiting for you," Flavial responded immediately.

"Good. Let's see what our sons have gotten us into."

CHAPTER 67

L ater that morning, when all the humans surrounded the breakfast table, Adaline updated everyone about what was happening with the royals. She also asked them to stay close to the palace and informed them about taking a guarded escort if they wandered far.

"Except me, right?" Asher asked.

"That goes double for you," Adaline joked. Asher's eyes narrowed on his twin. "You should come with me to see Sana today."

Asher nodded as he chewed his breakfast. He had a plan of his own after they visited with Sana, but he wasn't going to ask for permission to do it. Asher wasn't great with rules, just like his twin.

"I spoke to Theodon about fishing on the Ieobu River and wanted to take Tobey with me this morning," Jim admitted.

Adaline nodded and reiterated her earlier statement, "Take two guards with you." Jim glanced at Tobey, who was excited about his fishing adventure.

Adaline was surprised at how empty the palace felt without the royals in it. Thankfully, the day passed quickly. After she and

Asher checked in with Sana, whose pregnancy was progressing as planned, Asher wandered off. Adaline wasn't surprised, nor did it matter because Asher could be summoned at a moment's notice. Tessa ended up sticking with Adaline for the remainder of the day, and she was noticeably disappointed that Flavial rescheduled their date.

"I'm sure he will make it worth the wait," Adaline said to her friend as they sat in the garden as the sun set on the horizon.

"I know," Tessa whined. "I was looking forward to it."

"Well, I'm going to check in with Aureon," Adaline shared. "Would you like to come with me so you can see Flavial?"

"Is it safe?" Tessa asked.

Adaline swallowed a smile. "I'll do my best."

"Yes!" Tessa cheered. "Let's go."

Adaline faced the guards that flanked them and told them, "We'll be back within the hour." Tessa grabbed Adaline's hand, and the two females disappeared. The startled guards weren't prepared for their sudden departure and alerted their captain.

The girls appeared hand in hand in the king's tent, shrouded in Adaline's force field. There was a large table covered in maps surrounded by officers of the king's army, along with Theodon, Forb, Flavial, and Aureon. All of them looked up to see who had entered. The females gave a small smile, not meaning to interrupt.

"Let's wait outside," Adaline said as she led her friend out of the tent. Dozens of tents surrounded the king's, all in a similar format. Soldiers hustled back and forth to see to their duties, and Adaline asked one where they kept their wounded. The soldier gave her directions and continued with his assignments. Tessa stayed close to Adaline as they zigzagged through the tents until they found the infirmary. Adaline flipped open the door flap and peeked inside to see if it was a scene Tessa could handle.

"Welcome, Dr. Adaline," Iliana's voice whispered from the far end of the tent. Adaline's eyes shifted to the apprentice healer, and she nodded her greeting.

"Come in, but stay quiet, okay?" Adaline whispered to Tessa. Tessa followed her friend inside, and she was surprised to see the number of full beds of injured soldiers packed inside. Most of them didn't make a sound as they rested, although uncomfortable due to their injuries. Adaline smiled softly as an idea surfaced, and she began to sway to music no one could hear.

"Tess," Adaline whispered. "What was the song you used to sing? The one you said your aunt always sang to you."

Tessa's eyes widened. "Why?"

"Would you sing for me?" Adaline asked mischievously. Tessa's eyes narrowed on her friend. "Please?" Adaline asked as she continued to sway to the beat of the song Tessa refused to sing. Tessa shook her head. "Fine," Adaline said. "I'll start." Adaline hummed the soft tune, hoping to encourage her friend to join in. The gentle song did what she thought it would. The soldiers relaxed in their beds at the sound of a gentle voice, and it kept Adaline in a joyful state.

Adaline wandered to the bedside of the elf that struggled with the most severe injuries. He had bandages wrapped over one eye and another securing his arm to his chest, and one of his legs lay elevated under the blanket. Adaline continued to hum as she covered his heart with her illuminated hand, and the soldier's eyes flew open.

"Shh," she whispered. "Just listen to my voice and relax." She saw him give a slight nod as he coughed uncontrollably. Her hand wrapped around his throat and flooded his body with light. His crushed throat expanded, and the soldier gasped for air. "Easy," Adaline said to him. "Concentrate on breathing normally." The soldier ceased to struggle and regained his breath. Adaline smiled when Tessa hummed the song after Adaline stopped. "There, that's better," Adaline said. Her hand scanned his ribs. Two snapped back into place and mended immediately. The soldier's lungs inflated without pain as Adaline reached for his bandaged shoulder.

"That one hurts the most," he warned her.

She scanned over his shoulder before saying, "Yeah, it tends to hurt when it's out of the socket, and your ligaments are shredded." She gripped his shoulder as gently as she could. She locked eyes with him and counted, "On three. One, two-" SNAP! The soldier sagged in relief. "Now," she said, as she looked him over, "just the leg, and that's it?" He nodded. She scanned his leg and was surprised that it was a clean break through his kneecap, and his ankle was shattered but beginning to mend. She wrapped her hands around his kneecap, healing it in seconds, and she moved down to his ankle to speed the process along. The ankle regenerated, and the soldier regained full mobility. Adaline waved for him to stand and helped him remove his bandages. She held his chin as she blew light into his injured eye. The tissues regenerated swiftly, and the soldier blinked over his healed eye, amazed that he could see again. "Okay," she said. "Check your range of motion." He stretched and rotated his limbs before looking at Adaline in amazement. "Cool, huh?" she said with a smile. It took Adaline by surprise when he wrapped his arms around her and picked her up off the ground.

"Thank you," he whispered gratefully.

"You're welcome," she said. "You can put me down, now." He gently set her down, understanding how awkward he had made the moment. Adaline just smiled and shooed him along, "Now get out of here. This tent is for injured people."

"That was amazing," Tessa said.

"It truly was," Iliana added.

"Ladies, I'm going to need you to leave the tent," Adaline said, not paying attention to their wonder.

"Why?" Tessa asked.

"Because I'm going to heal the rest of them in one swift move, but I might accidentally burn down the tent," Adaline admitted since her holy fire energy was recently upgraded. "If I do, it would be best if you weren't inside it since it's fewer people for me to evacuate."

Tessa didn't question her friend and grabbed Iliana's hand before leading the she-elf outside without a word.

"Do you think she'll burn it down?" Iliana asked Tessa.

Tessa shrugged. "I think it's better to be safe than sorry."

"Fair point," Iliana admitted.

Tessa heard Adaline continue to hum the song inside the tent, and she smiled. Inside, Adaline flicked her hand to suspend the soldiers in the air. A few felt out of balance until Adaline calmed them. "This will be over in a minute, and then you can return to your duties," Adaline told them. They floated around her as if she were a centrifugal force, as she radiated white light in a giant sphere, covering each soldier. Their aches, pains, wounds, and broken bones healed. Her light illuminated the tent like a beacon, and it darkened just as quickly. She set the soldiers on their feet and surveyed their results as Aureon threw open the door flap to the tent. The soldiers immediately acknowledged the king, who nodded at them in return.

"Everyone back to their stations," Aureon said to them in Tear, and the soldiers quickly vacated the tent. Aureon took measured steps toward Adaline, relieved that she was in his sights. As much as he knew he had to send her away soon, he would deny it for as long as possible.

She looked at him knowingly. "Did my light show give away your position?"

Aureon shook his head before his lips dove for hers. He kissed her hard, grabbing her by the shoulders. She reached for his armor-covered chest and pulled him closer. Adaline knew that war brought forth a plethora of emotions to those who fought in it. She could feel his desire for control, and then she teleported them into his tent. He glanced around to see no one present. "No one is to enter," he said, at a normal volume with his lips inches from hers.

"Yes, My Lord," echoed the two guards posted outside of his tent.

"Where's Tessa?" Adaline asked.

"With Flavial," he answered before he covered her mouth with his kiss. He picked her up and walked over to the table covered in maps, setting her on the edge of it. He tore at her clothes until he had her down to her panties, then spun her to bend her over the table. He stopped with his hand over the small of her back. He intended to push her down against the table, but he wrestled with being greedy about what he needed. He stepped away from her to regain control over his thoughts.

Oh, no, no, no, Adaline knew she was losing him because he focused on the wrong need. He needed to devour, to be greedy, and he was wavering. She covered them in her force field and got his attention.

"Aureon," she said in a whiskey voice.

Aureon dropped his hand from his face and refocused on her. She stood with her hips against the table before pushing up onto her toes as her hot gaze stayed on him. She leaned against the edge of the table, crossing her wrists behind the small of her back. She gave him an elevator stare before slowly bending over the table. Her large breasts pushed against the table as she lifted her bottom into the air. His gaze zeroed in on her perfect ass, but still, he withheld.

Okay, a hail Mary, then, Adaline decided, as she shimmied her legs. Her curves jiggled, beckoning his touch. He stood over her a moment later with his hands on her hips. His chest was heaving as he tore away her panties and unlaced the front of his pants. He covered her crossed wrists with one hand and guided his shaft past her folds with the other.

"I am sorry, Addy," he whispered before he slammed home.

Adaline cried out at the blatant invasion, and her walls tensed in surprise. "C'mon," she gasped as her breasts heaved against the table. "More."

Aureon pounded into her from behind, growling the whole time. His grip sank into her hips so hard it would leave bruises that would last minutes. She decided she wanted the mate bond before he took her ravenously. She was willing, but she didn't think now was the time to discuss something so romantic during a time of war, when his needs were more carnal. She focused on the headache as he moved, feeling the thud against the spot in her brain where the bond tried pushing through. She closed her eyes as she thought of accepting the bond, and it immediately broke through the discomfort. She winced through gritted teeth, and her body tensed in orgasm, but it had the opposite reaction in him. His back bowed in ecstasy as he emptied his body into hers. The pressure in his mind gave way due to extending the bond to her. When he was finished and clearheaded, he stared at her, baffled.

"Addy?" he asked tenderly. "Did you?"

"Yes," she breathed as she peeled her cheek off the table, as she felt his joy and worry.

Aureon planned for her acceptance of the bond to be a gentler experience, not this ravaging of her body he'd done. Adaline said nothing as she caught her breath, so he picked her up and put her on her back on the table. He lifted her ankles back to his shoulders as he pushed inside of her again. Aureon was gentler with his movements to make up for her experience. He lifted her hips off the edge of the table and thrust deeply, stroking her G-spot. Her legs shook, and she moaned.

"Yes, little human," he rumbled as he kissed the inside of her ankle. "Let me give to you. You have given me so much."

"Almost there," Adaline struggled to say.

He kissed the inside of her other ankle. "Take all the time you need." He decided to change tactics. "Wrap your legs around me." Once she did, he picked her up and brought her against his chest until their foreheads touched. He pushed her up against the large pillar that held up the center of his tent before he shifted his grip and continued to pump his length into her slowly, gently.

Adaline's body clenched his before her eyes flashed open. "Don't stop."

"Not stopping, Addy," Aureon said in her mind. Her eyes widened in surprise. It was their first telepathic conversation. "Yes, my darling," he said in her mind, as he continued to thrust deep within her. "You have made me so happy." Love and longing filled his eyes as this was the moment he'd patiently waited for without ceasing. The connection with her was deep and eternal, setting his nerve endings aflame with desire. "I want to show you everything."

Adaline's brow drew tight as the tension in her body was about to break free. He lifted her hips a little higher as he picked up his pace. Adaline's eyes widened as her orgasm rushed over her. She moaned his name as he continued to thrust into her. Once she felt boneless, he slowed his ministrations and stepped backward to slide into his chair. He leaned back so she could sprawl on him while she regained her breath. He finally hooked his finger under her chin and brought her face. A dark, sated gaze looked back at him before she kissed him. He rested his forehead against hers, and she felt his energy radiate through her, noticing it was far greater than it had been before due to their new bond.

"That's new," Adaline whispered.

Aureon's eyes reopened. "There are many new things for us to explore."

She cupped his face and kissed him. "We will have lots of time for that when you return."

"Yes," he agreed as her force field came down.

"Addy?" Tessa called from outside the tent.

Adaline's eyes widened at how close her friend sounded. "Thank goodness for the force field." Aureon chuckled as he picked her up by her waist and set her on her feet. He helped her with her clothes, and she was lost in thought as he helped her pull her shirt over her head. "So, I couldn't tell you this before because when you wear it, it's because of a serious situation," Adaline rambled before making her point. "But you look sexy in your armor."

"Do I?" he asked, amused, as he pulled her in closer and placed a kiss on her forehead. She shivered.

"Yes," she said. "I didn't think I would find the right moment to say that."

"Come on in, Tess," Adaline called to her friend. Tessa cautiously wandered into the tent, all smiles as well. Curiosity nudged Adaline as she prepared to bombard Tessa with questions about Flavial after they returned home. "Are you ready to go?"

Tessa sighed. "If we must."

Adaline chuckled as she moved to step away from Aureon, but he caught her.

"I will be in connection with you always," Aureon said into Adaline's mind as he looked at her.

She nodded. "Let me know if you want me to return." He kissed her then reluctantly retracted his touch.

"Be safe," Aureon said to them both.

"We will," Tessa said with a smile as she reached for Adaline's hand.

Adaline winked at Aureon before they teleported. They appeared on the balcony off the throne room. Before Adaline could rib her friend for rounding a base or two with Flavial, her attention snapped to the throne room. She heard the clashing of swords and the yelling of voices; voices, snarling threats, and weapons hurled in all directions. "Go hide in your room," Adaline said to Tessa before covering her friend in her force field. Tessa hesitated, so Adaline gently pushed her toward the direction of her suite. Tessa ran and barricaded herself inside.

Adaline entered the throne room to see royal guards engaged in hand-to-hand combat with males of a short, stocky variety. Black smoke spilled from their noses, they had sharp teeth, and their eyes were fiery red. *So those are Shadow Dwarves,* she guessed. She saw one teleport around the room, delivering impactful blows to guards, before moving on to its next target.

The Shadow Dwarves were burly, mean and delivered powerful blows to the guards. She saw one dwarf knock a guard off his feet. He stepped forward with his large, spiked hammer raised to execute a killing blow to the elf. Adaline teleported in front of him and grasped the hammer over the dwarf's hand.

"Well, that's not very nice," she said in a condescending tone, as her eyes blazed white. The dwarf's red eyes flooded with surprise before she snatched the hammer from his hand. She let her energy cover the weapon, transforming it into her new fiery mallet.

"The human!" the dwarf exclaimed.

Adaline's brow furrowed. *He knows English?*

"Definitely human," Adaline confirmed before she kicked him in the chest, sending him crashing into the far wall.

"Dr. Adaline, behind you!" Iventuil yelled.

Adaline froze whoever was behind her and turned to look her assailant in the eye. It was the teleporter. She kissed her palm then blew the kiss to the dwarf, encasing him in a large light ball, prohibiting him from teleporting. "Fun's over, jerk," Adaline muttered as she continued to fight the dwarves rushing the throne room from all areas of the palace. Her new weapon sent dwarves flying from the room, or else her fire incinerated them. A few dwarves fled at the sight of her, but the rest kept coming. Eventually, she and Iventuil fought back to back.

"Can you get the guards to jump at once?" Adaline asked Iventuil as they continued to fight through the waves of dwarves flooding the palace.

"Yes," Iventuil said through gritted teeth.

"Okay," Adaline said, her feet had already left the ground. "Command them to jump... now!"

Iventuil yelled the command, and all the guards jumped. Adaline impacted the floor hard, sending a tremor through the ground, causing all standing dwarves to lose footing. The guard's feet hit the steady ground a moment later and slew their opponents at an increased speed.

"Well done," Iventuil commended.

"Why, thank you," Adaline smirked. "Have you told the king what's happening?"

"I was just doing that," Iventuil admitted as he cut through another dwarf.

Aureon spoke into her mind a moment later, "What are you doing to my throne room, little human?"

Adaline chuckled. "Not much. You might need a new floor, though."

"How many are there?"

"They just keep coming," Adaline admitted. "We're holding them back, but they're like cockroaches."

The king guessed cockroaches to be some sort of resilient species on Earth. "Can you get somewhere safe?"

"No," Adaline said with attitude. "I don't know where Jim and Tobey are, and I don't know where Asher is, and Tessa is barricaded in her room. I'm not going to flee when too many innocents are variables in the decision."

"All right," he said. "I am coming for you."

"Wait, let me get Asher," she said.

The dwarves spilled into the throne room as she telepathically reached for her twin, swaying her focus from the fight for a split second. It was long enough for the Shadow Dwarf king to sneak up behind her and bring his hammer down on the back of her head, making her world go black in an instant.

Aureon's expression filled with horror at the excruciating pain as the mate bond tore from his mind, his connection with Adaline gone. *Not this*, he thought. *Not this, again.* He had lost one mate while away at war. *This part was not supposed to repeat.*

Flavial shot up from his chair. "What's happened?"

Rage filled Aureon as he knew someone had gotten to Adaline. Someone hurt her badly to sever their bond. His fists clenched as his eyes swirled with emotions that he allowed to consume him. His head fell back, and a loud warrior cry ripped from his throat. His soldiers were awake and standing, ready for orders. "Get me my son and his team. We leave, now!" Aureon ordered, as his unrealized abilities activated within him simultaneously.

"Yes, Your Ma-" Flavial's words died as he saw the king, his longtime friend, transform into something else.

THE TWINS RETURN!

While King Aureon deals with new… changes, Theris battles upheaval as Asher rushes to save Adaline by taking her back to Earth.

Stay updated about the Everlys and the Sleones on Facebook:

ABOUT THE AUTHOR

With over a decade of experience bouncing between the entertainment and fashion industries of Los Angeles, Allison Fagundes is a creative professional with her sights set on entrepreneurship. When she left her corporate job for swimwear design, she managed to shuffle away from a car accident that changed the order of her creative expression. During the recovery process, Allison awakened one morning after an incredible dream and dream-journaled the adventure for four weeks. At the end of that time, she finished the first draft of Goddess Save the King. Seven months later, she completed the final draft of the project and self-published it through Amazon.

Allison now lives in Los Banos, California, and spends her free time playing beach volleyball in Carmel and learning to play golf with her uncle.

Find out more at arfagundes.com.